A THIEF AMONG THE TREES

BASED ON THE NOVEL SERIES *AN EMBER IN THE ASHES* BY

SABAA TAHIR

Published by
ARCHAIA™

A THIE

THE

AMONG TREES

STORY BY

SABAA TAHIR

SCRIPT BY

NICOLE ANDELFINGER

ART BY

SONIA LIAO

COLORS BY

KIERAN QUIGLEY

LETTERS BY

MIKE FIORENTINO

ARCHAIA
Los Angeles, California

COVER BY
SONIA LIAO

LIMITED EDITION COVER BY
QISTINA KHALIDAH

EDITOR
AMANDA LaFRANCO

DESIGNER
JILLIAN CRAB

EXECUTIVE EDITOR
SIERRA HAHN

Ross Richie CEO & Founder
Joy Huffman CFO
Matt Gagnon Editor-in-Chief
Filip Sablik President, Publishing & Marketing
Stephen Christy President, Development
Lance Kreiter Vice President, Licensing & Merchandising
Arune Singh Vice President, Marketing
Bryce Carlson Vice President, Editorial & Creative Strategy
Kate Henning Director, Operations
Spencer Simpson Director, Sales
Scott Newman Manager, Production Design
Elyse Strandberg Manager, Finance
Sierra Hahn Executive Editor
Jeanine Schaefer Executive Editor
Dafna Pleban Senior Editor
Shannon Watters Senior Editor
Eric Harburn Senior Editor
Matthew Levine Editor
Sophie Philips-Roberts Associate Editor
Amanda LaFranco Associate Editor
Jonathan Manning Associate Editor
Gavin Gronenthal Assistant Editor

Gwen Waller Assistant Editor
Allyson Gronowitz Assistant Editor
Shelby Netschke Editorial Assistant
Jillian Crab Design Coordinator
Michelle Ankley Design Coordinator
Marie Krupina Production Designer
Grace Park Production Designer
Chelsea Roberts Production Designer
Samantha Knapp Production Design Assistant
José Meza Live Events Lead
Stephanie Hocutt Digital Marketing Lead
Esther Kim Marketing Coordinator
Cat O'Grady Digital Marketing Coordinator
Amanda Lawson Marketing Assistant
Holly Aitchison Digital Sales Coordinator
Morgan Perry Retail Sales Coordinator
Megan Christopher Operations Coordinator
Rodrigo Hernandez Operations Coordinator
Zipporah Smith Operations Assistant
Jason Lee Senior Accountant
Sabrina Lesin Accounting Assistant
Breanna Sarpy Executive Assistant

**A THIEF AMONG THE TREES: AN EMBER IN THE ASHES GRAPHIC NOVEL,
July 2020.** Published by Archaia, a division of Boom Entertainment, Inc. An Ember in the Ashes is ™ & © 2020 Sabaa Tahir. All rights reserved. Archaia™ and the Archaia logo are trademarks of Boom Entertainment, Inc., registered in various countries and categories. All characters, events, and institutions depicted herein are fictional. Any similarity between any of the names, characters, persons, events, and/or institutions in this publication to actual names, characters, and persons, whether living or dead, events, and/or institutions is unintended and purely coincidental.

BOOM! Studios, 5670 Wilshire Boulevard, Suite 400, Los Angeles, CA 90036-5679. Printed in China. First Printing.

ISBN: 978-1-68415-524-8, eISBN: 978-1-64144-690-7

Limited Edition
ISBN: 978-1-68415-639-9

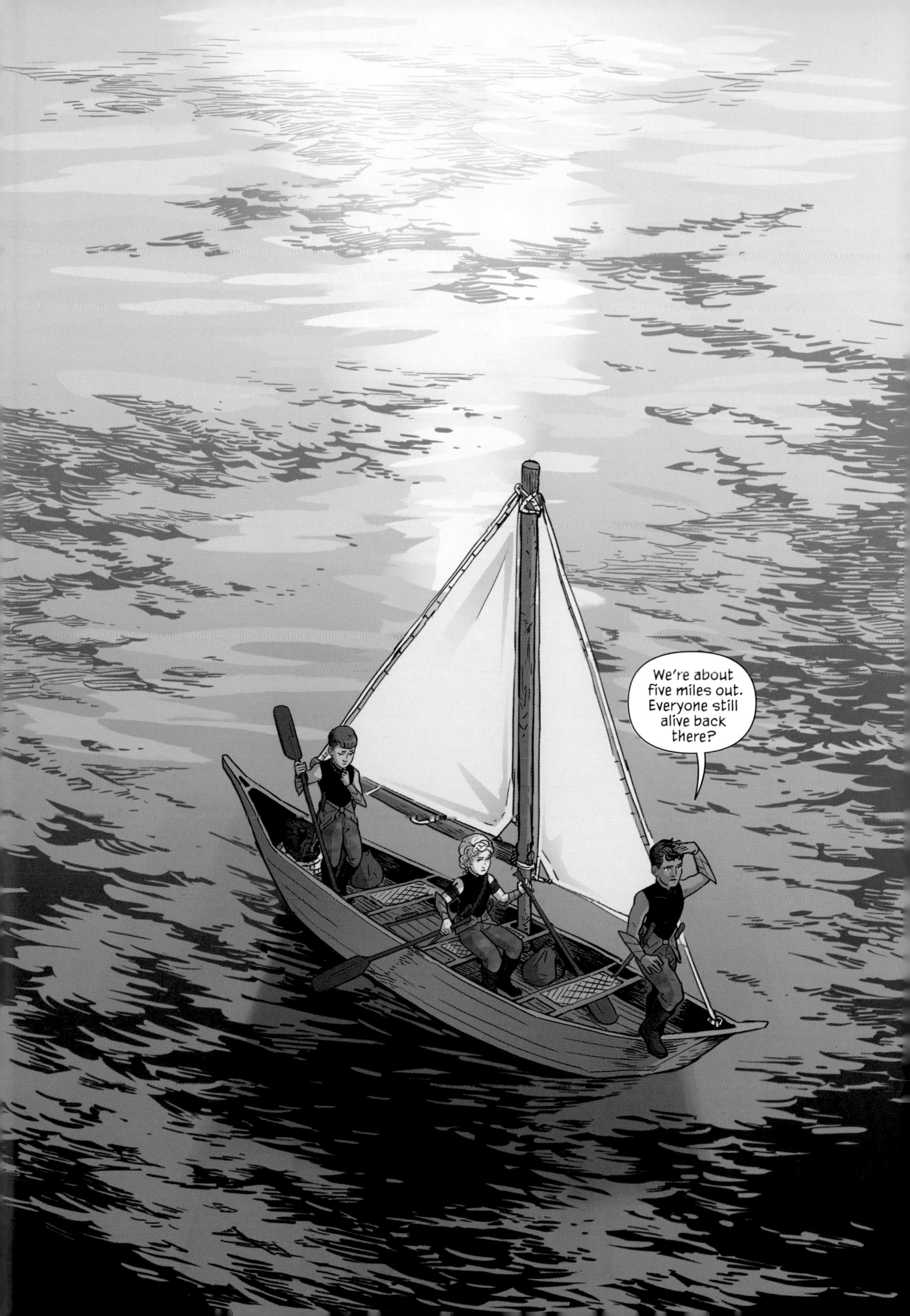
We're about five miles out. Everyone still alive back there?

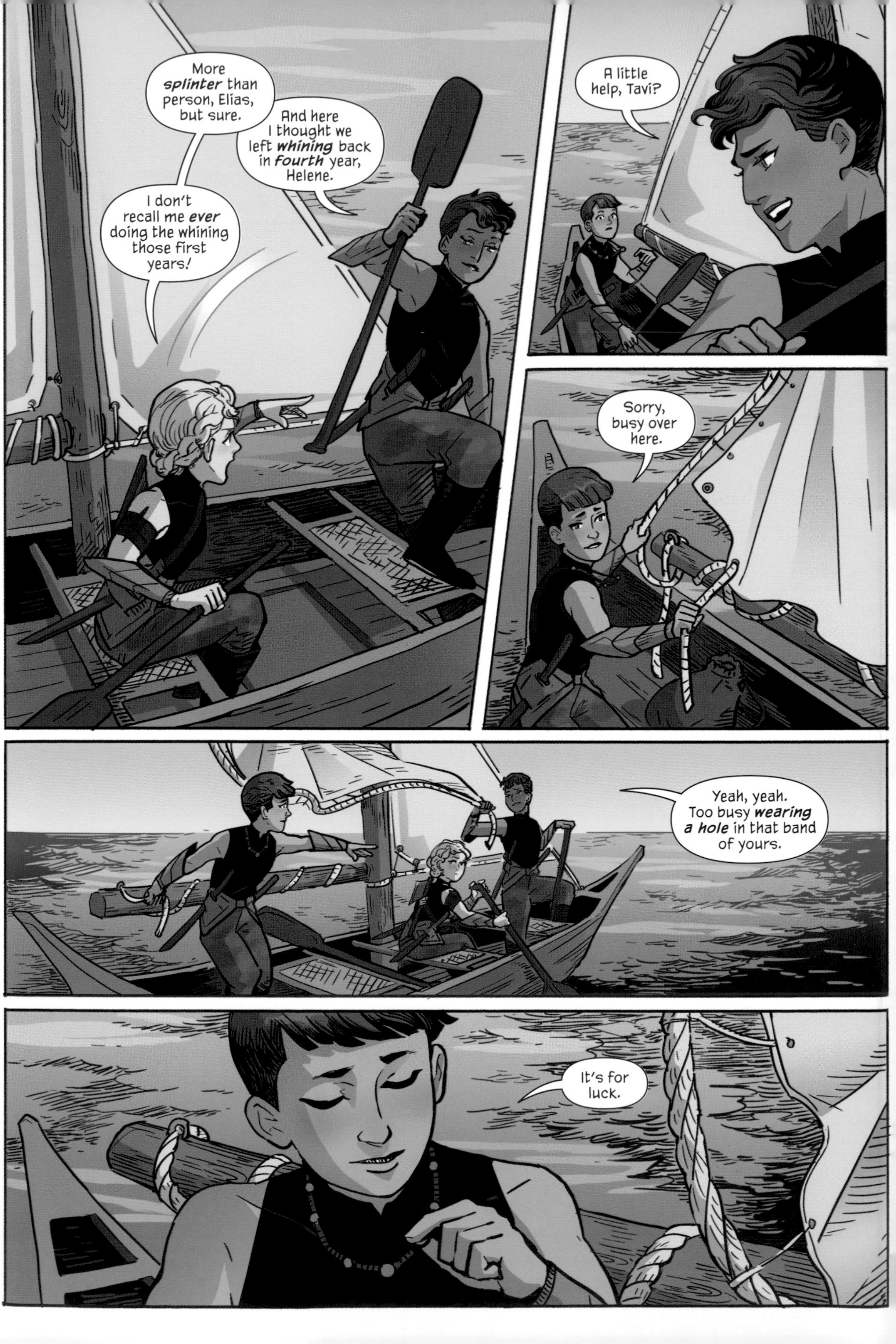
More *splinter* than person, Elias, but sure.
And here I thought we left *whining* back in *fourth* year, Helene.
I don't recall me *ever* doing the whining those first years!
A little help, Tavi?
Sorry, busy over here.
Yeah, yeah. Too busy *wearing a hole* in that band of yours.
It's for luck.

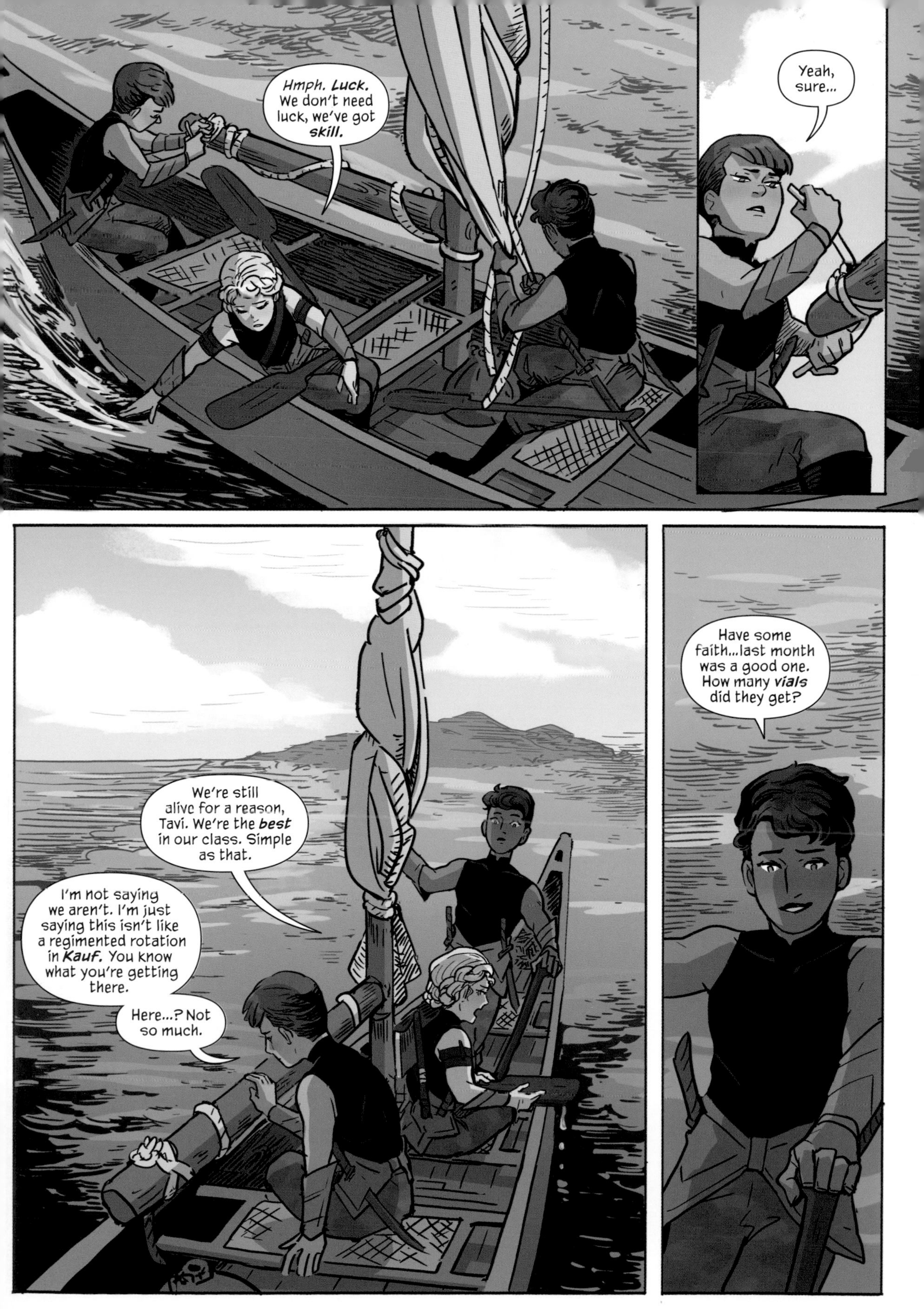
Hmph. Luck. We don't need luck, we've got skill.
Yeah, sure...
Have some faith...last month was a good one. How many vials did they get?
We're still alive for a reason, Tavi. We're the best in our class. Simple as that.
I'm not saying we aren't. I'm just saying this isn't like a regimented rotation in Kauf. You know what you're getting there.
Here...? Not so much.

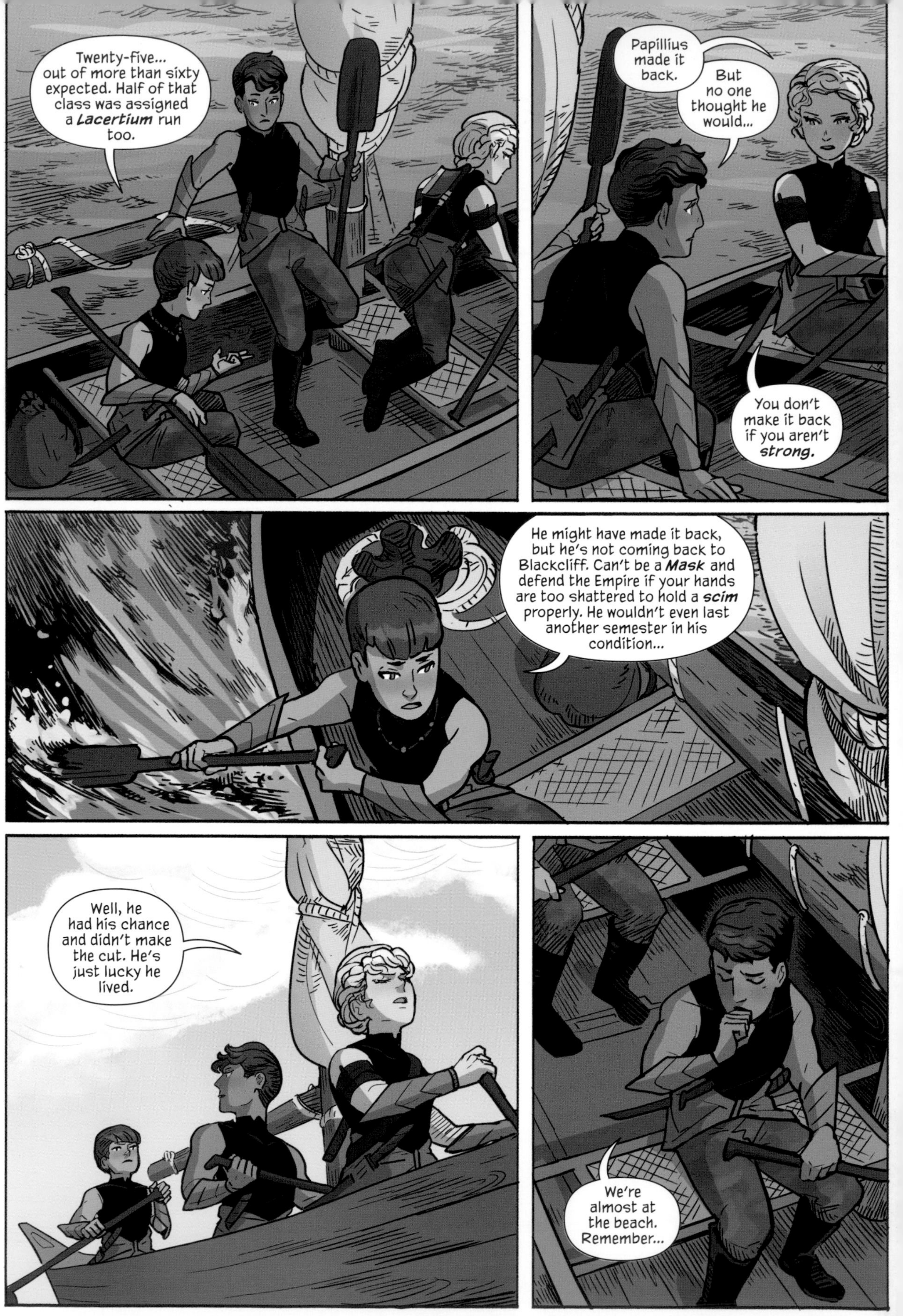
Twenty-five... out of more than sixty expected. Half of that class was assigned a *Lacertium* run too.
Papillius made it back.
But no one thought he would...
You don't make it back if you aren't **strong.**
He might have made it back, but he's not coming back to Blackcliff. Can't be a **Mask** and defend the Empire if your hands are too shattered to hold a **scim** properly. He wouldn't even last another semester in his condition...
Well, he had his chance and didn't make the cut. He's just lucky he lived.
We're almost at the beach. Remember...

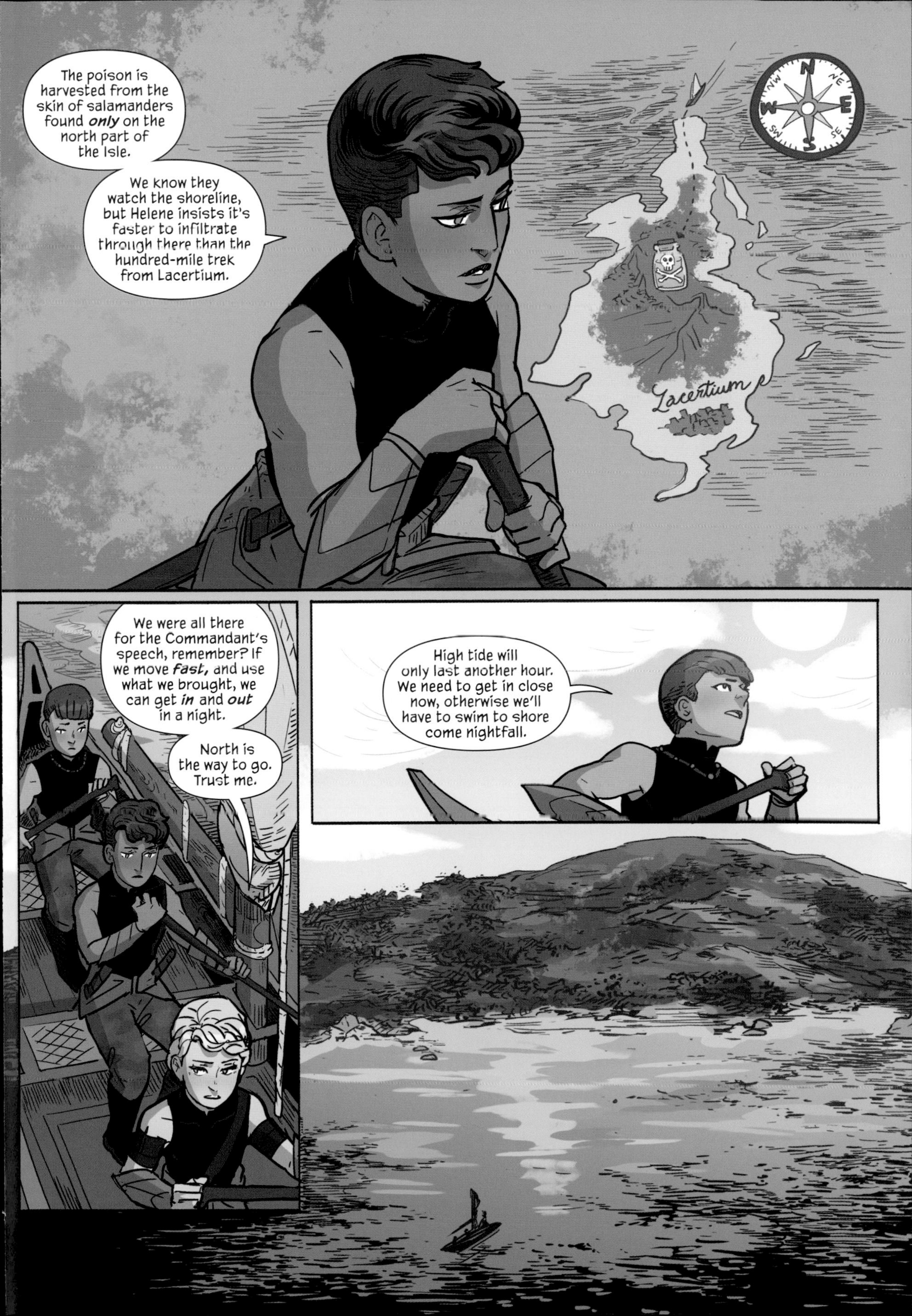
The poison is harvested from the skin of salamanders found *only* on the north part of the Isle.
We know they watch the shoreline, but Helene insists it's faster to infiltrate through there than the hundred-mile trek from Lacertium.
N
NE
E
SE
S
SW
W
NW
Lacertium
We were all there for the Commandant's speech, remember? If we move *fast,* and use what we brought, we can get *in* and *out* in a night.
North is the way to go. Trust me.
High tide will only last another hour. We need to get in close now, otherwise we'll have to swim to shore come nightfall.

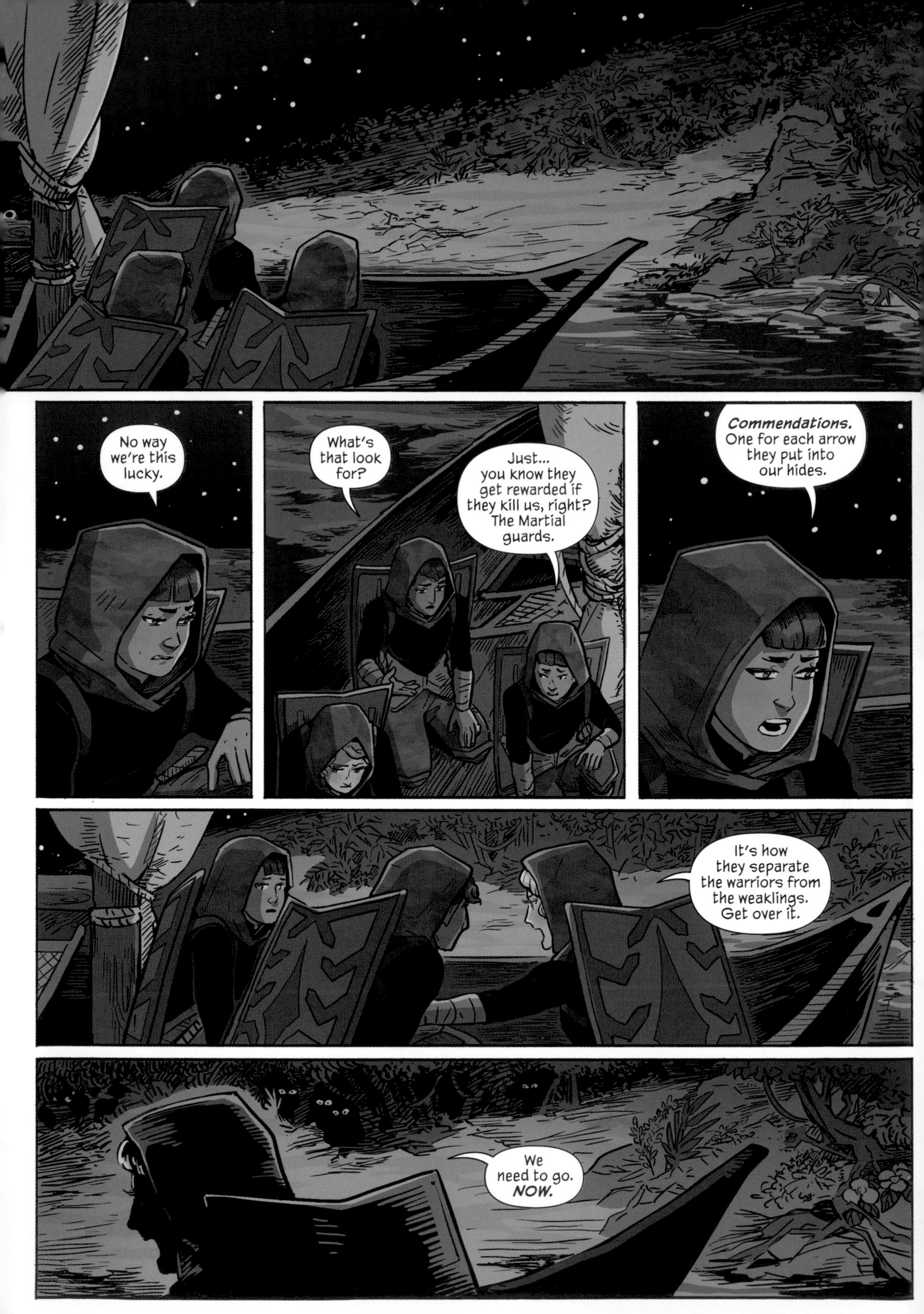
No way we're this lucky.
What's that look for?
Just... you know they get rewarded if they kill us, right? The Martial guards.
Commendations. One for each arrow they put into our hides.
It's how they separate the warriors from the weaklings. Get over it.
We need to go. ***NOW.***

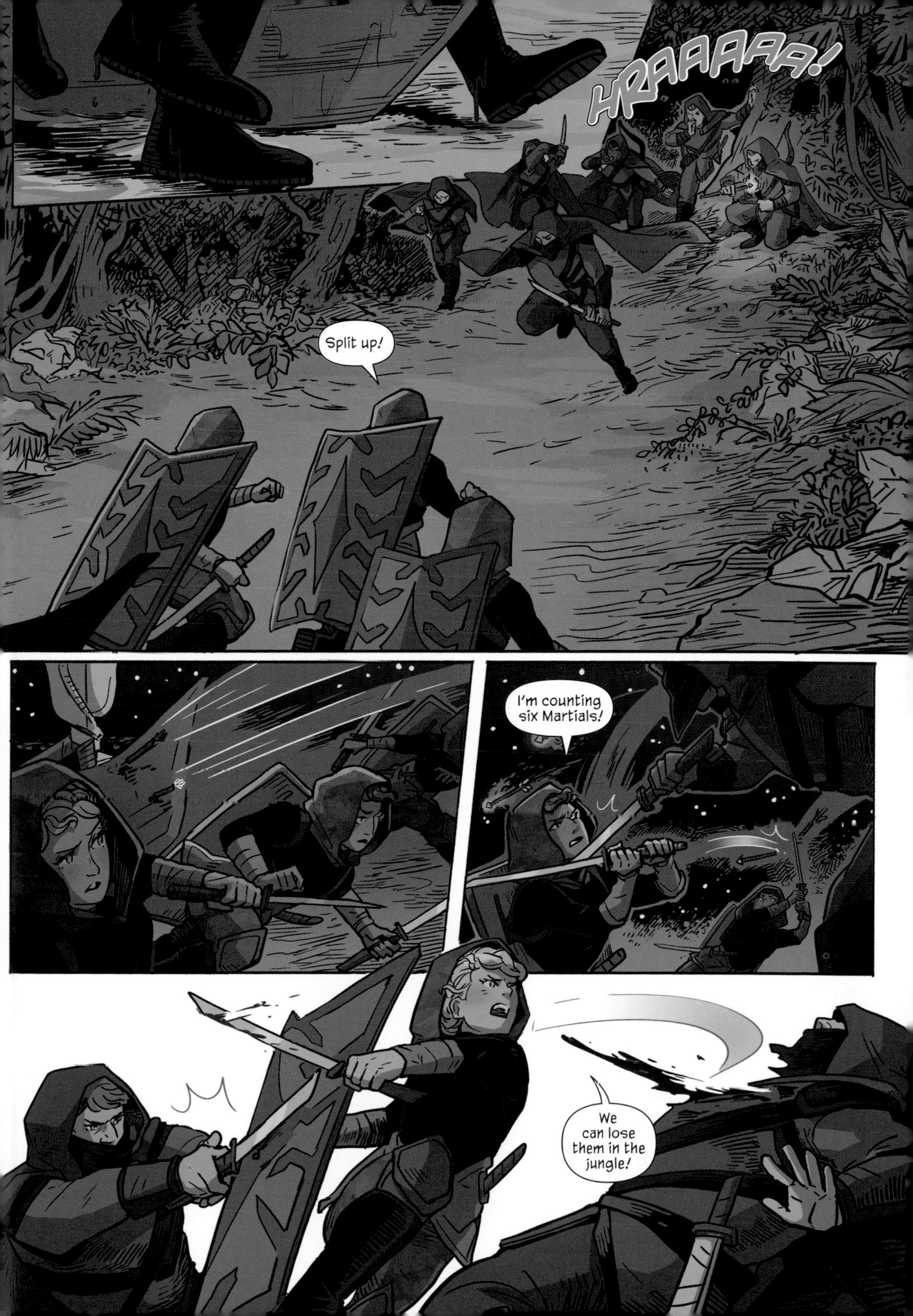
HRAAAAAA!
Split up!
I'm counting six Martials!
We can lose them in the jungle!

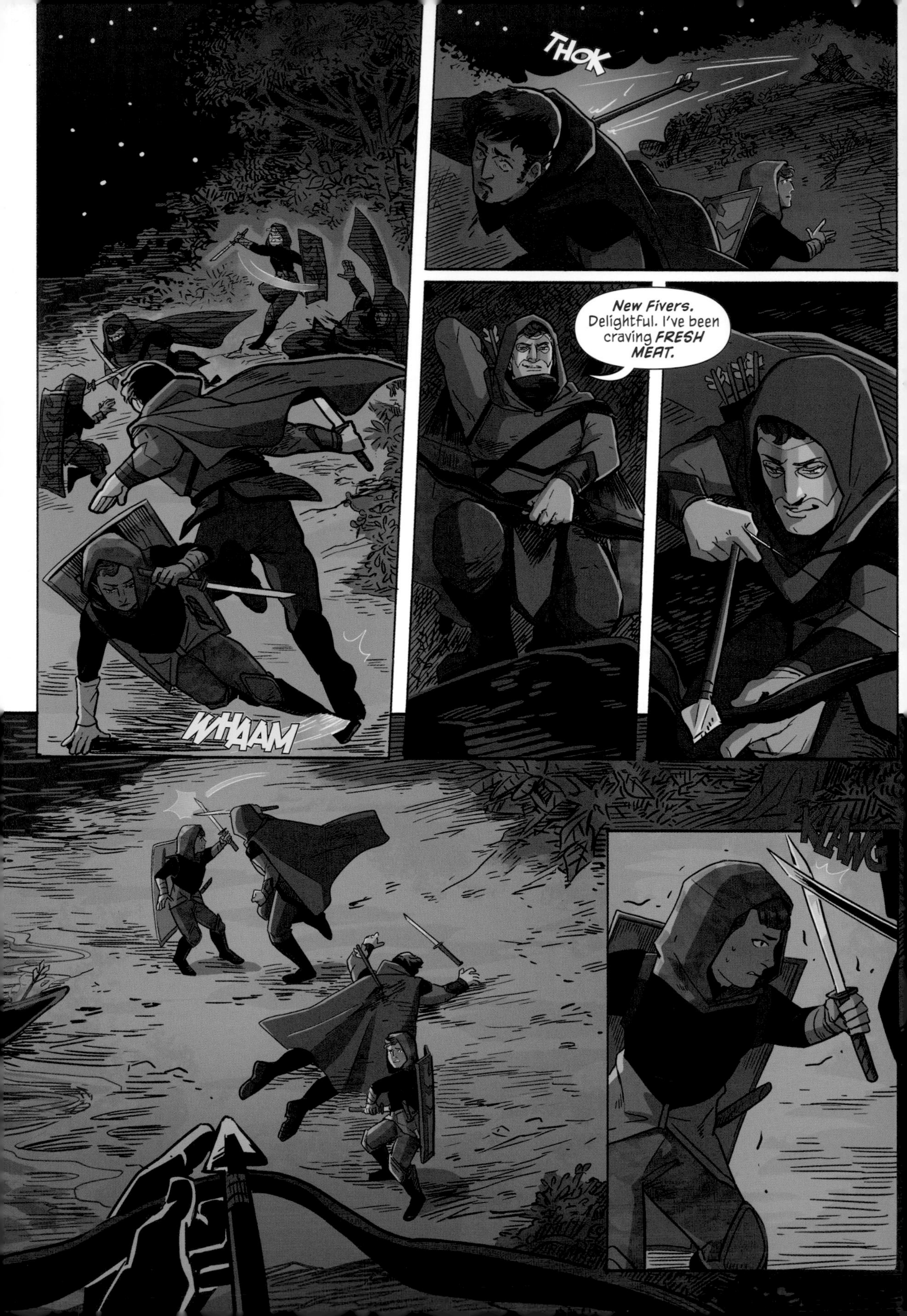
THOK
New Fivers. Delightful. I've been craving FRESH MEAT.
WHAAM
KLANG

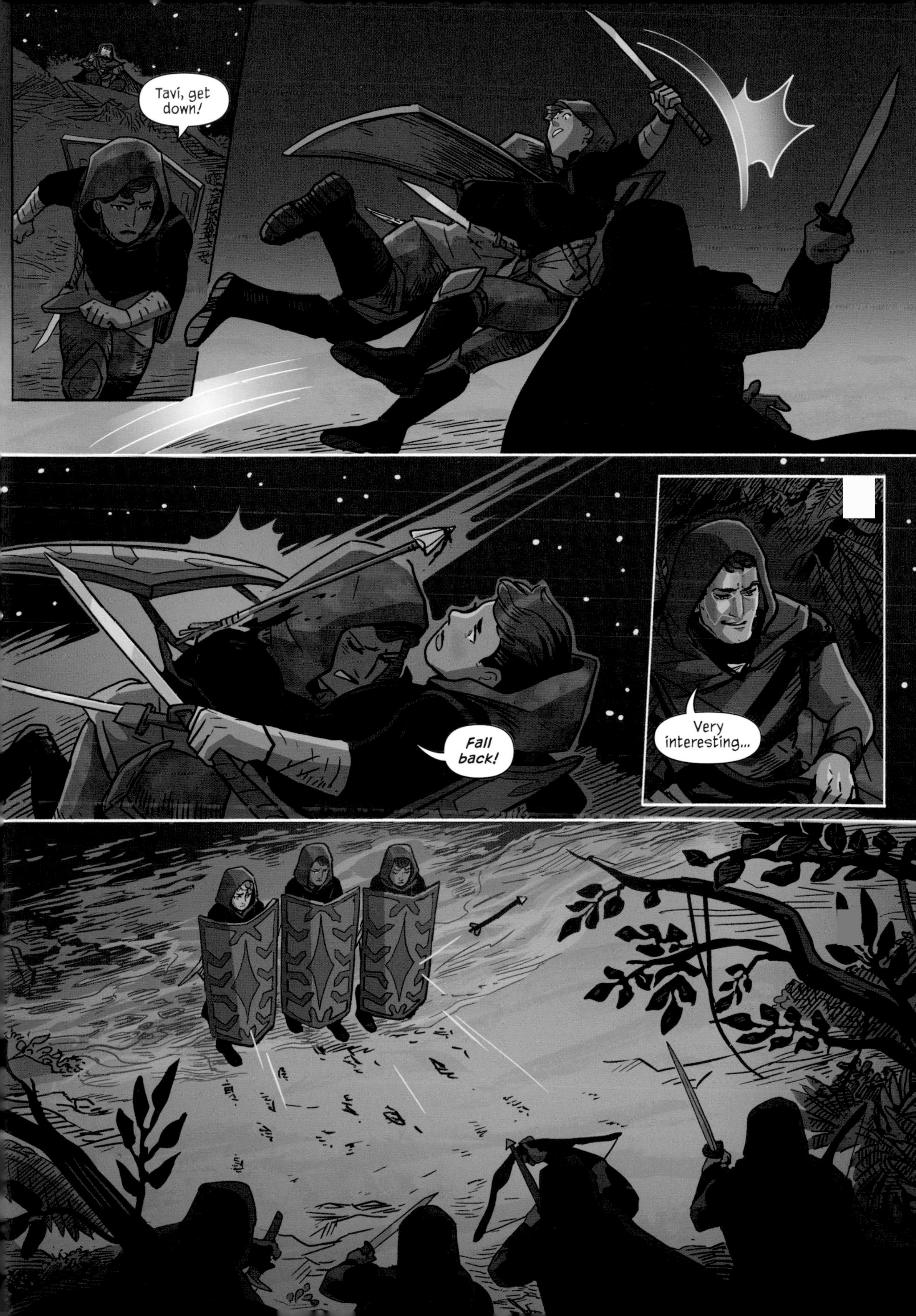
Tavi, get down!
Fall back!
Very interesting...

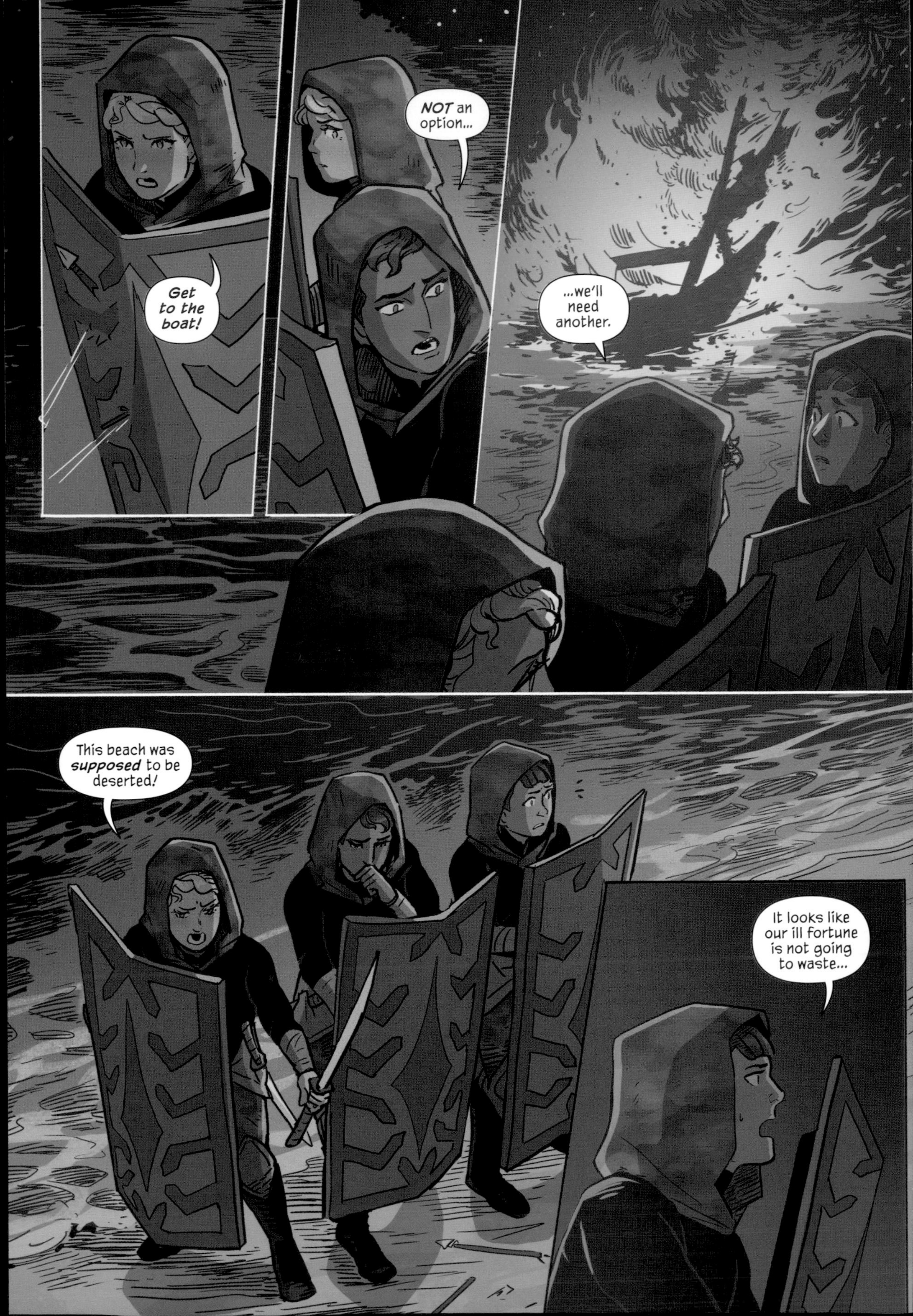
Get to the boat!
NOT an option...
...we'll need another.
This beach was supposed to be deserted!
It looks like our ill fortune is not going to waste...

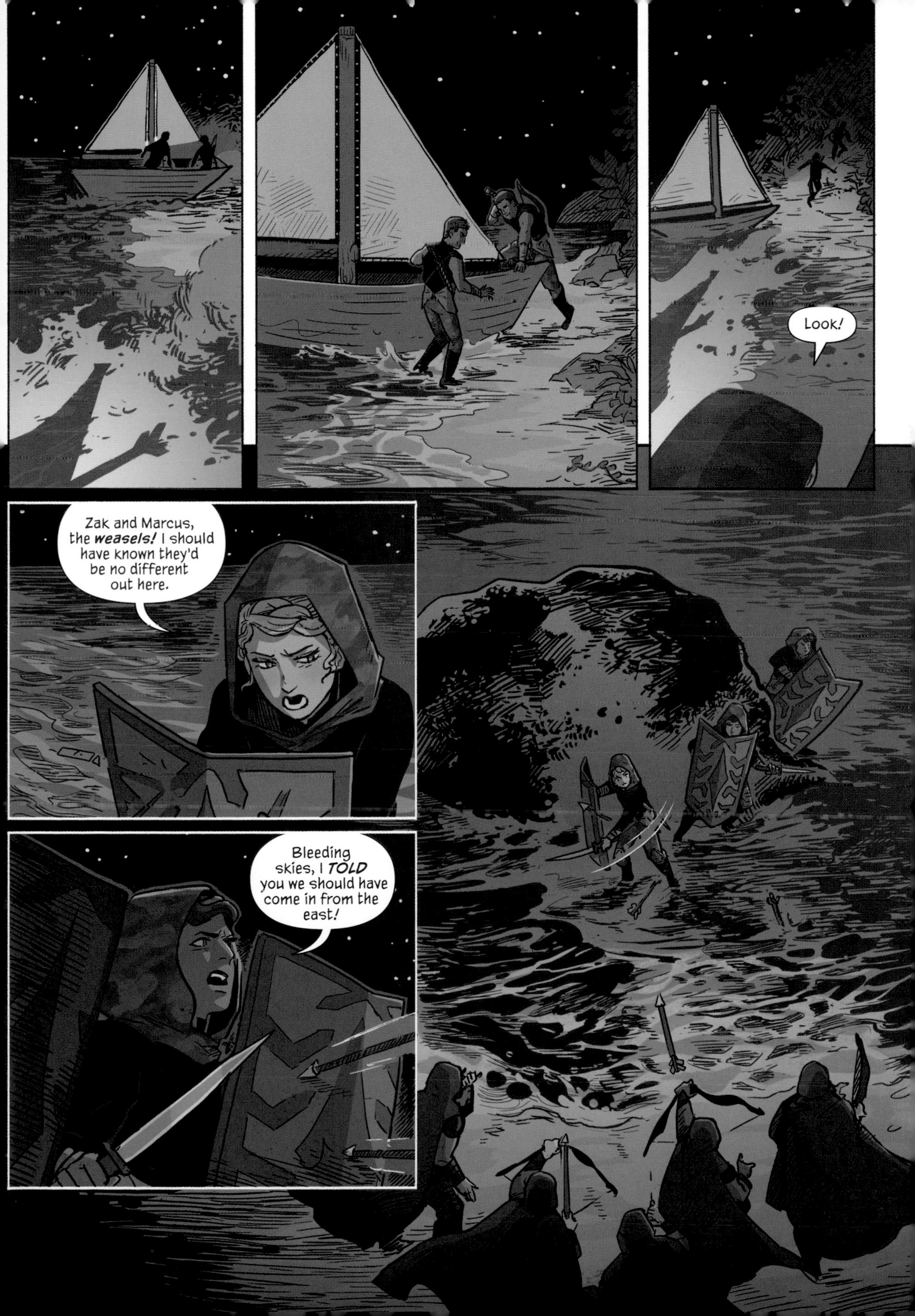
Look!
Zak and Marcus, the *weasels!* I should have known they'd be no different out here.
Bleeding skies, I *TOLD* you we should have come in from the east!

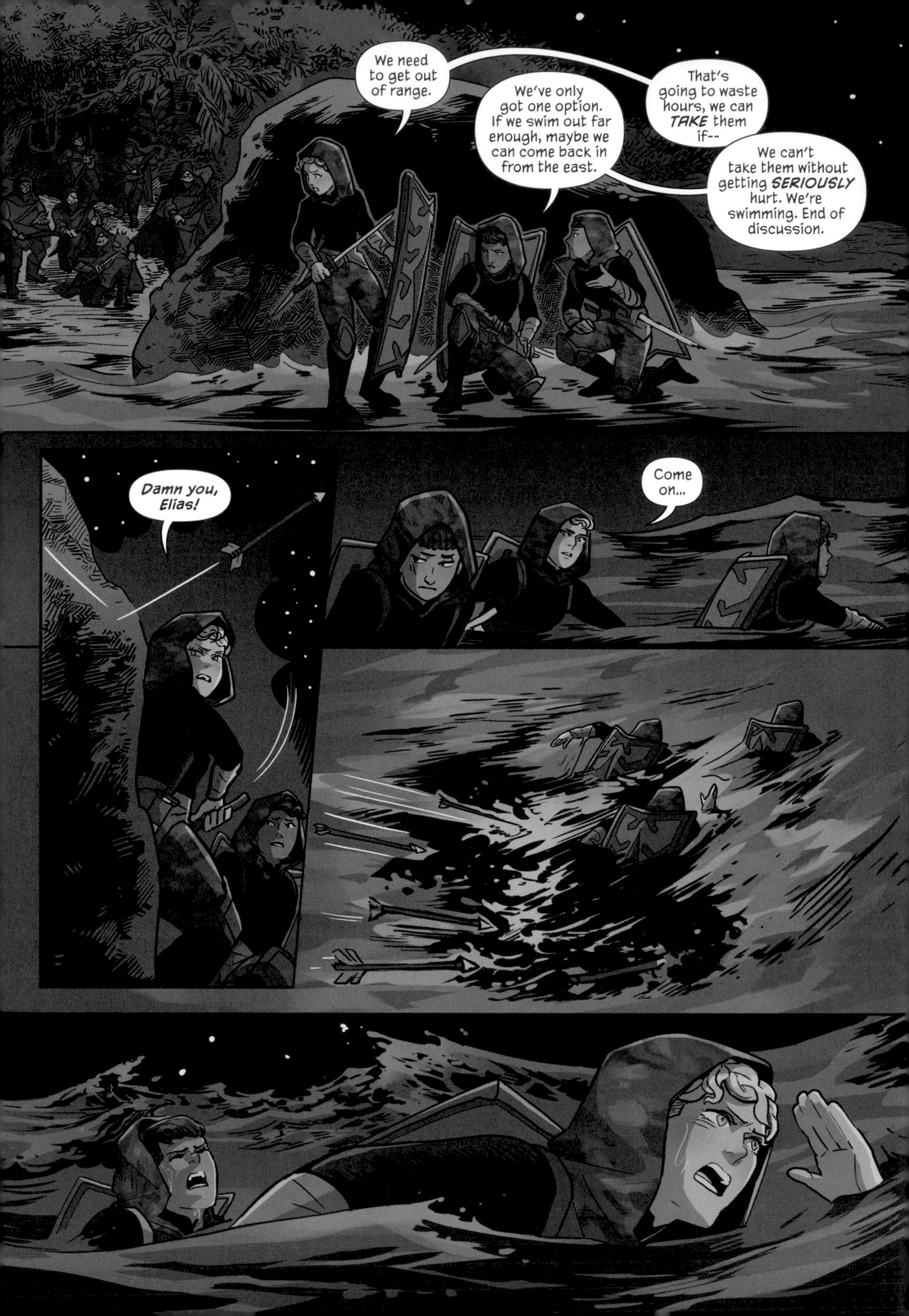

We need to get out of range.
We've only got one option. If we swim out far enough, maybe we can come back in from the east.
That's going to waste hours, we can *TAKE* them if--
We can't take them without getting ***SERIOUSLY*** hurt. We're swimming. End of discussion.
Damn you, Elias!
Come on...

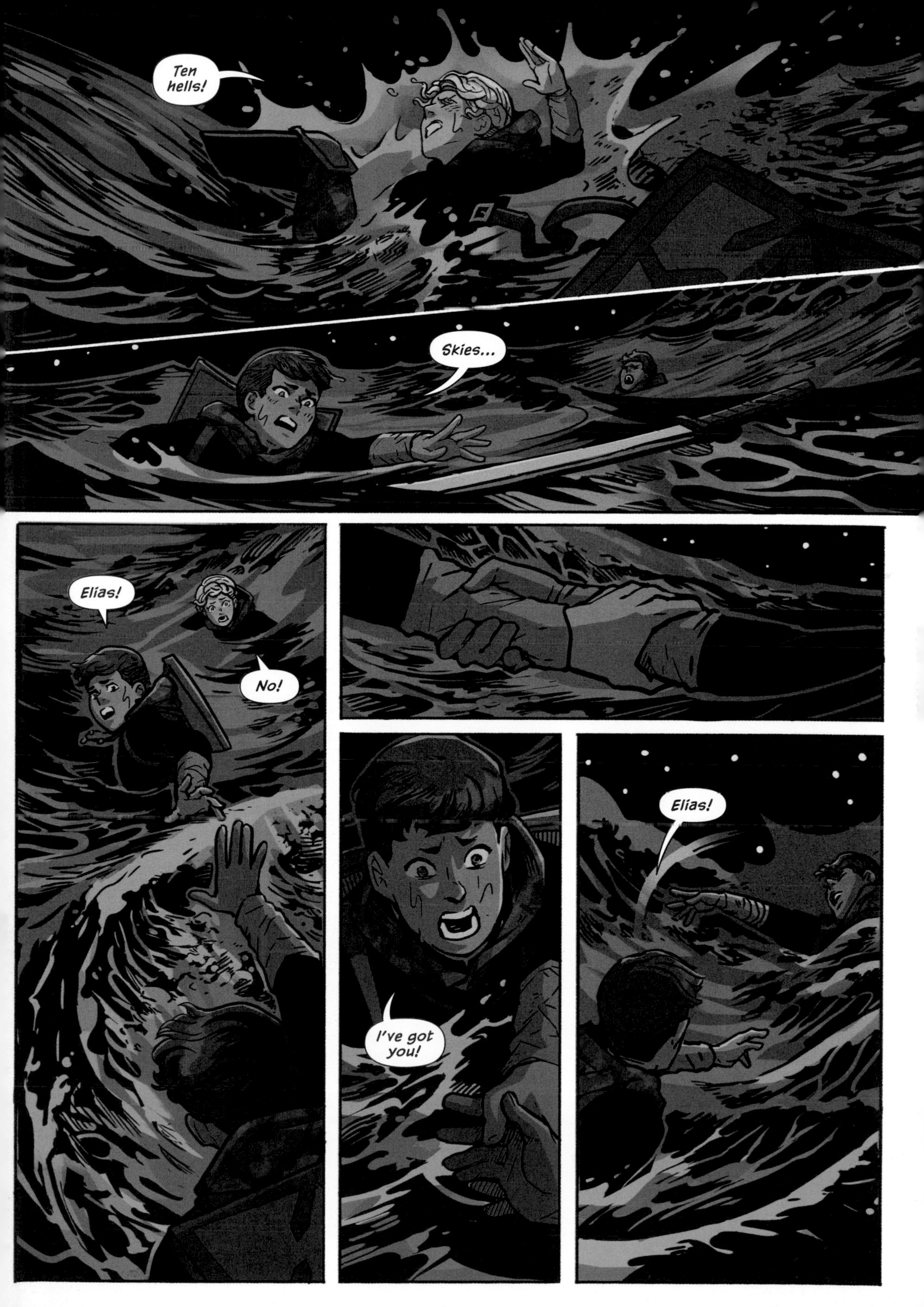
Ten hells!
Skies...
Elias!
No!
I've got you!
Elias!

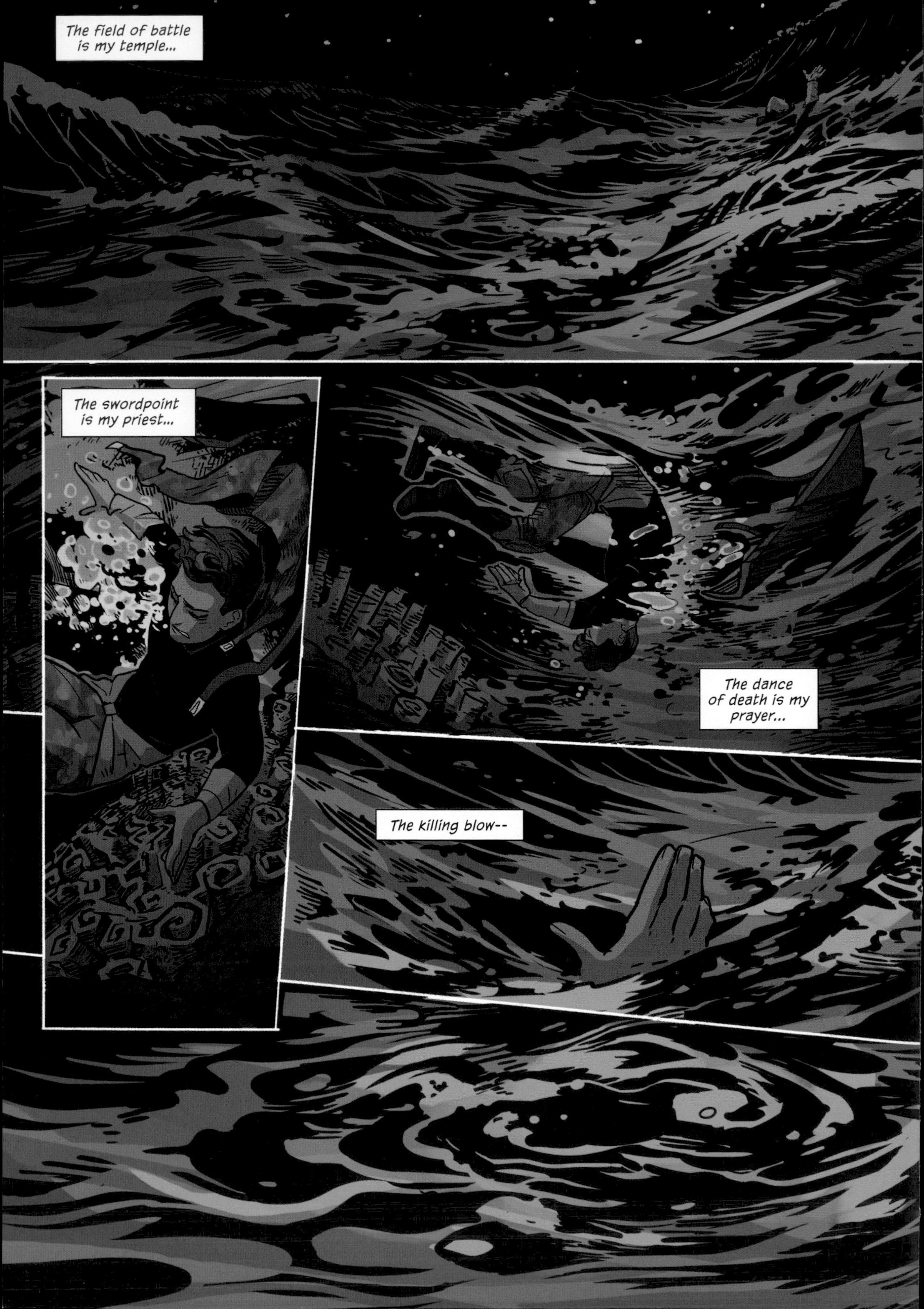
The field of battle is my temple...
The swordpoint is my priest...
The dance of death is my prayer...
The killing blow--

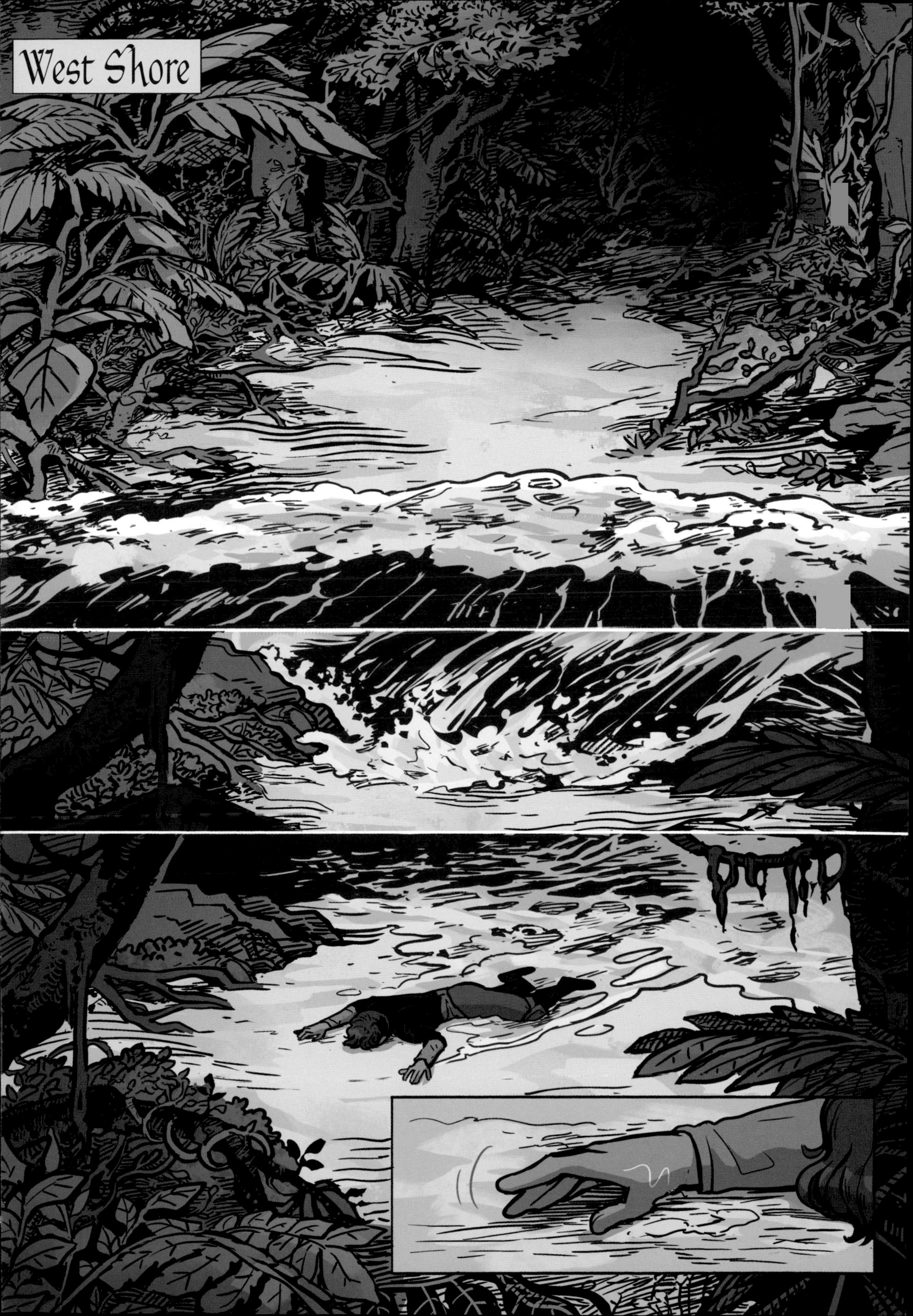
West Shore

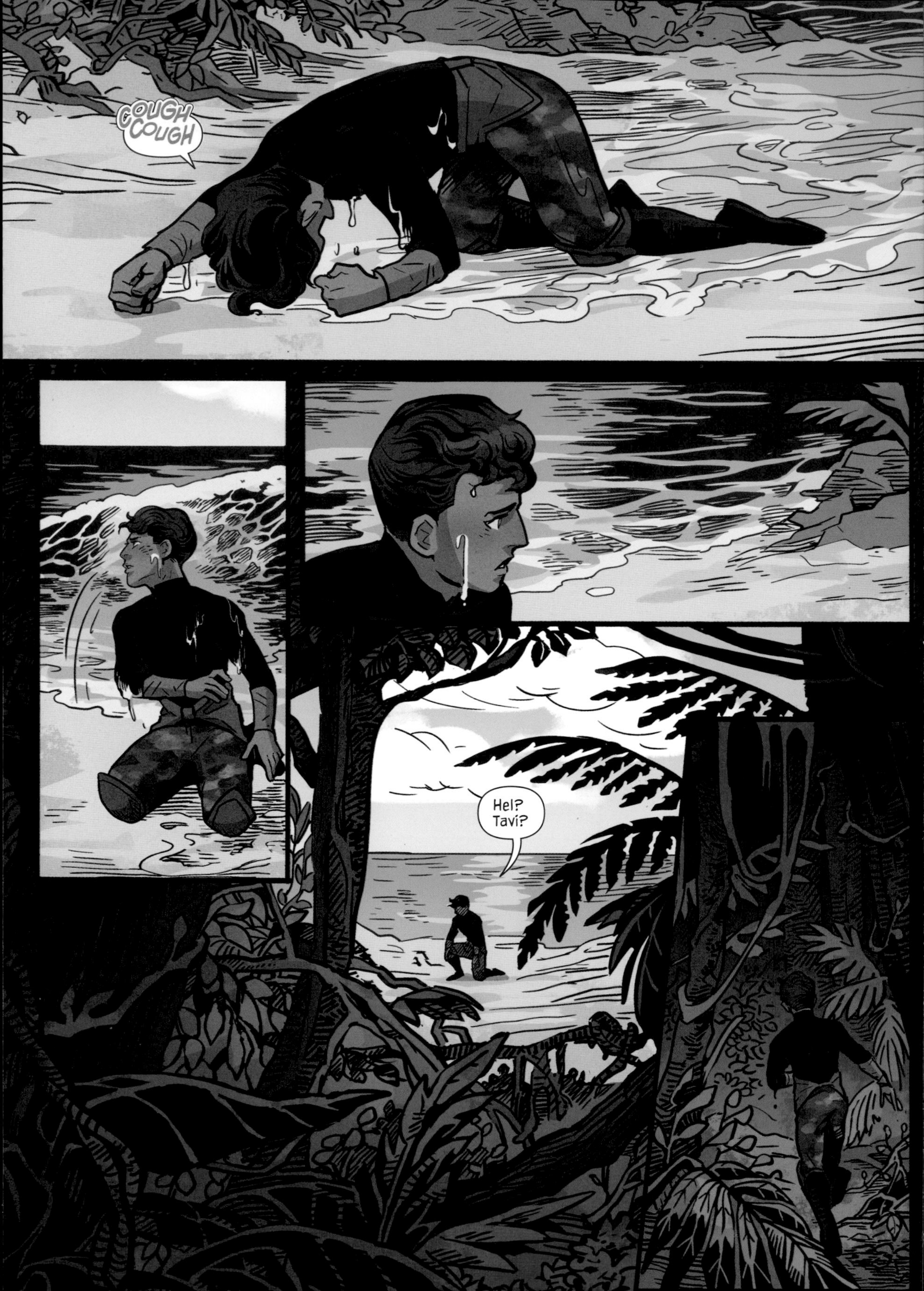
COUGH COUGH
Hel? Tavi?

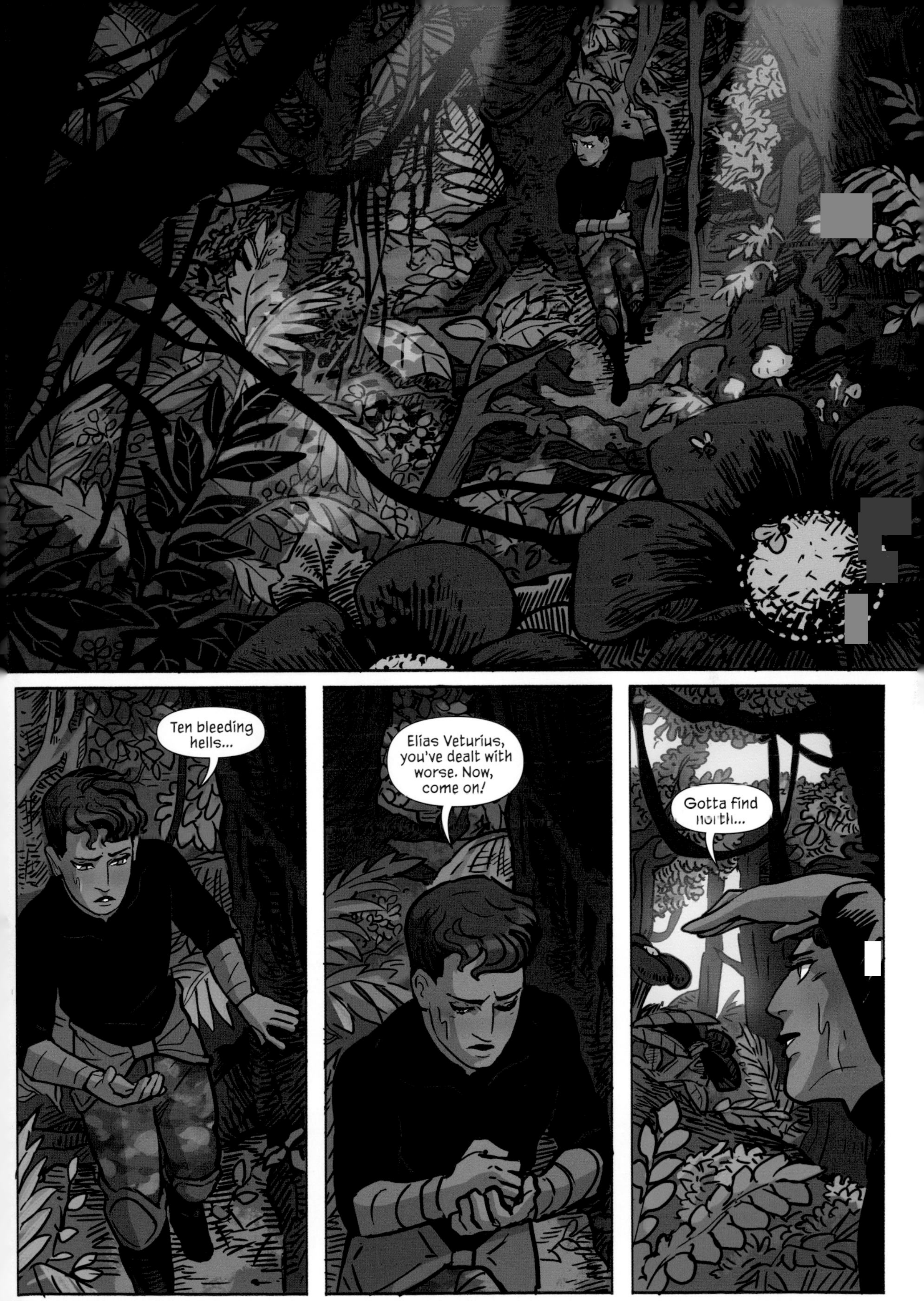
Ten bleeding hells...
Elias Veturius, you've dealt with worse. Now, come on!
Gotta find north...

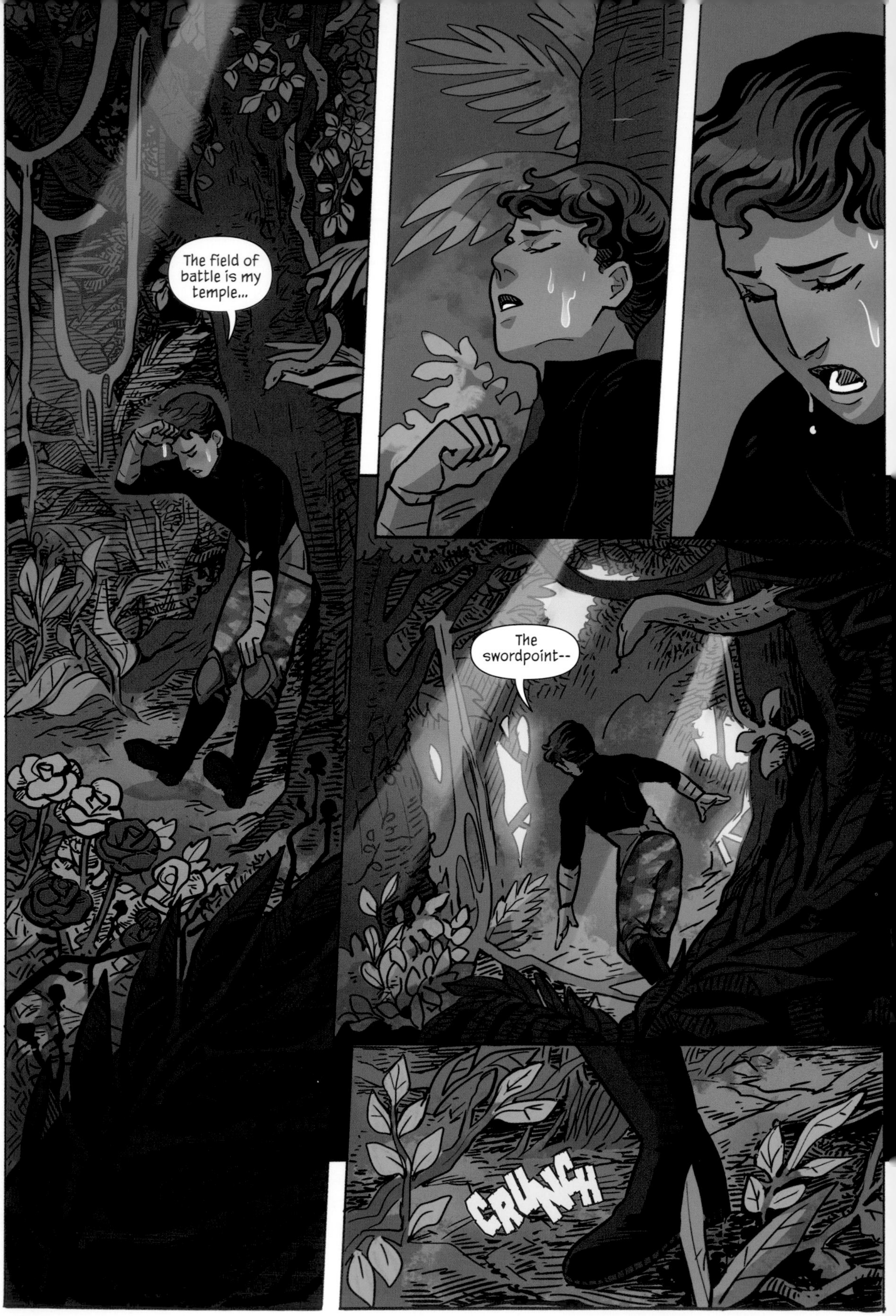
The field of battle is my temple...
The swordpoint--
CRUNCH

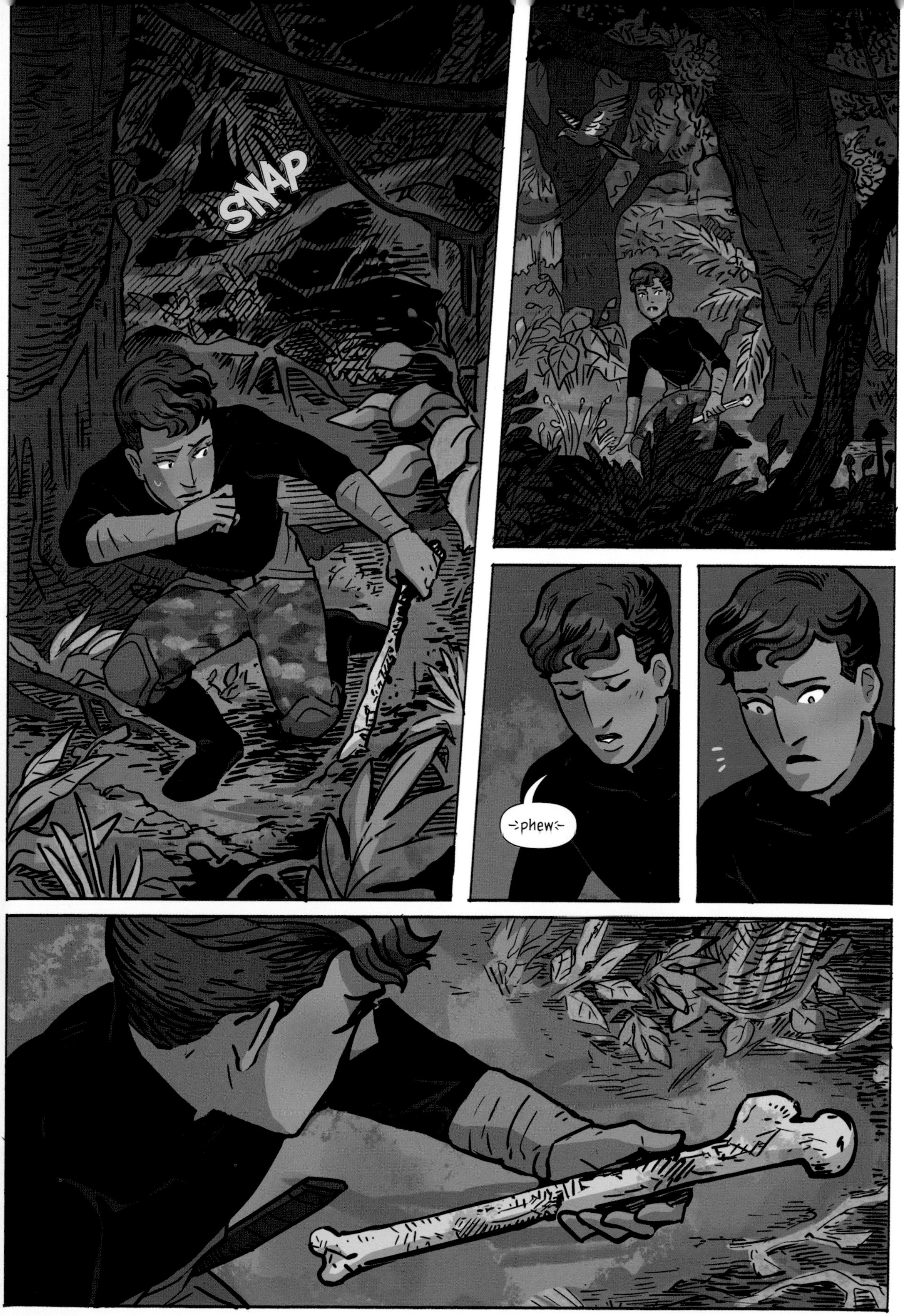
SNAP
phew

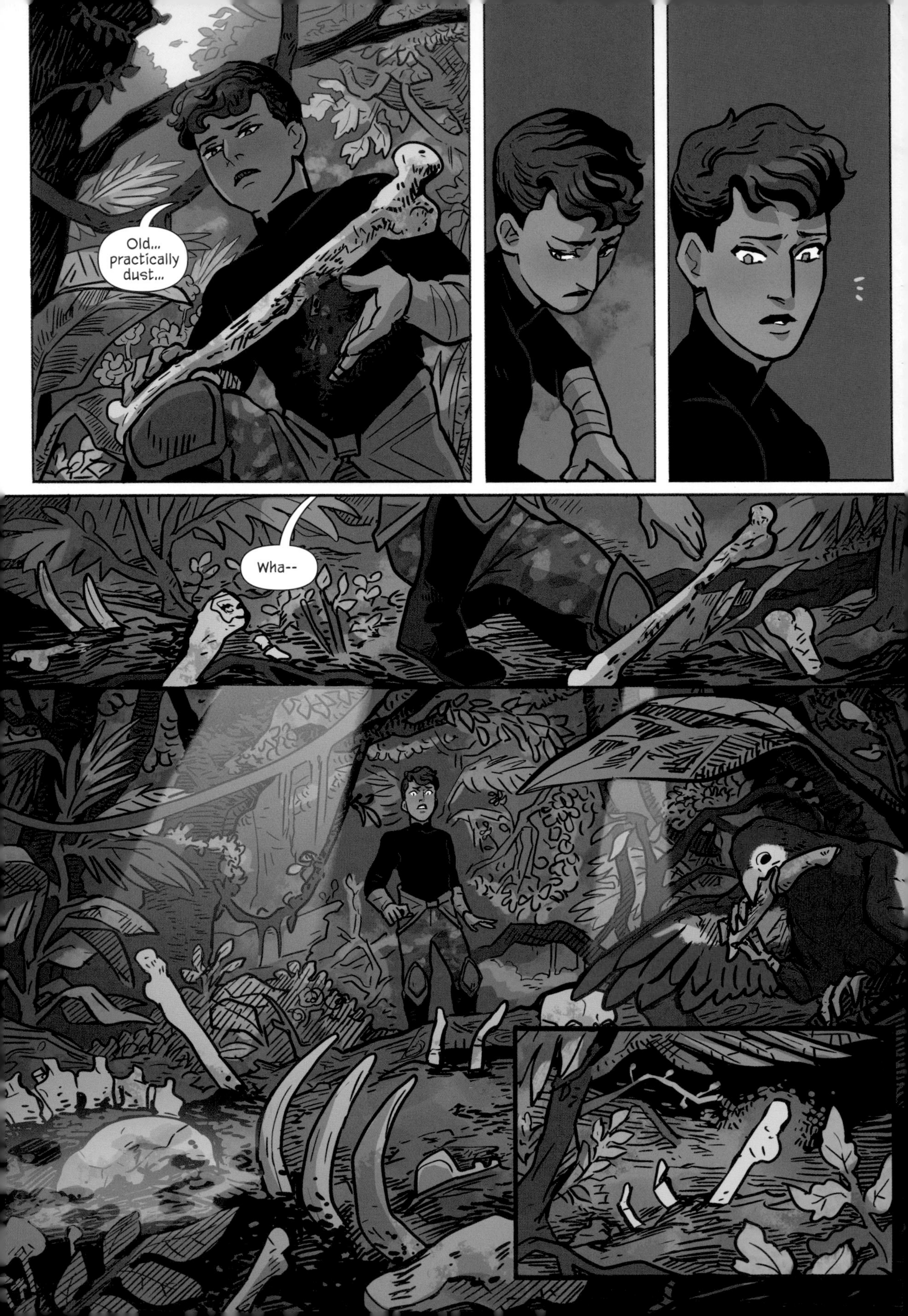
Old... practically dust...
Wha--

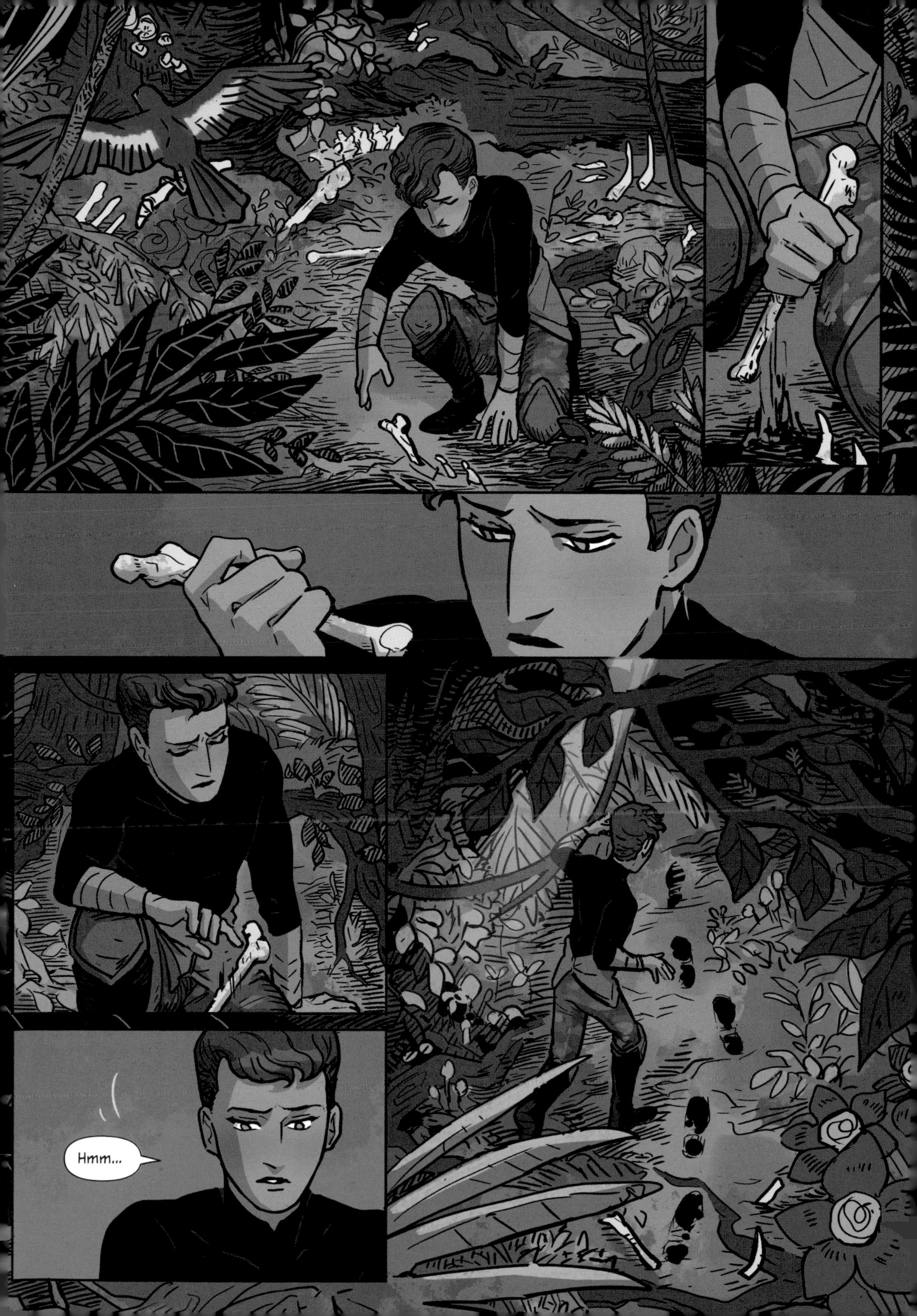
Hmm...

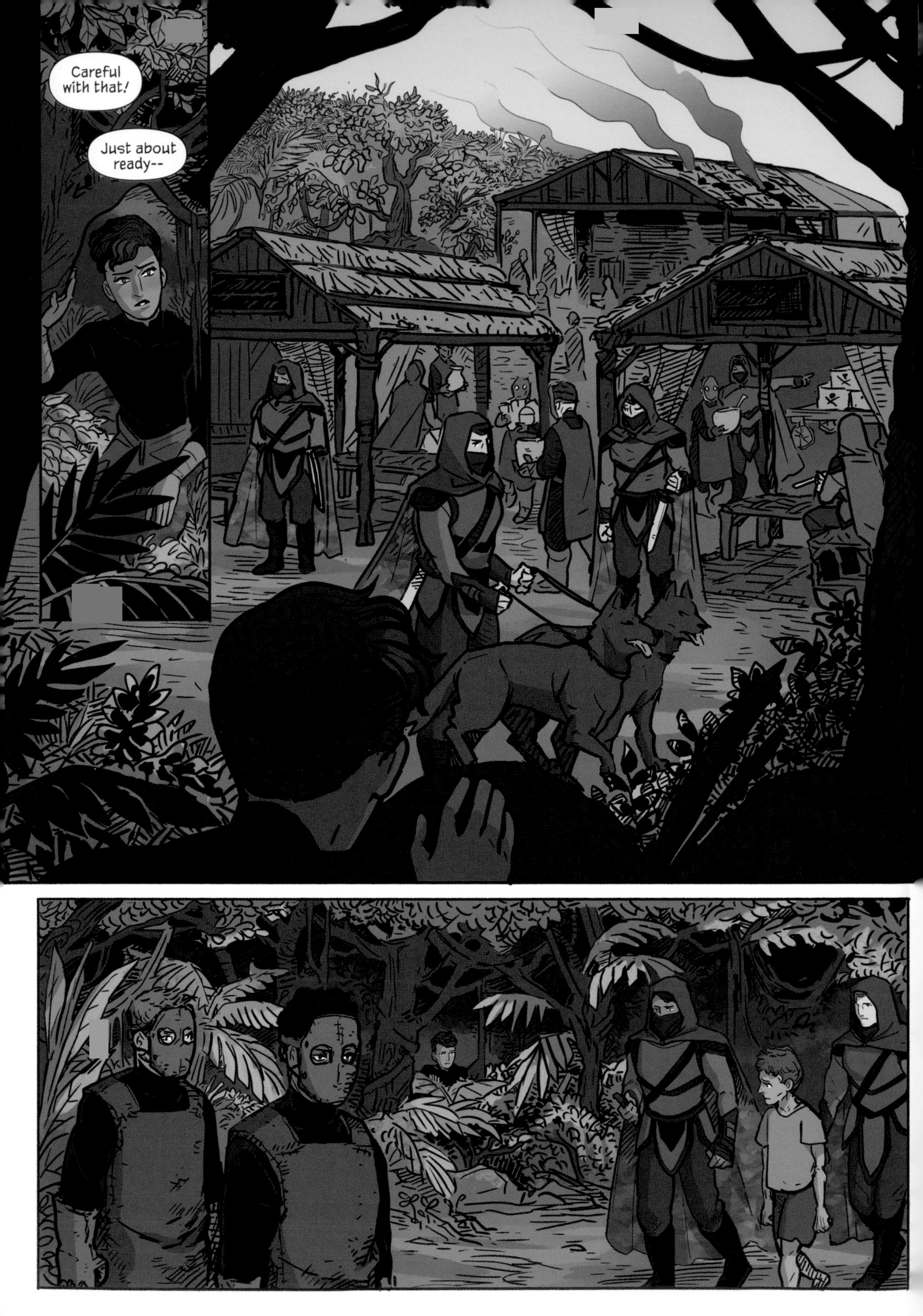
Careful with that!
Just about ready--

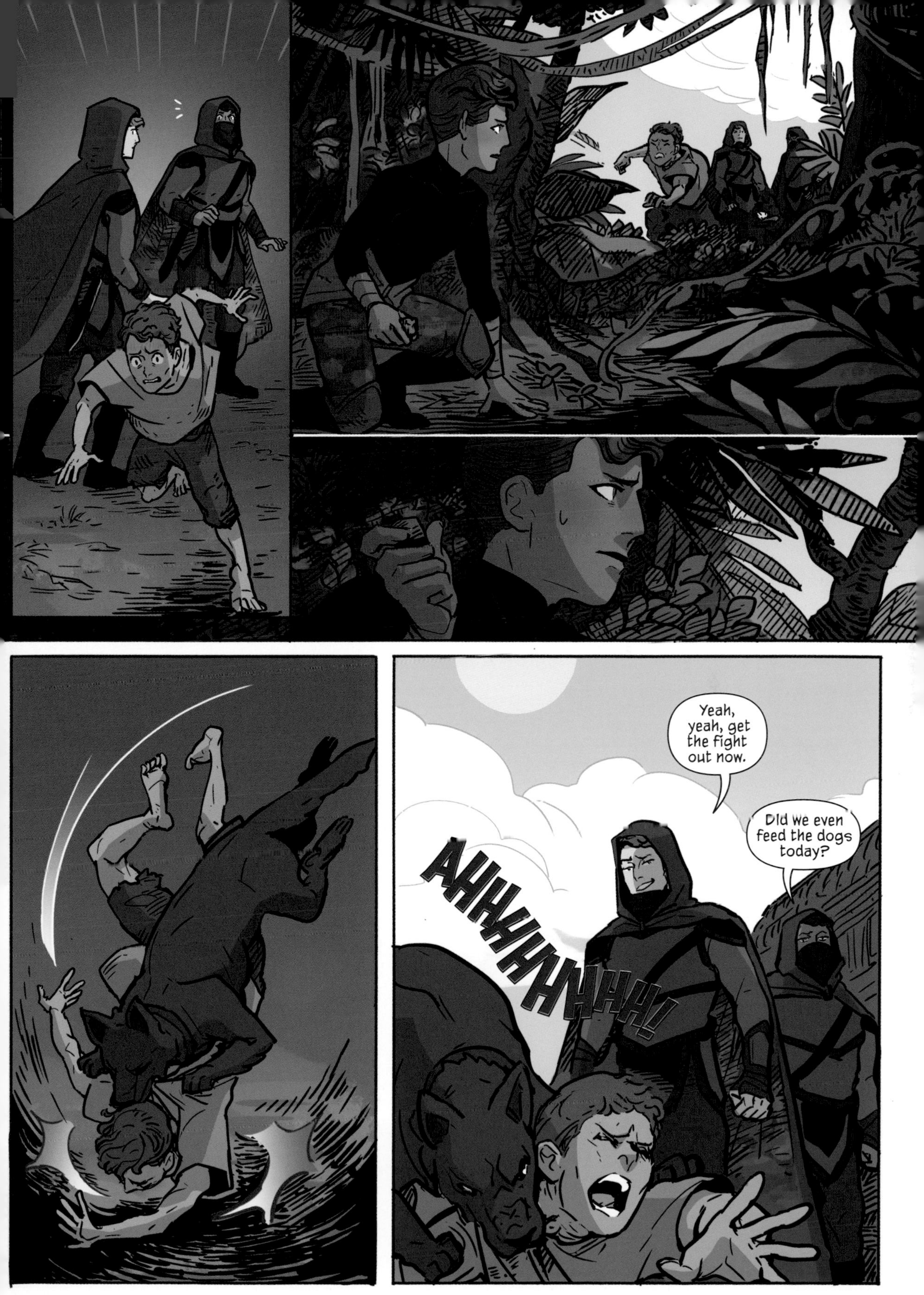
AHHHHHHHHH!
Yeah, yeah, get the fight out now.
Did we even feed the dogs today?

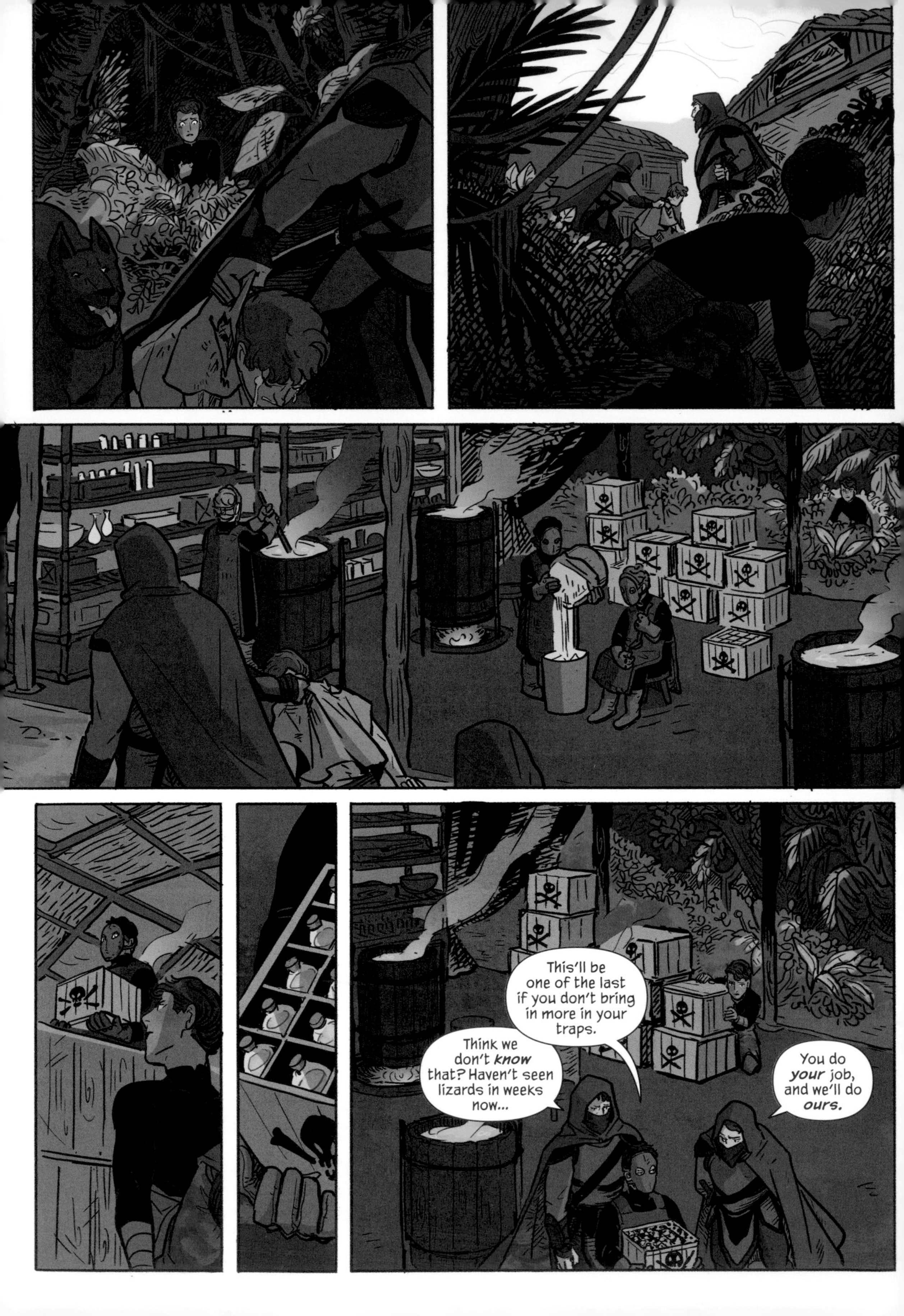

This'll be one of the last if you don't bring in more in your traps.
Think we don't *know* that? Haven't seen lizards in weeks now...
You do *your* job, and we'll do *ours.*

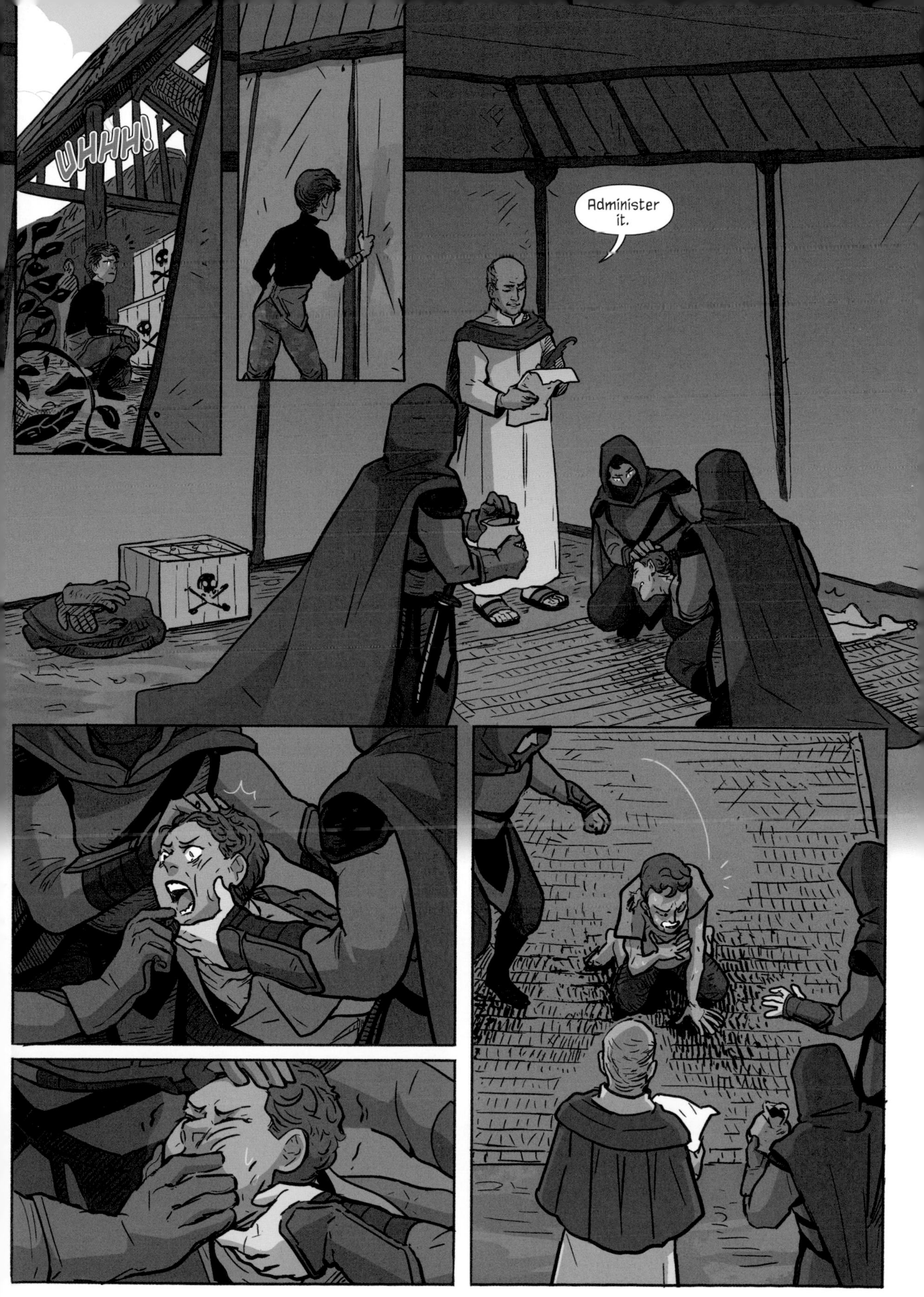
UHHH!
Administer it.

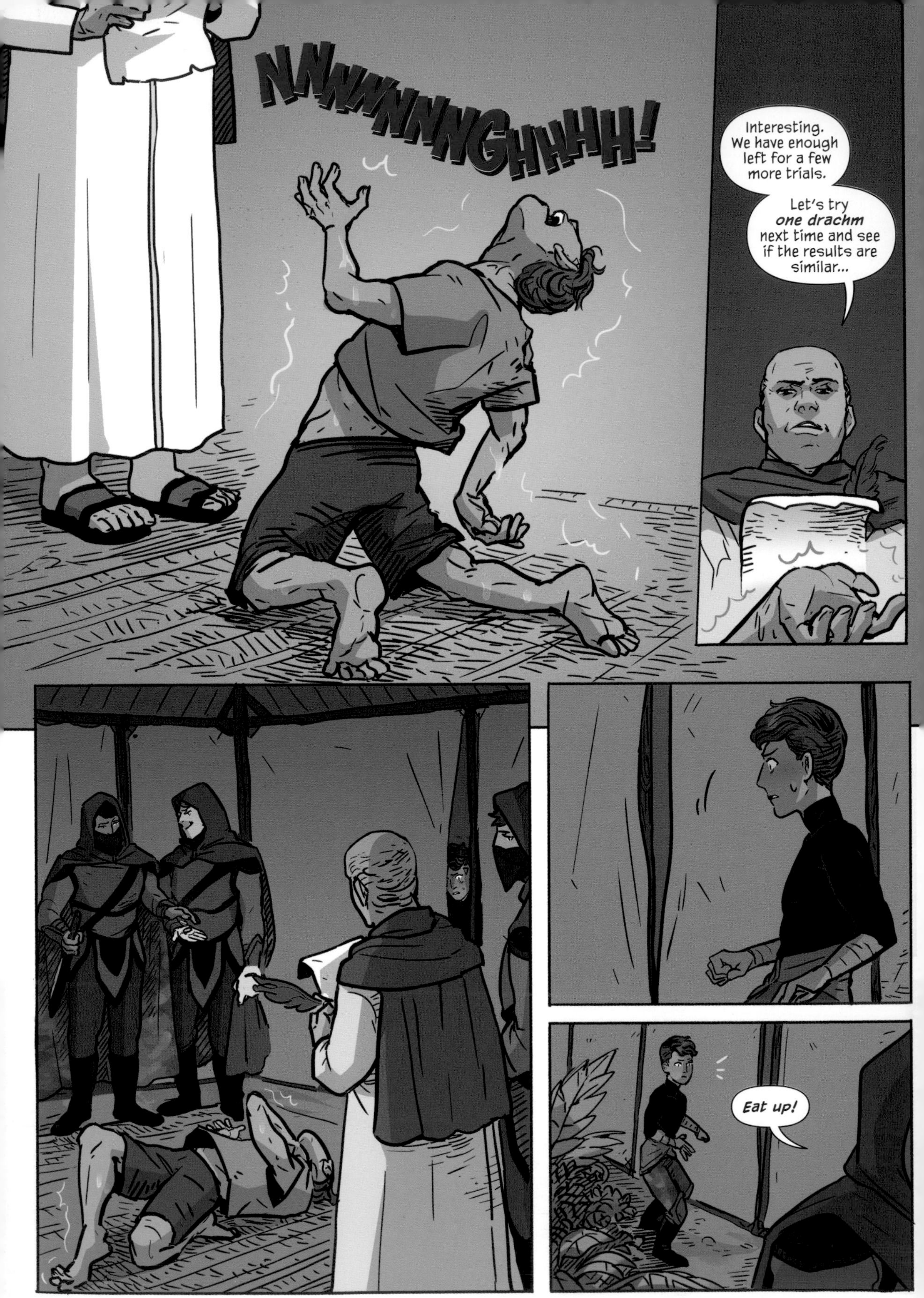
NNNNNNNNGHHHH!
Interesting. We have enough left for a few more trials.
Let's try *one drachm* next time and see if the results are similar...
Eat up!

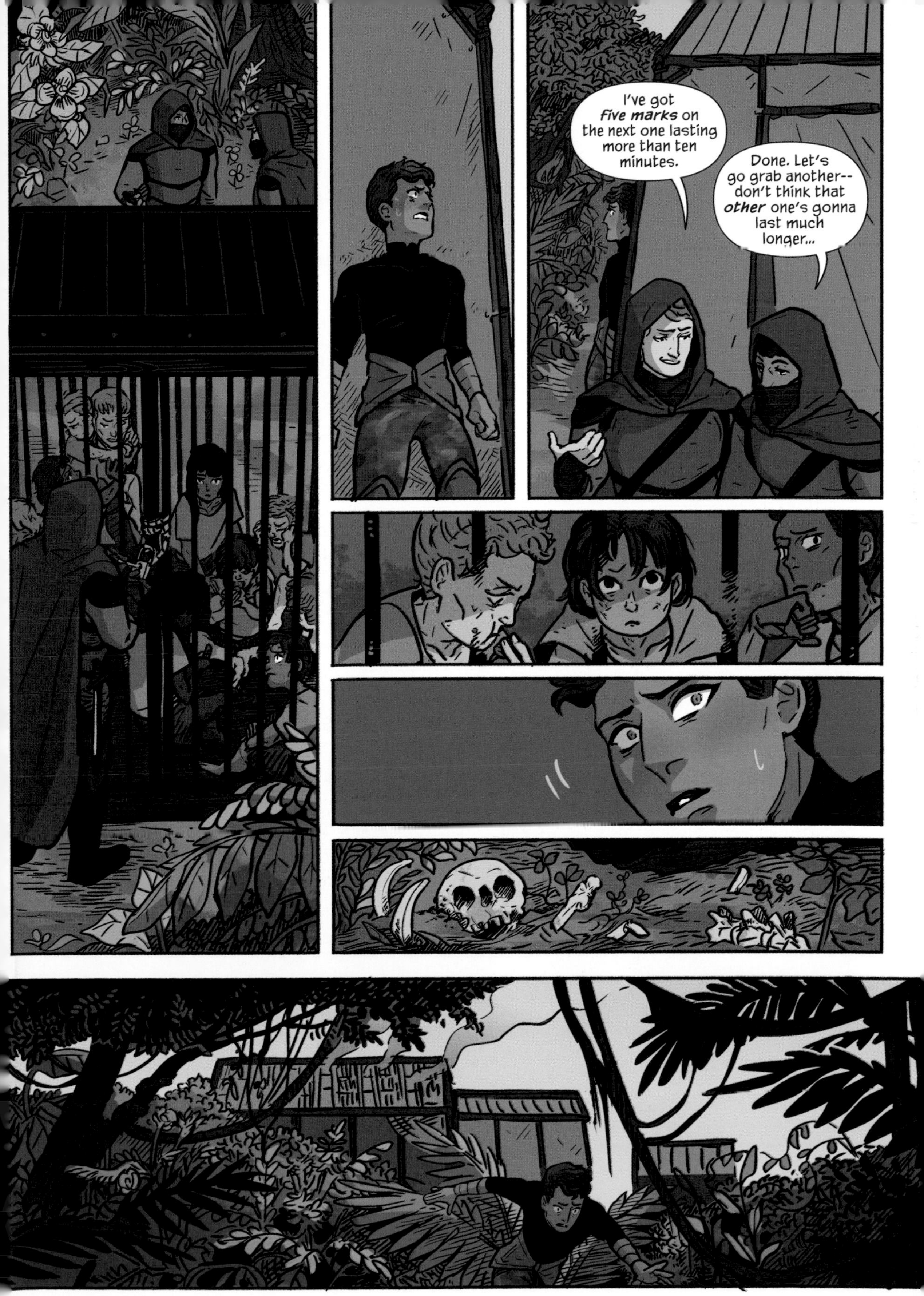
I've got *five marks* on the next one lasting more than ten minutes.
Done. Let's go grab another-- don't think that *other* one's gonna last much longer...

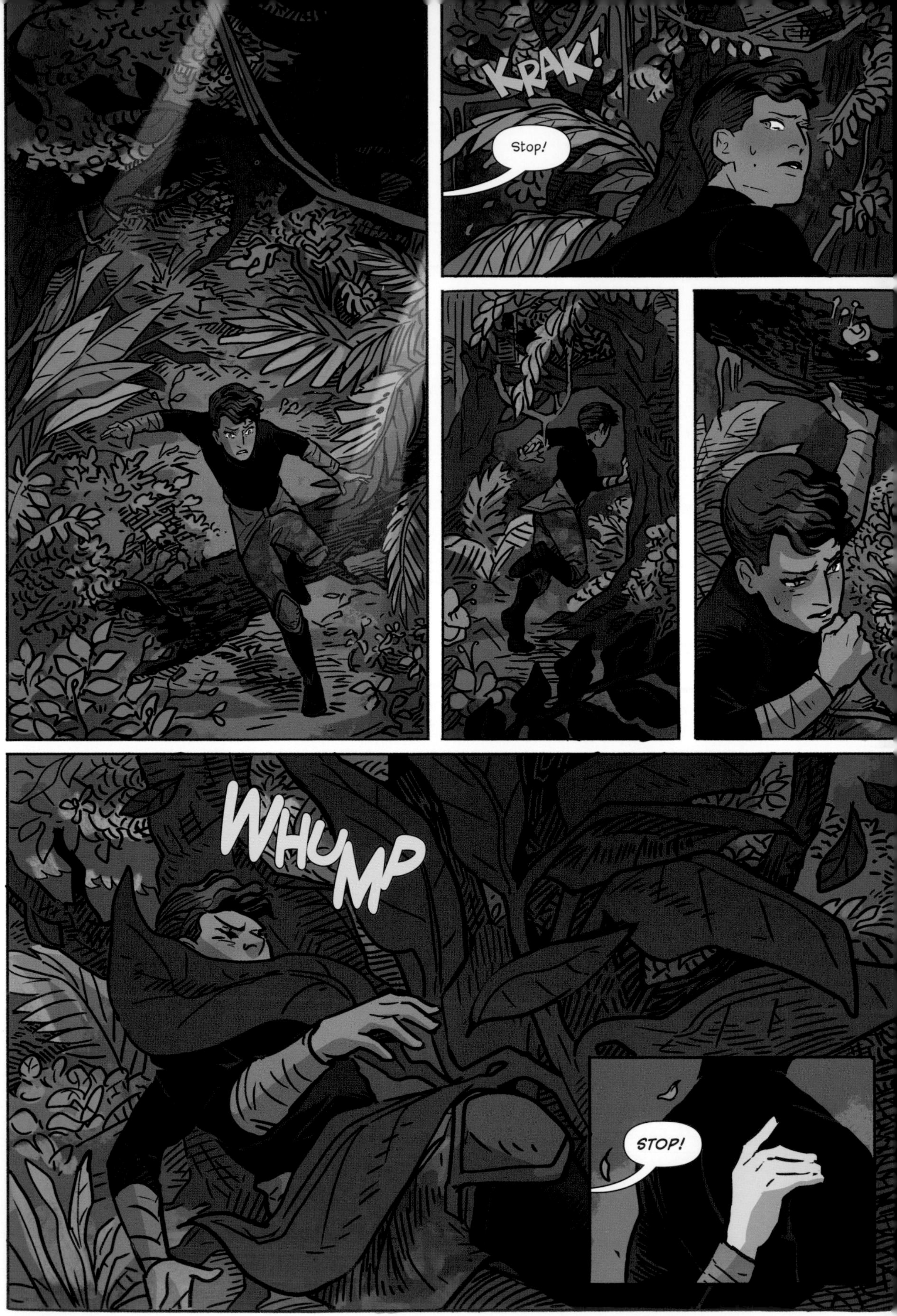
KRAK!
Stop!
WHUMP
STOP!

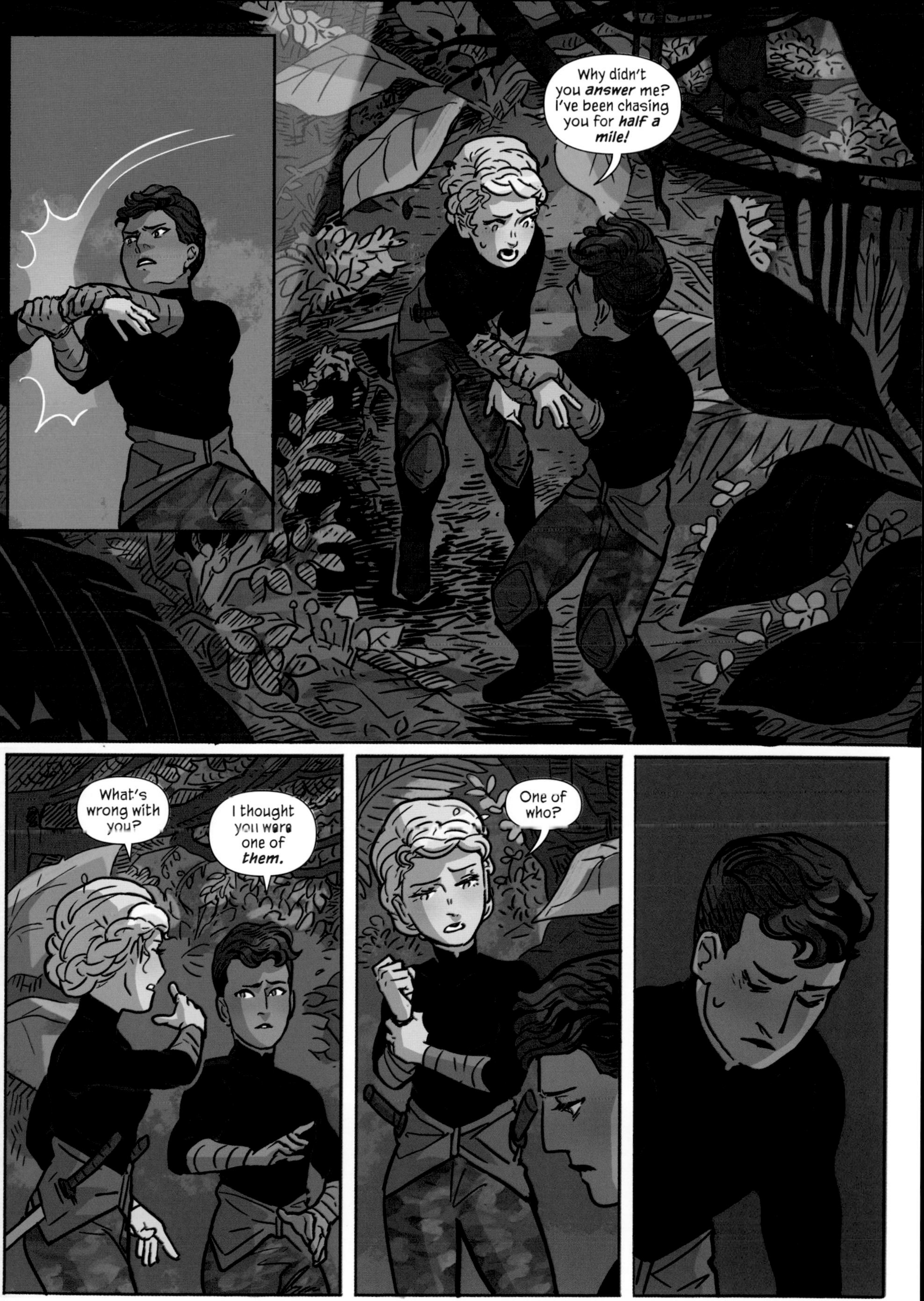

Why didn't you *answer* me? I've been chasing you for *half a mile!*
What's wrong with you?
I thought you were one of *them.*
One of who?

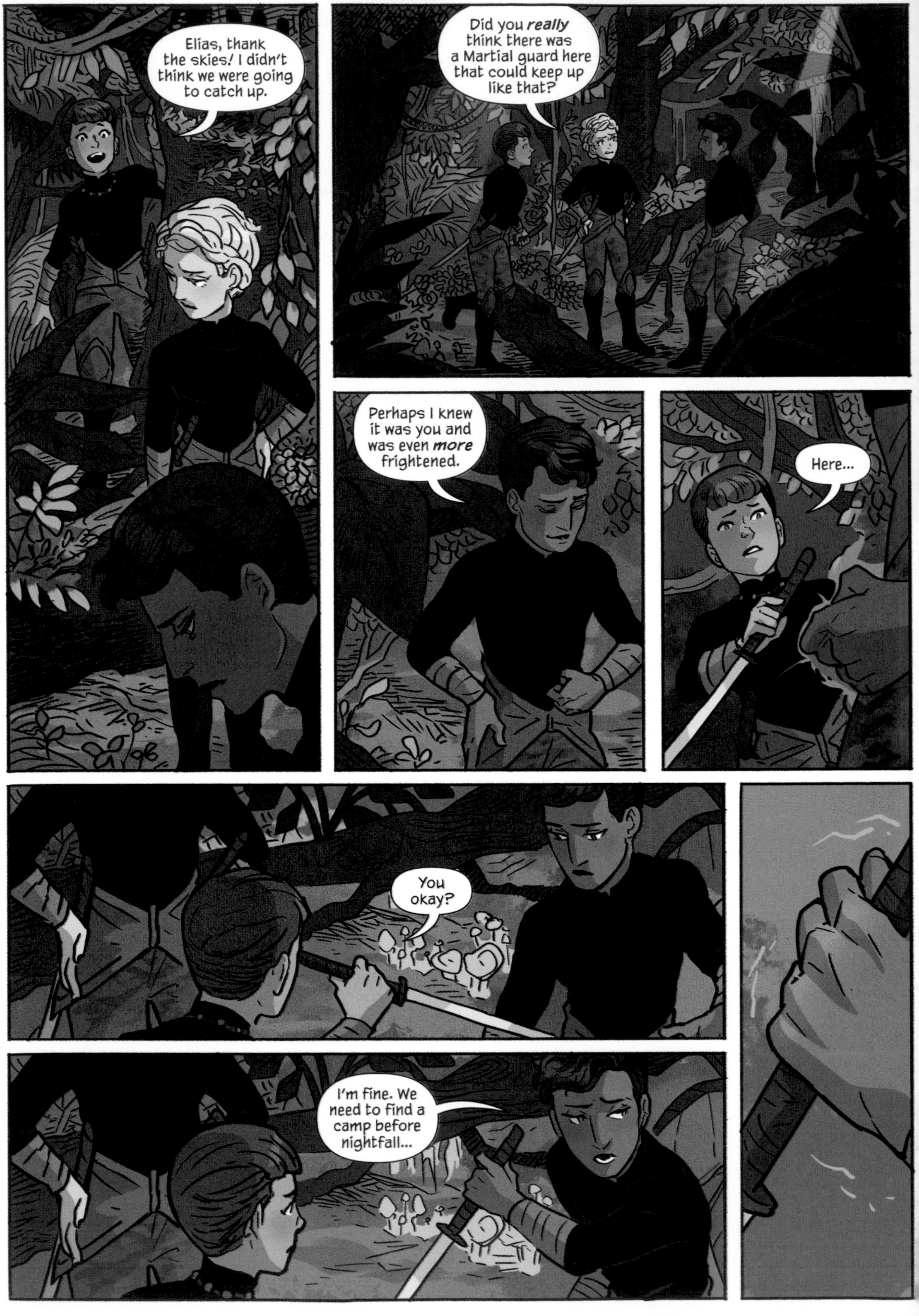
Elias, thank the skies! I didn't think we were going to catch up.
Did you *really* think there was a Martial guard here that could keep up like that?
Perhaps I knew it was you and was even *more* frightened.
Here...
You okay?
I'm fine. We need to find a camp before nightfall...

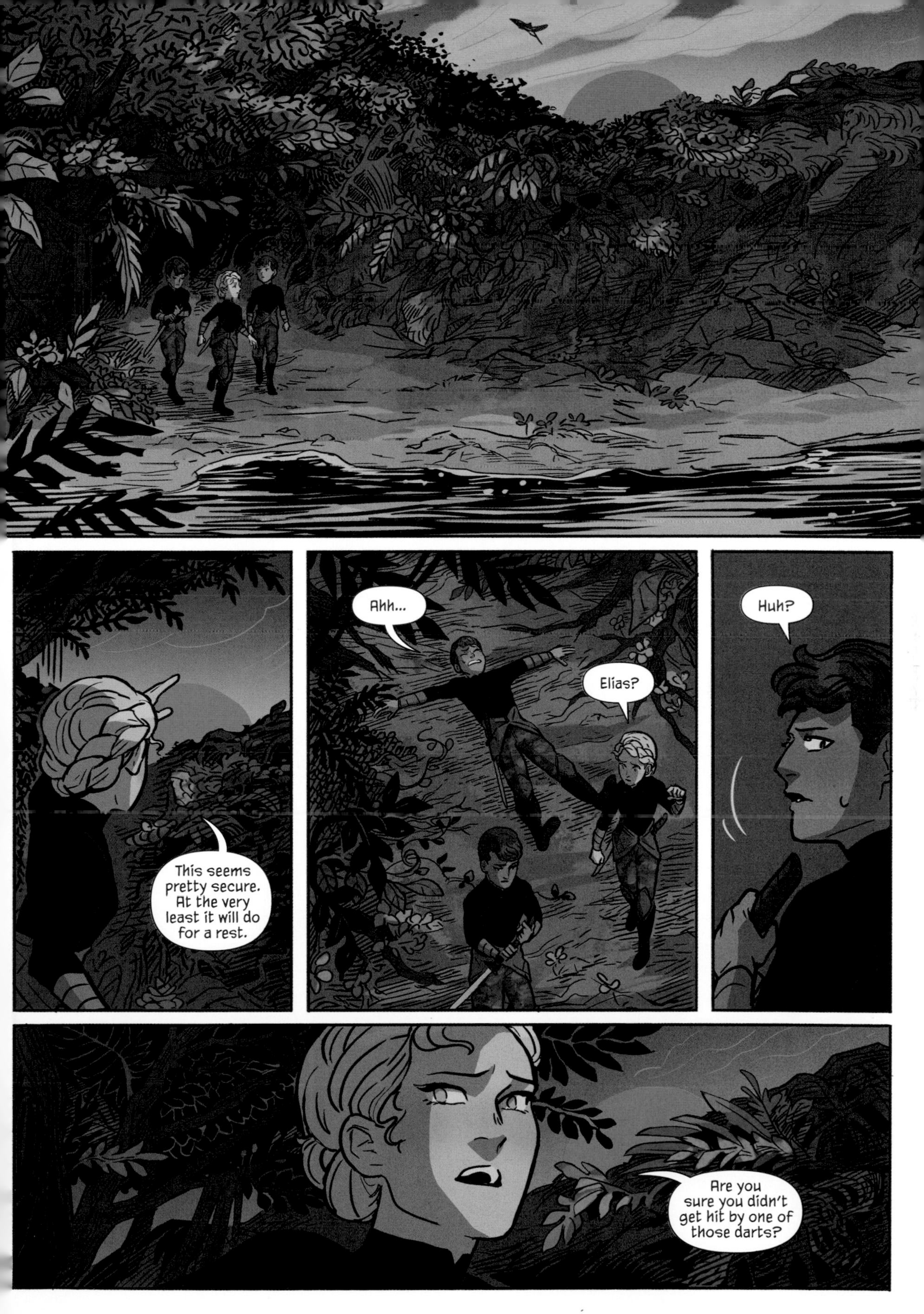
This seems pretty secure. At the very least it will do for a rest.
Ahh...
Elias?
Huh?
Are you sure you didn't get hit by one of those darts?

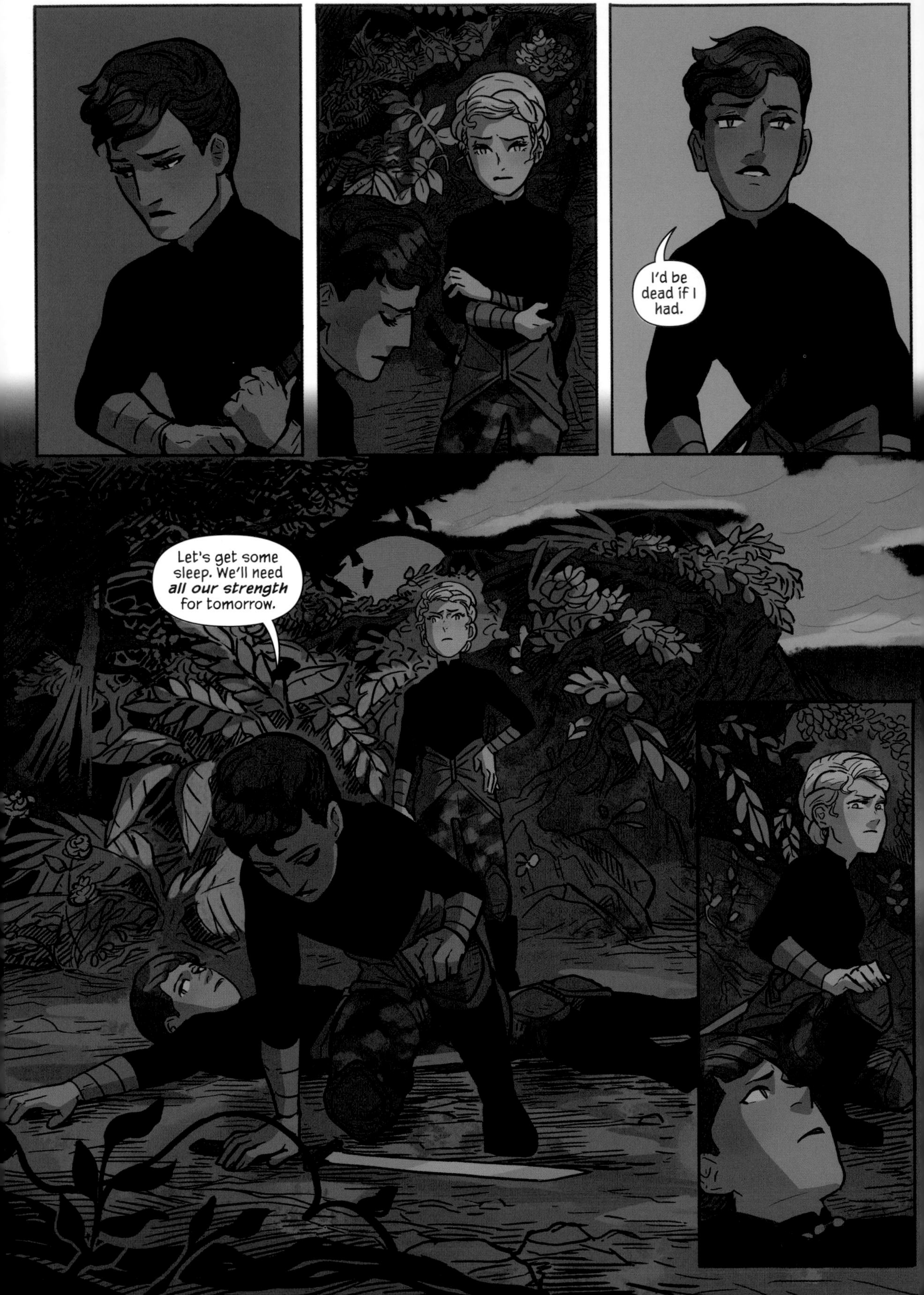
I'd be dead if I had.
Let's get some sleep. We'll need **all our strength** for tomorrow.

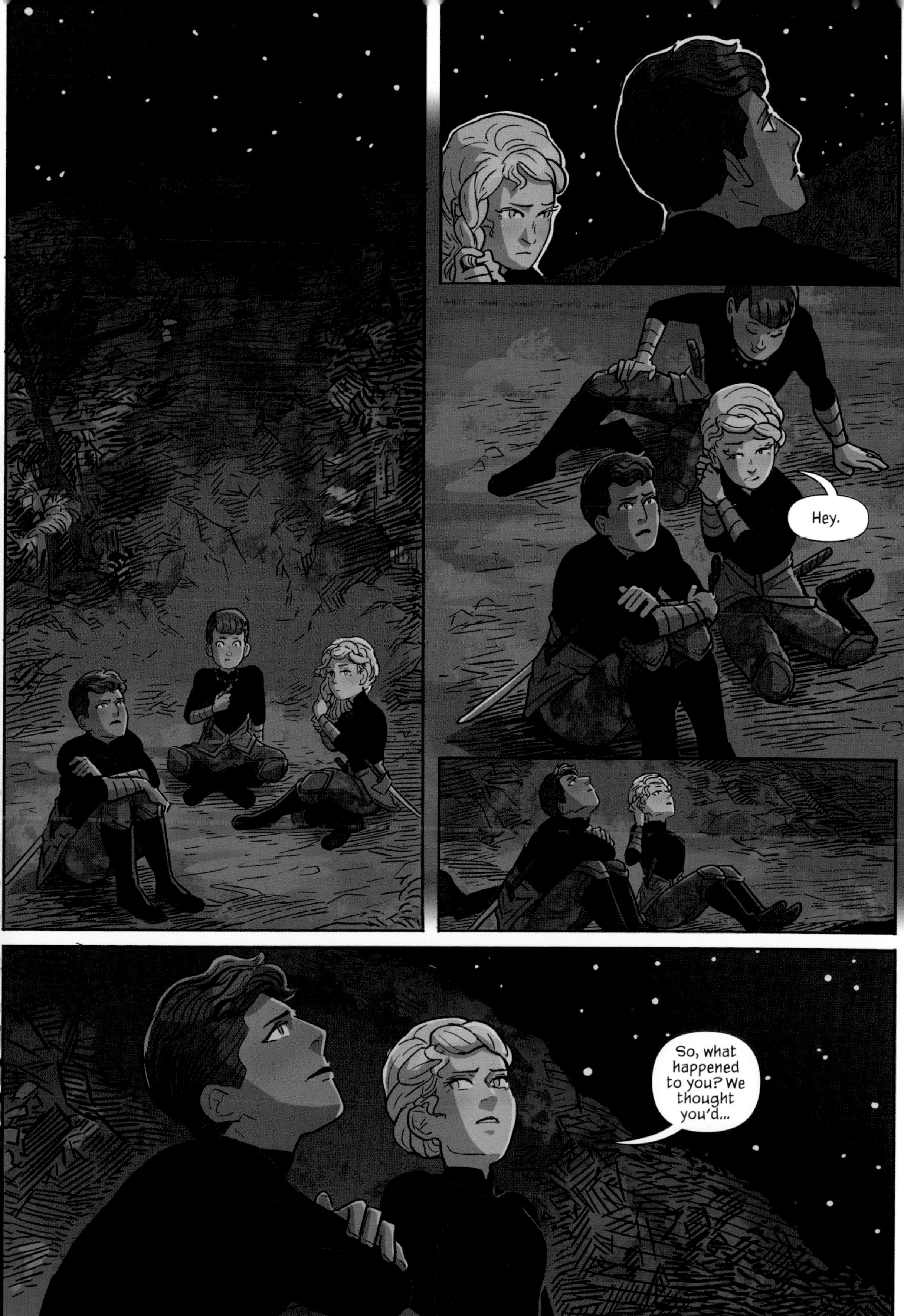
Hey.
So, what happened to you? We thought you'd...

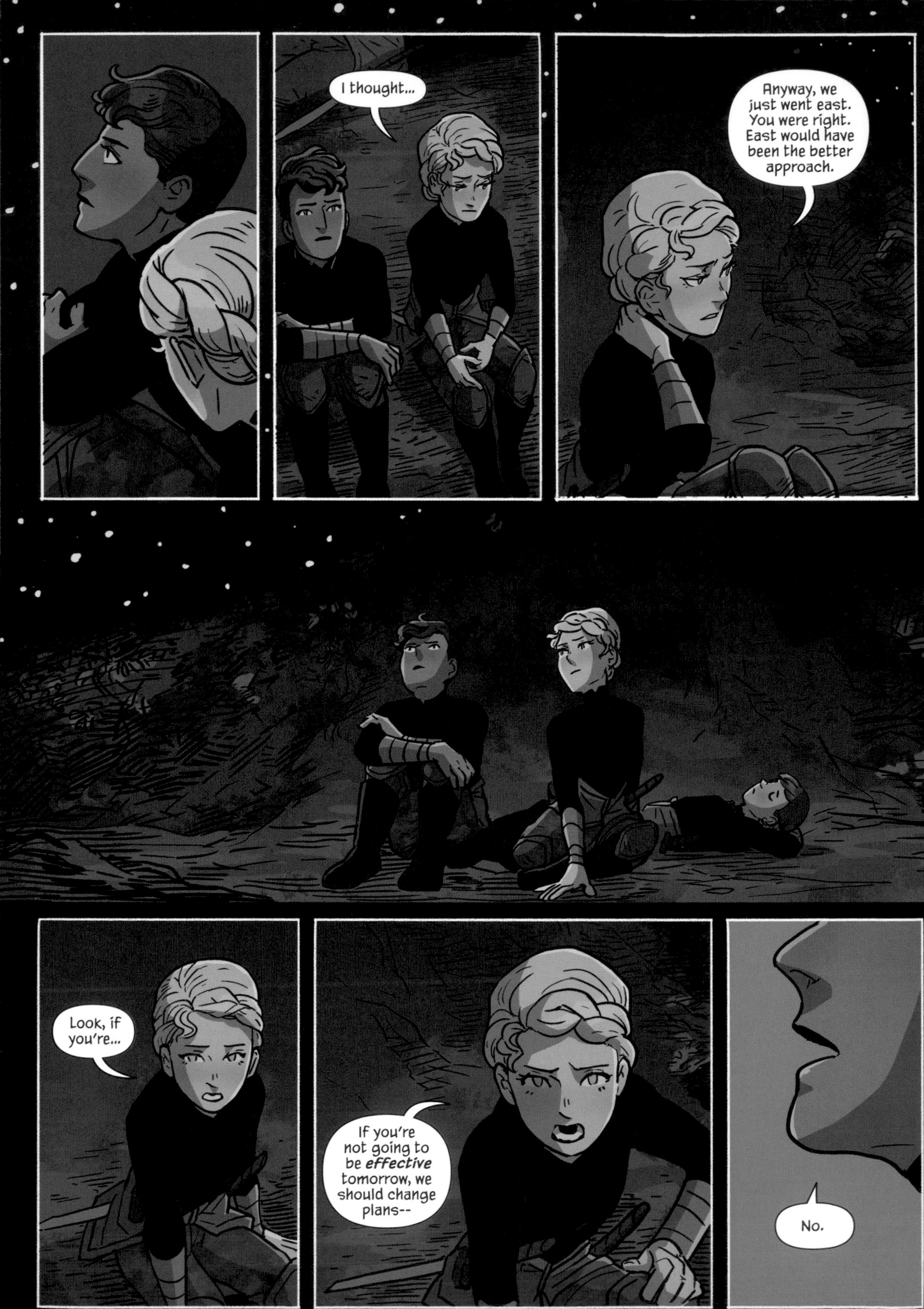
I thought...
Anyway, we just went east. You were right. East would have been the better approach.
Look, if you're...
If you're not going to be *effective* tomorrow, we should change plans--
No.

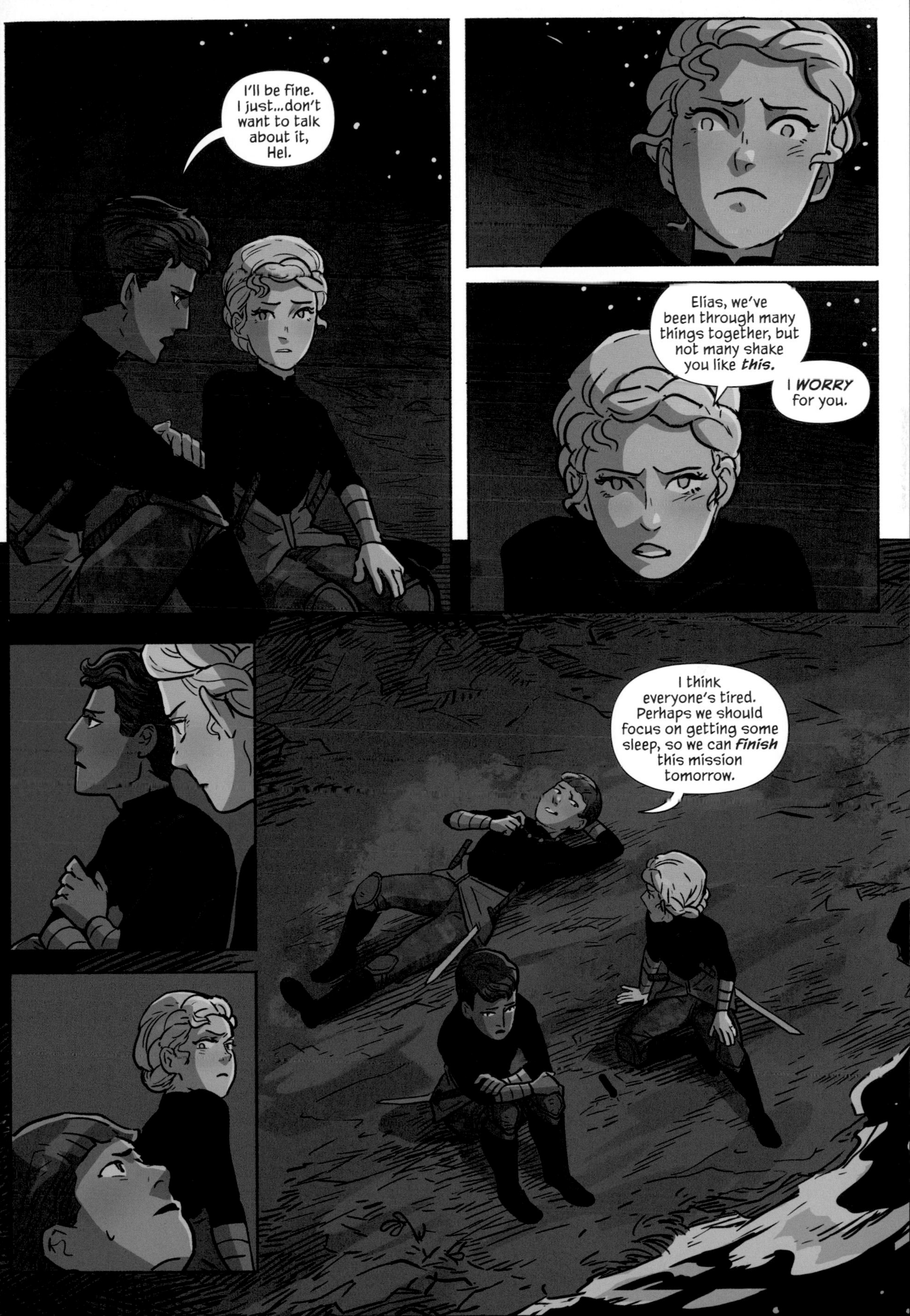
I'll be fine. I just...don't want to talk about it, Hel.
Elias, we've been through many things together, but not many shake you like *this.*
I **WORRY** for you.
I think everyone's tired. Perhaps we should focus on getting some sleep, so we can *finish* this mission tomorrow.

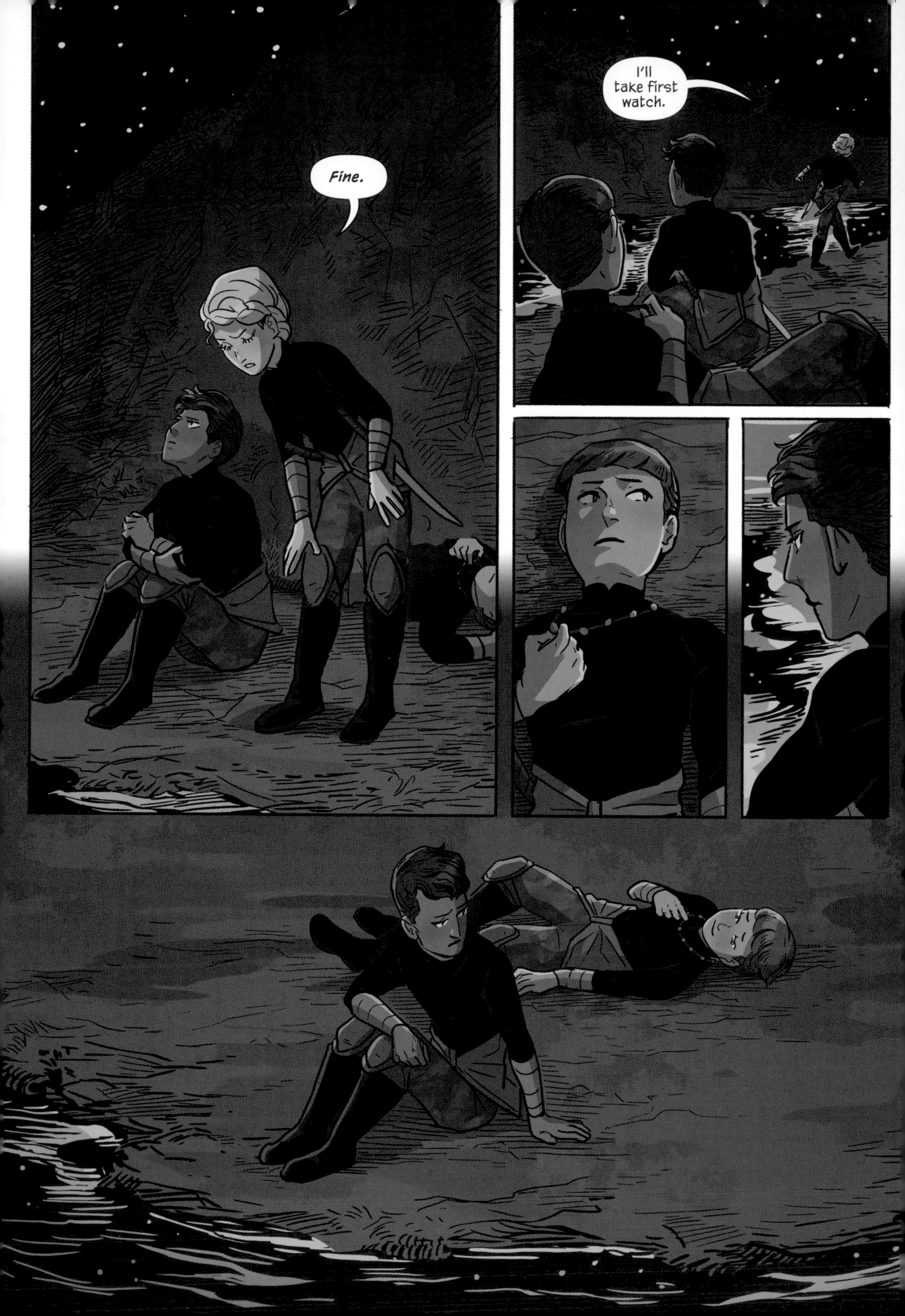
Fine.
I'll take first watch.

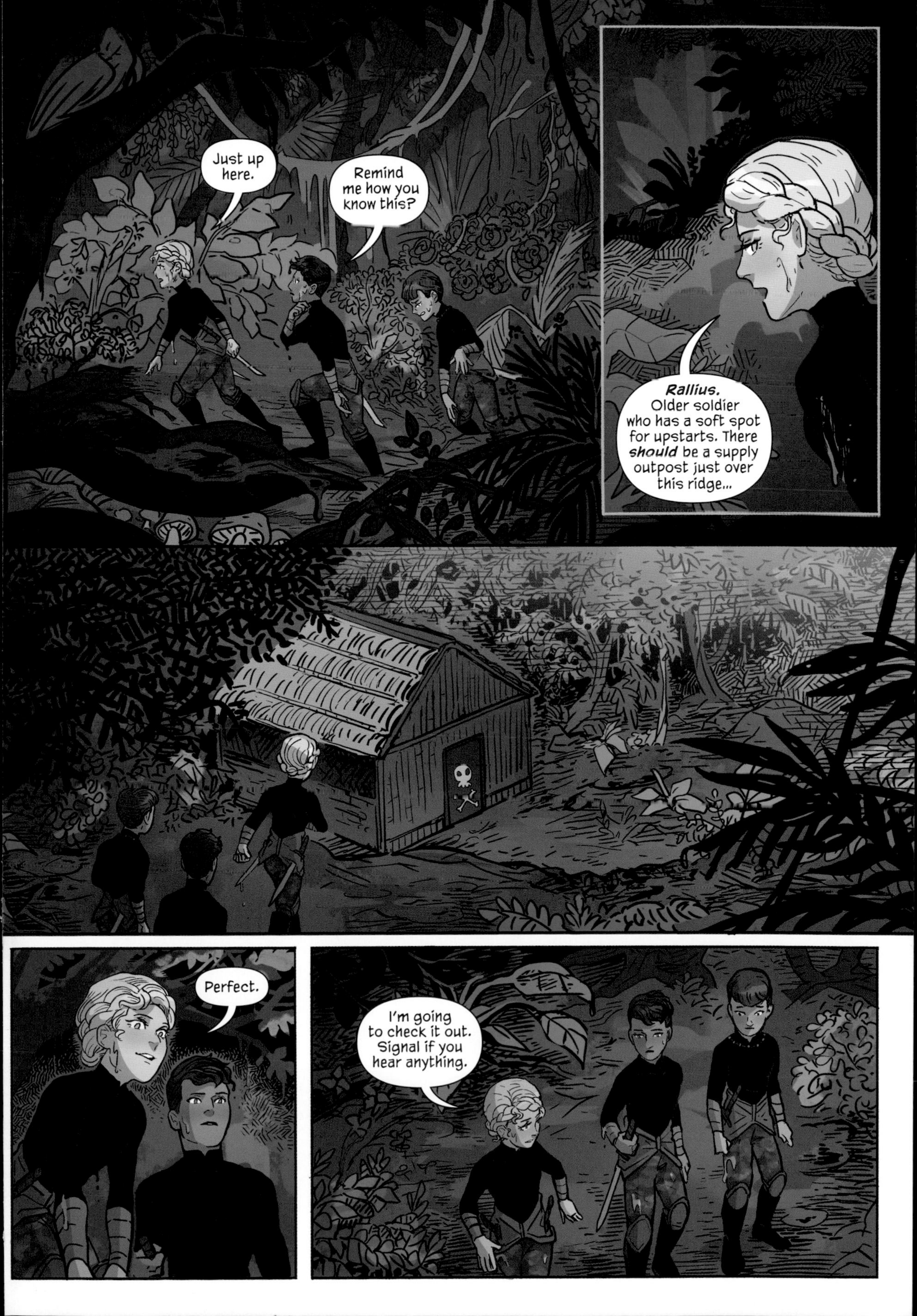
Just up here.
Remind me how you know this?
Rallius. Older soldier who has a soft spot for upstarts. There should be a supply outpost just over this ridge...
Perfect.
I'm going to check it out. Signal if you hear anything.

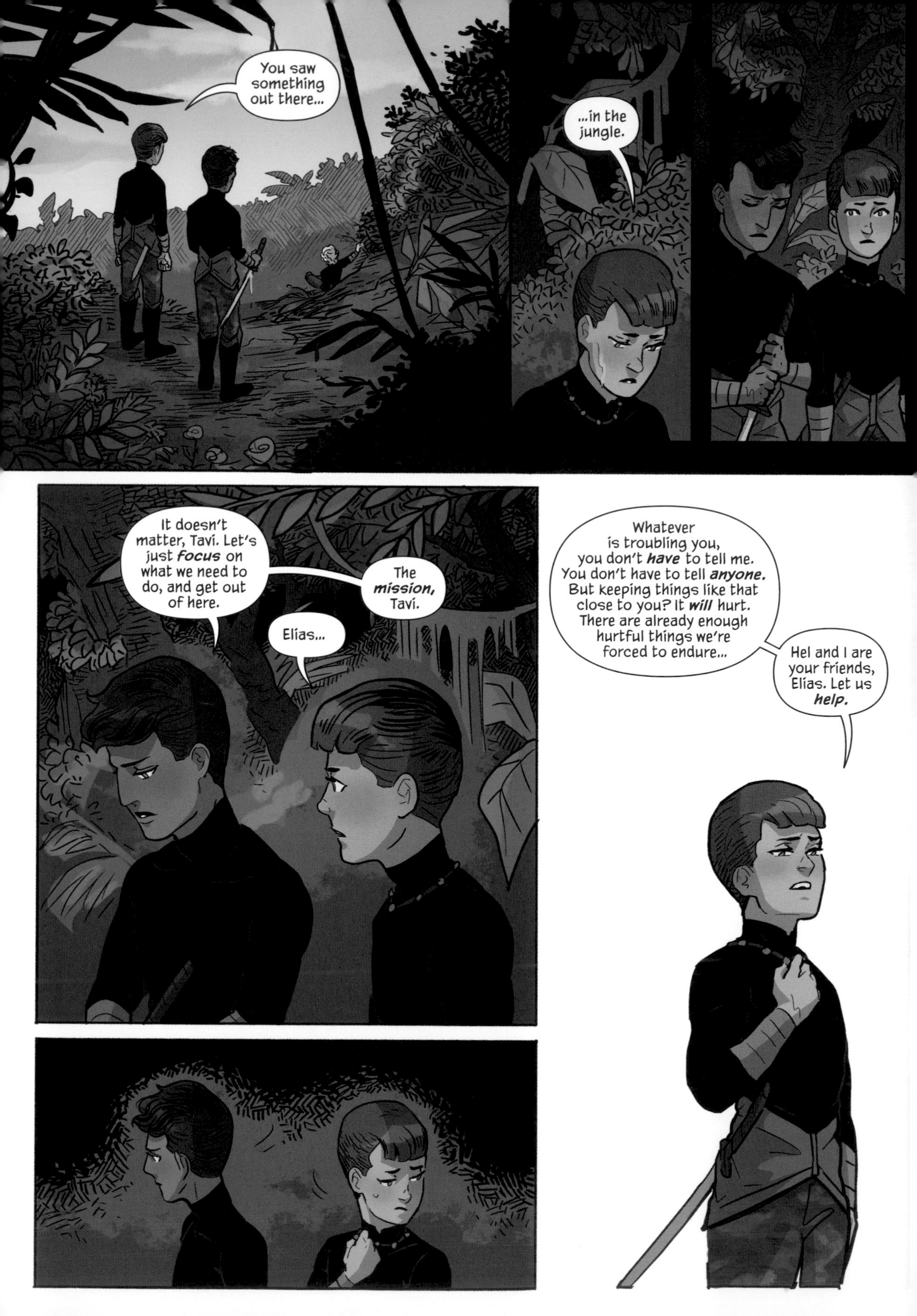
You saw something out there...
...in the jungle.
It doesn't matter, Tavi. Let's just *focus* on what we need to do, and get out of here.
The *mission,* Tavi.
Elías...
Whatever is troubling you, you don't *have* to tell me. You don't have to tell *anyone.* But keeping things like that close to you? It *will* hurt. There are already enough hurtful things we're forced to endure...
Hel and I are your friends, Elías. Let us *help.*

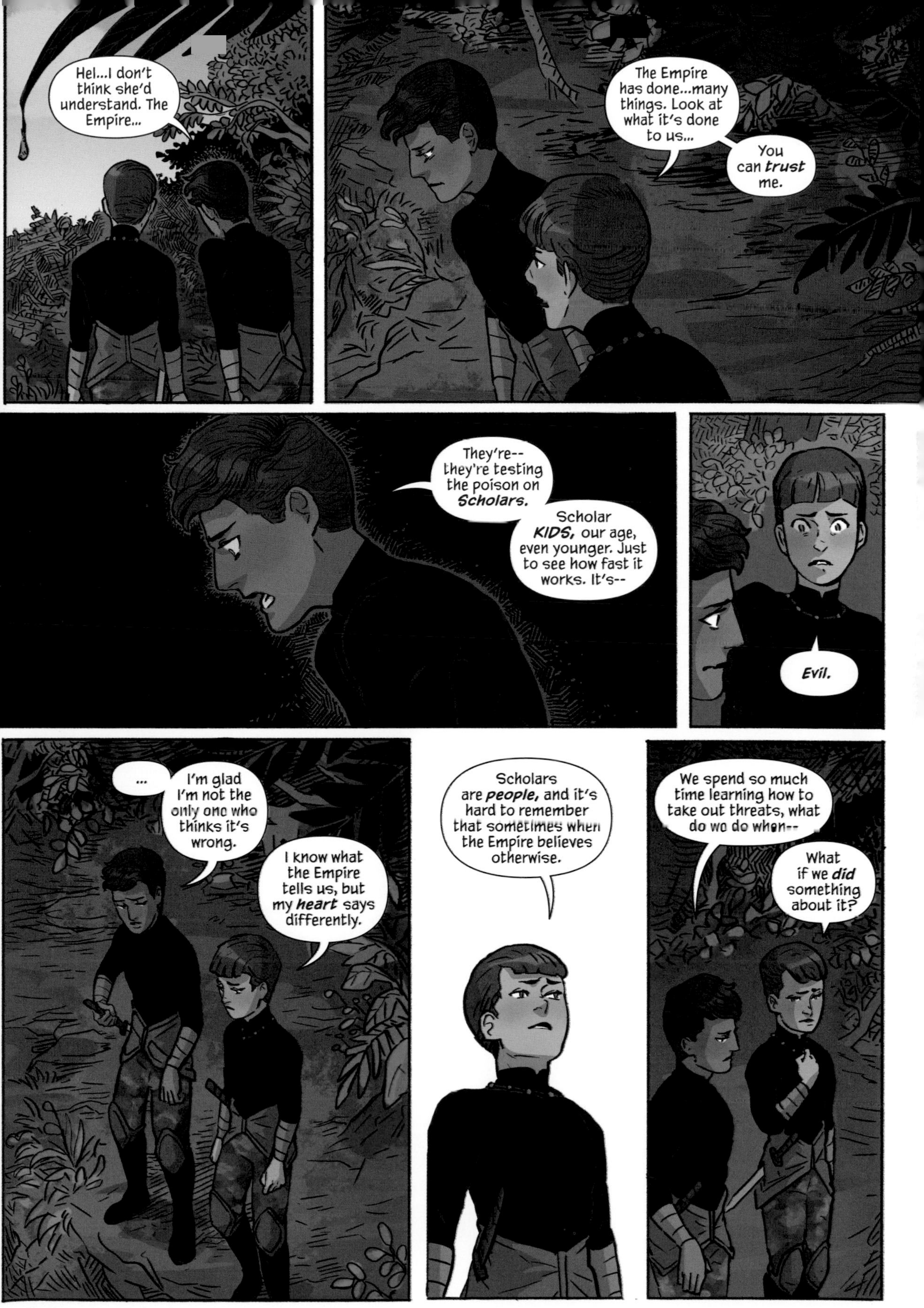
Hel...I don't think she'd understand. The Empire...
The Empire has done...many things. Look at what it's done to us...
You can *trust* me.
They're-- they're testing the poison on *Scholars.*
Scholar *KIDS,* our age, even younger. Just to see how fast it works. It's--
Evil.
...
I'm glad I'm not the only one who thinks it's wrong.
I know what the Empire tells us, but my *heart* says differently.
Scholars are *people,* and it's hard to remember that sometimes when the Empire believes otherwise.
We spend so much time learning how to take out threats, what do we do when--
What if we *did* something about it?

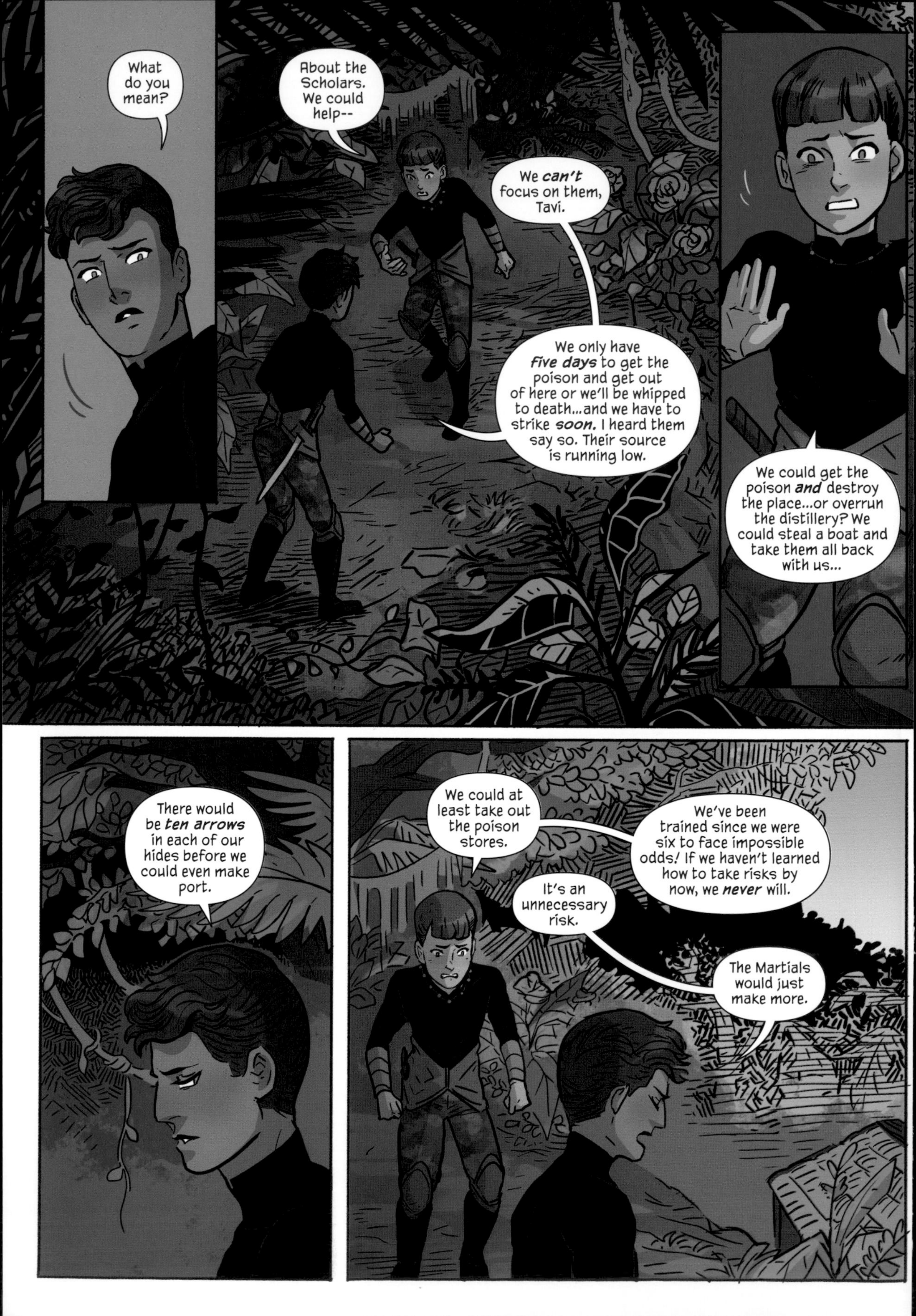
What do you mean?
About the Scholars. We could help--
We *can't* focus on them, Tavi.
We only have *five days* to get the poison and get out of here or we'll be whipped to death...and we have to strike *soon.* I heard them say so. Their source is running low.
We could get the poison *and* destroy the place...or overrun the distillery? We could steal a boat and take them all back with us...
There would be *ten arrows* in each of our hides before we could even make port.
We could at least take out the poison stores.
We've been trained since we were six to face impossible odds! If we haven't learned how to take risks by now, we *never* will.
It's an unnecessary risk.
The Martials would just make more.

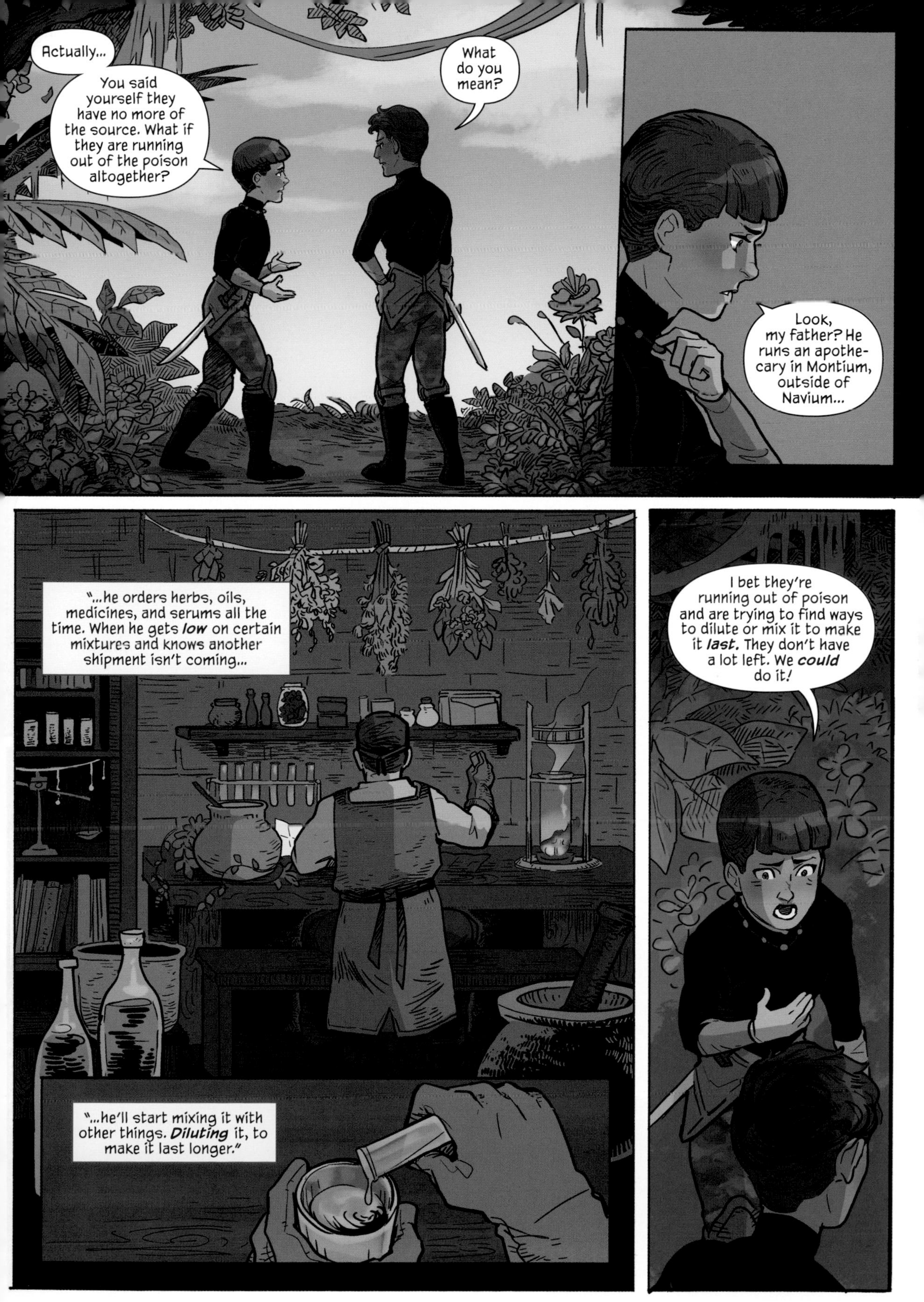
Actually...
You said yourself they have no more of the source. What if they are running out of the poison altogether?
What do you mean?
Look, my father? He runs an apothecary in Montium, outside of Navium...
"...he orders herbs, oils, medicines, and serums all the time. When he gets *low* on certain mixtures and knows another shipment isn't coming...
"...he'll start mixing it with other things. *Diluting* it, to make it last longer."
I bet they're running out of poison and are trying to find ways to dilute or mix it to make it *last.* They don't have a lot left. We *could* do it!

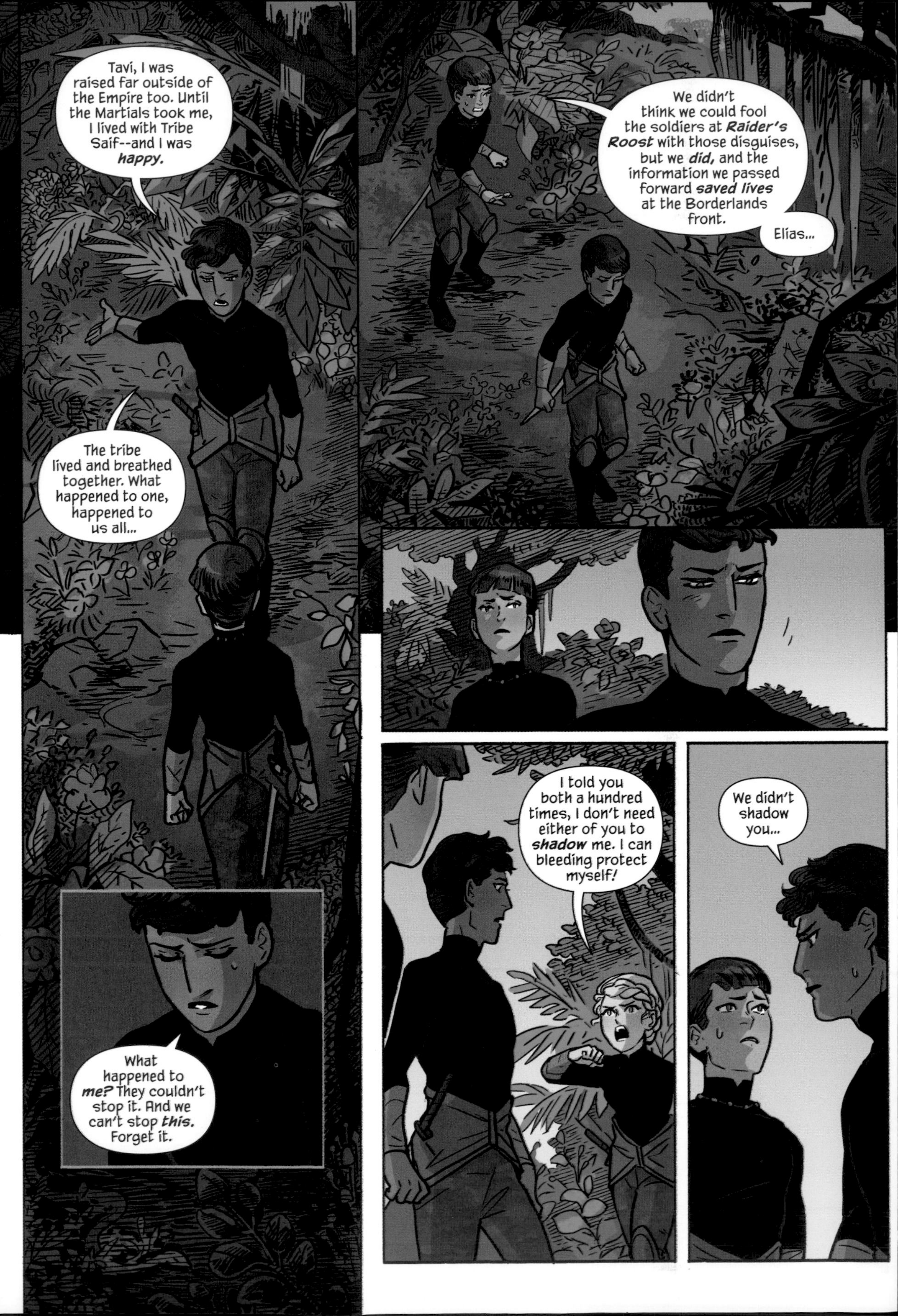

Tavi, I was raised far outside of the Empire too. Until the Martials took me, I lived with Tribe Saif--and I was *happy.*
The tribe lived and breathed together. What happened to one, happened to us all...
What happened to *me?* They couldn't stop it. And we can't stop *this.* Forget it.
We didn't think we could fool the soldiers at *Raider's Roost* with those disguises, but we *did,* and the information we passed forward *saved lives* at the Borderlands front.
Elias...
I told you both a hundred times, I don't need either of you to *shadow* me. I can bleeding protect myself!
We didn't shadow you...

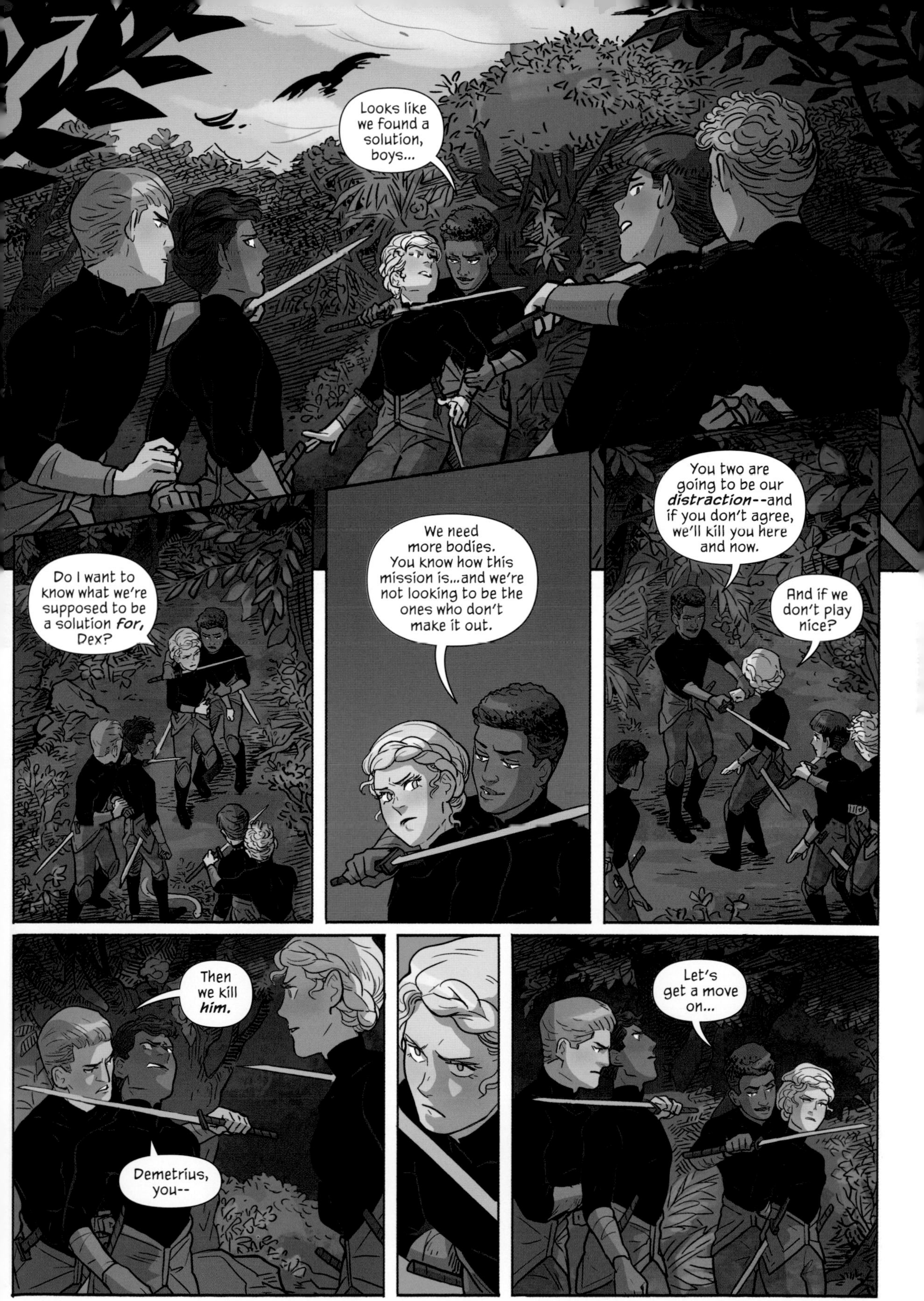

Looks like we found a solution, boys...
Do I want to know what we're supposed to be a solution *for*, Dex?
We need more bodies. You know how this mission is...and we're not looking to be the ones who don't make it out.
You two are going to be our ***distraction***--and if you don't agree, we'll kill you here and now.
And if we don't play nice?
Then we kill ***him.***
Demetrius, you--
Let's get a move on...

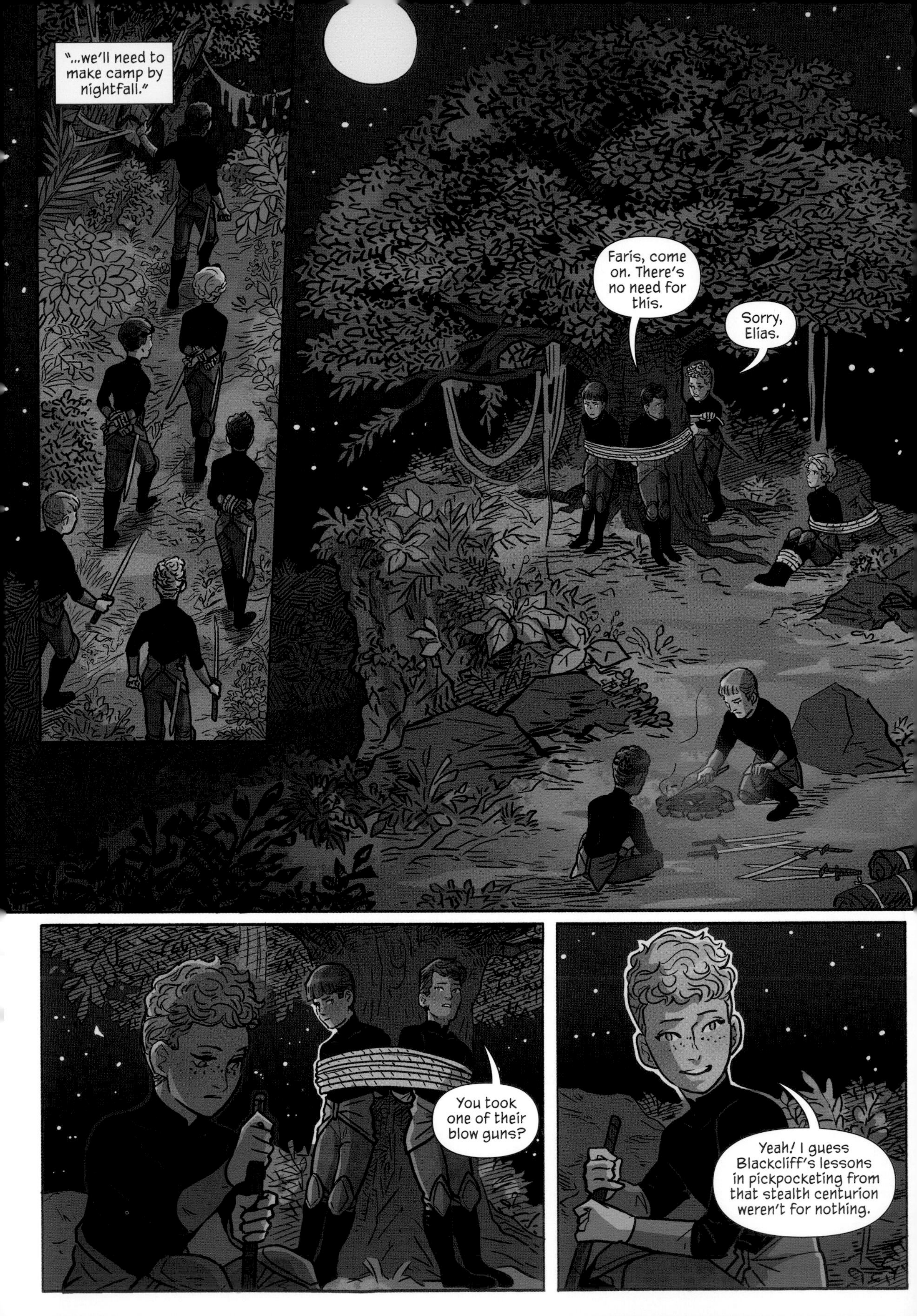
"...we'll need to make camp by nightfall."
Faris, come on. There's no need for this.
Sorry, Elias.
You took one of their blow guns?
Yeah! I guess Blackcliff's lessons in pickpocketing from that stealth centurion weren't for nothing.

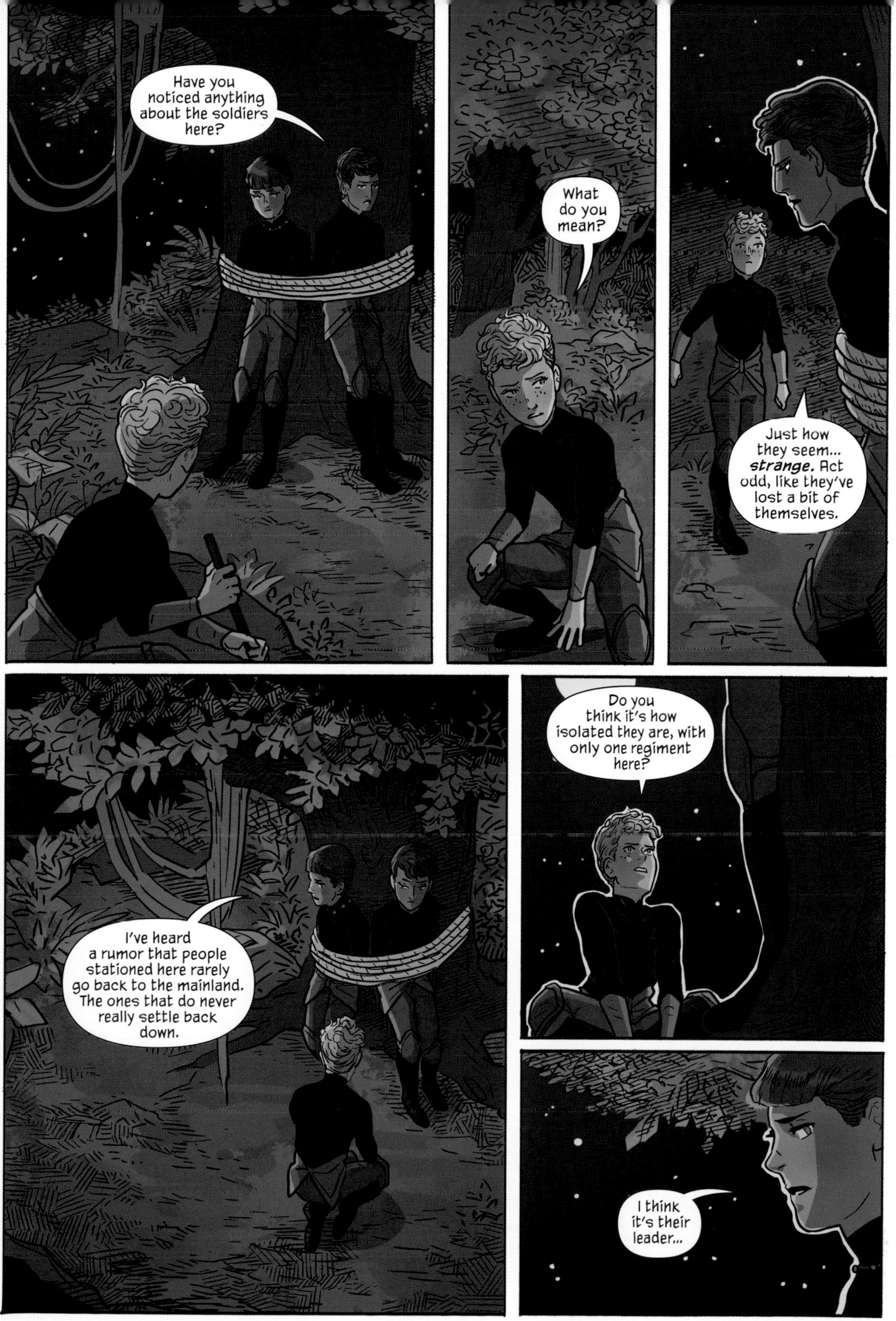
Have you noticed anything about the soldiers here?
What do you mean?
Just how they seem... ***strange.*** Act odd, like they've lost a bit of themselves.
I've heard a rumor that people stationed here rarely go back to the mainland. The ones that do never really settle back down.
Do you think it's how isolated they are, with only one regiment here?
I think it's their leader...

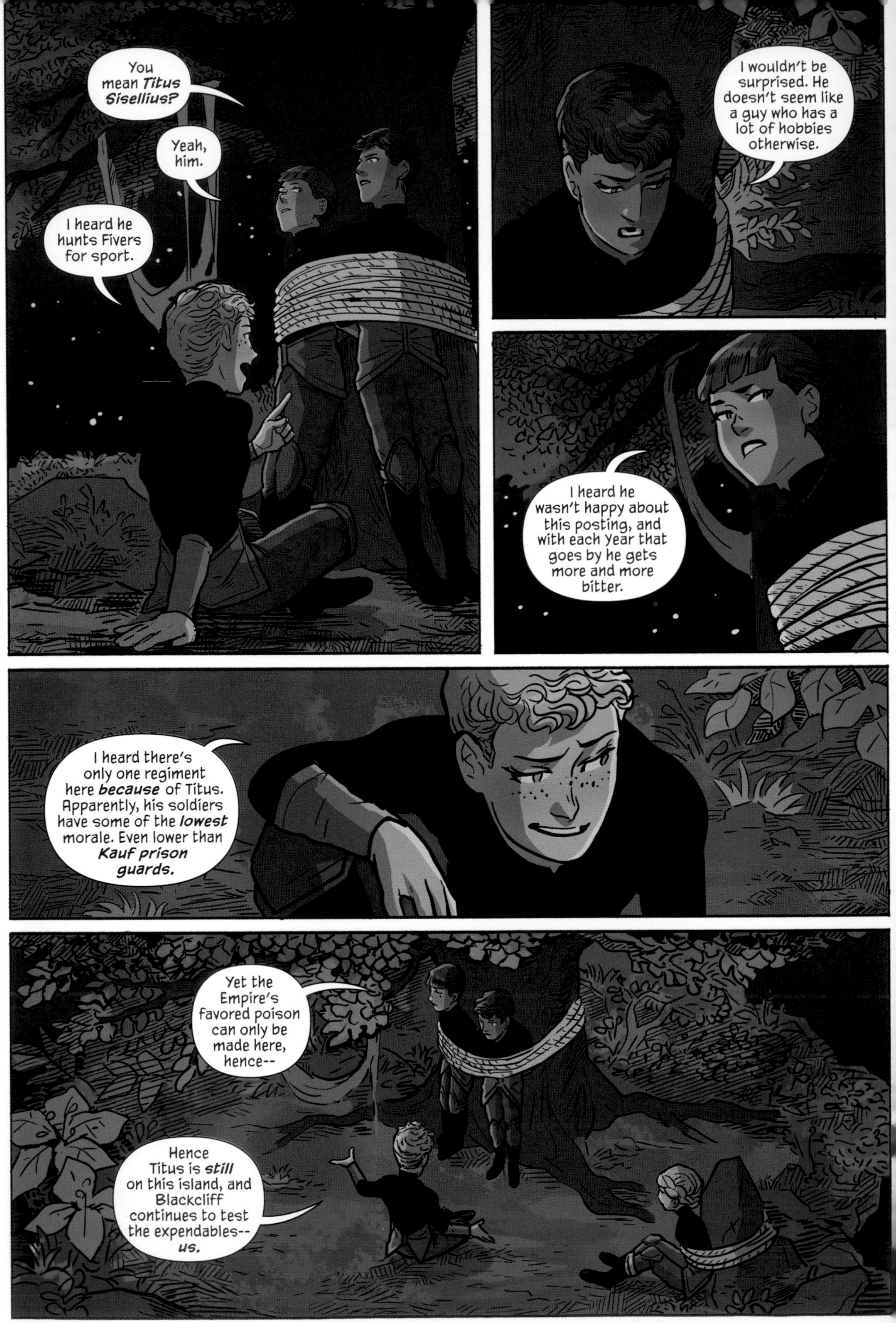

You mean *Titus Sisellius?*
Yeah, him.
I heard he hunts Fivers for sport.
I wouldn't be surprised. He doesn't seem like a guy who has a lot of hobbies otherwise.
I heard he wasn't happy about this posting, and with each Year that goes by he gets more and more bitter.
I heard there's only one regiment here *because* of Titus. Apparently, his soldiers have some of the *lowest* morale. Even lower than *Kauf prison guards.*
Yet the Empire's favored poison can only be made here, hence--
Hence Titus is *still* on this island, and Blackcliff continues to test the expendables-- *us.*

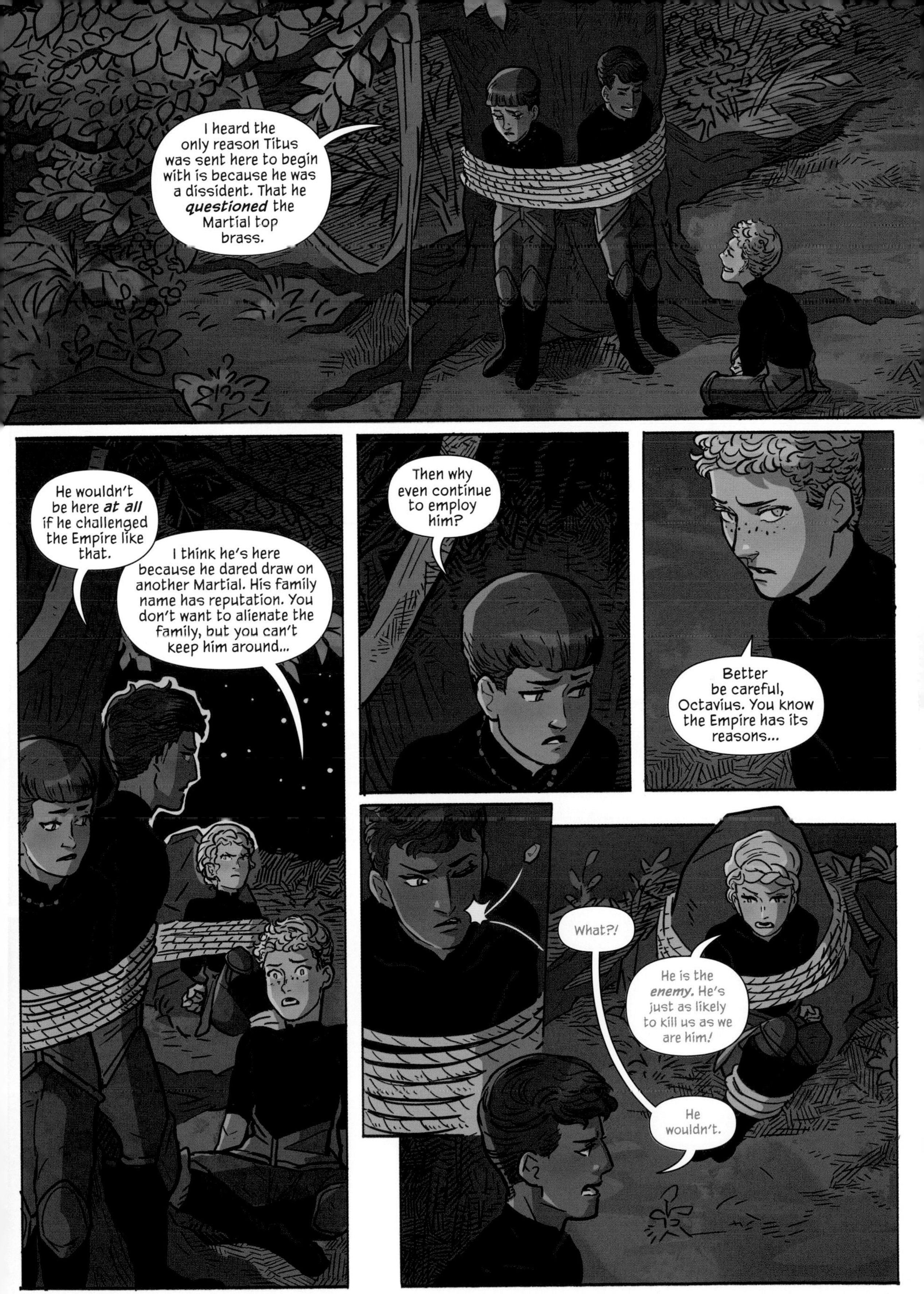
I heard the only reason Titus was sent here to begin with is because he was a dissident. That he ***questioned*** the Martial top brass.
He wouldn't be here ***at all*** if he challenged the Empire like that.
I think he's here because he dared draw on another Martial. His family name has reputation. You don't want to alienate the family, but you can't keep him around...
Then why even continue to employ him?
Better be careful, Octavius. You know the Empire has its reasons...
What?!
He is the ***enemy.*** He's just as likely to kill us as we are him!
He wouldn't.

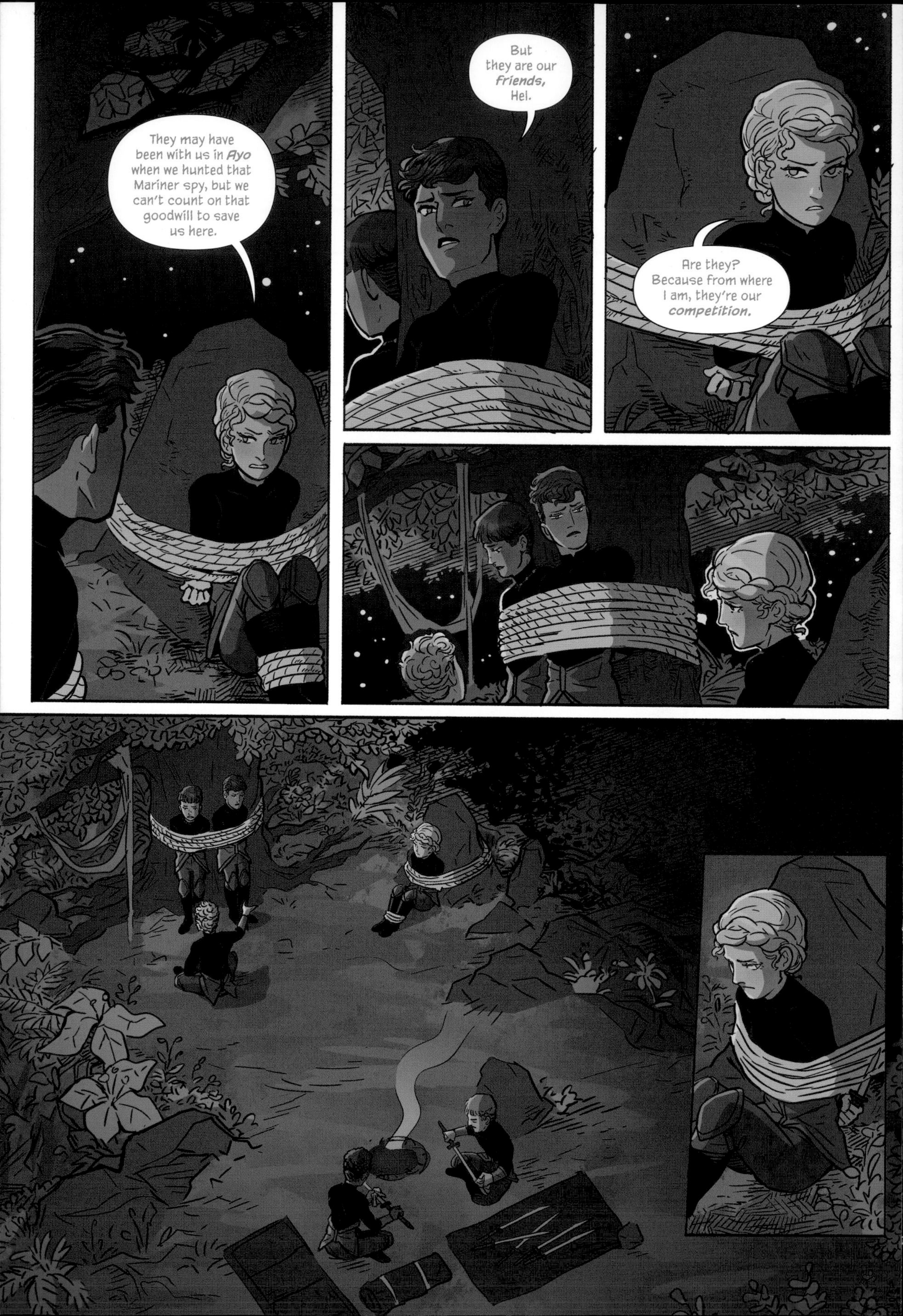

They may have been with us in *Ayo* when we hunted that Mariner spy, but we can't count on that goodwill to save us here.
But they are our *friends,* Hel.
Are they? Because from where I am, they're our ***competition.***

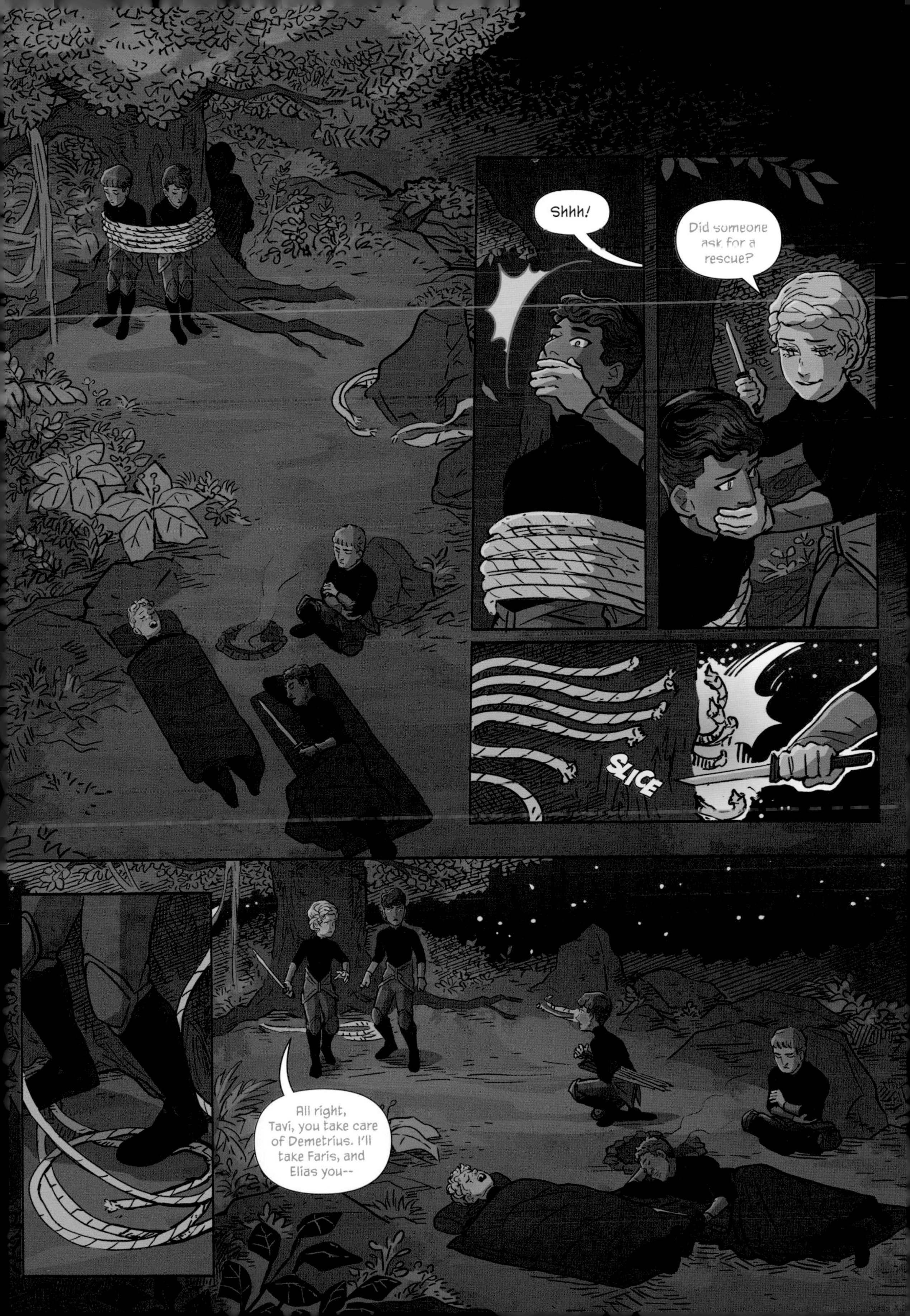
Shhh!
Did someone ask for a rescue?
SLICE
All right, Tavi, you take care of Demetrius. I'll take Faris, and Elias you--

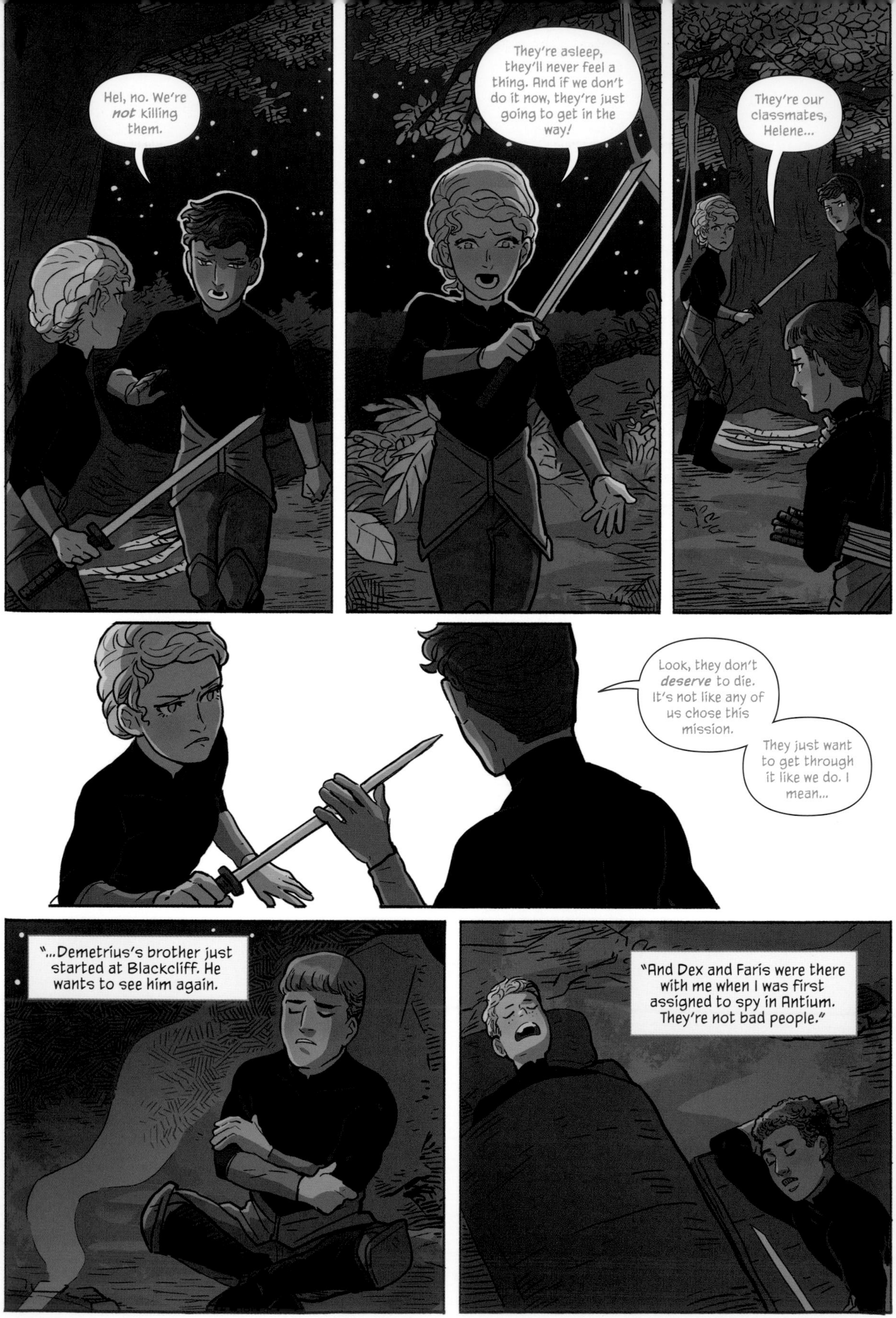

Hel, no. We're *not* killing them.
They're asleep, they'll never feel a thing. And if we don't do it now, they're just going to get in the way!
They're our classmates, Helene...
Look, they don't *deserve* to die. It's not like any of us chose this mission.
They just want to get through it like we do. I mean...
"...Demetrius's brother just started at Blackcliff. He wants to see him again.
"And Dex and Faris were there with me when I was first assigned to spy in Antium. They're not bad people."

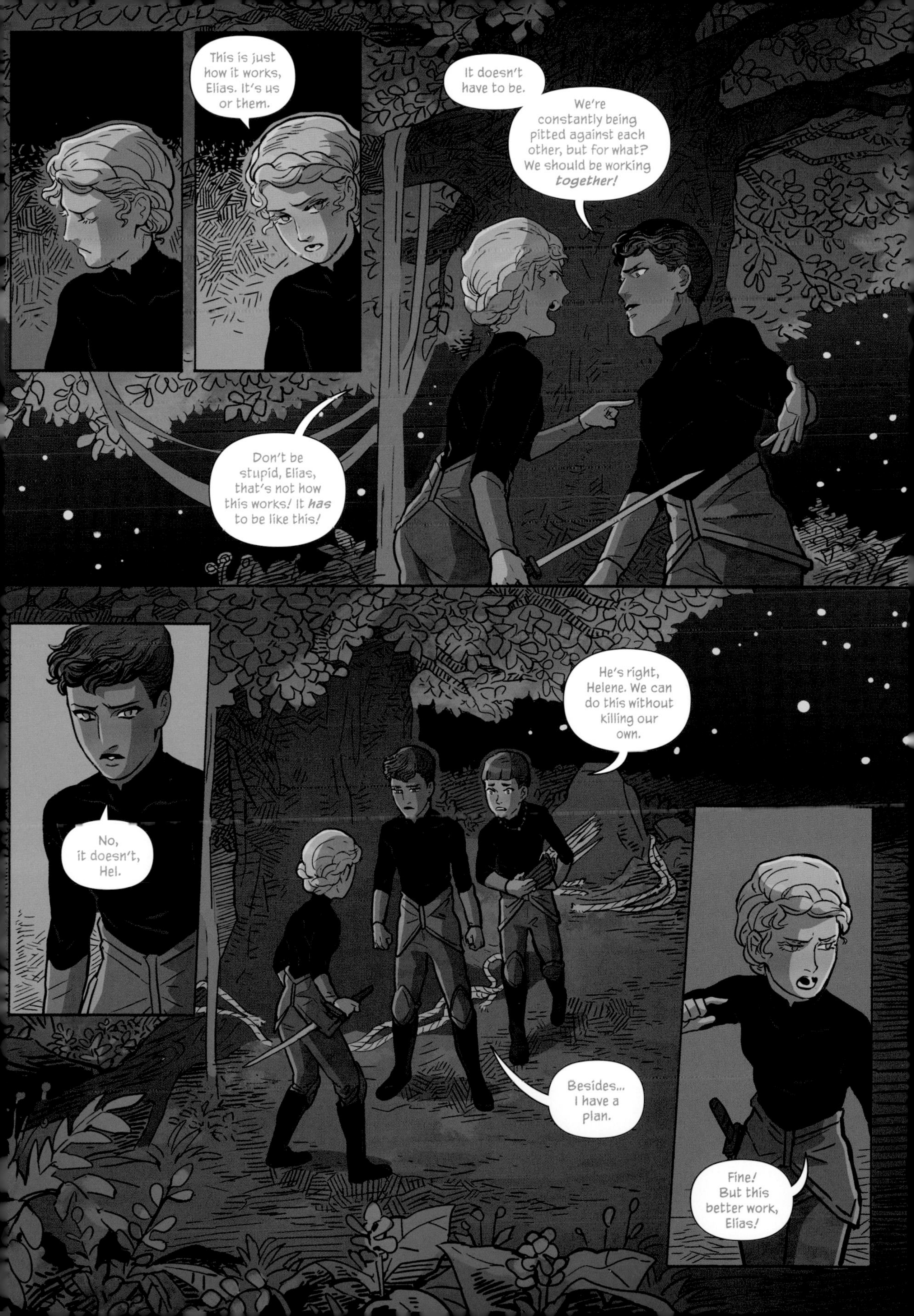
This is just how it works, Elias. It's us or them.
It doesn't have to be.
We're constantly being pitted against each other, but for what? We should be working *together!*
Don't be stupid, Elias, that's not how this works! It *has* to be like this!
No, it doesn't, Hel.
He's right, Helene. We can do this without killing our own.
Besides... I have a plan.
Fine! But this better work, Elias!

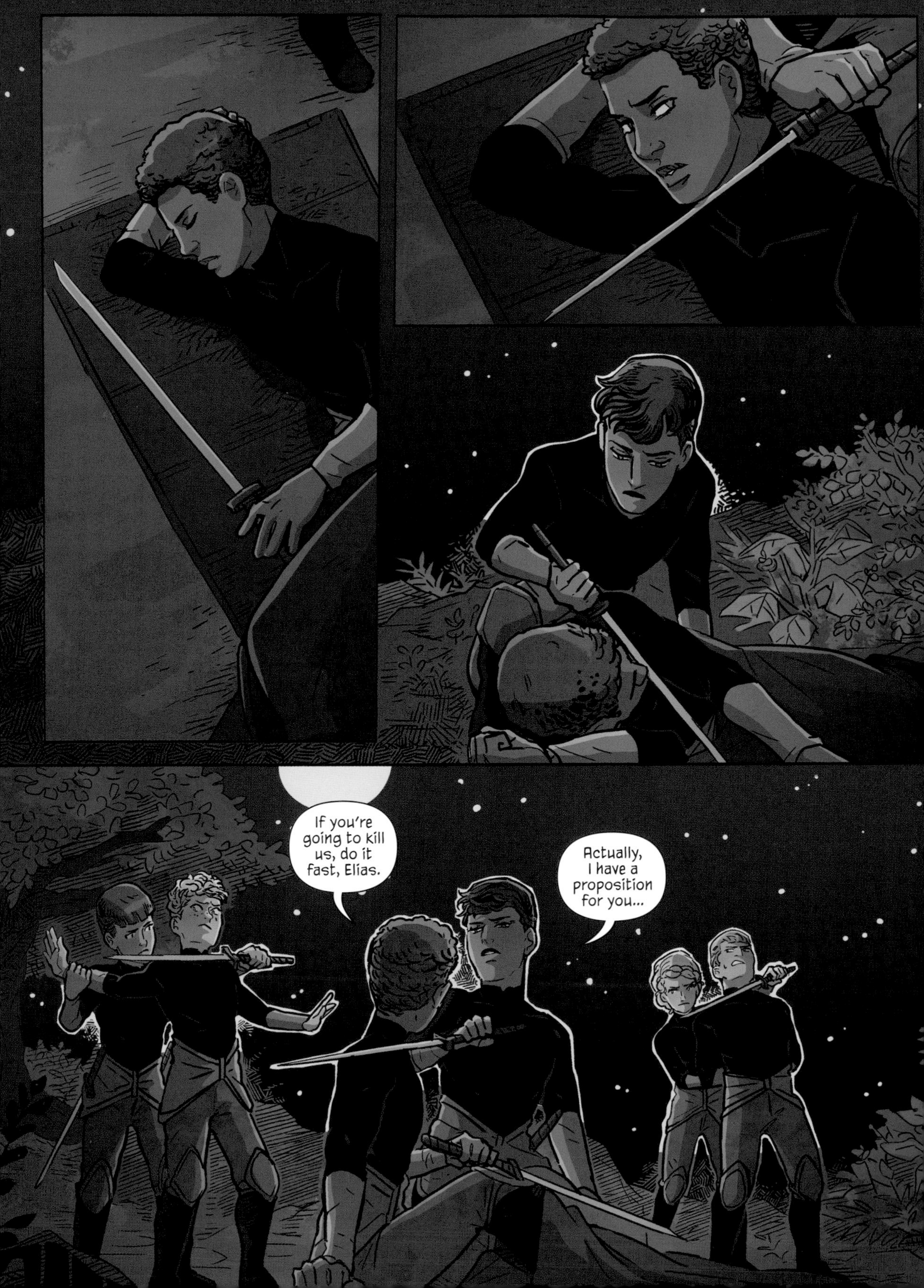
If you're going to kill us, do it fast, Elias.
Actually, I have a proposition for you...

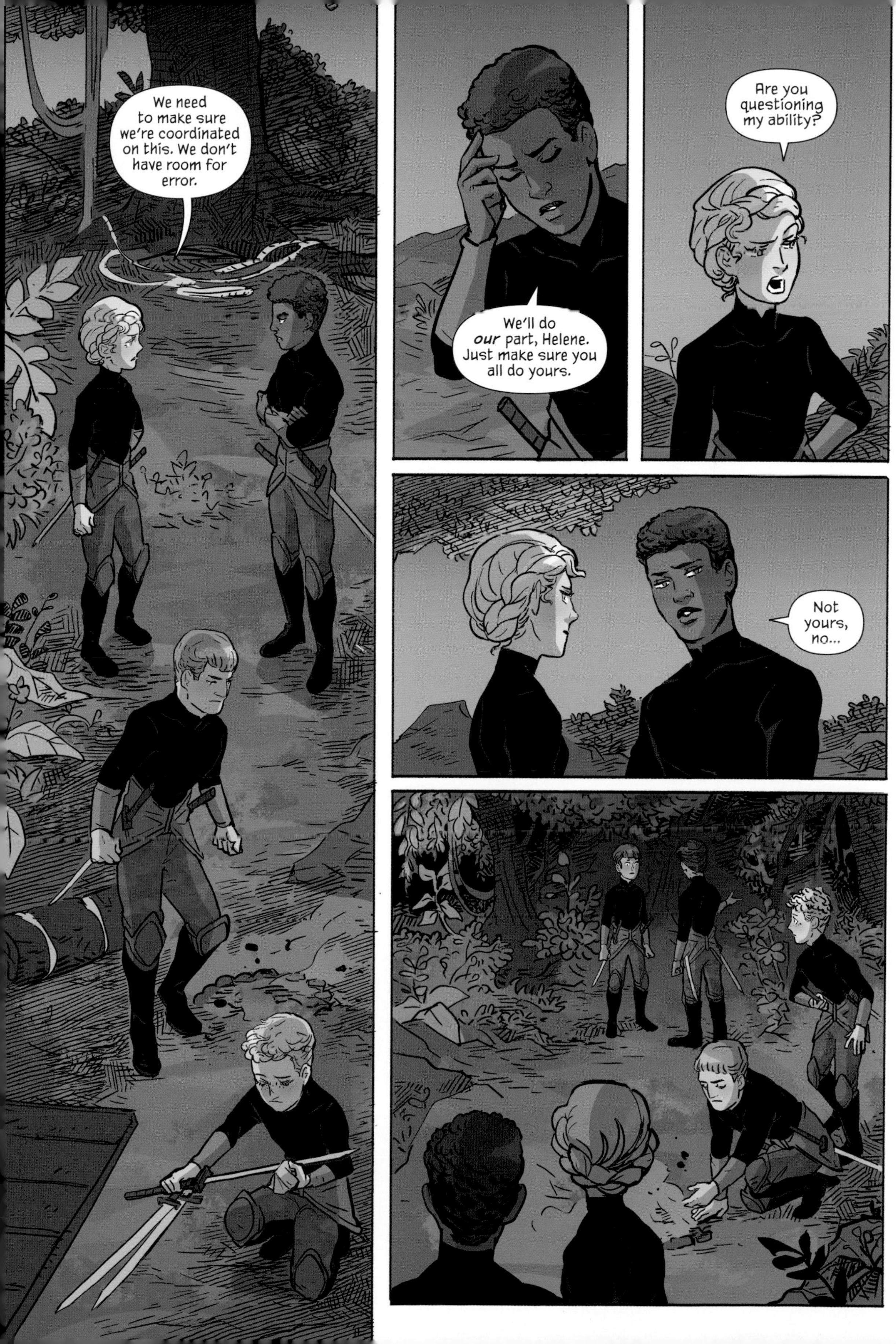
We need to make sure we're coordinated on this. We don't have room for error.
We'll do *our* part, Helene. Just make sure you all do yours.
Are you questioning my ability?
Not yours, no...

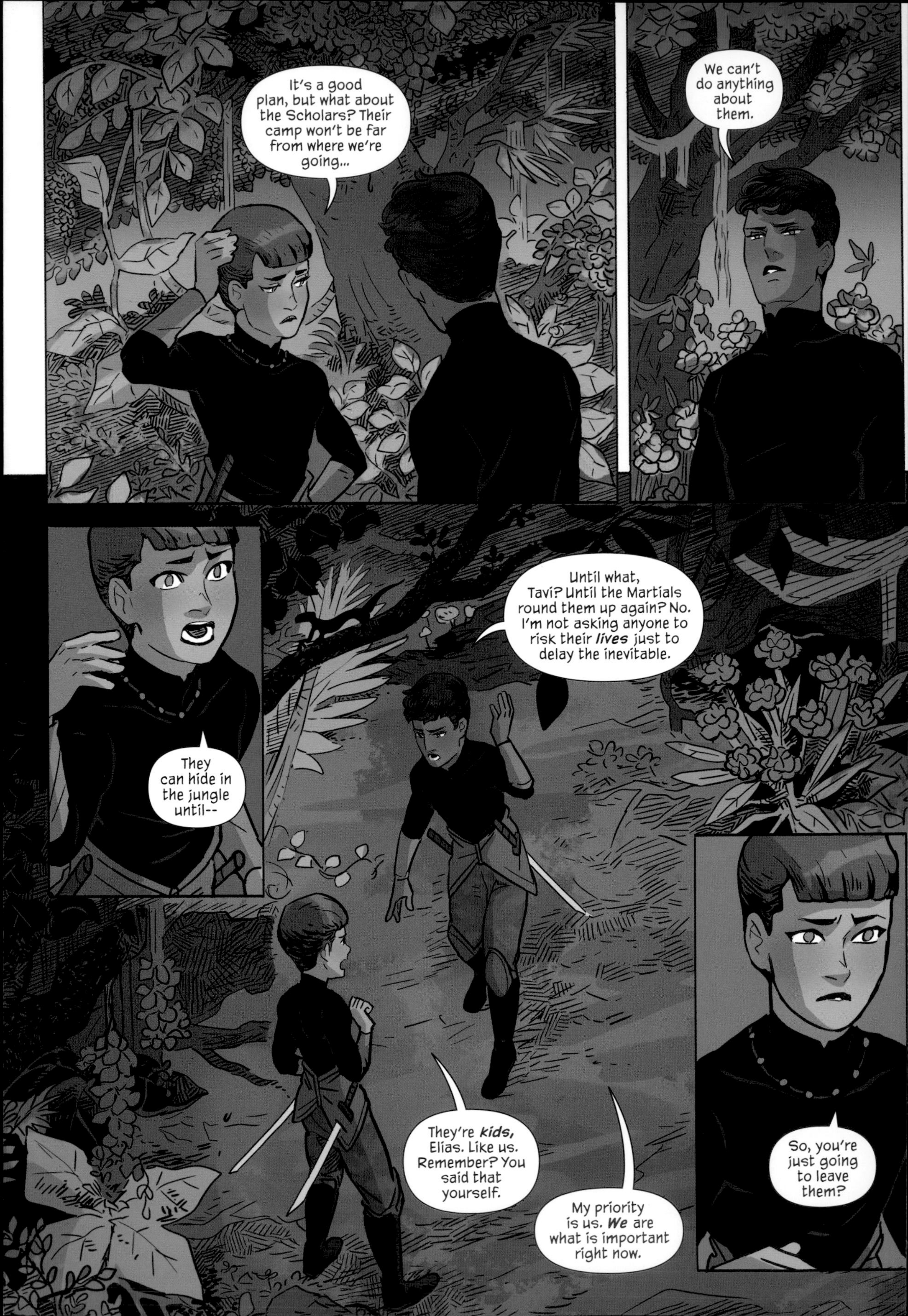

It's a good plan, but what about the Scholars? Their camp won't be far from where we're going...
We can't do anything about them.
They can hide in the jungle until--
Until what, Tavi? Until the Martials round them up again? No. I'm not asking anyone to risk their *lives* just to delay the inevitable.
So, you're just going to leave them?
My priority is us. *We* are what is important right now.
They're *kids,* Elias. Like us. Remember? You said that yourself.

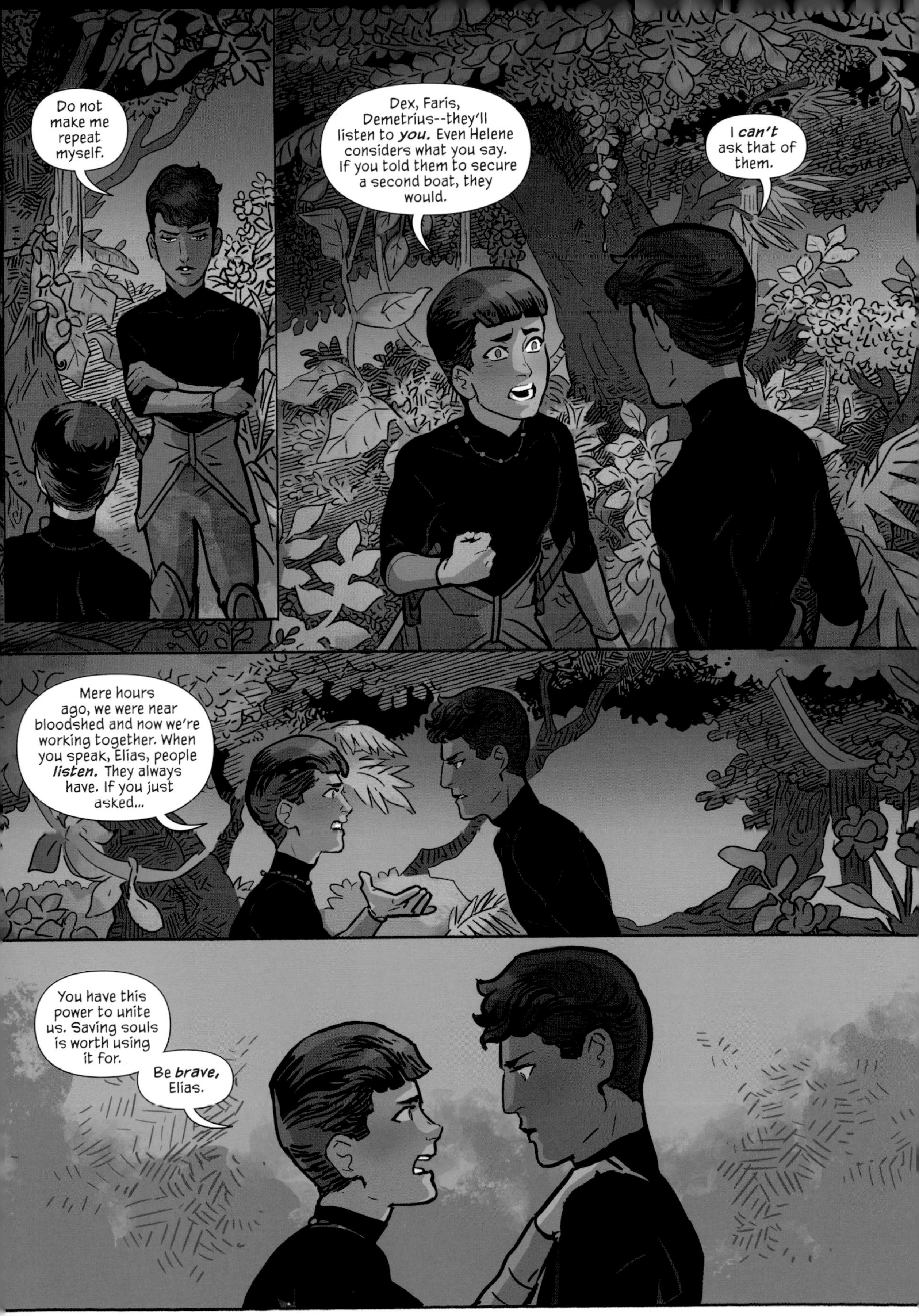
Do not make me repeat myself.
Dex, Faris, Demetrius--they'll listen to *you.* Even Helene considers what you say. If you told them to secure a second boat, they would.
I *can't* ask that of them.
Mere hours ago, we were near bloodshed and now we're working together. When you speak, Elias, people *listen.* They always have. If you just asked...
You have this power to unite us. Saving souls is worth using it for.
Be *brave,* Elias.

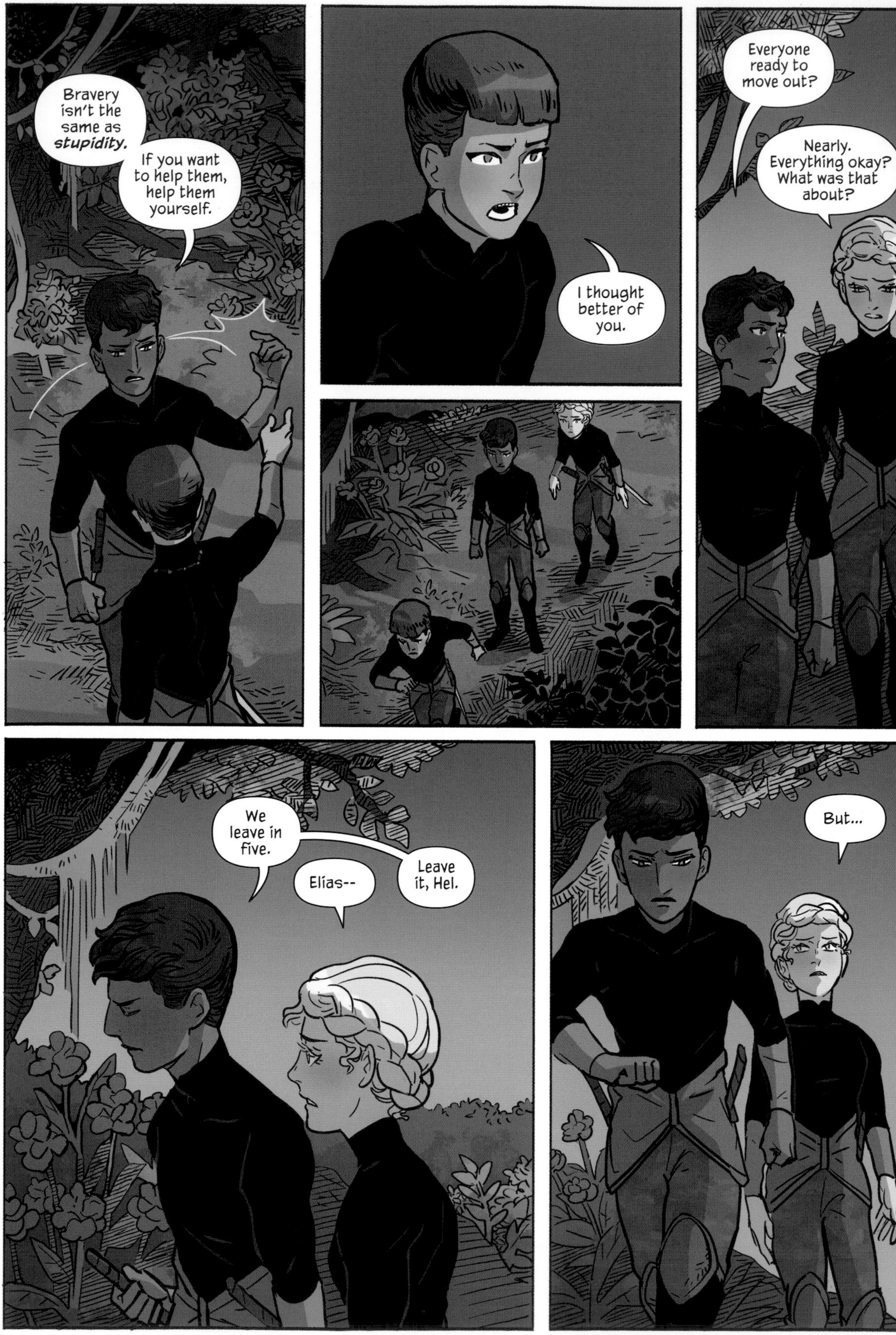
Bravery isn't the same as *stupidity*.
If you want to help them, help them yourself.
I thought better of you.
Everyone ready to move out?
Nearly. Everything okay? What was that about?
We leave in five.
Elias--
Leave it, Hel.
But...

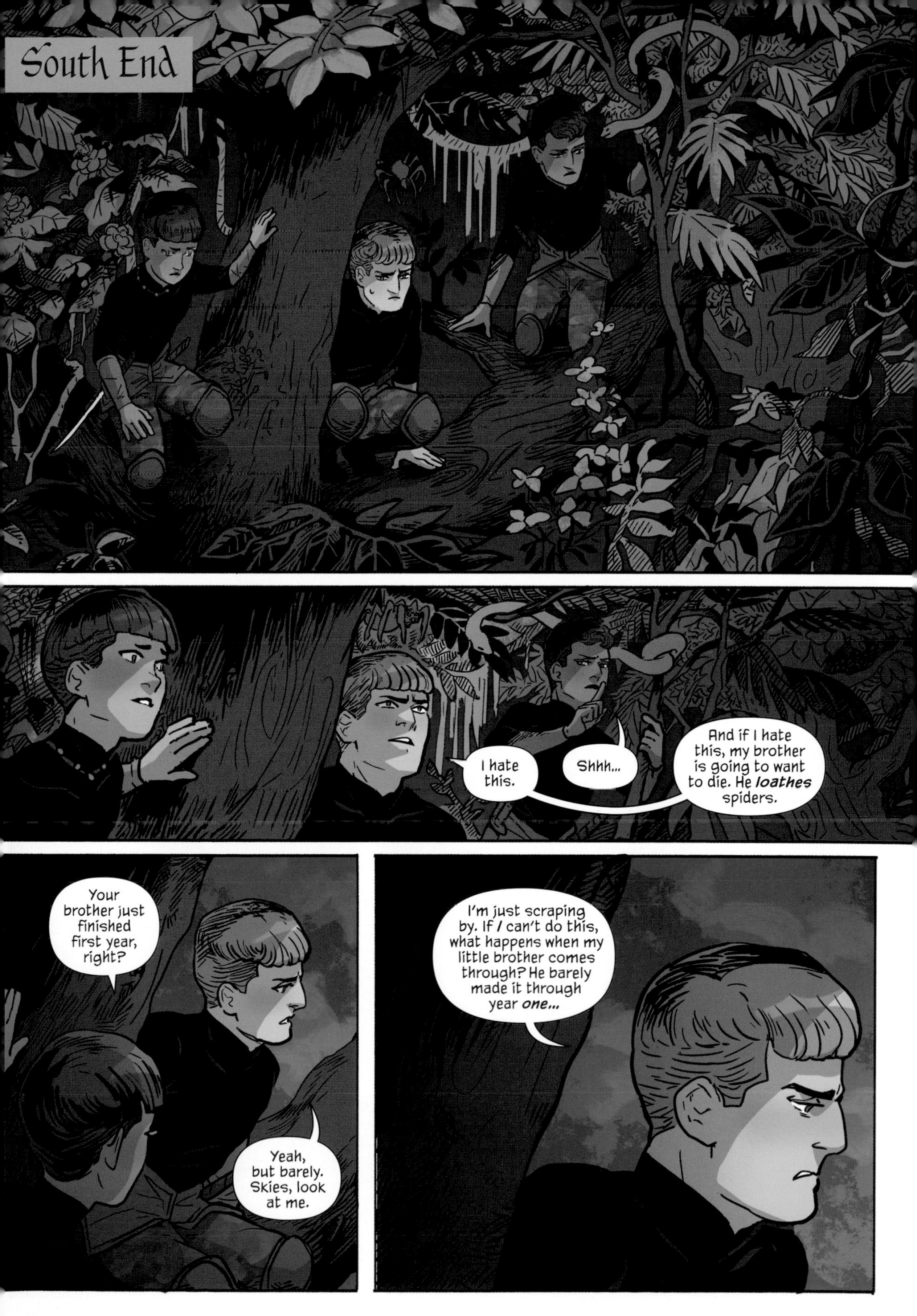
South End
I hate this.
Shhh...
And if I hate this, my brother is going to want to die. He *loathes* spiders.
Your brother just finished first year, right?
Yeah, but barely. Skies, look at me.
I'm just scraping by. If *I* can't do this, what happens when my little brother comes through? He barely made it through year *one*...

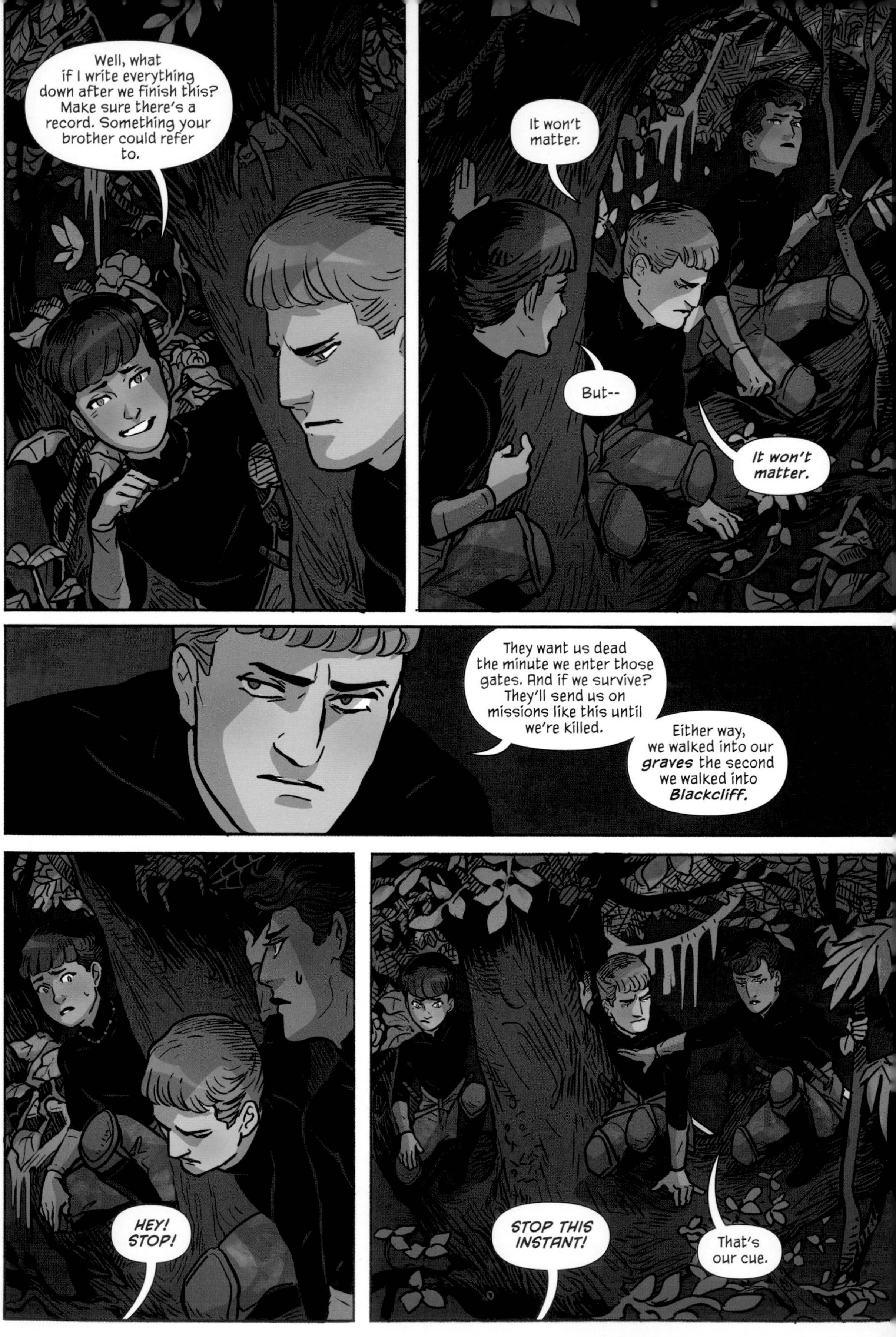
Well, what if I write everything down after we finish this? Make sure there's a record. Something your brother could refer to.
It won't matter.
But--
It won't matter.
They want us dead the minute we enter those gates. And if we survive? They'll send us on missions like this until we're killed.
Either way, we walked into our ***graves*** the second we walked into ***Blackcliff.***
HEY! STOP!
STOP THIS INSTANT!
That's our cue.

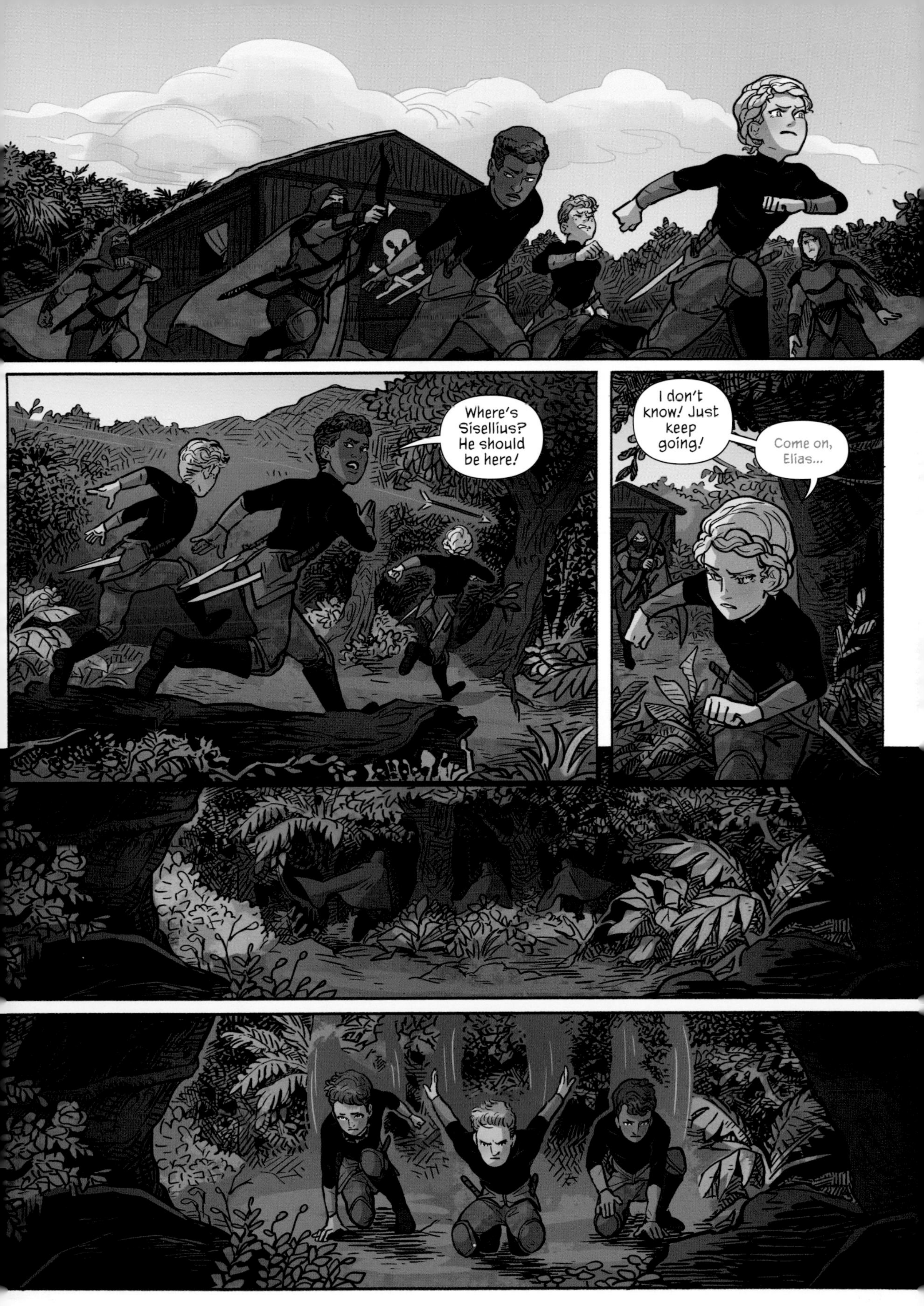
Where's Sisellius? He should be here!
I don't know! Just keep going!
Come on, Elias...

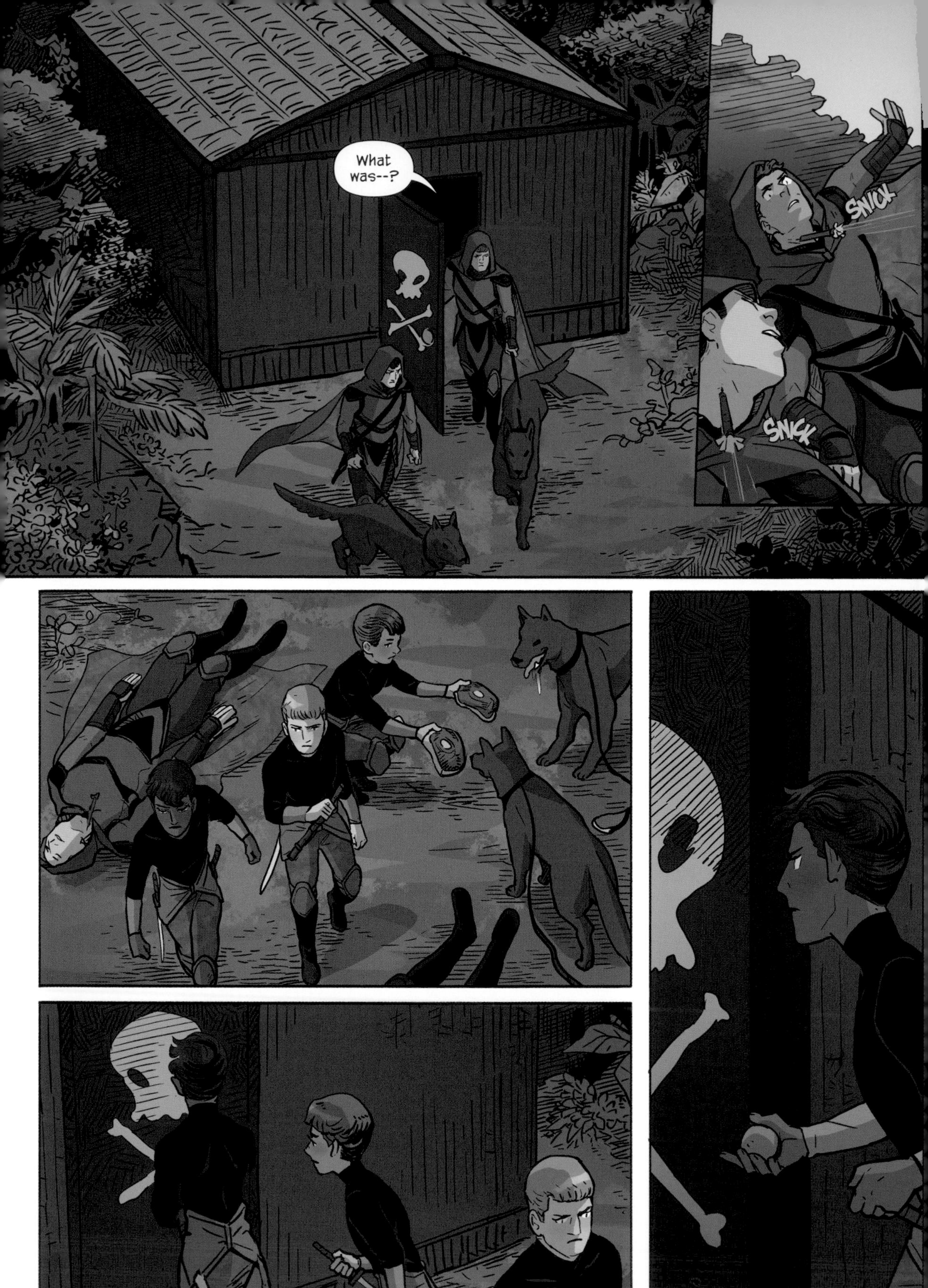

What was--?
SNICK
SNICK

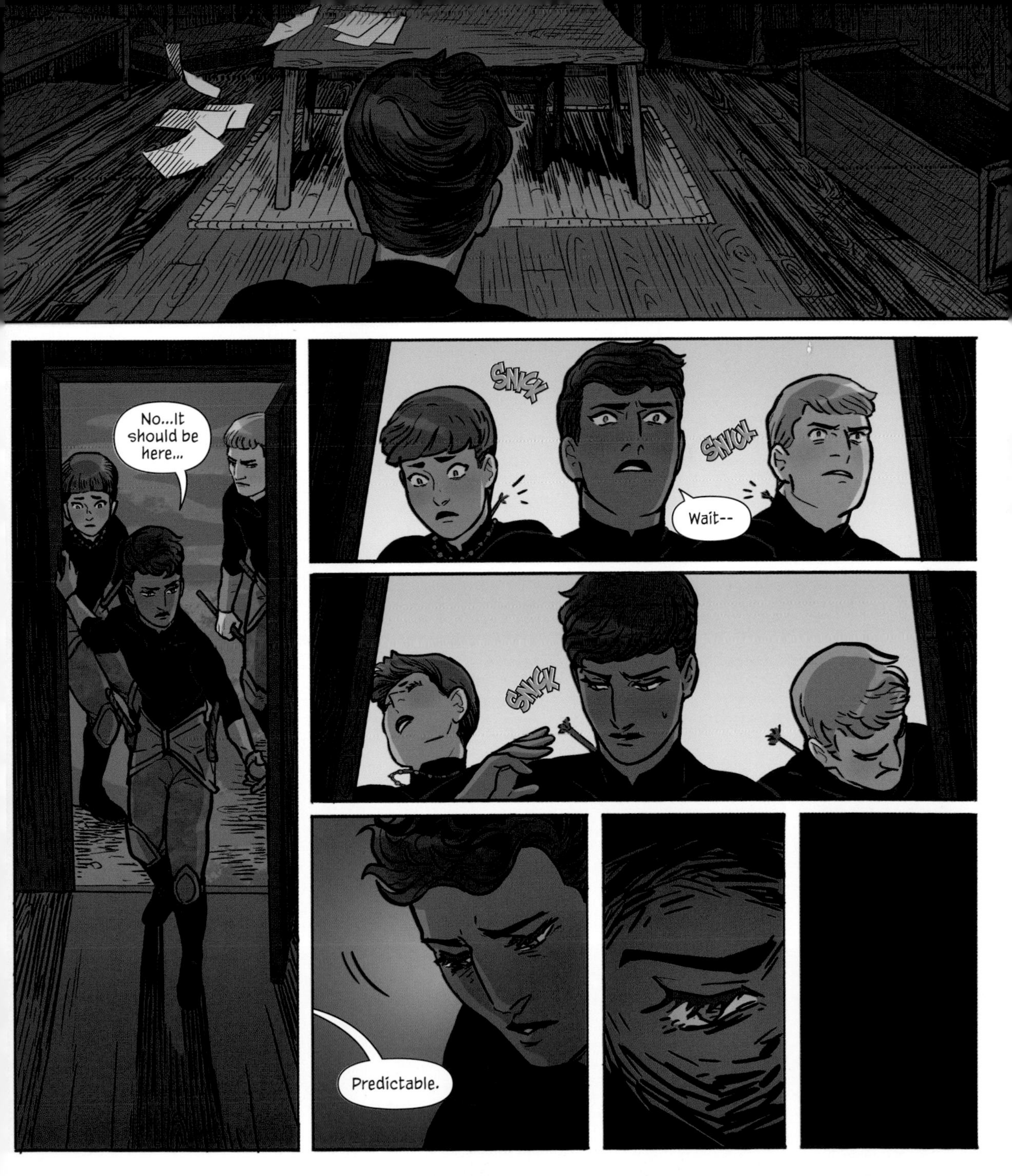
No...It should be here...
SNICK
SNICK
Wait--
SNICK
Predictable.

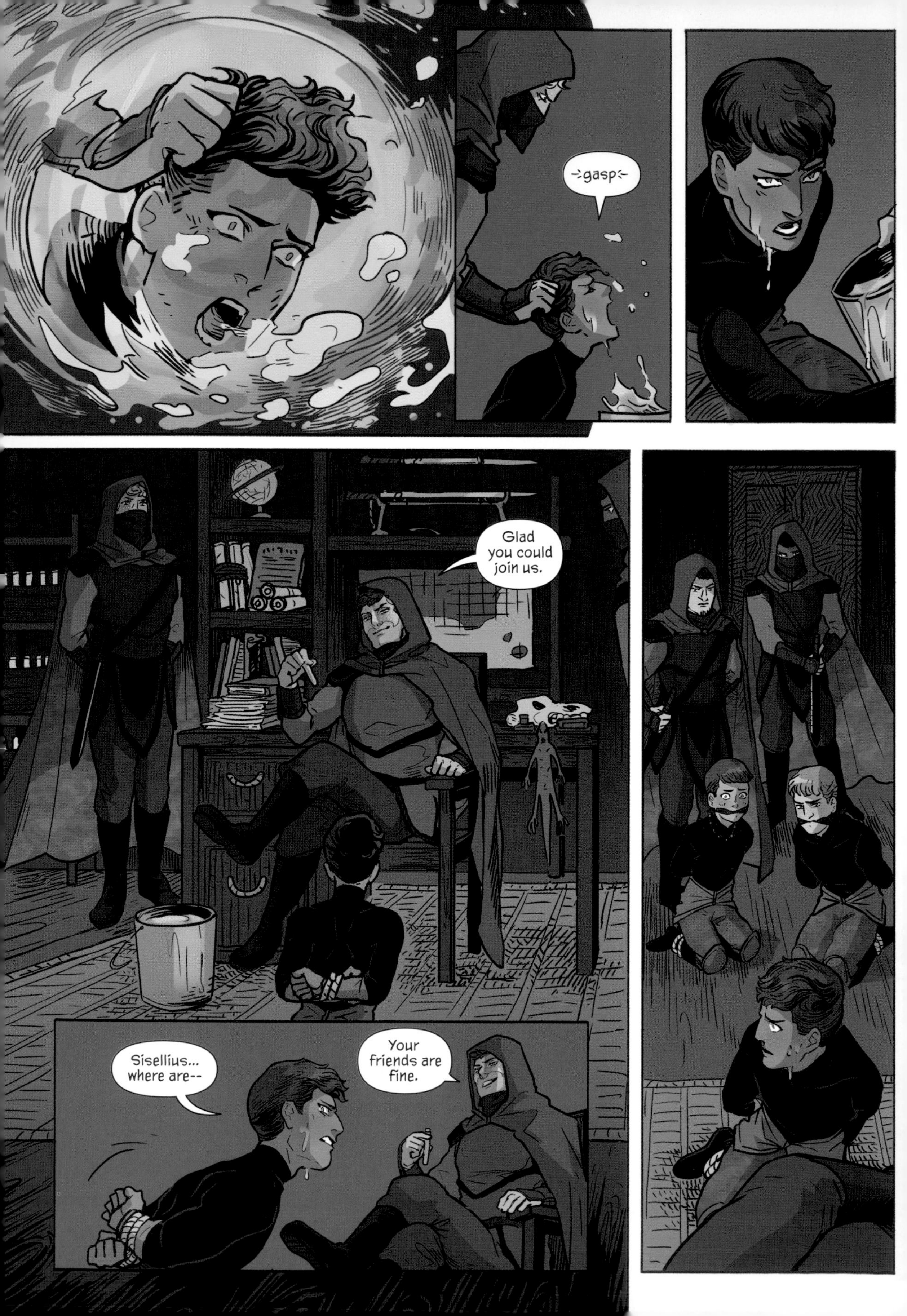
gasp
Glad you could join us.
Sisellius... where are--
Your friends are fine.

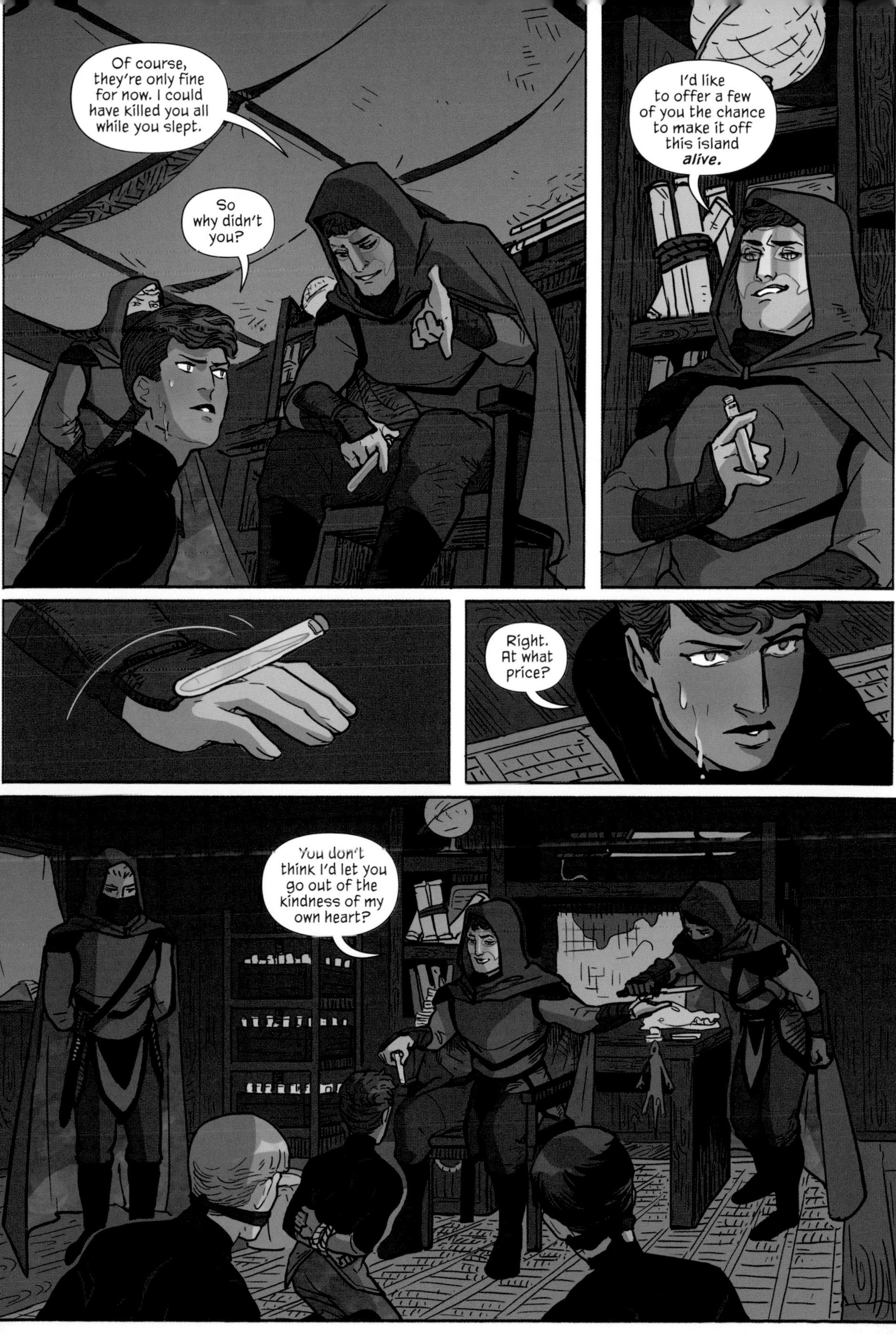
Of course, they're only fine for now. I could have killed you all while you slept.
So why didn't you?
I'd like to offer a few of you the chance to make it off this island *alive.*
Right. At what price?
You don't think I'd let you go out of the kindness of my own heart?

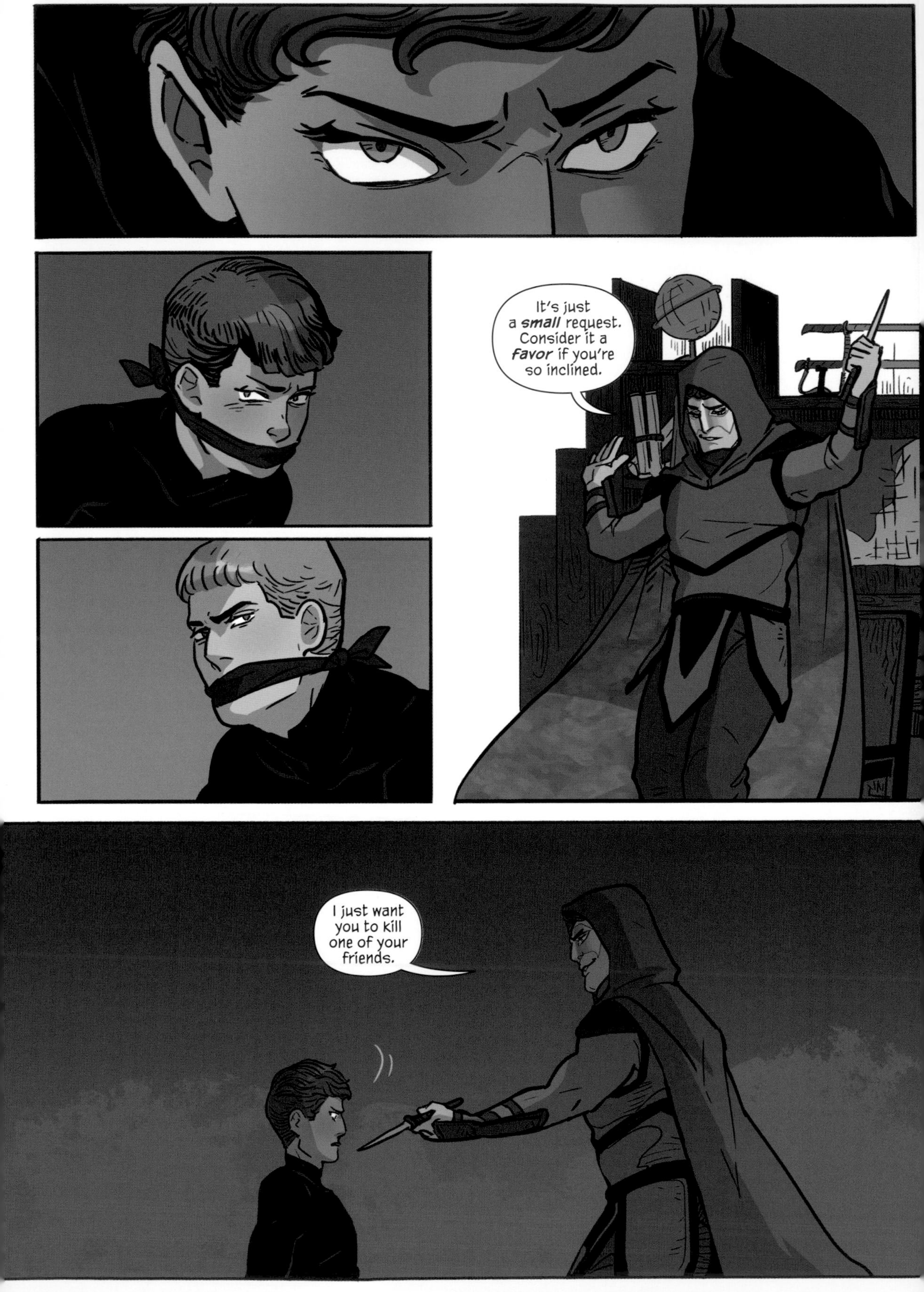
It's just a *small* request. Consider it a *favor* if you're so inclined.
I just want you to kill one of your friends.

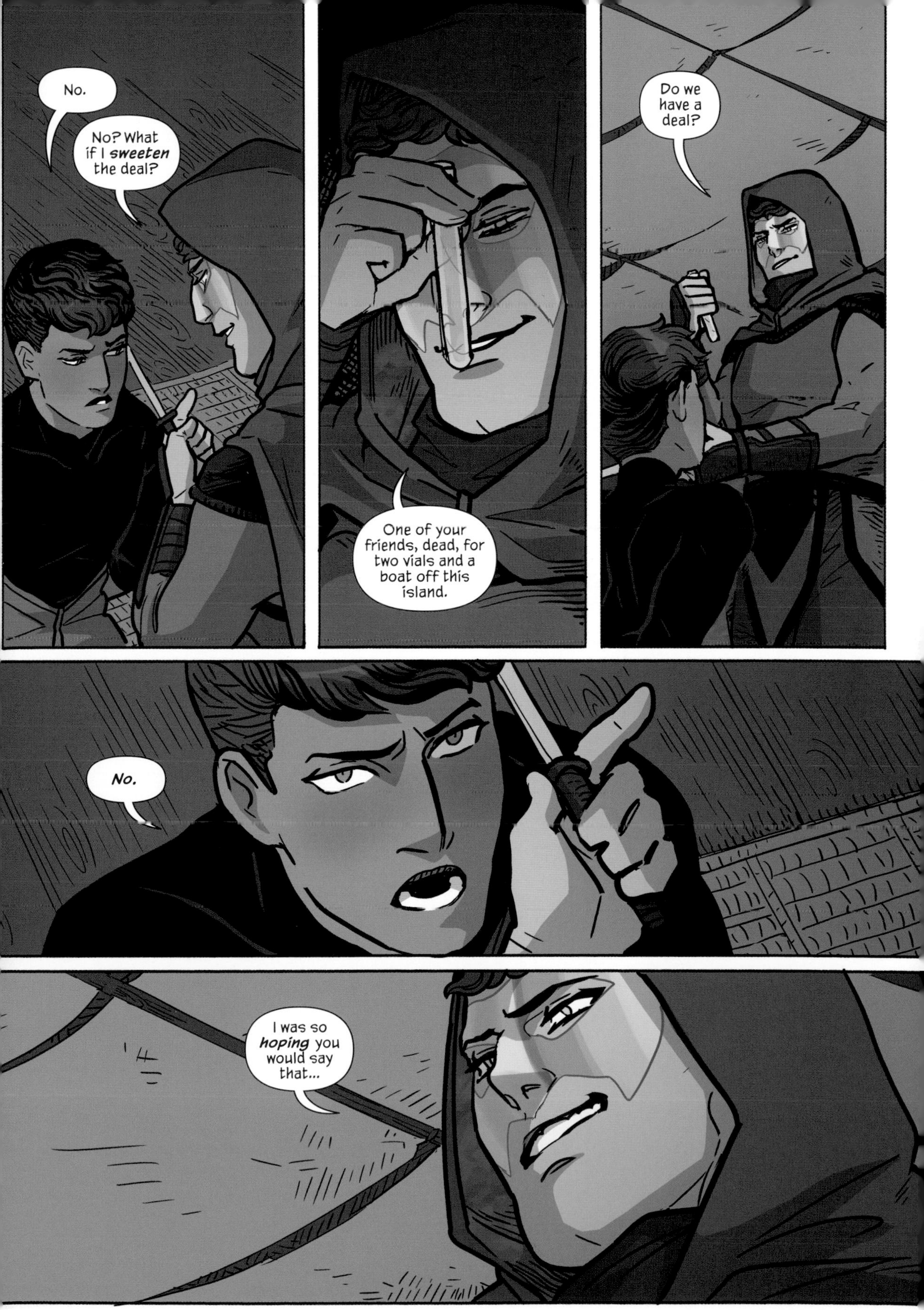
No.
No? What if I *sweeten* the deal?
One of your friends, dead, for two vials and a boat off this island.
Do we have a deal?
No.
I was so *hoping* you would say that...

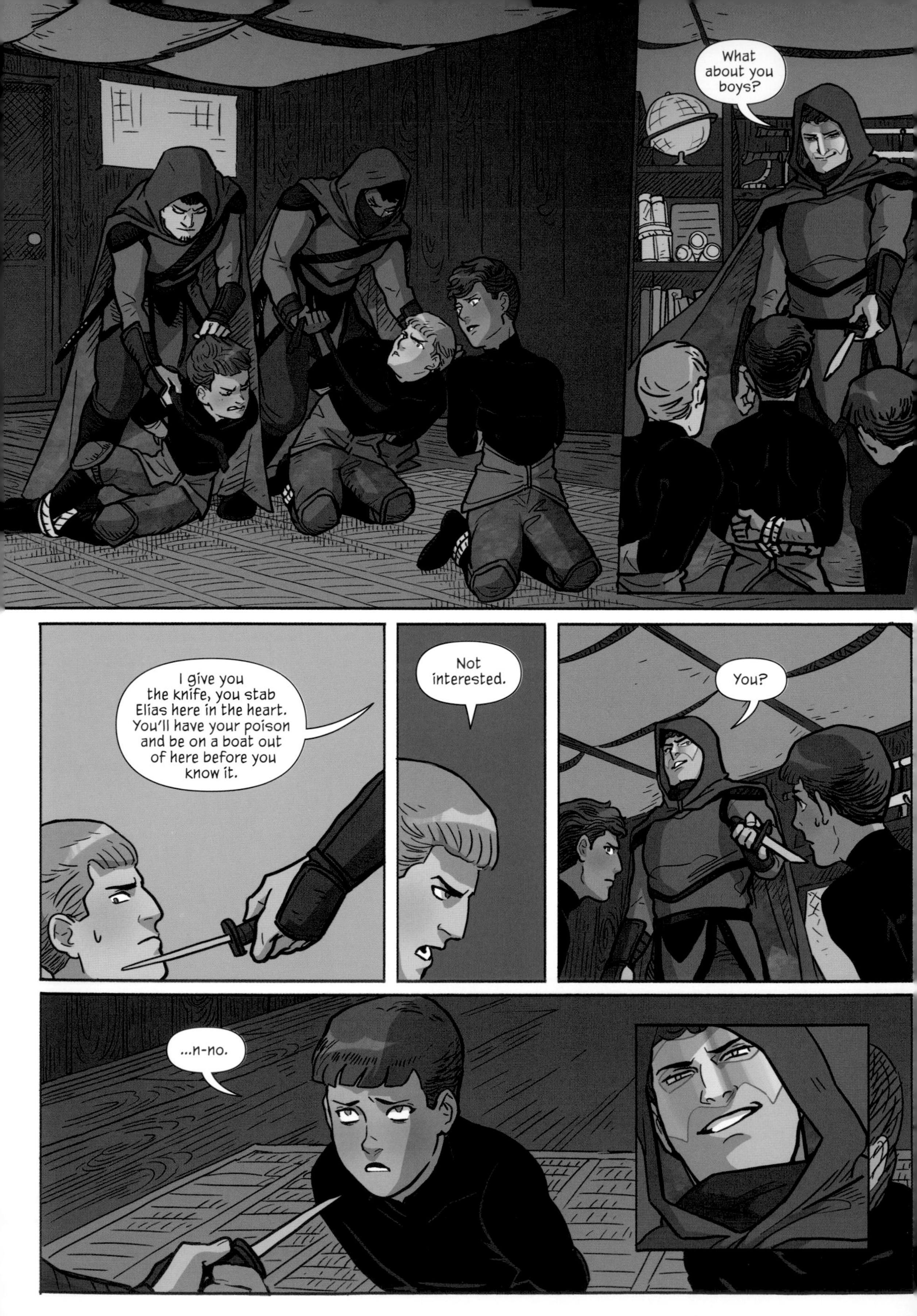
What about you boys?
I give you the knife, you stab Elias here in the heart. You'll have your poison and be on a boat out of here before you know it.
Not interested.
You?
...n-no.

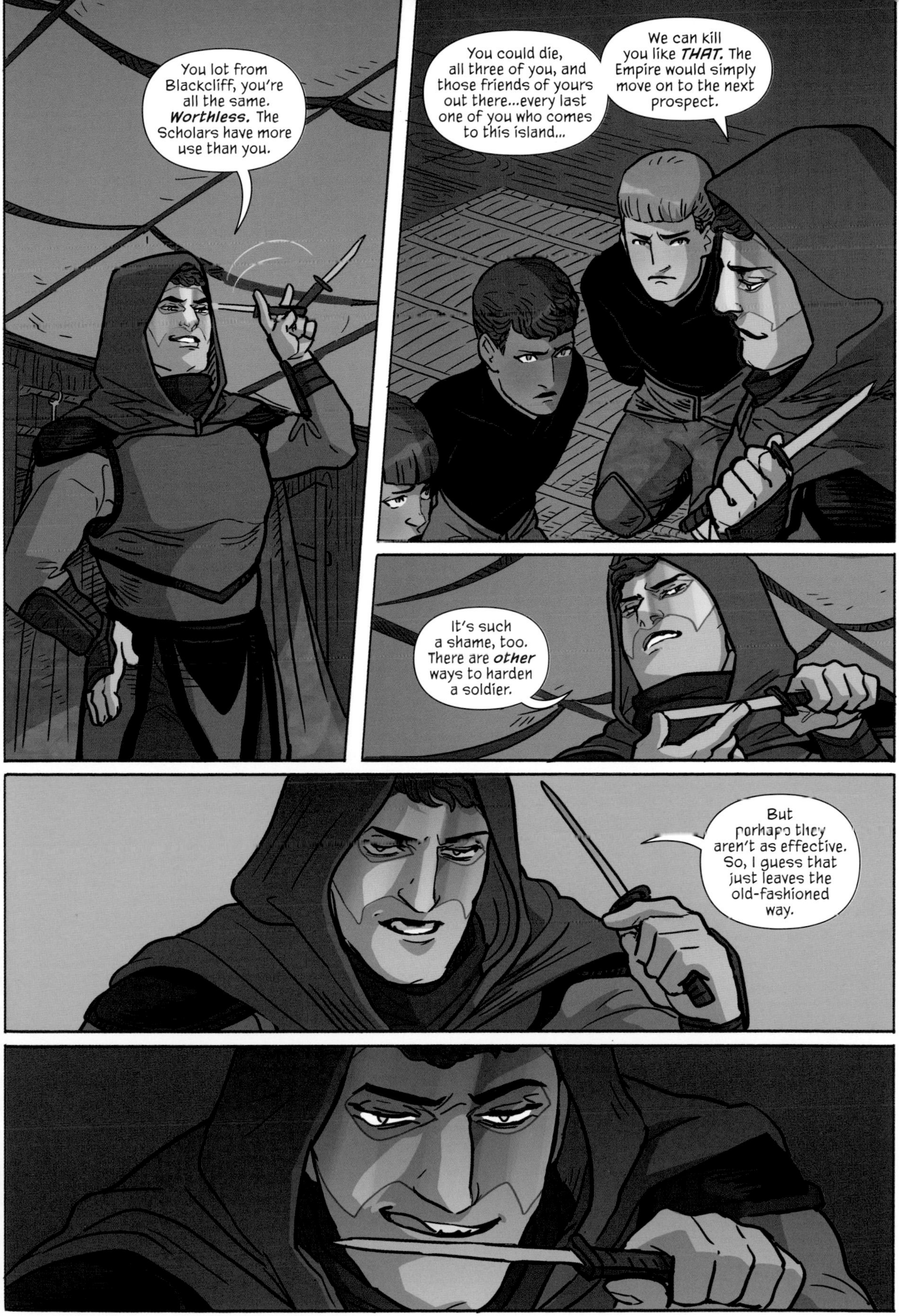
You lot from Blackcliff, you're all the same. **Worthless.** The Scholars have more use than you.
You could die, all three of you, and those friends of yours out there...every last one of you who comes to this island...
We can kill you like ***THAT.*** The Empire would simply move on to the next prospect.
It's such a shame, too. There are ***other*** ways to harden a soldier.
But perhaps they aren't as effective. So, I guess that just leaves the old-fashioned way.

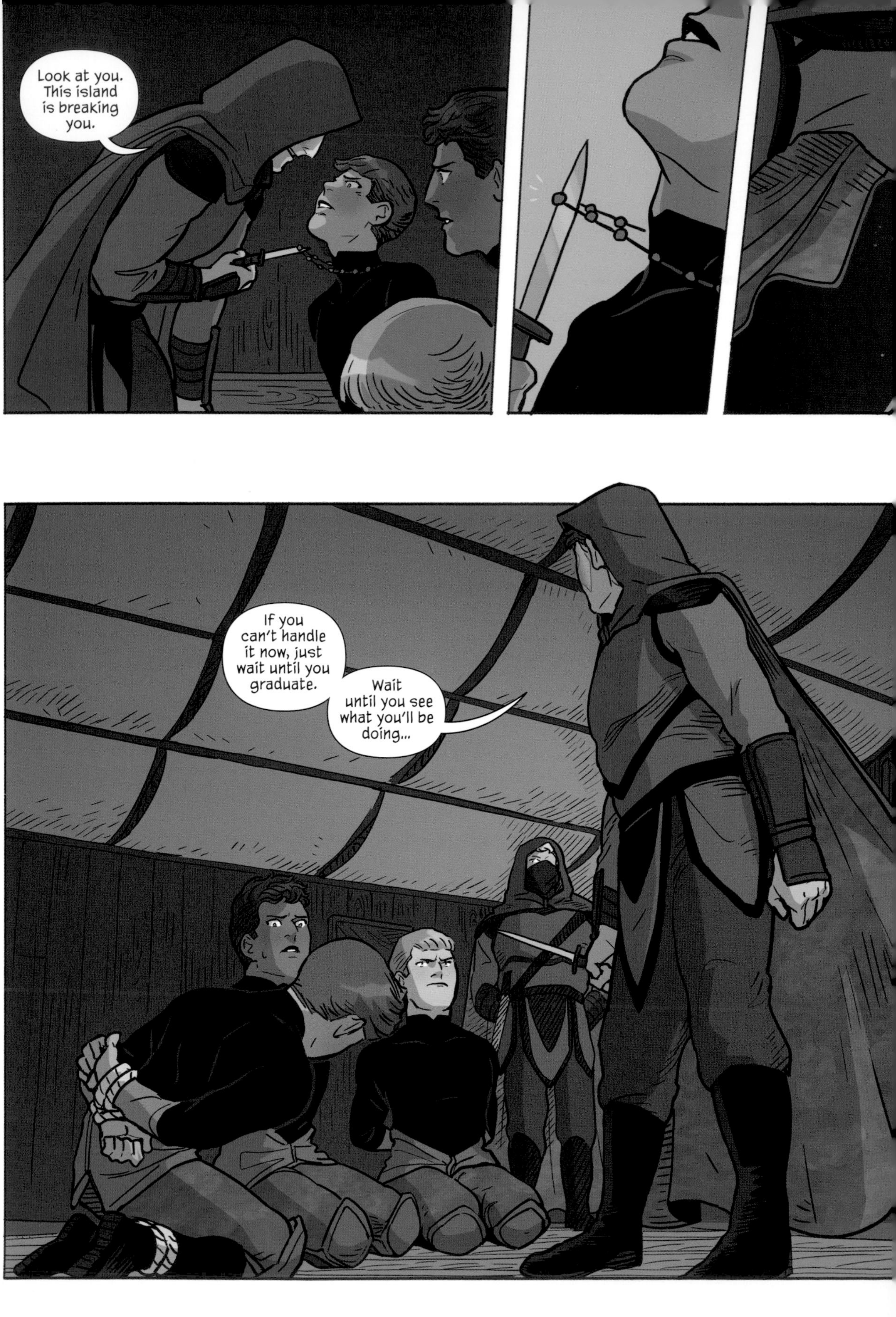
Look at you. This island is breaking you.
If you can't handle it now, just wait until you graduate.
Wait until you see what you'll be doing...

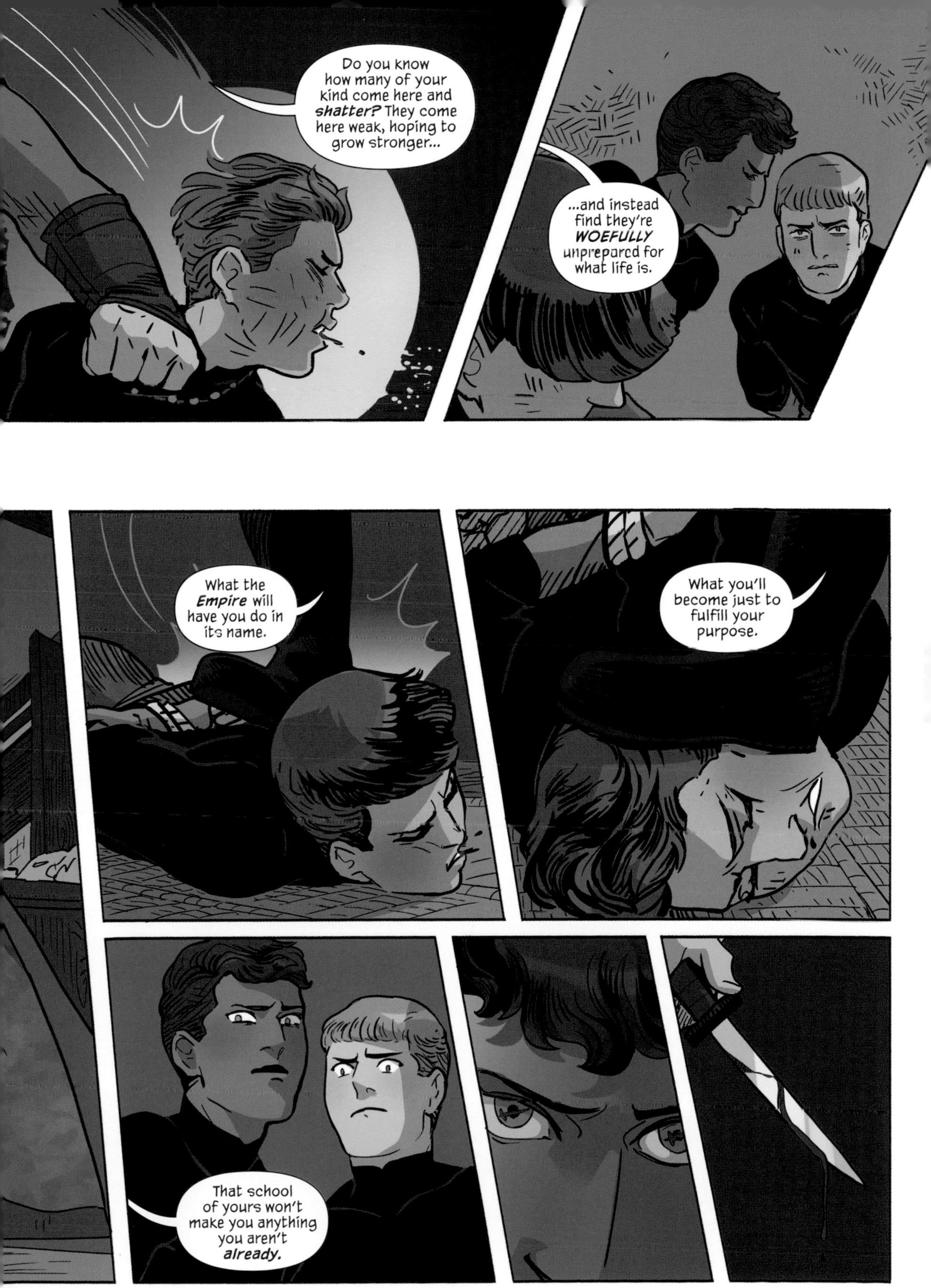
Do you know how many of your kind come here and *shatter?* They come here weak, hoping to grow stronger...
...and instead find they're ***WOEFULLY*** unprepared for what life is.
What the *Empire* will have you do in its name.
What you'll become just to fulfill your purpose.
That school of yours won't make you anything you aren't ***already.***

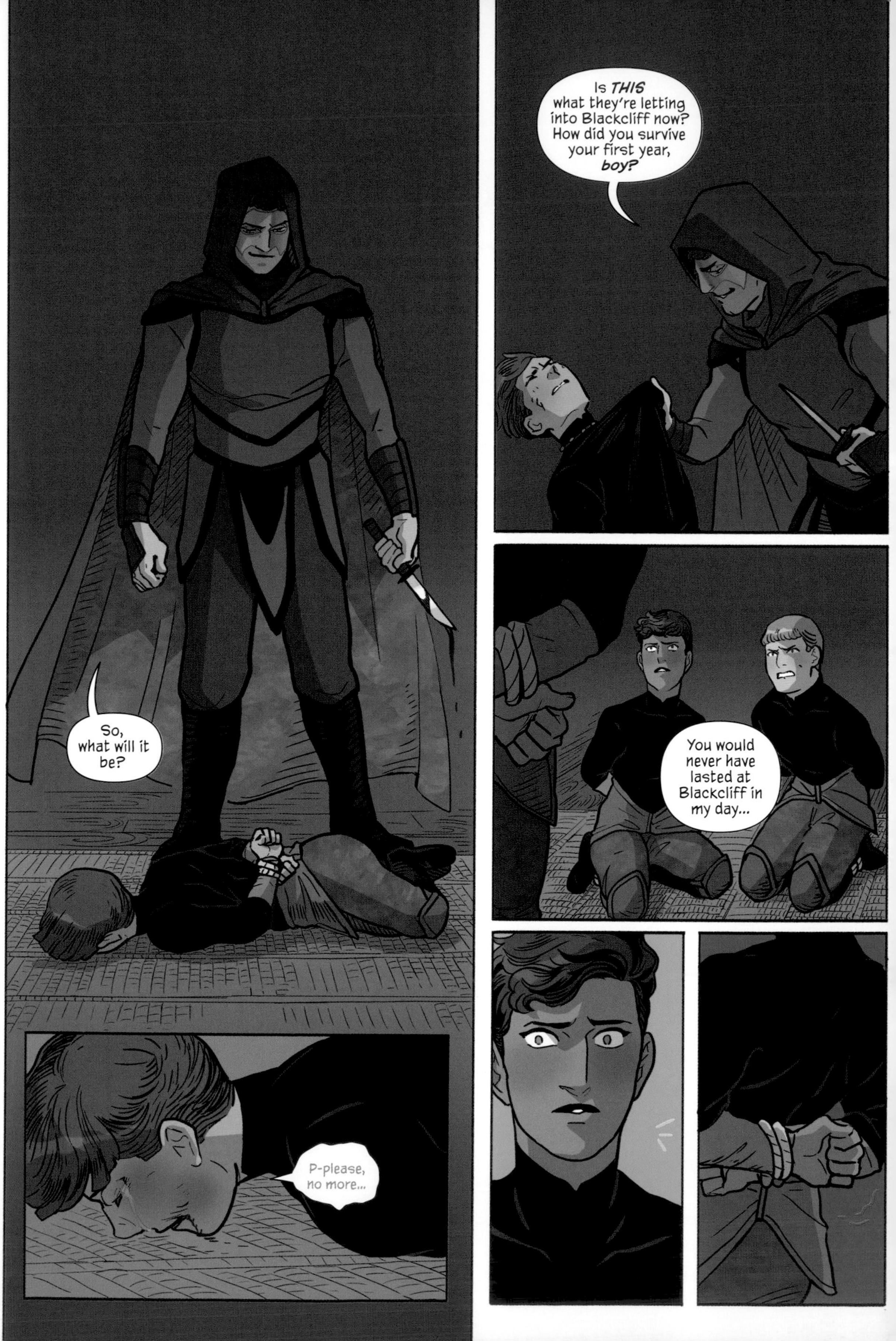

So, what will it be?
P-please, no more...
Is *THIS* what they're letting into Blackcliff now? How did you survive your first year, *boy?*
You would never have lasted at Blackcliff in my day...

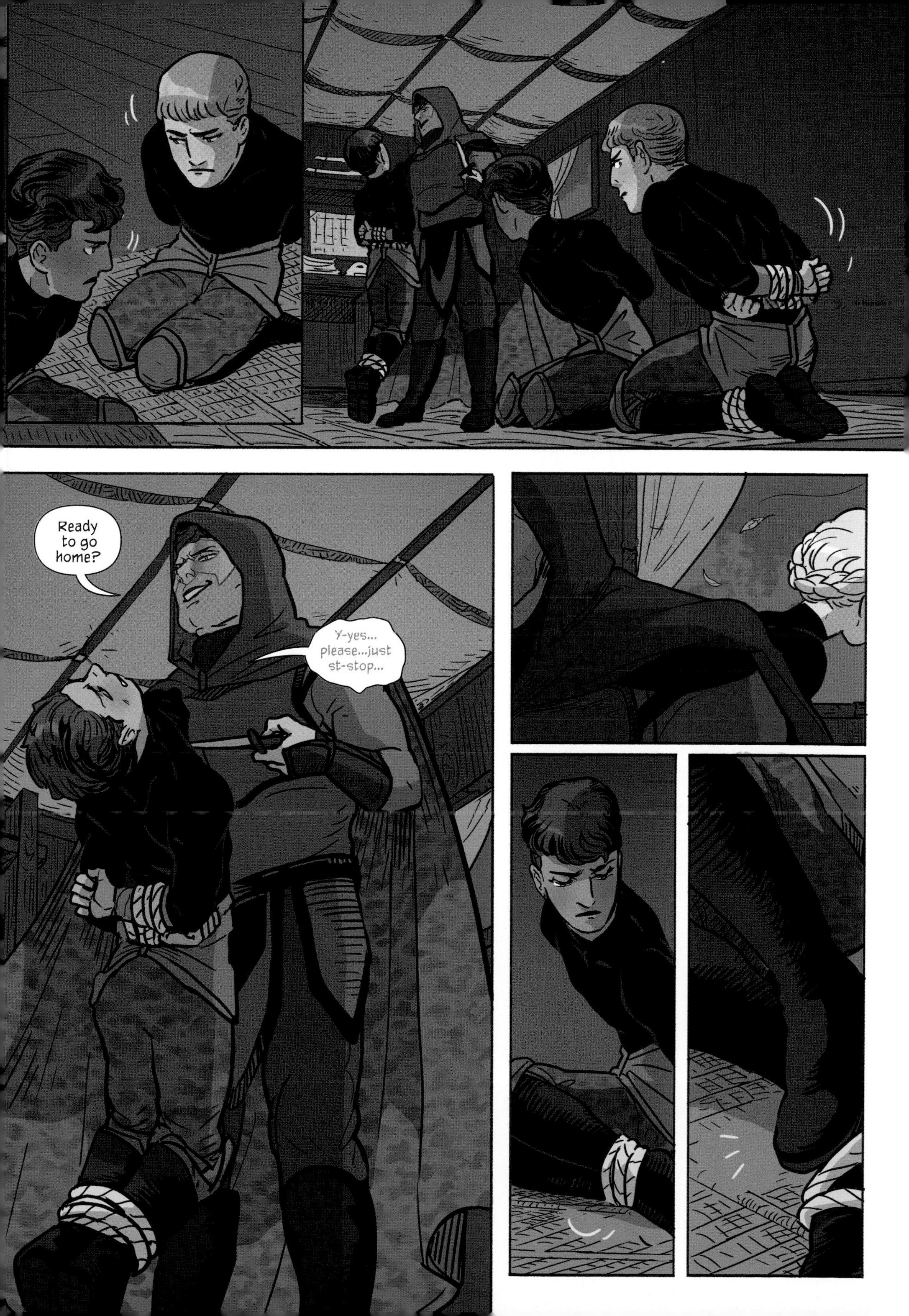
Ready to go home?
Y-yes... please...just st-stop...

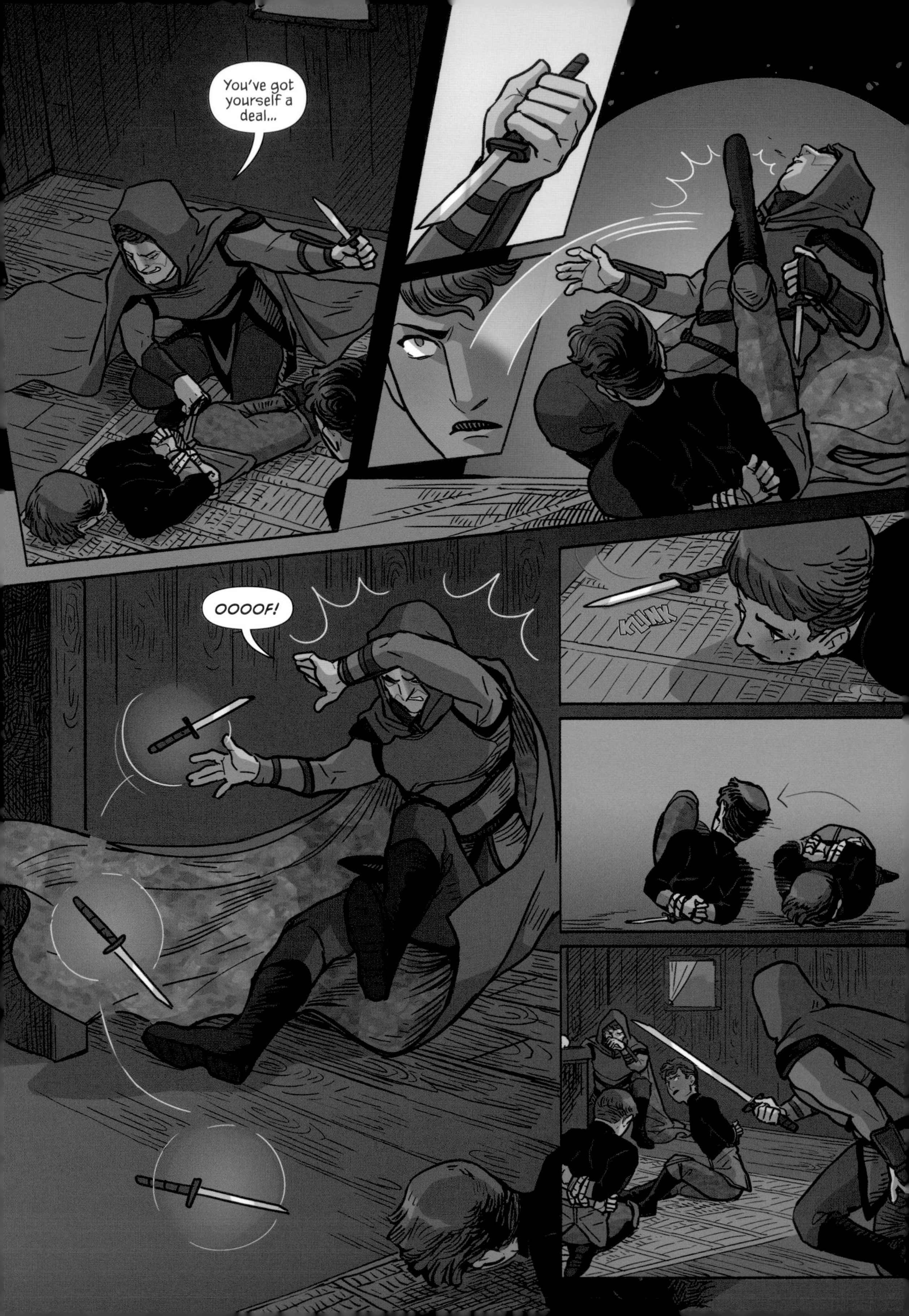
You've got yourself a deal...
OOOOF!
KLUNK

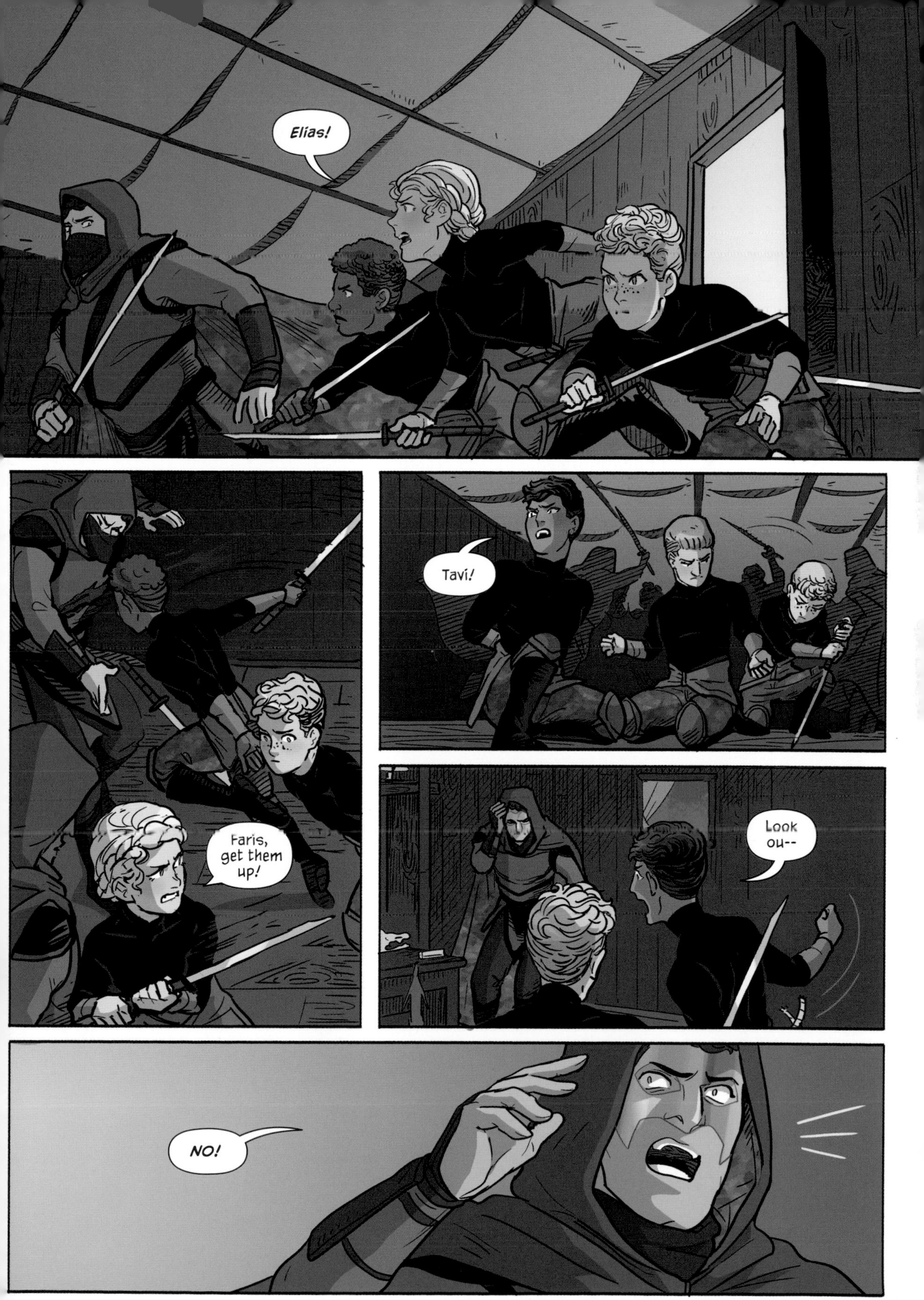

Elias!
Faris, get them up!
Tavi!
Look ou--
NO!

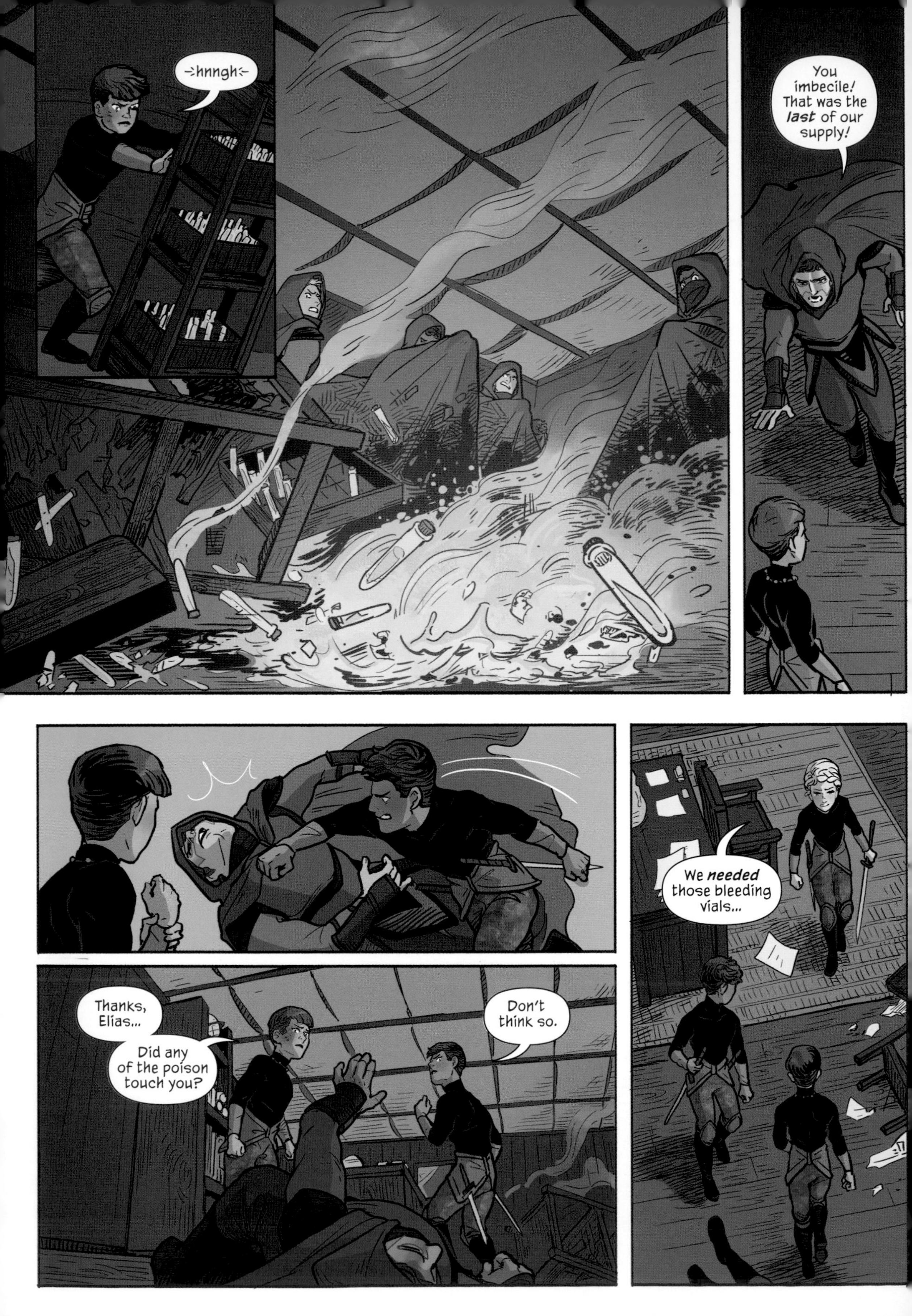

-hnngh-
You imbecile! That was the *last* of our supply!
We *needed* those bleeding vials...
Thanks, Elias...
Did any of the poison touch you?
Don't think so.

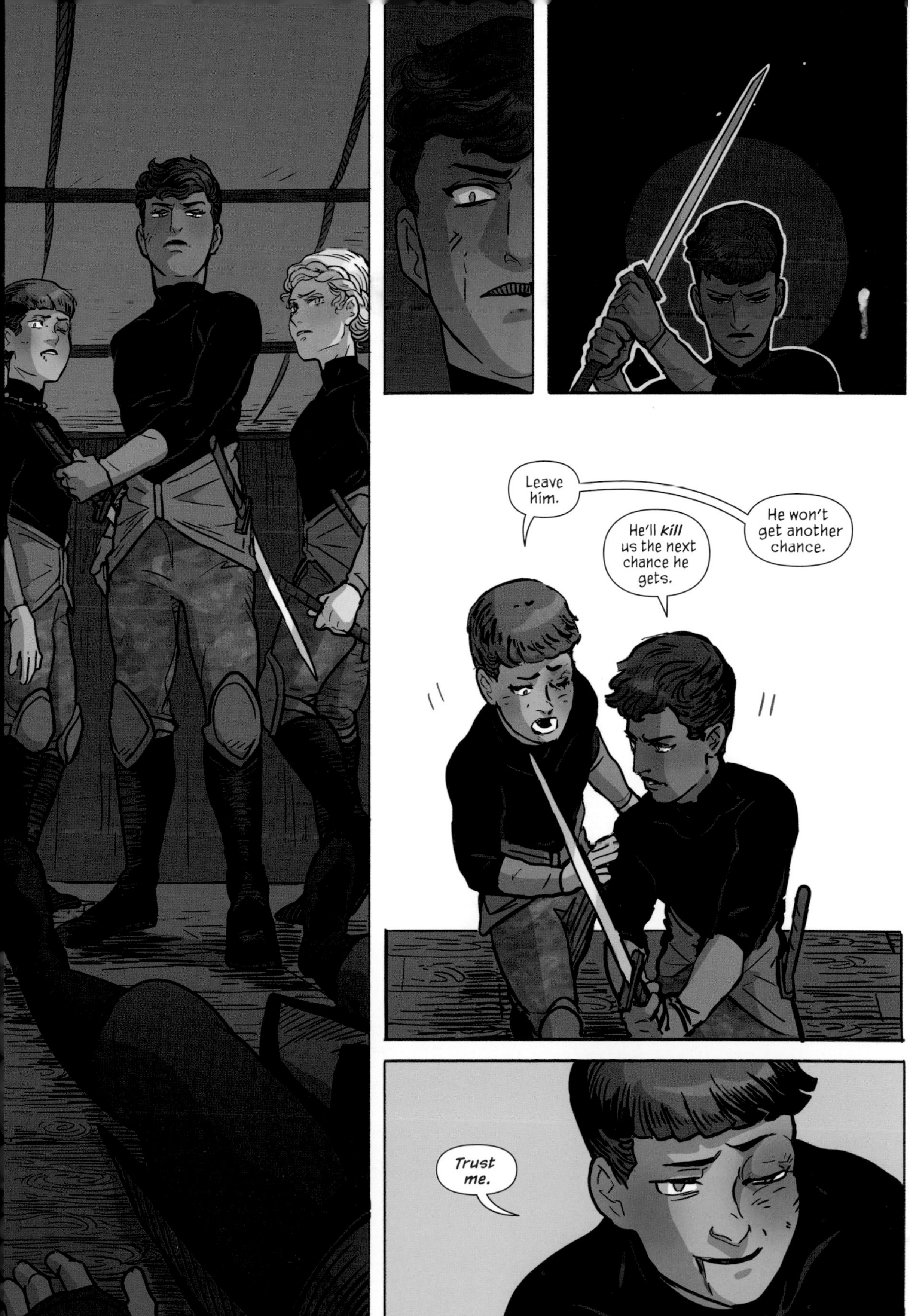
Leave him.
He won't get another chance.
He'll *kill* us the next chance he gets.
Trust me.

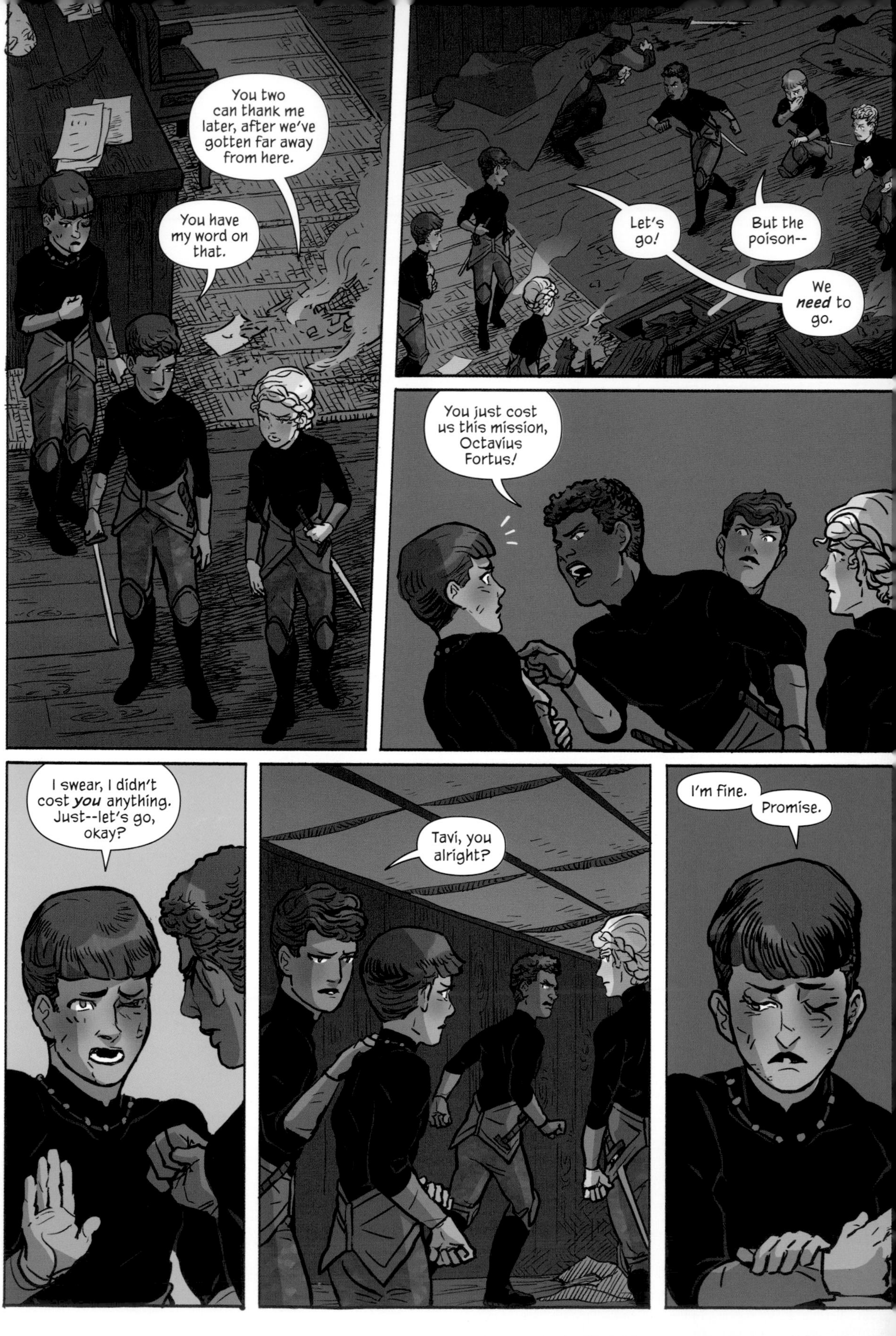
You two can thank me later, after we've gotten far away from here.
You have my word on that.
Let's go!
But the poison--
We *need* to go.
You just cost us this mission, Octavius Fortus!
I swear, I didn't cost *you* anything. Just--let's go, okay?
Tavi, you alright?
I'm fine.
Promise.

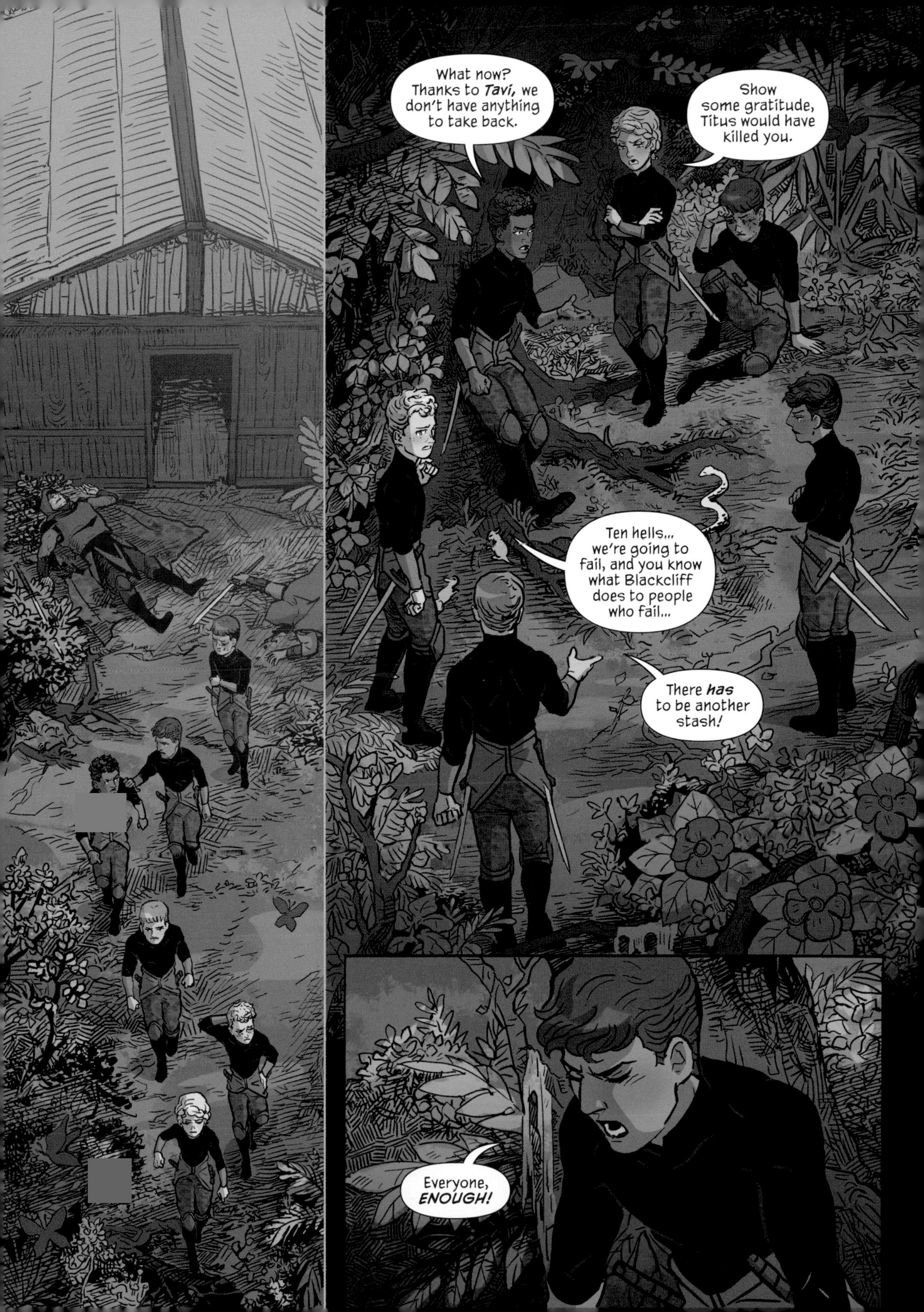
What now? Thanks to *Tavi,* we don't have anything to take back.
Show some gratitude, Titus would have killed you.
Ten hells... we're going to fail, and you know what Blackcliff does to people who fail...
There *has* to be another stash!
Everyone, *ENOUGH!*

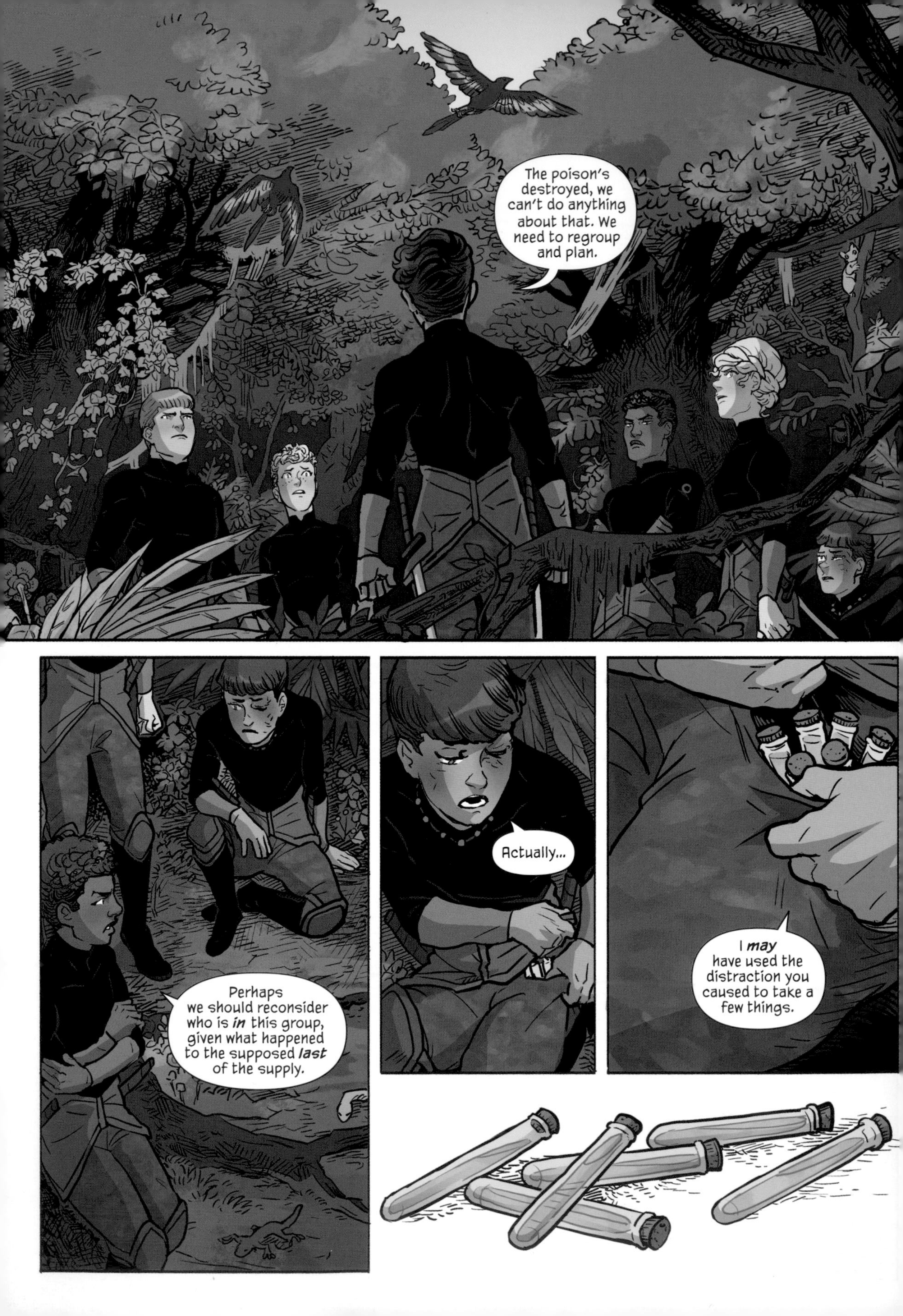
The poison's destroyed, we can't do anything about that. We need to regroup and plan.
Perhaps we should reconsider who is *in* this group, given what happened to the supposed *last* of the supply.
Actually...
I *may* have used the distraction you caused to take a few things.

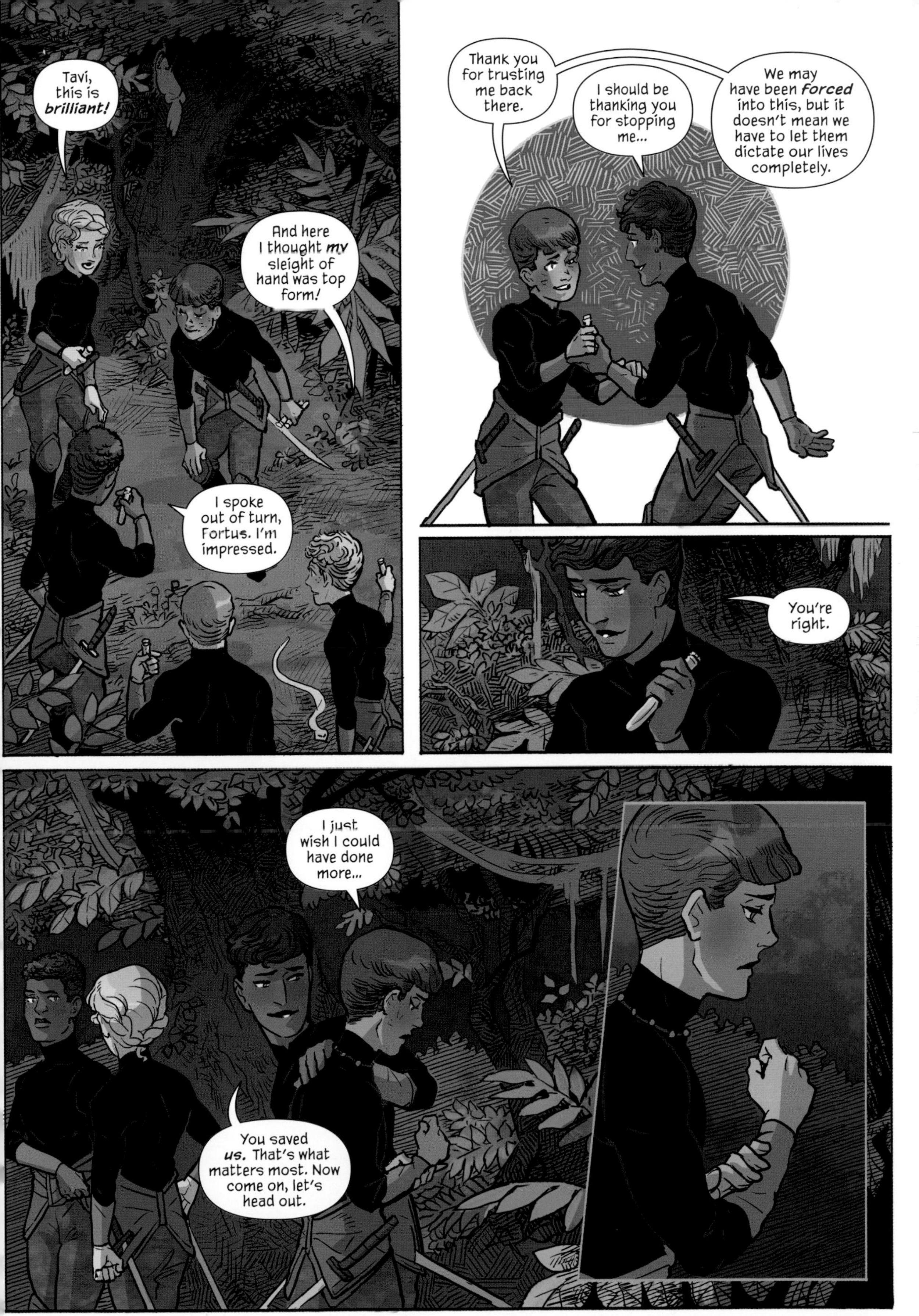
Tavi, this is **brilliant!**
And here I thought ***my*** sleight of hand was top form!
I spoke out of turn, Fortus. I'm impressed.
Thank you for trusting me back there.
I should be thanking you for stopping me...
We may have been ***forced*** into this, but it doesn't mean we have to let them dictate our lives completely.
You're right.
I just wish I could have done more...
You saved ***us.*** That's what matters most. Now come on, let's head out.

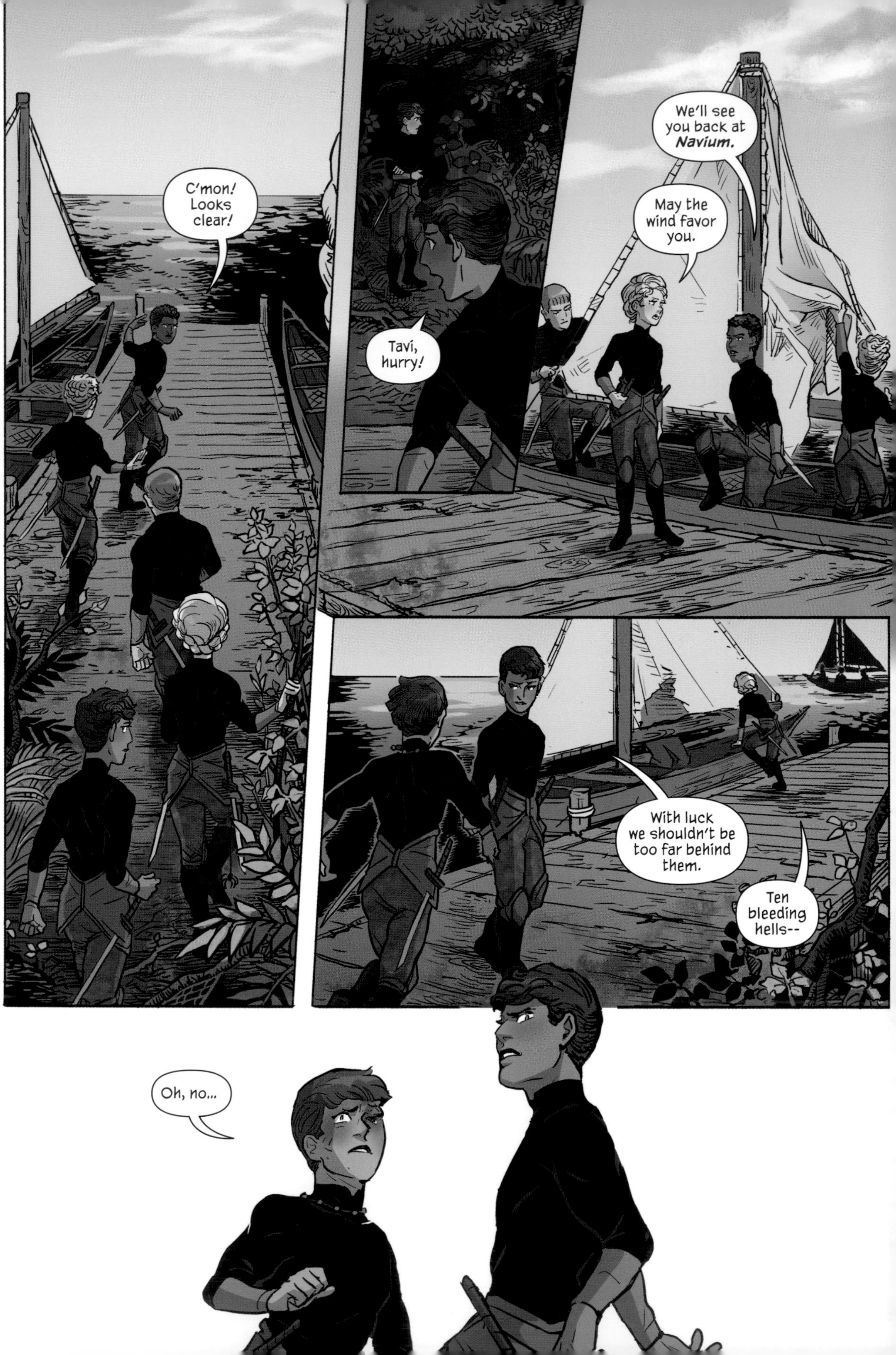
C'mon! Looks clear!
Tavi, hurry!
We'll see you back at **Navium.**
May the wind favor you.
With luck we shouldn't be too far behind them.
Ten bleeding hells--
Oh, no...

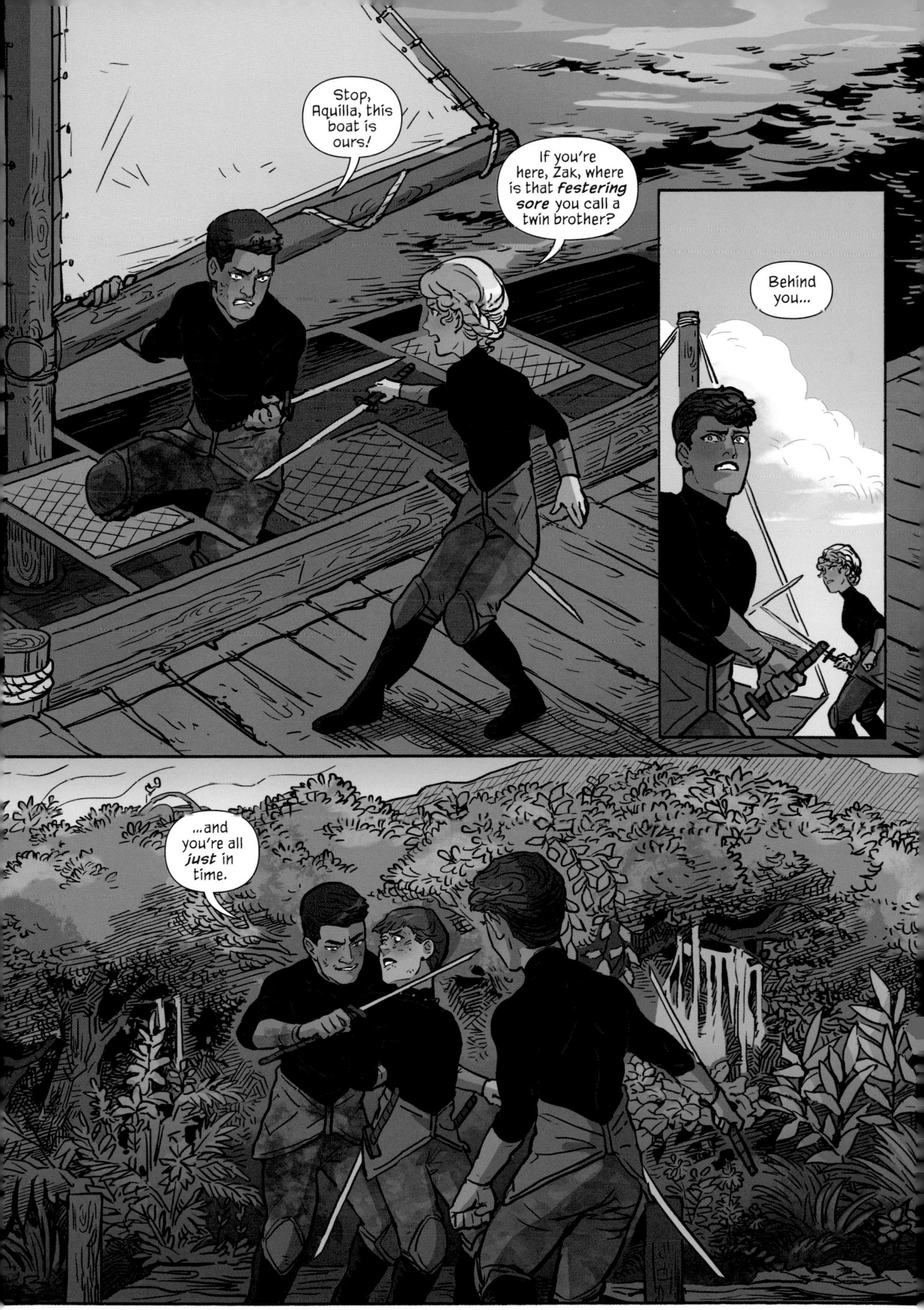
Stop, Aquilla, this boat is ours!
If you're here, Zak, where is that *festering sore* you call a twin brother?
Behind you...
...and you're all *just* in time.

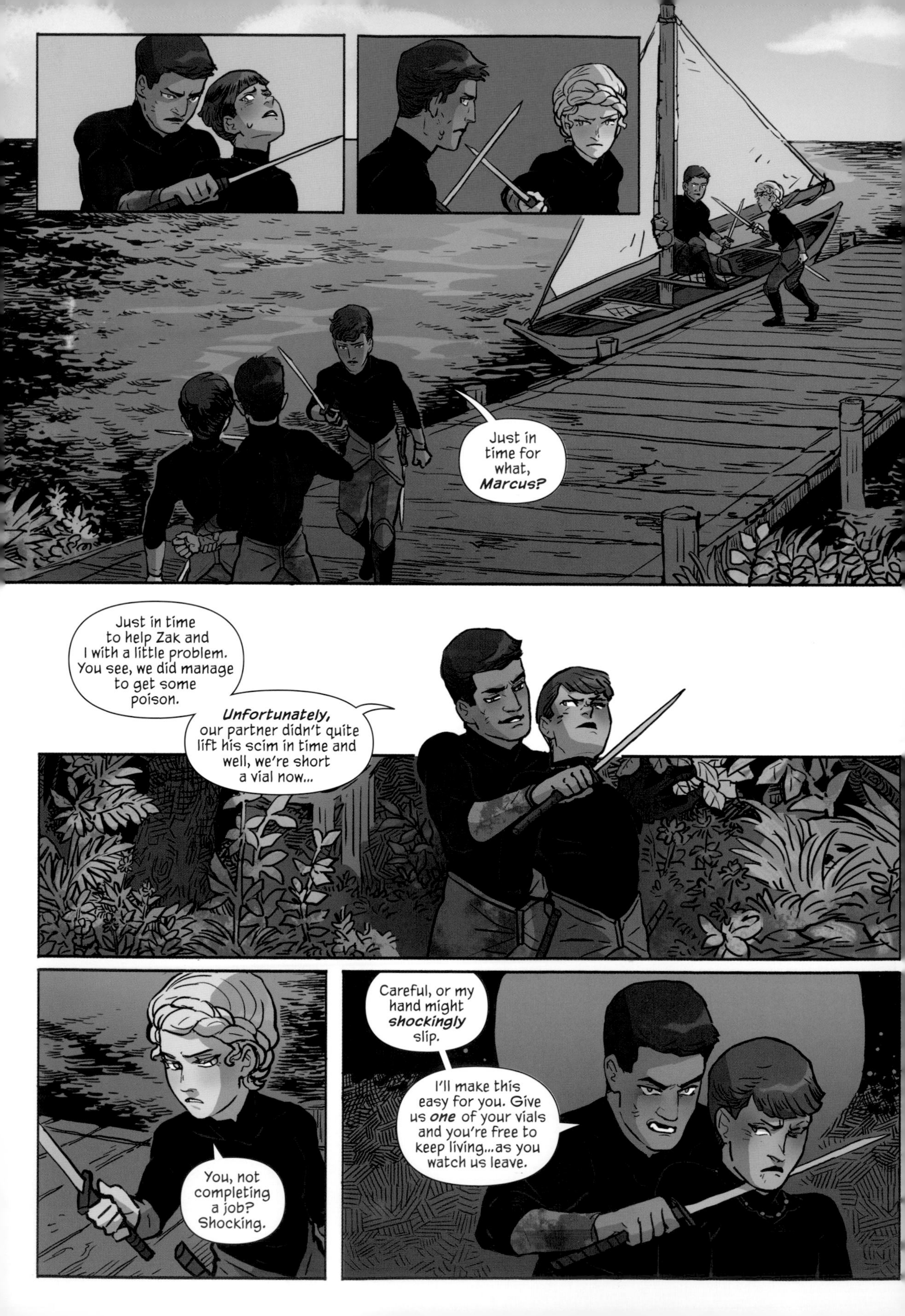
Just in time for what, *Marcus?*
Just in time to help Zak and I with a little problem. You see, we did manage to get some poison.
Unfortunately, our partner didn't quite lift his scim in time and well, we're short a vial now...
You, not completing a job? Shocking.
Careful, or my hand might *shockingly* slip.
I'll make this easy for you. Give us *one* of your vials and you're free to keep living...as you watch us leave.

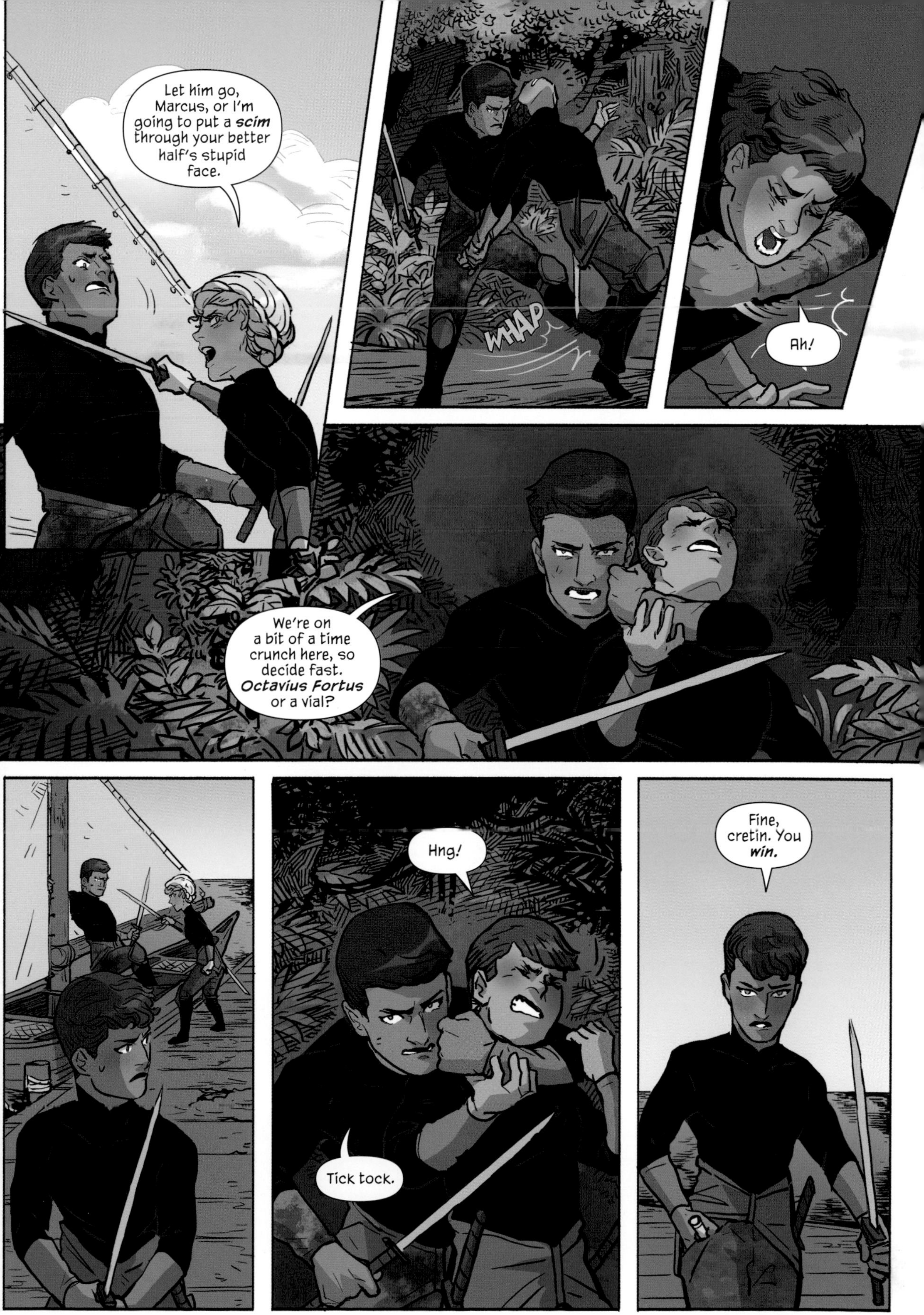
Let him go, Marcus, or I'm going to put a ***scim*** through your better half's stupid face.
WHAP
Ah!
We're on a bit of a time crunch here, so decide fast. ***Octavius Fortus*** or a vial?
Hng!
Tick tock.
Fine, cretin. You ***win.***

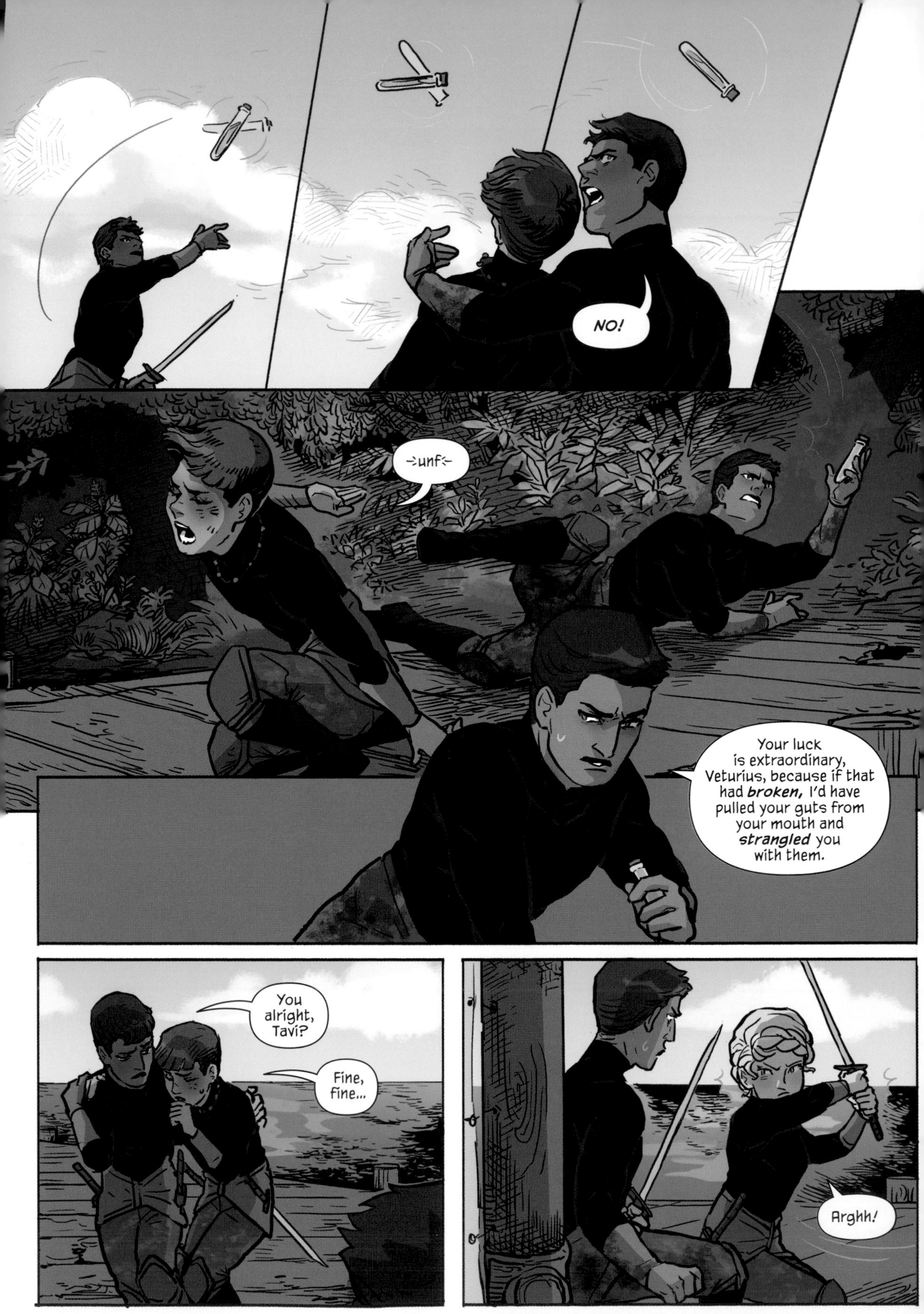
NO!
unf
Your luck is extraordinary, Veturius, because if that had **broken,** I'd have pulled your guts from your mouth and **strangled** you with them.
You alright, Tavi?
Fine, fine...
Arghh!

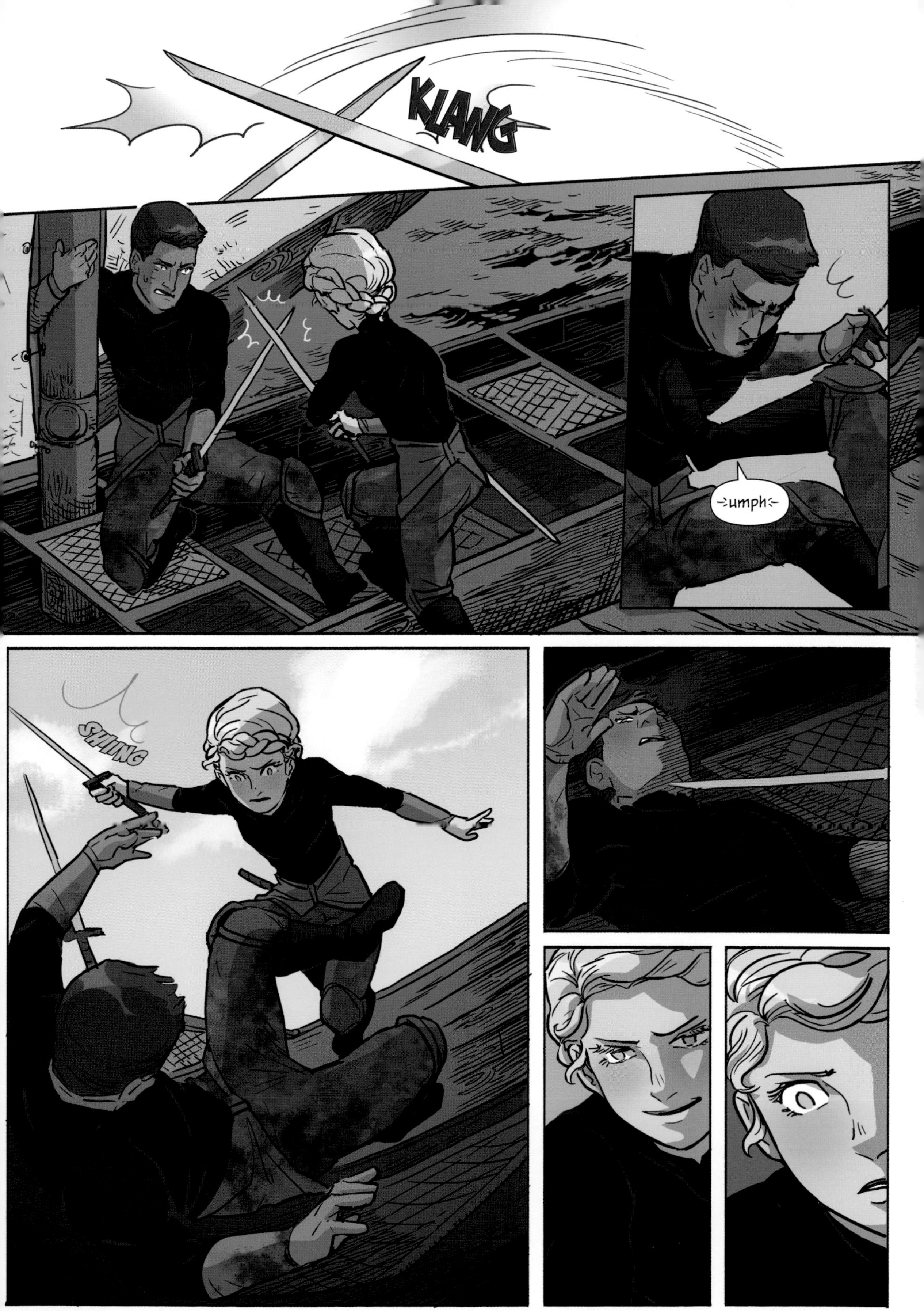
KLANG
umph
SHING

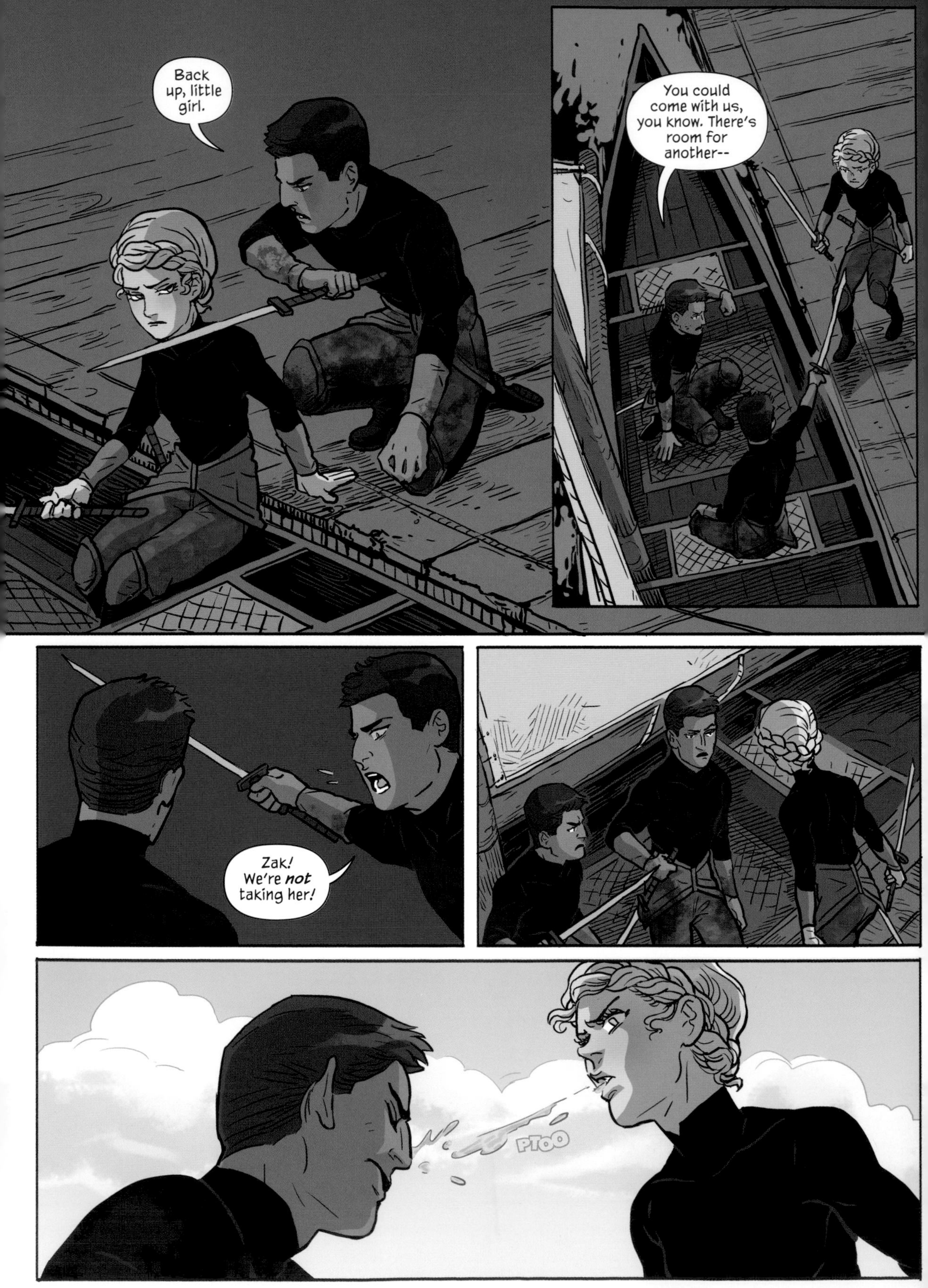
Back up, little girl.
You could come with us, you know. There's room for another--
Zak! We're *not* taking her!
PTOO

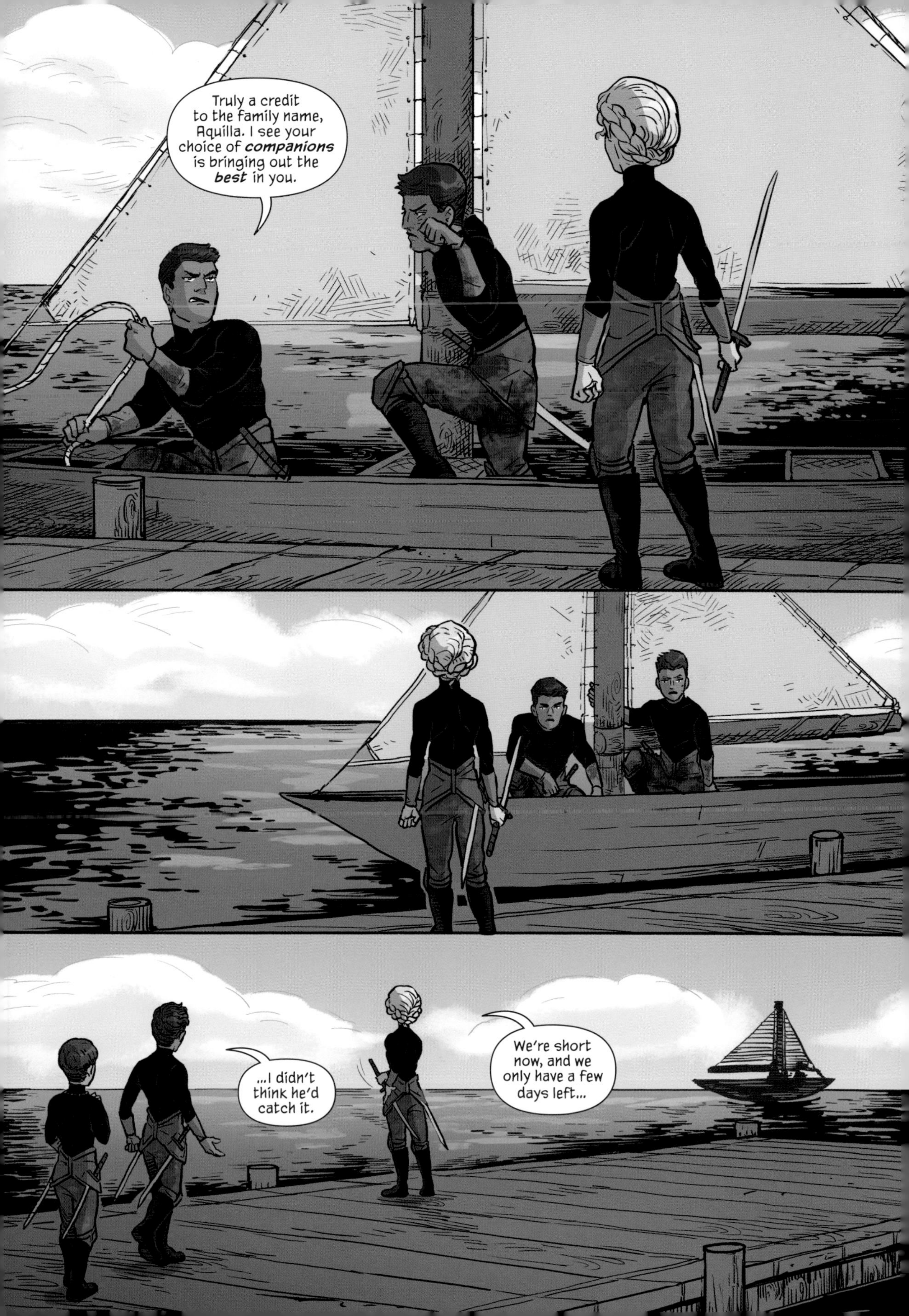
Truly a credit to the family name, Aquilla. I see your choice of *companions* is bringing out the *best* in you.
...I didn't think he'd catch it.
We're short now, and we only have a few days left...

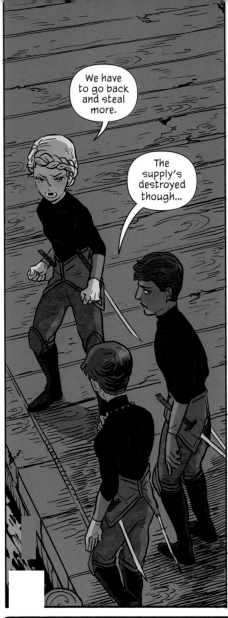

We have to go back and steal more.

The supply's destroyed though...

Maybe... maybe Titus has a personal store.

If Titus has anything left, I fear our escape may have put him on tighter lock down.

I think... we should go straight to the source.

What do you mean, Elias?

They distill the poison in the main camp, and they have all of the equipment needed to extract it *directly* from the source.

Tavi, you're home on leave *every year,* and you've seen your father do this countless times. You could do it.

Right?

Perhaps...

Absolutely *not!* We'd be up against far more than Titus's personal guard...

This is our *ONLY* option, Helene. The camp may have more people, but it's mostly civilians and Scholar slaves.

We've gone unseen in *far* bigger crowds. What's a handful of untrained eyes?

Elias is *right.* I've watched my father do it numerous times, I can dilute what we need. You just have to cook it to a certain point.

Besides, Titus won't see this coming. He'll be expecting us to target what he has, if he has anything at all.

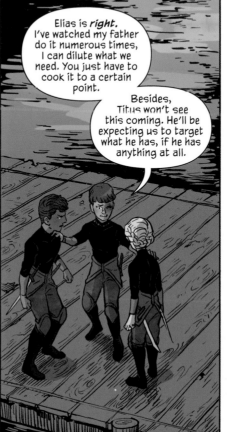

This is the *faster* way.

Hmph...

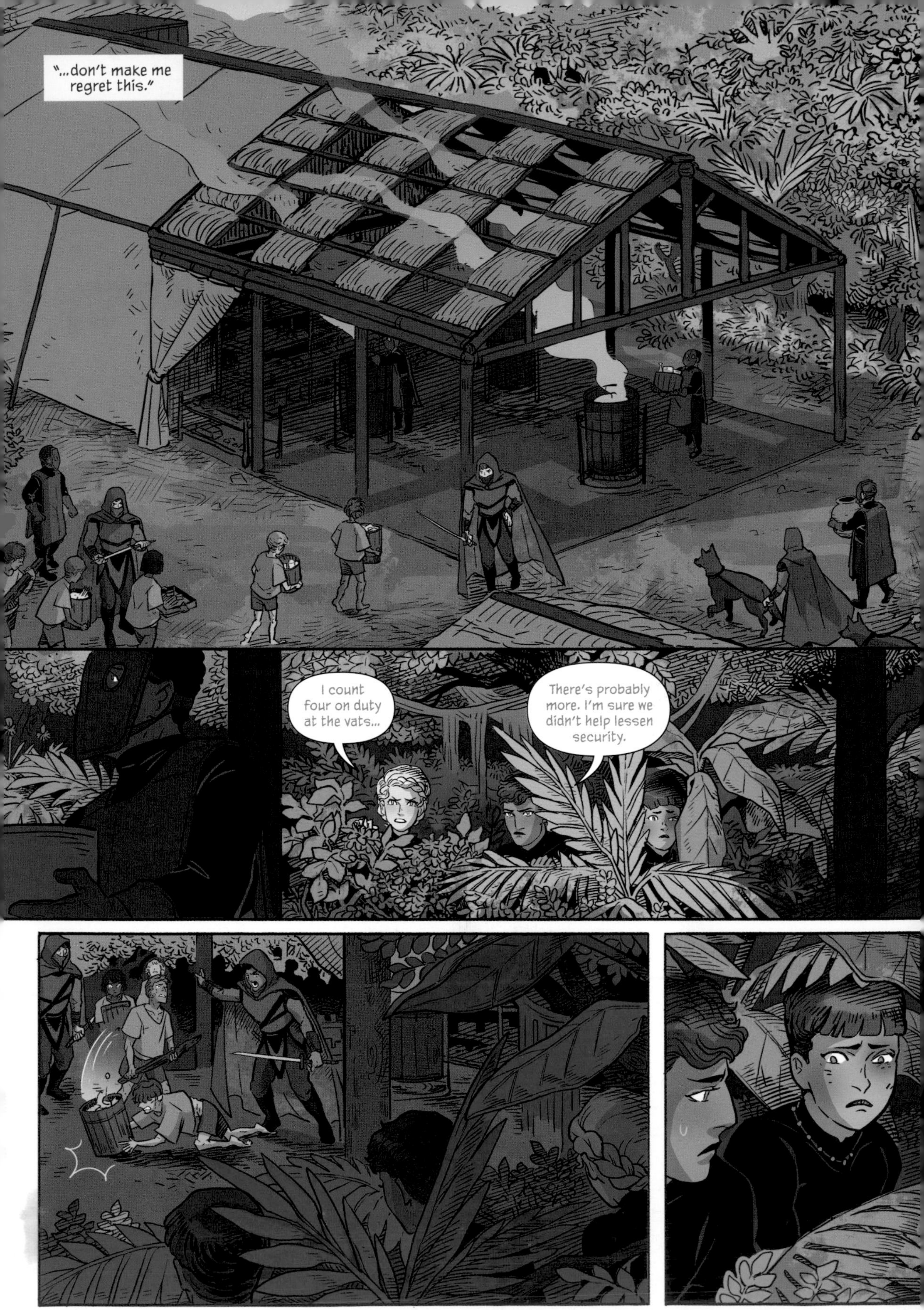
"...don't make me regret this."
I count four on duty at the vats...
There's probably more. I'm sure we didn't help lessen security.

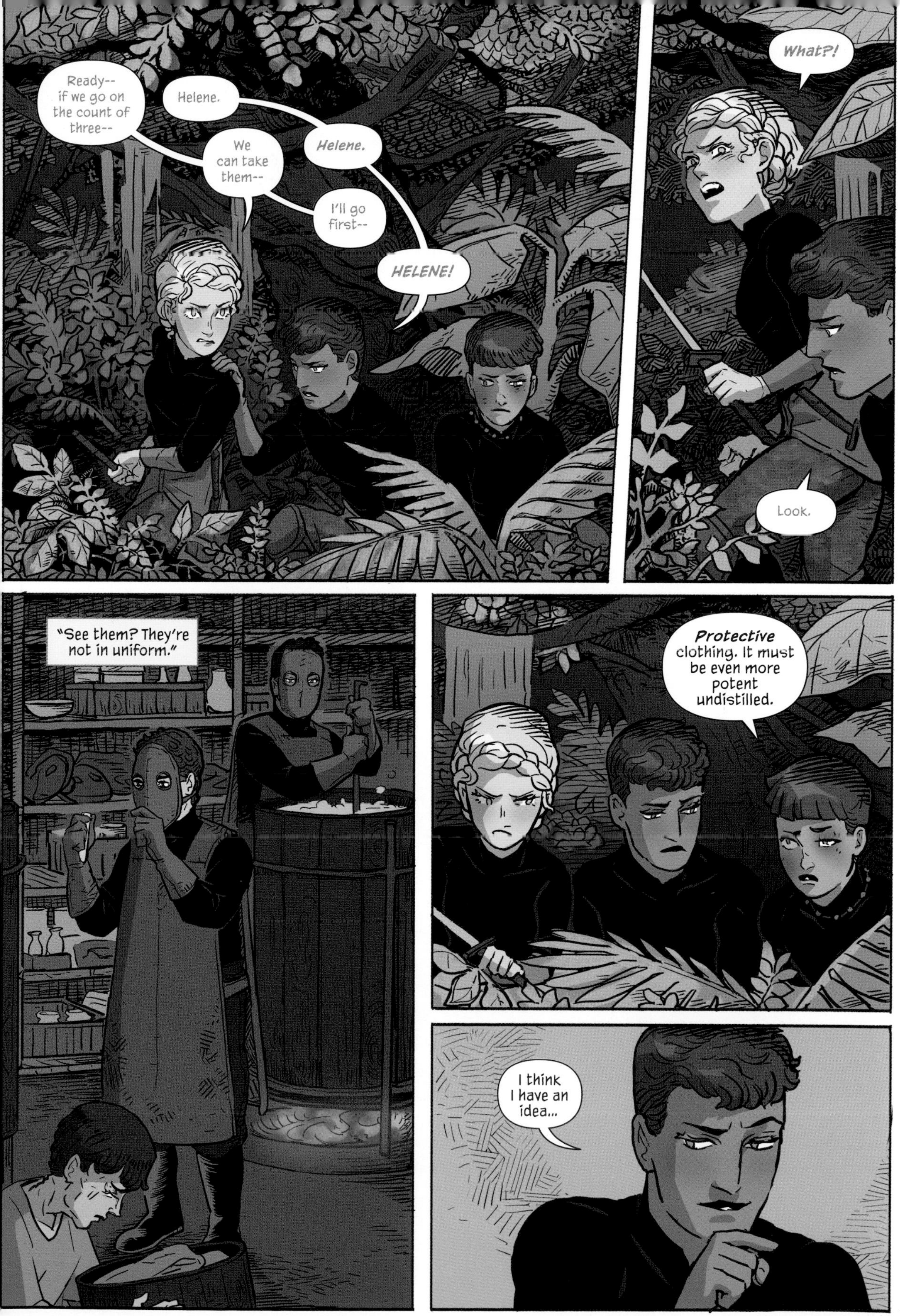
Ready-- if we go on the count of three--
Helene.
We can take them--
Helene.
I'll go first--
HELENE!
What?!
Look.
"See them? They're not in uniform."
Protective clothing. It must be even more potent undistilled.
I think I have an idea...

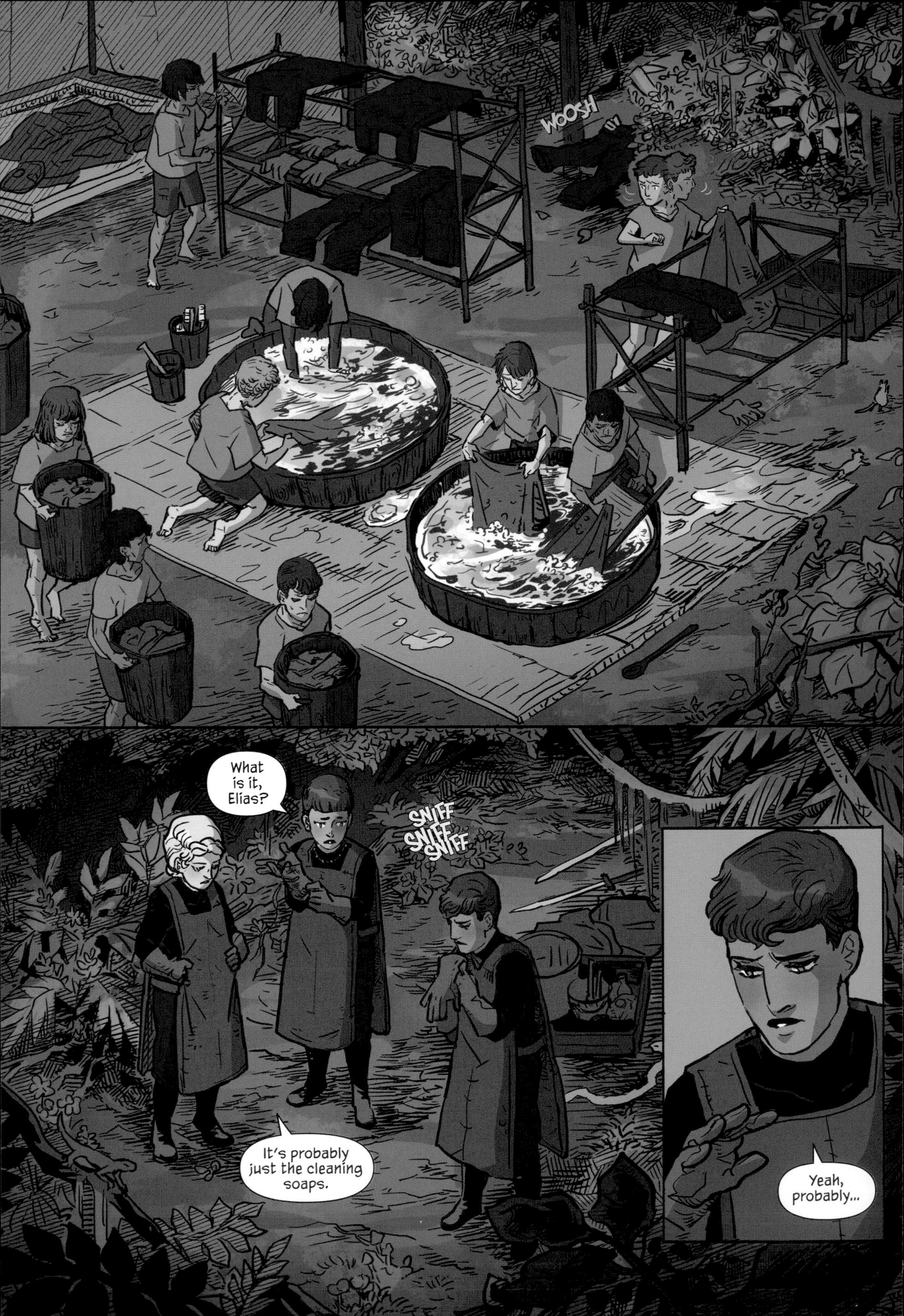
WOOSH
What is it, Elias?
SNIFF SNIFF SNIFF
It's probably just the cleaning soaps.
Yeah, probably...

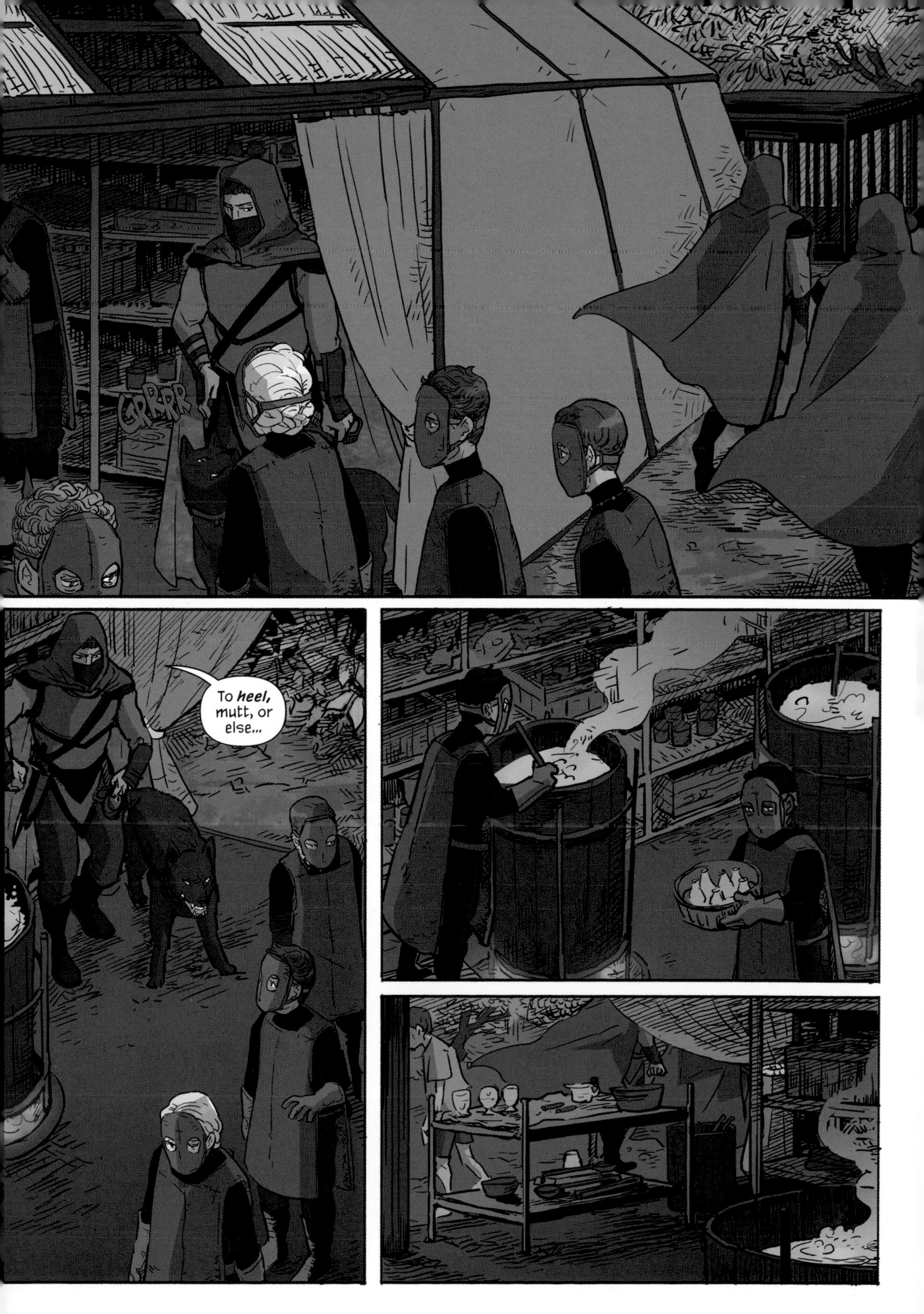
GRRRR
To heel, mutt, or else...

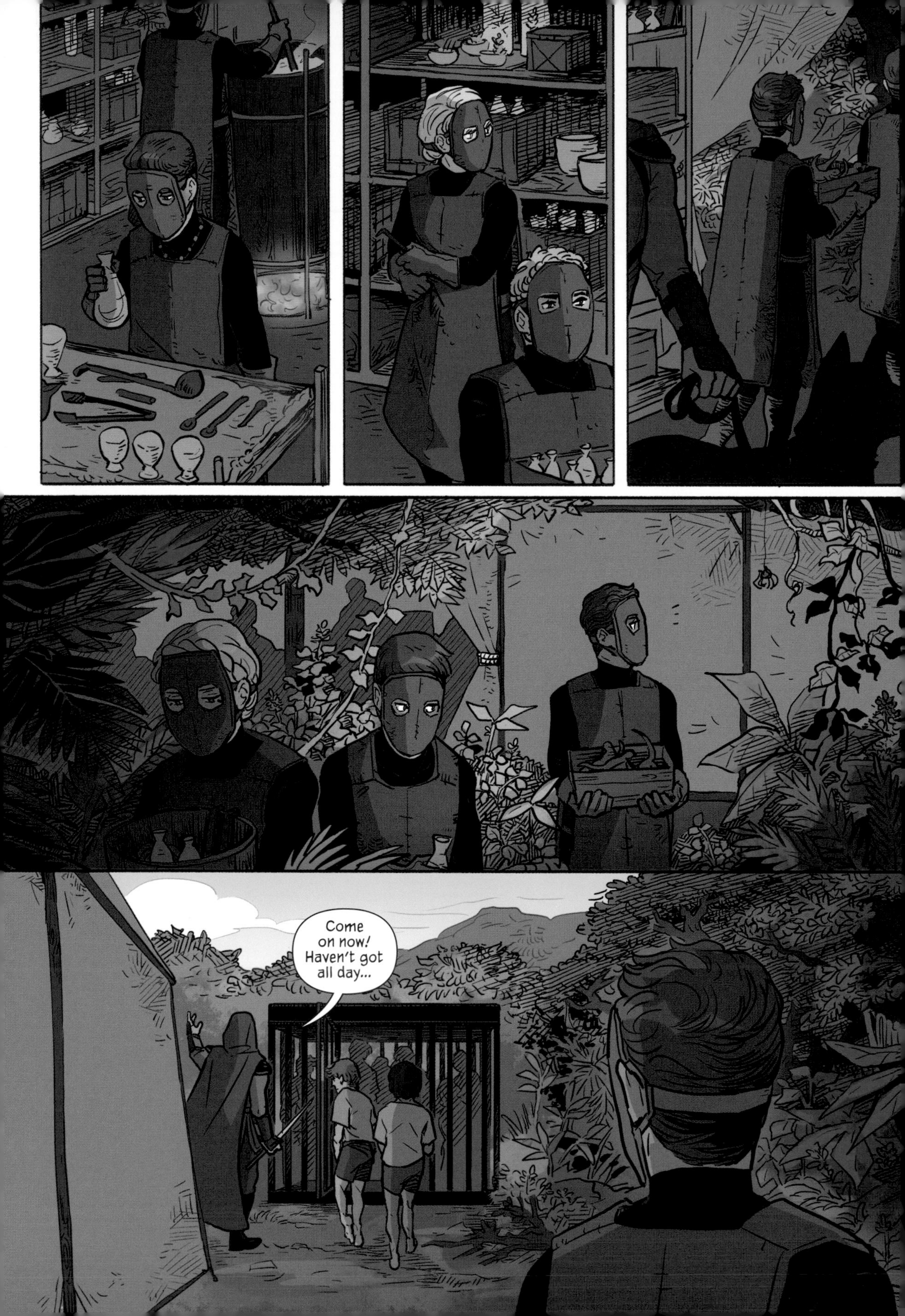
Come on now! Haven't got all day...

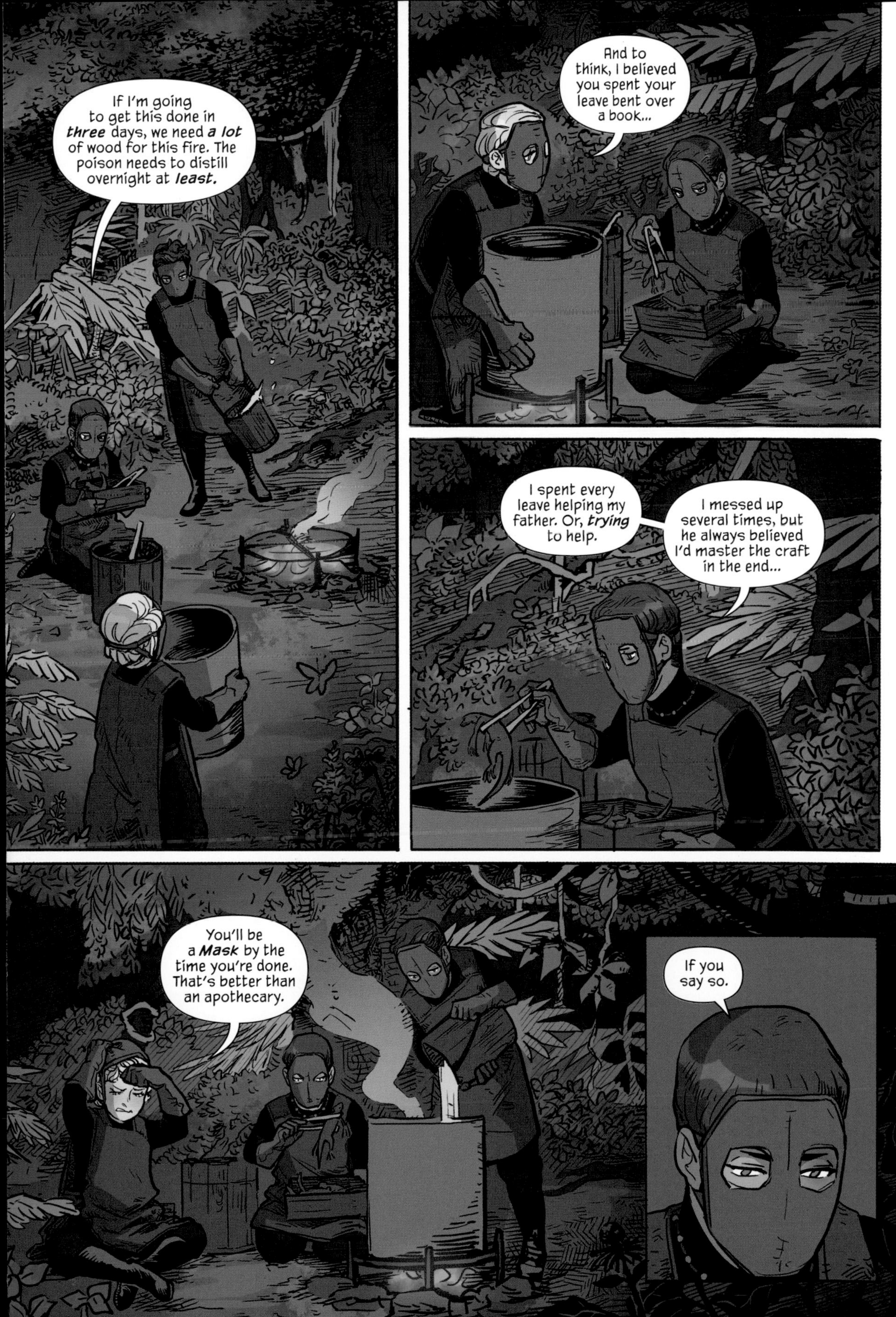
If I'm going to get this done in *three* days, we need *a lot* of wood for this fire. The poison needs to distill overnight at *least.*
And to think, I believed you spent your leave bent over a book...
I spent every leave helping my father. Or, *trying* to help.
I messed up several times, but he always believed I'd master the craft in the end...
You'll be a *Mask* by the time you're done. That's better than an apothecary.
If you say so.

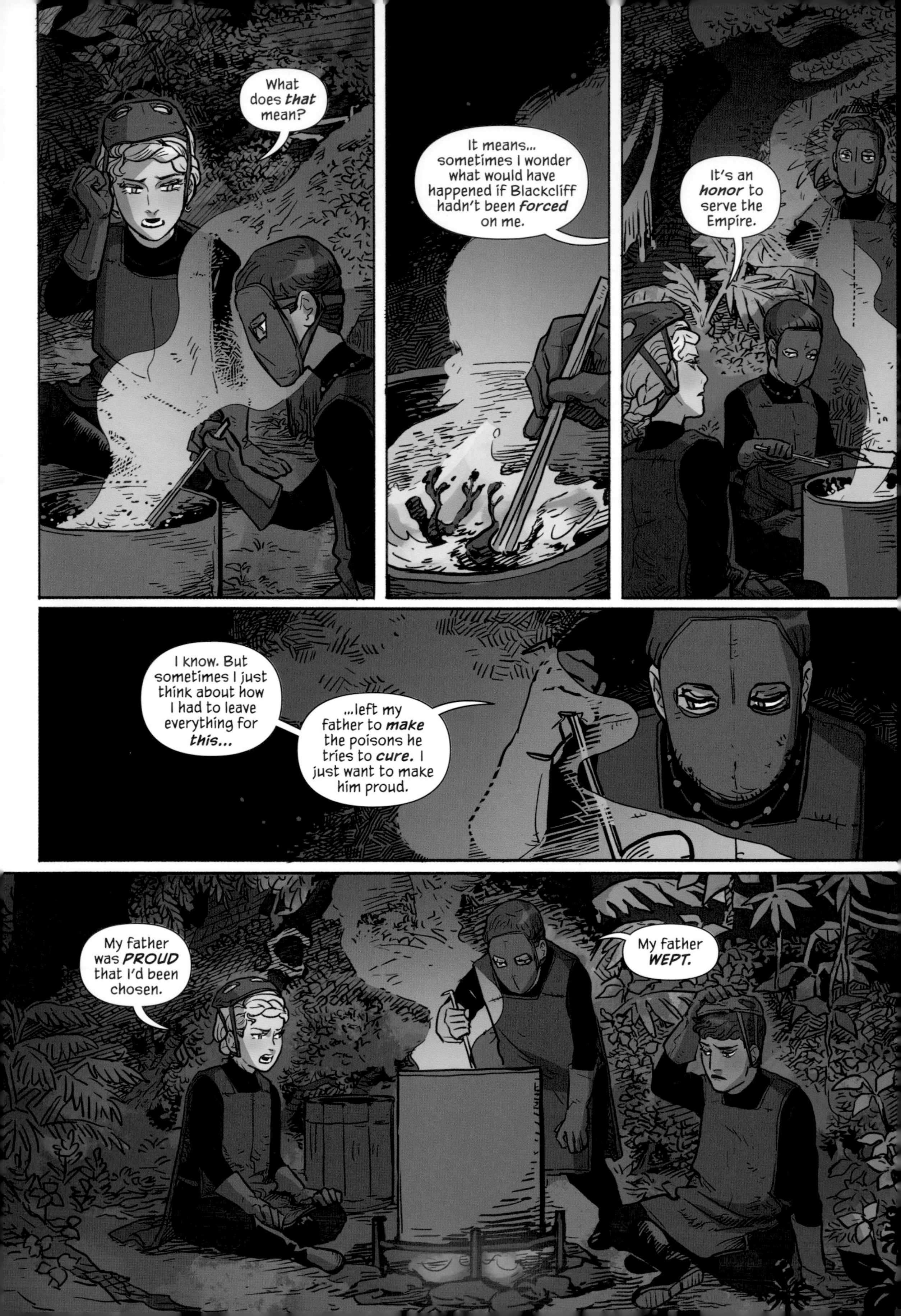
What does *that* mean?
It means... sometimes I wonder what would have happened if Blackcliff hadn't been *forced* on me.
It's an *honor* to serve the Empire.
I know. But sometimes I just think about how I had to leave everything for *this...*
...left my father to *make* the poisons he tries to *cure.* I just want to make him proud.
My father was *PROUD* that I'd been chosen.
My father *WEPT.*

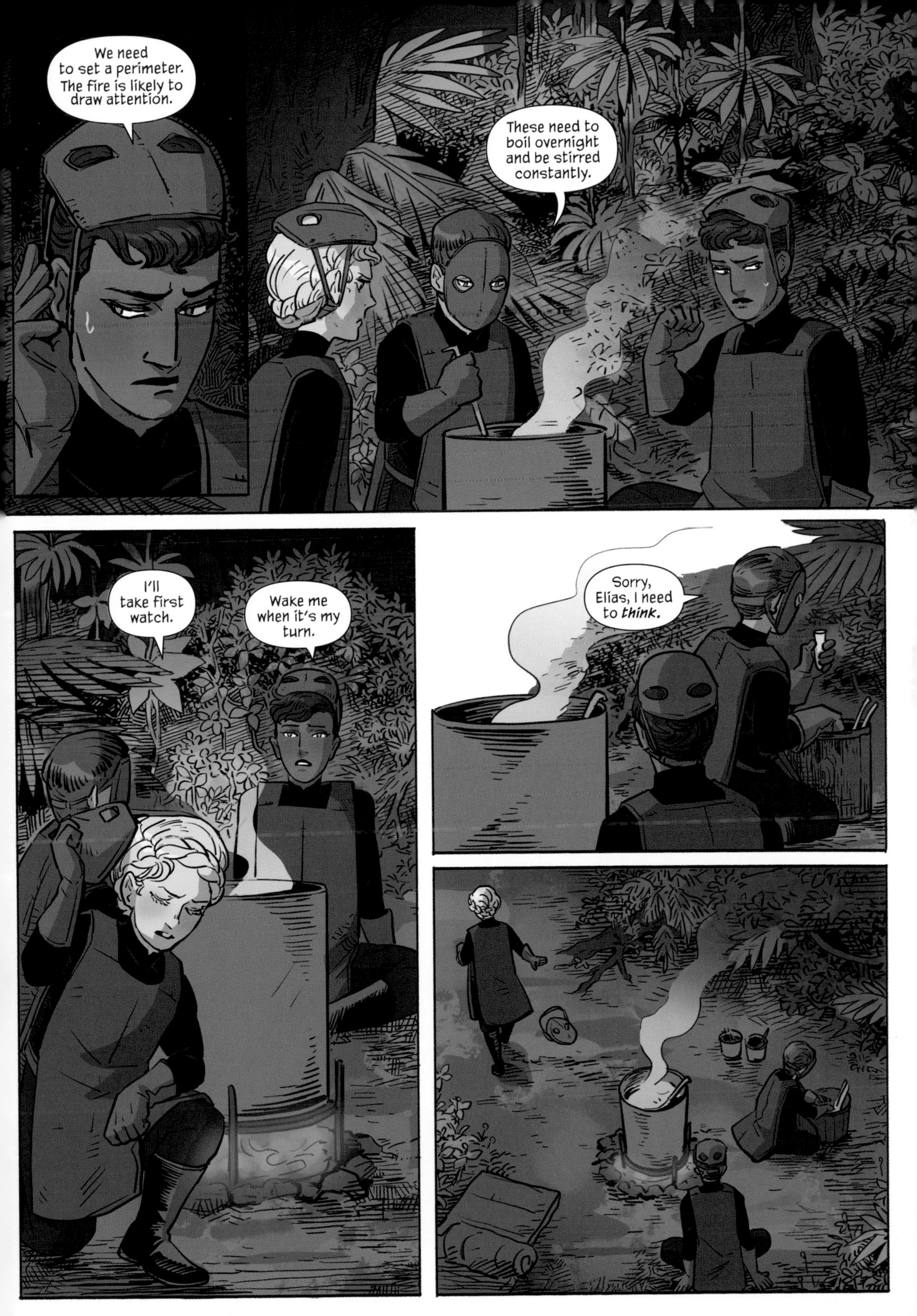
We need to set a perimeter. The fire is likely to draw attention.
These need to boil overnight and be stirred constantly.
I'll take first watch.
Wake me when it's my turn.
Sorry, Elias, I need to *think.*

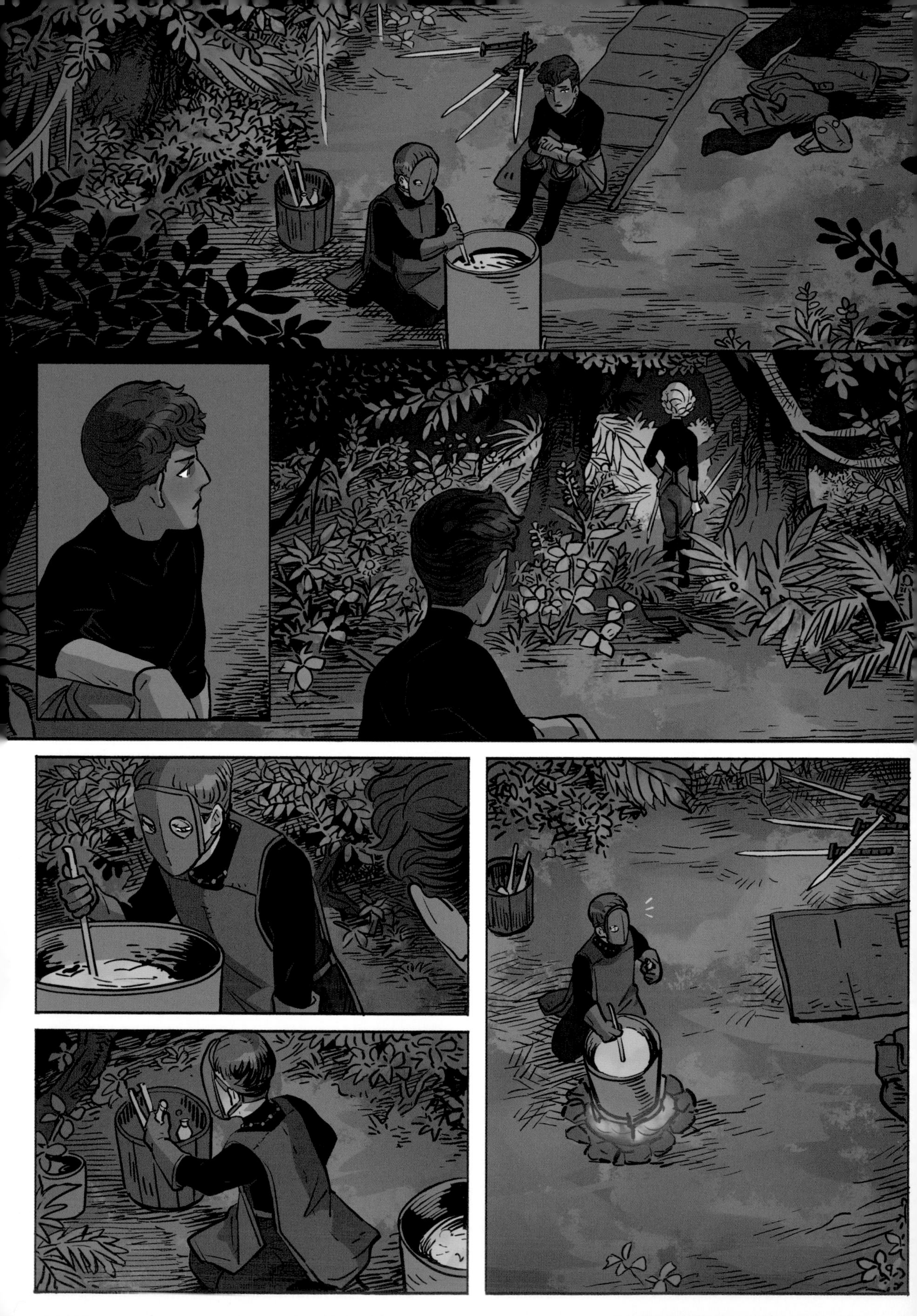

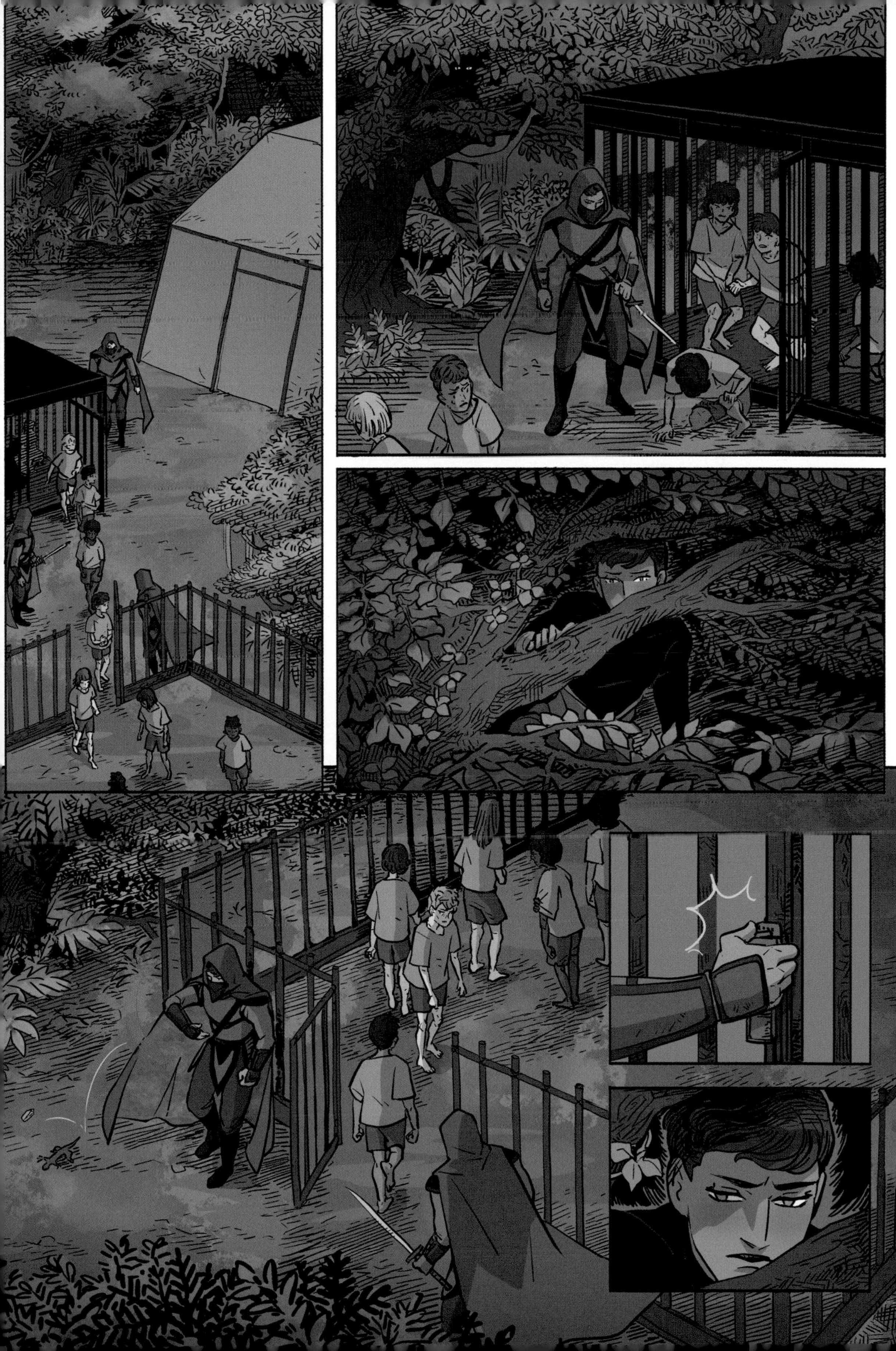

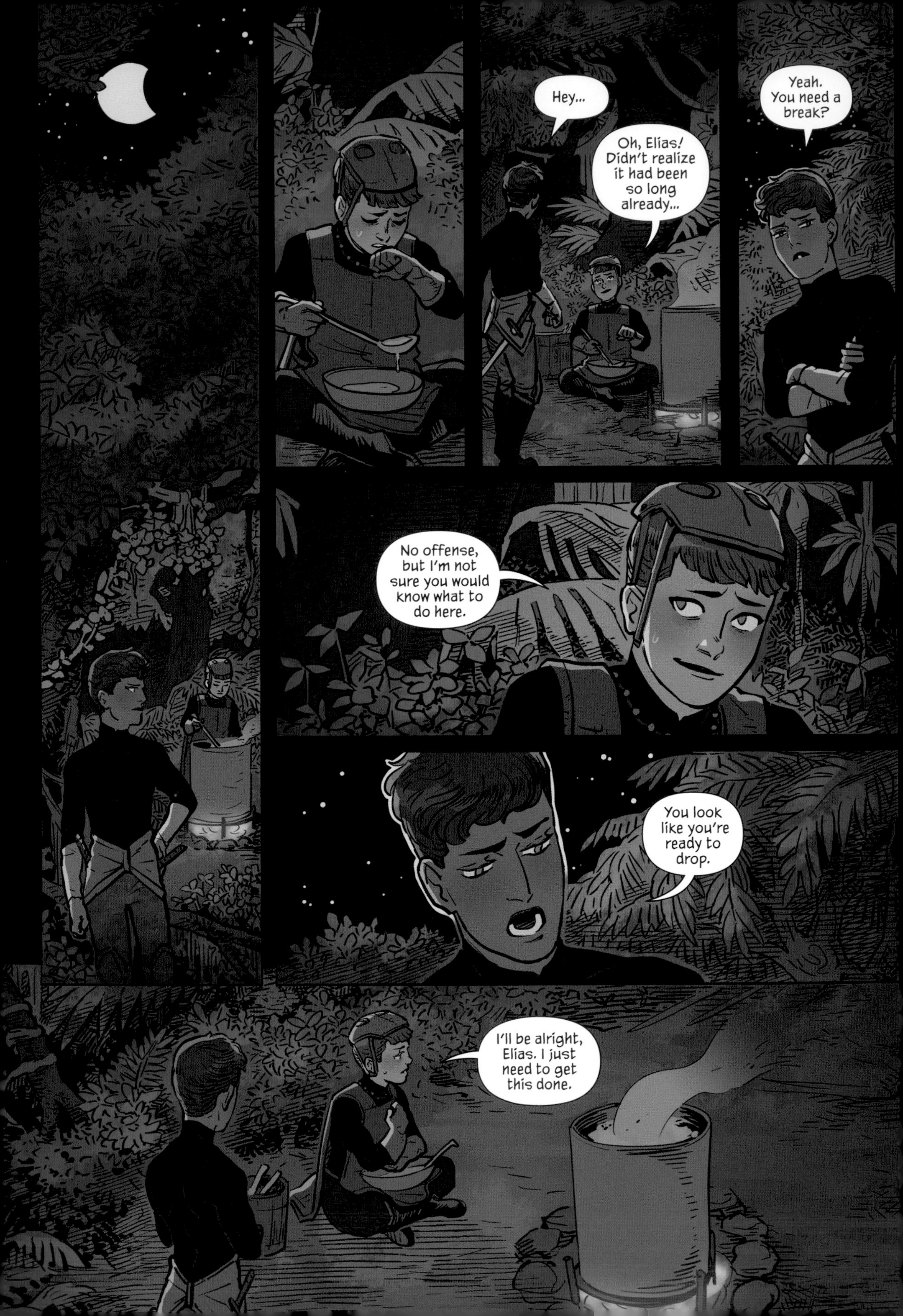
Hey...
Oh, Elías! Didn't realize it had been so long already...
Yeah. You need a break?
No offense, but I'm not sure you would know what to do here.
You look like you're ready to drop.
I'll be alright, Elías. I just need to get this done.

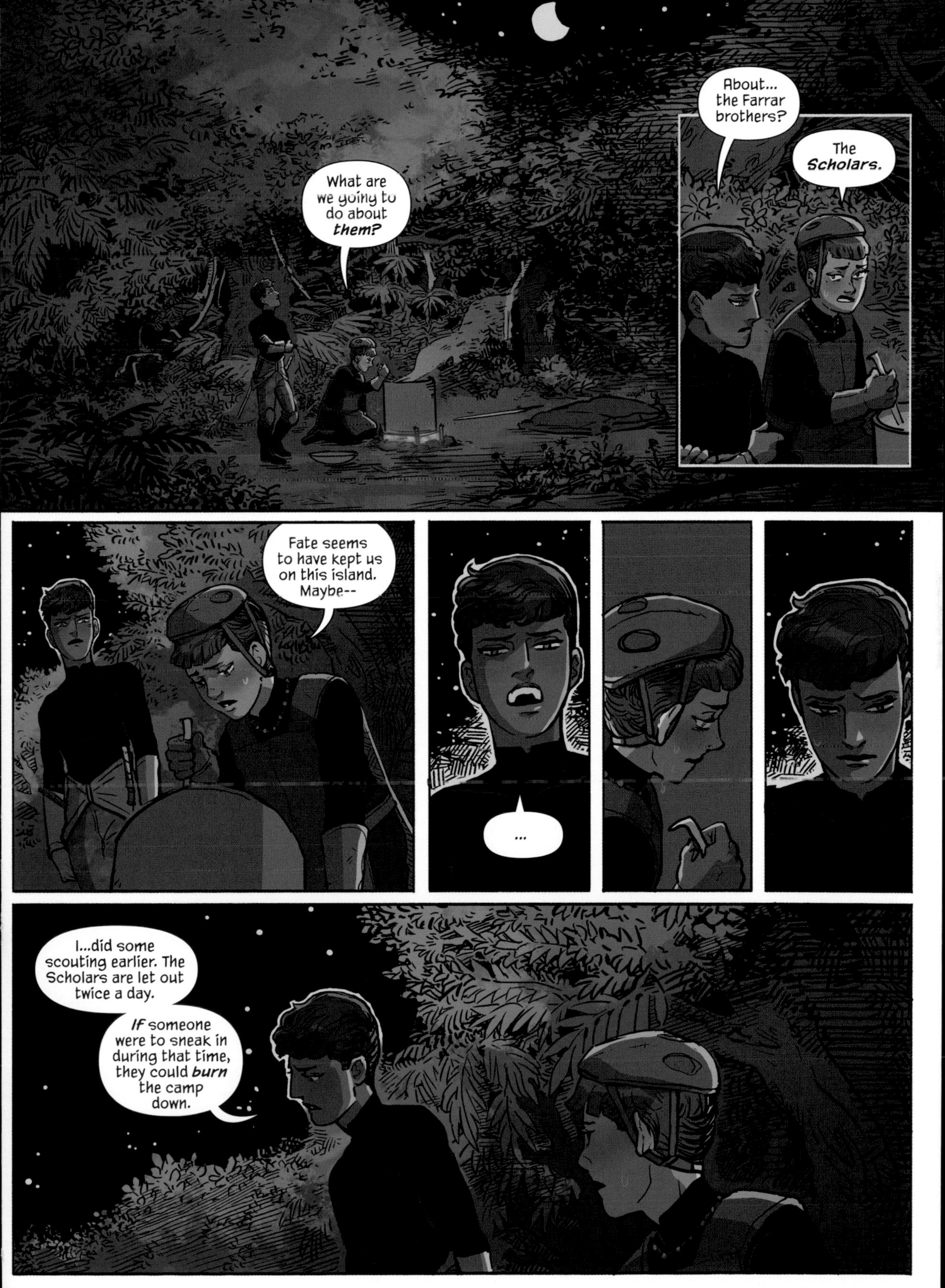
What are we going to do about *them?*
About... the Farrar brothers?
The *Scholars.*
Fate seems to have kept us on this island. Maybe--
...
I...did some scouting earlier. The Scholars are let out twice a day.
If someone were to sneak in during that time, they could *burn* the camp down.

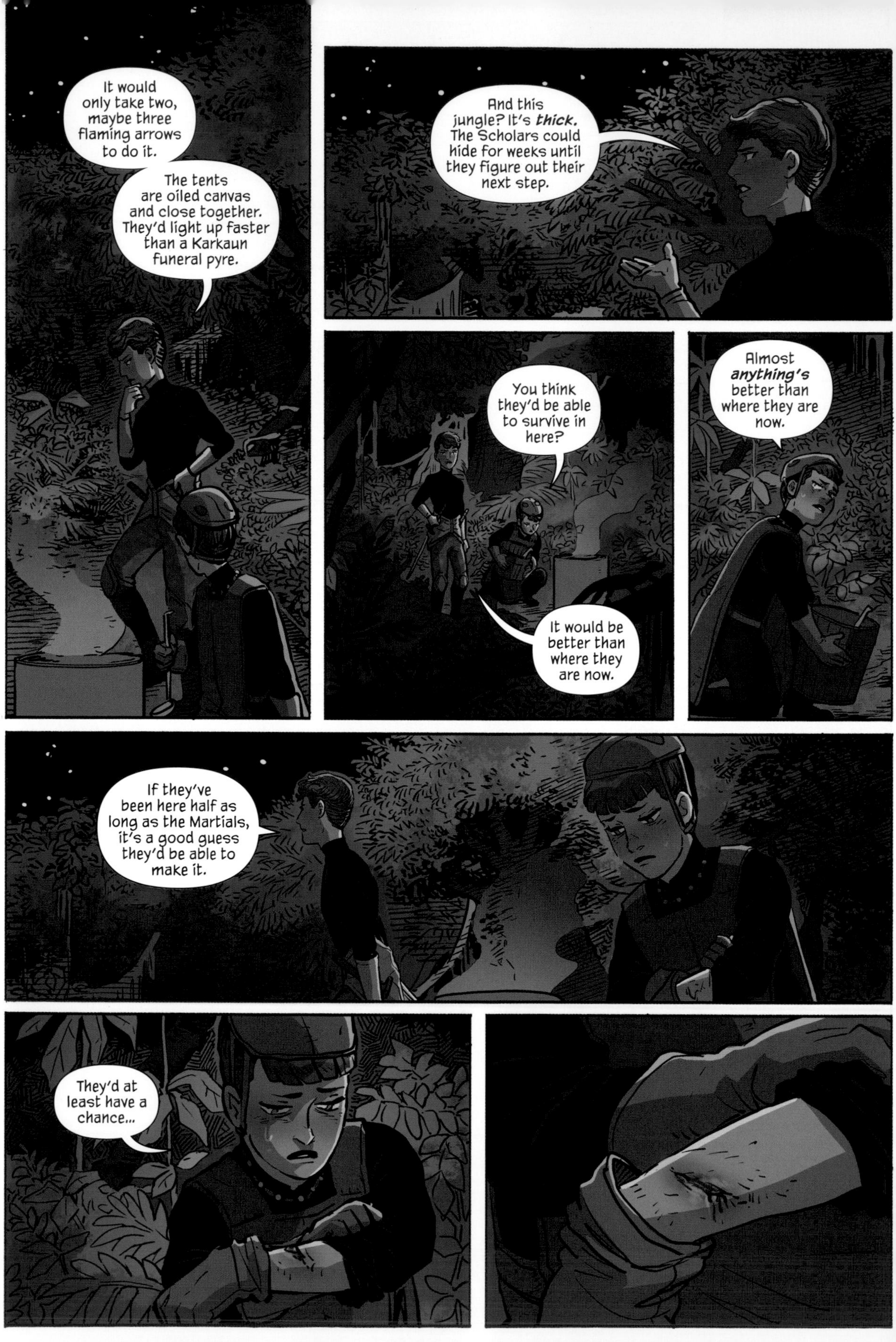
It would only take two, maybe three flaming arrows to do it.
The tents are oiled canvas and close together. They'd light up faster than a Karkaun funeral pyre.
And this jungle? It's *thick.* The Scholars could hide for weeks until they figure out their next step.
You think they'd be able to survive in here?
It would be better than where they are now.
Almost *anything's* better than where they are now.
If they've been here half as long as the Martials, it's a good guess they'd be able to make it.
They'd at least have a chance...

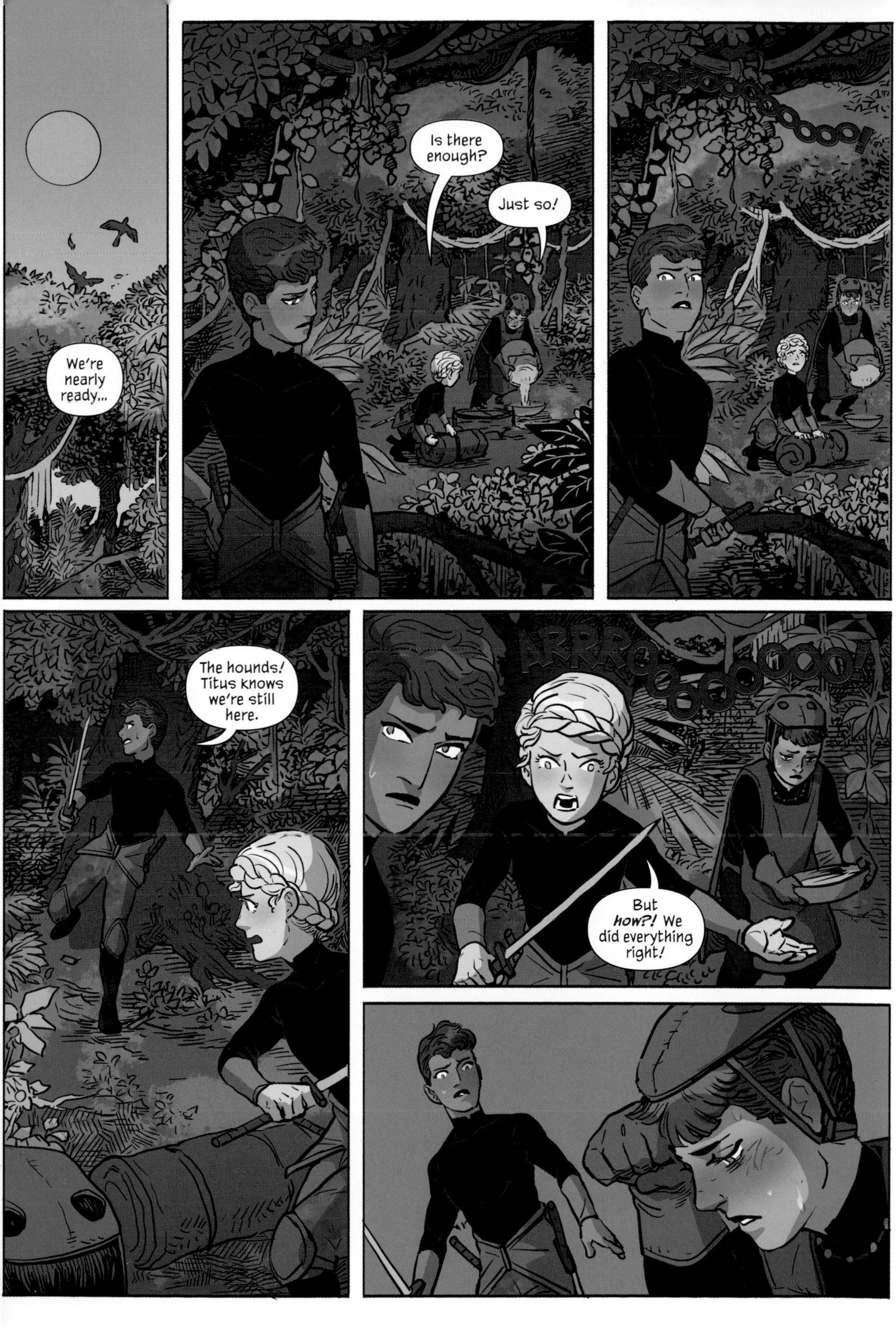
We're nearly ready...
Is there enough?
Just so!
ARRROOOOOOOOOOO!
The hounds! Titus knows we're still here.
ARRROOOOOOOOOO!
But *how?!* We did everything right!

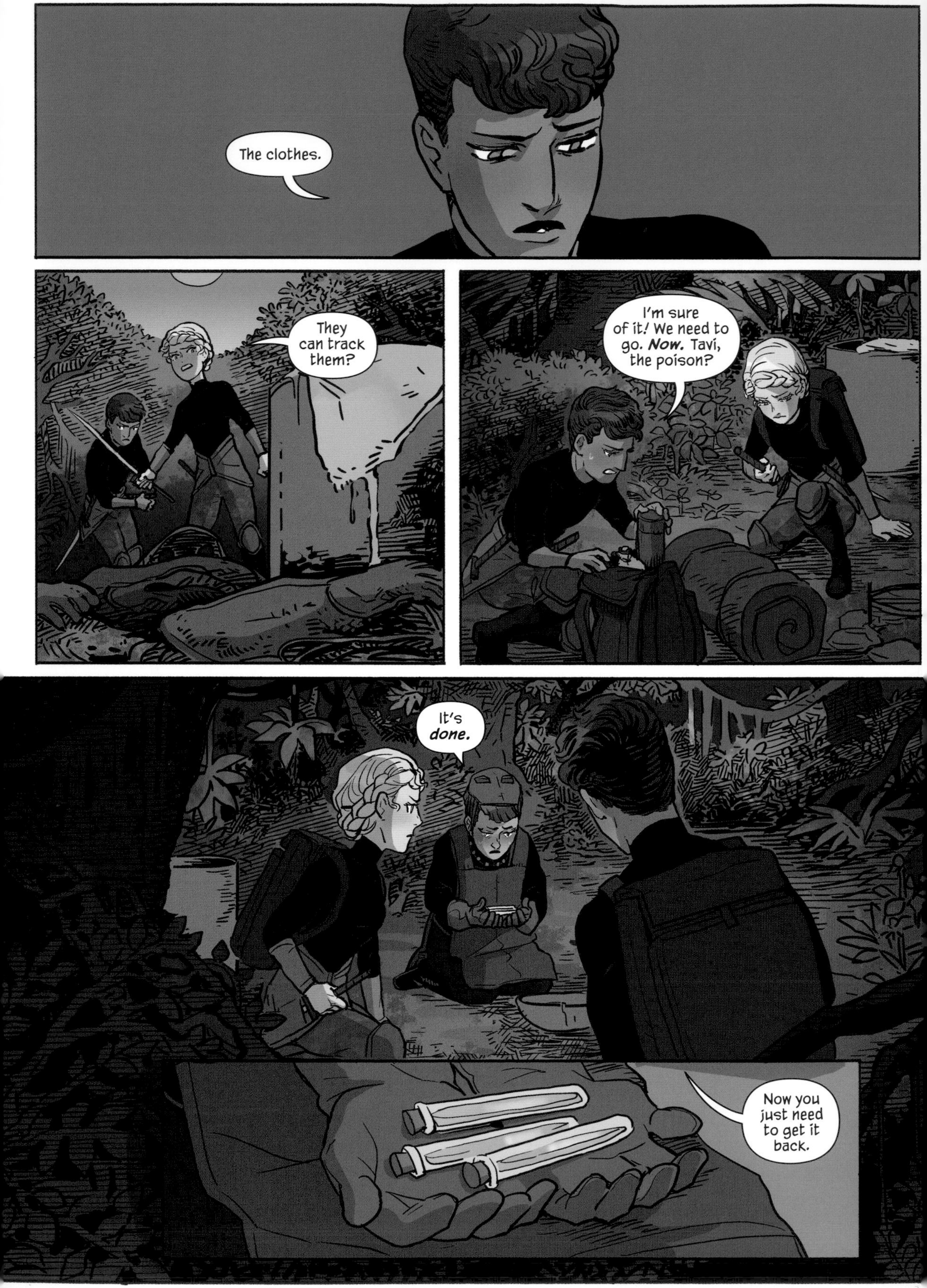
The clothes.
They can track them?
I'm sure of it! We need to go. *Now.* Tavi, the poison?
It's *done.*
Now you just need to get it back.

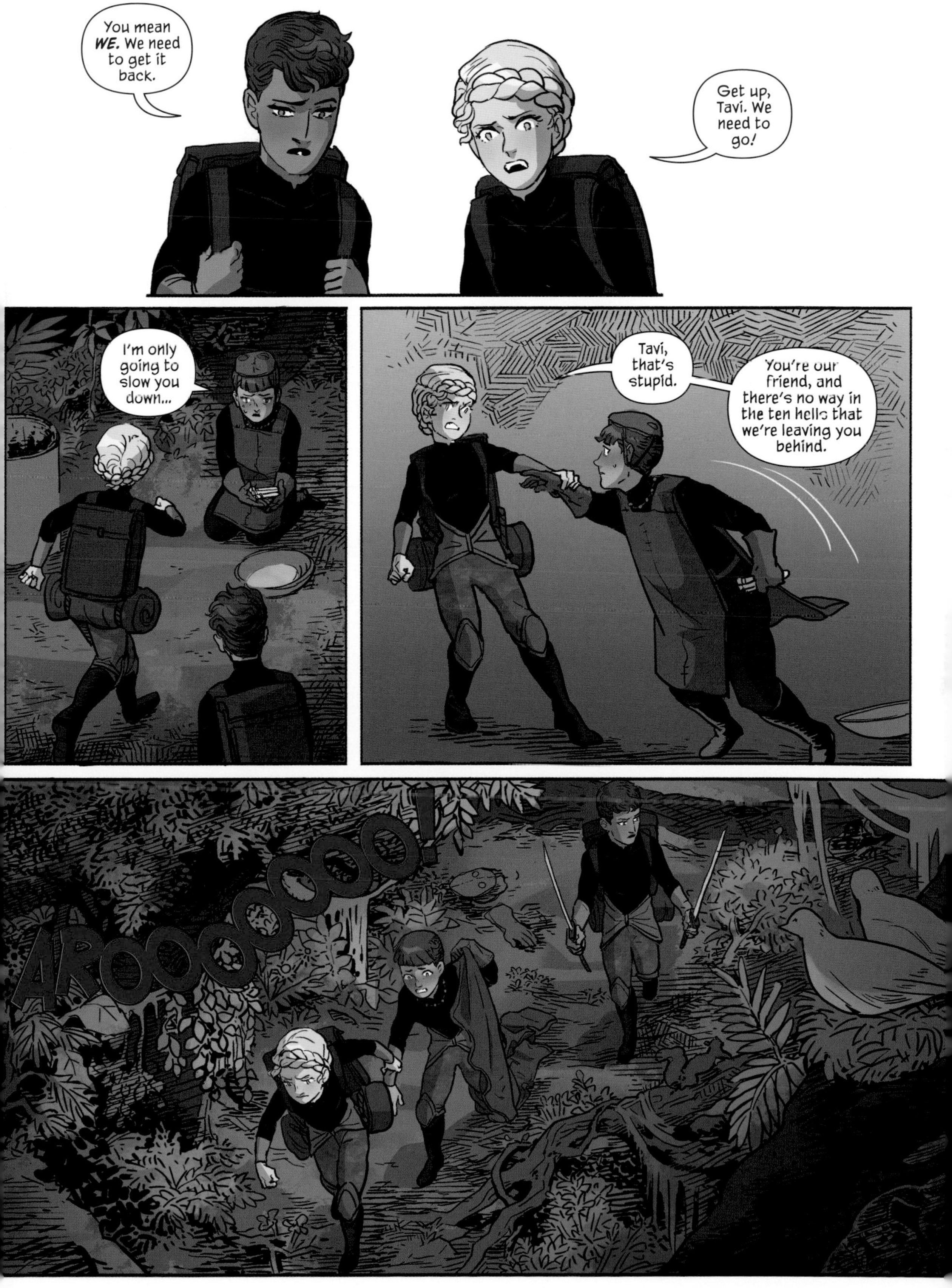
You mean **WE.** We need to get it back.
Get up, Tavi. We need to go!
I'm only going to slow you down...
Tavi, that's stupid.
You're our friend, and there's no way in the ten hells that we're leaving you behind.
AROOOOOOOOO!

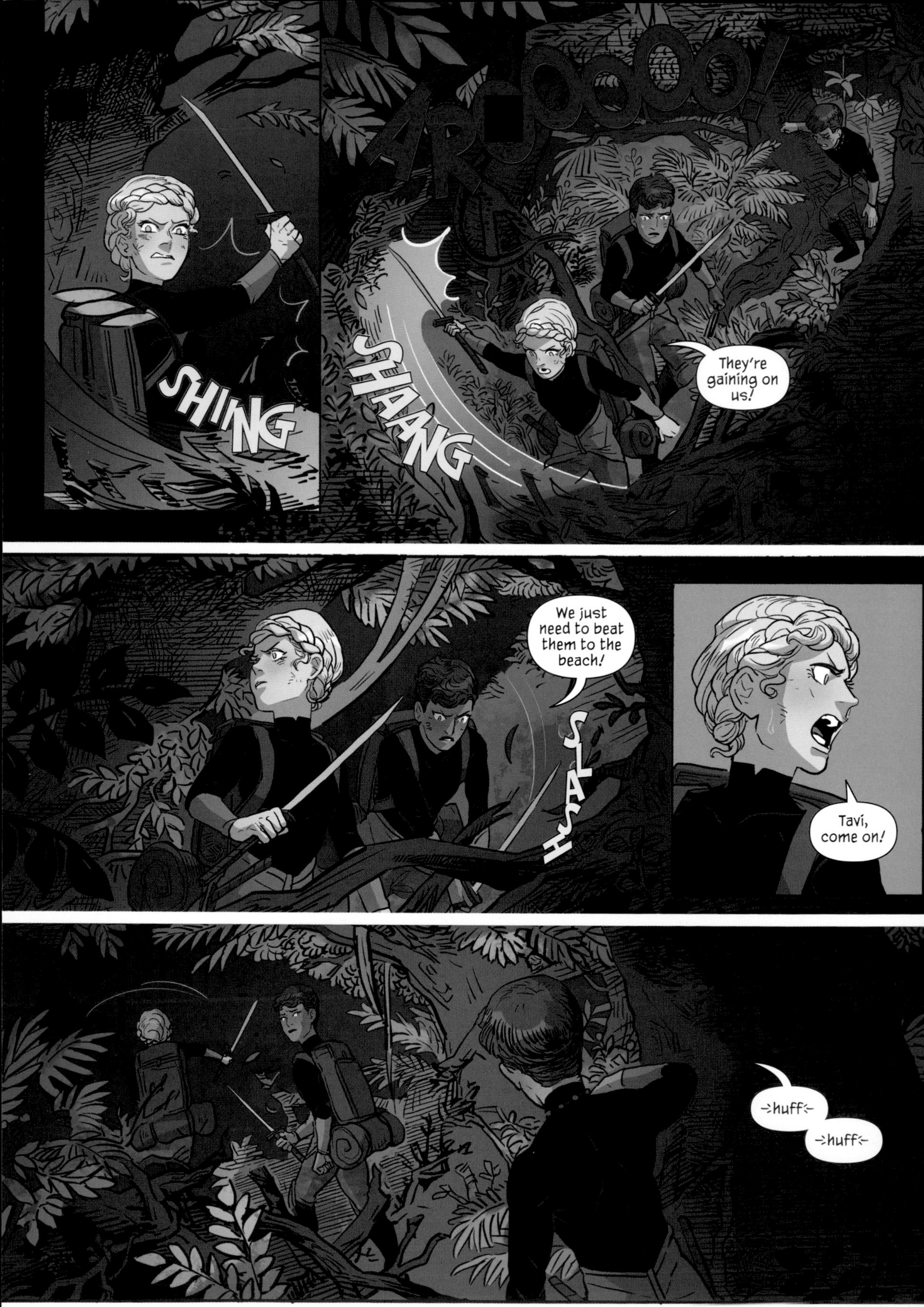
SHING
SHAANG
They're gaining on us!
We just need to beat them to the beach!
SLASH
Tavi, come on!
huff
huff

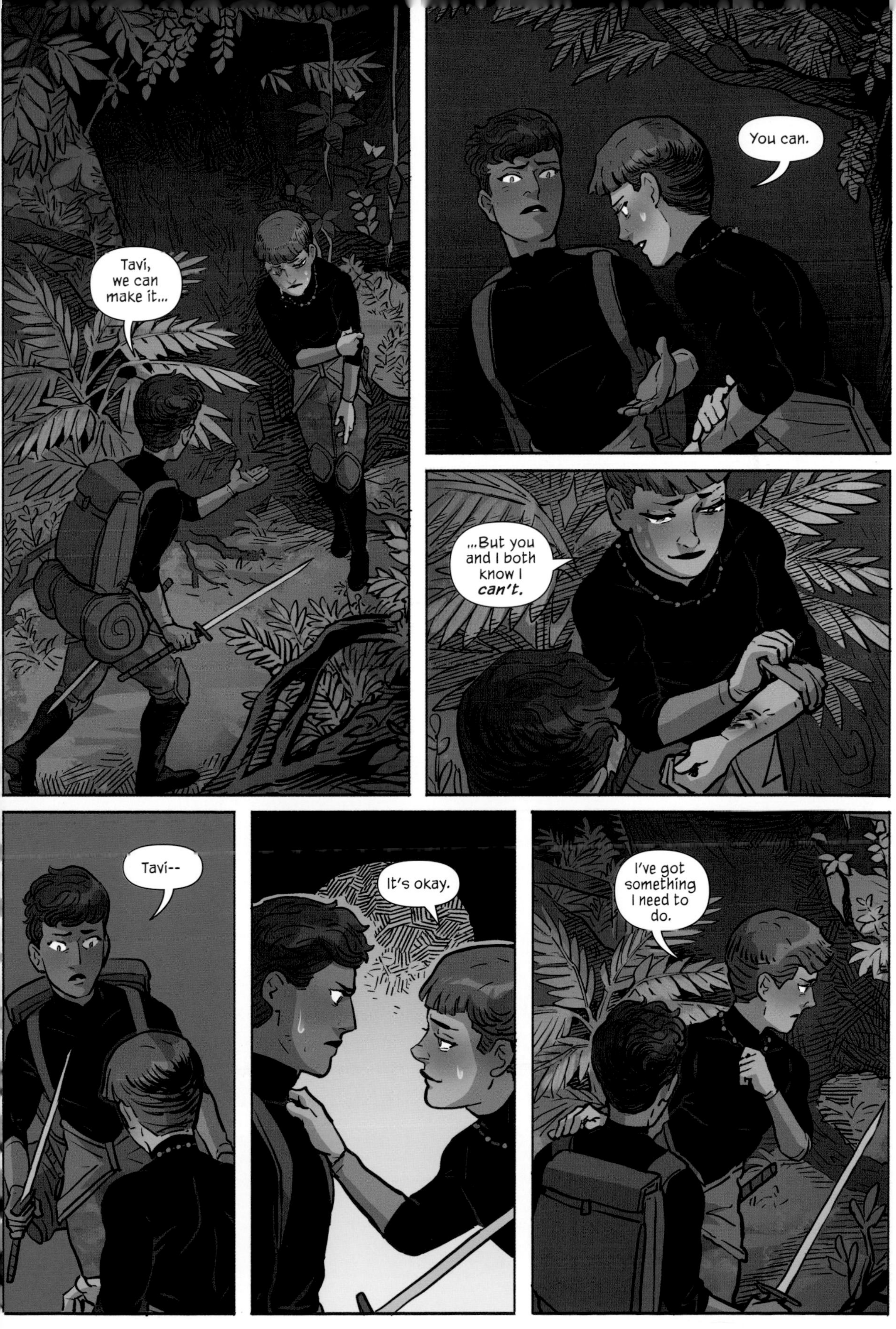
Tavi, we can make it...
You can.
...But you and I both know I *can't.*
Tavi--
It's okay.
I've got something I need to do.

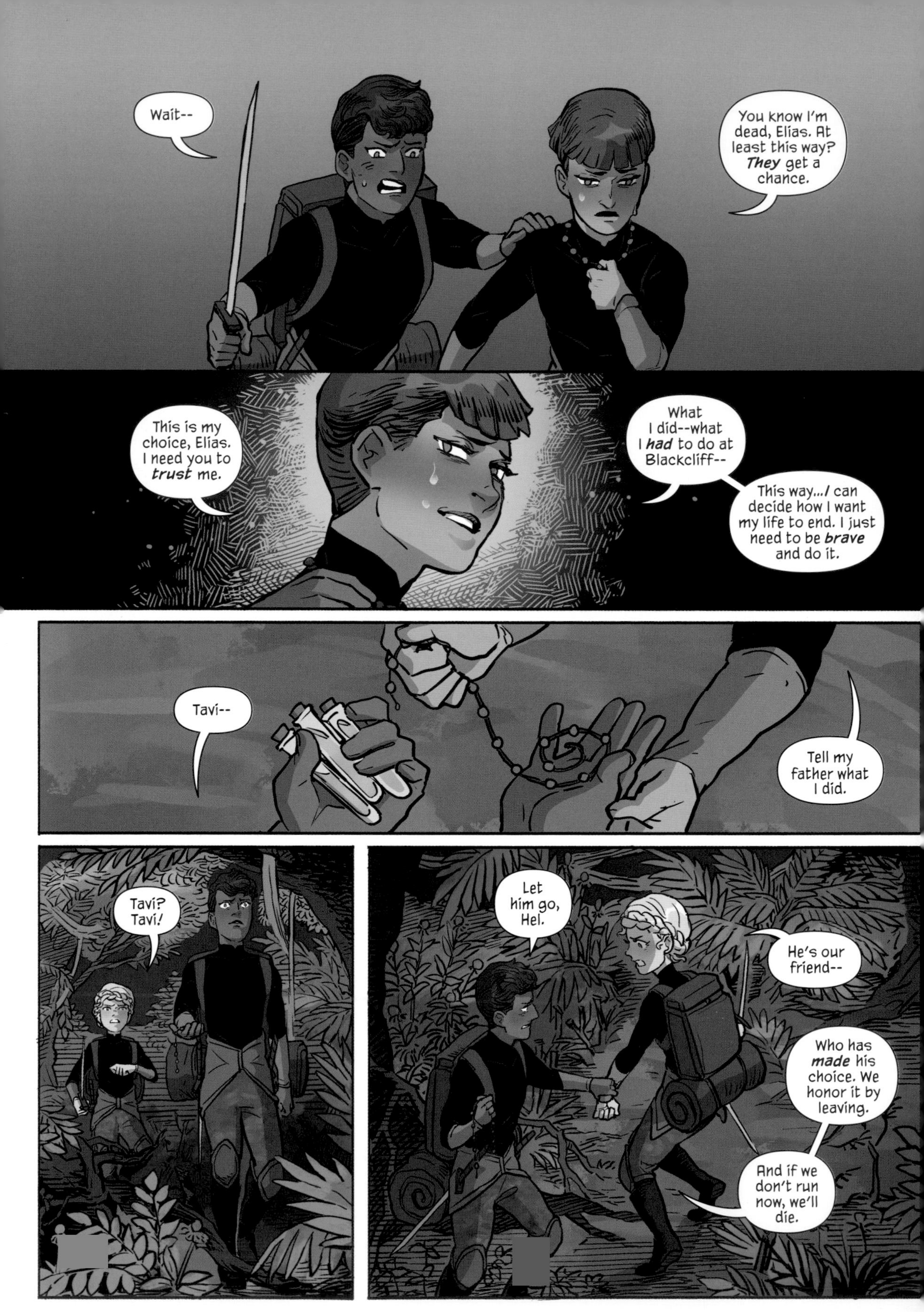
Wait--
You know I'm dead, Elias. At least this way? *They* get a chance.
This is my choice, Elias. I need you to *trust* me.
What I did--what I *had* to do at Blackcliff--
This way.../ can decide how I want my life to end. I just need to be *brave* and do it.
Tavi--
Tell my father what I did.
Tavi? Tavi!
Let him go, Hel.
He's our friend--
Who has *made* his choice. We honor it by leaving.
And if we don't run now, we'll die.

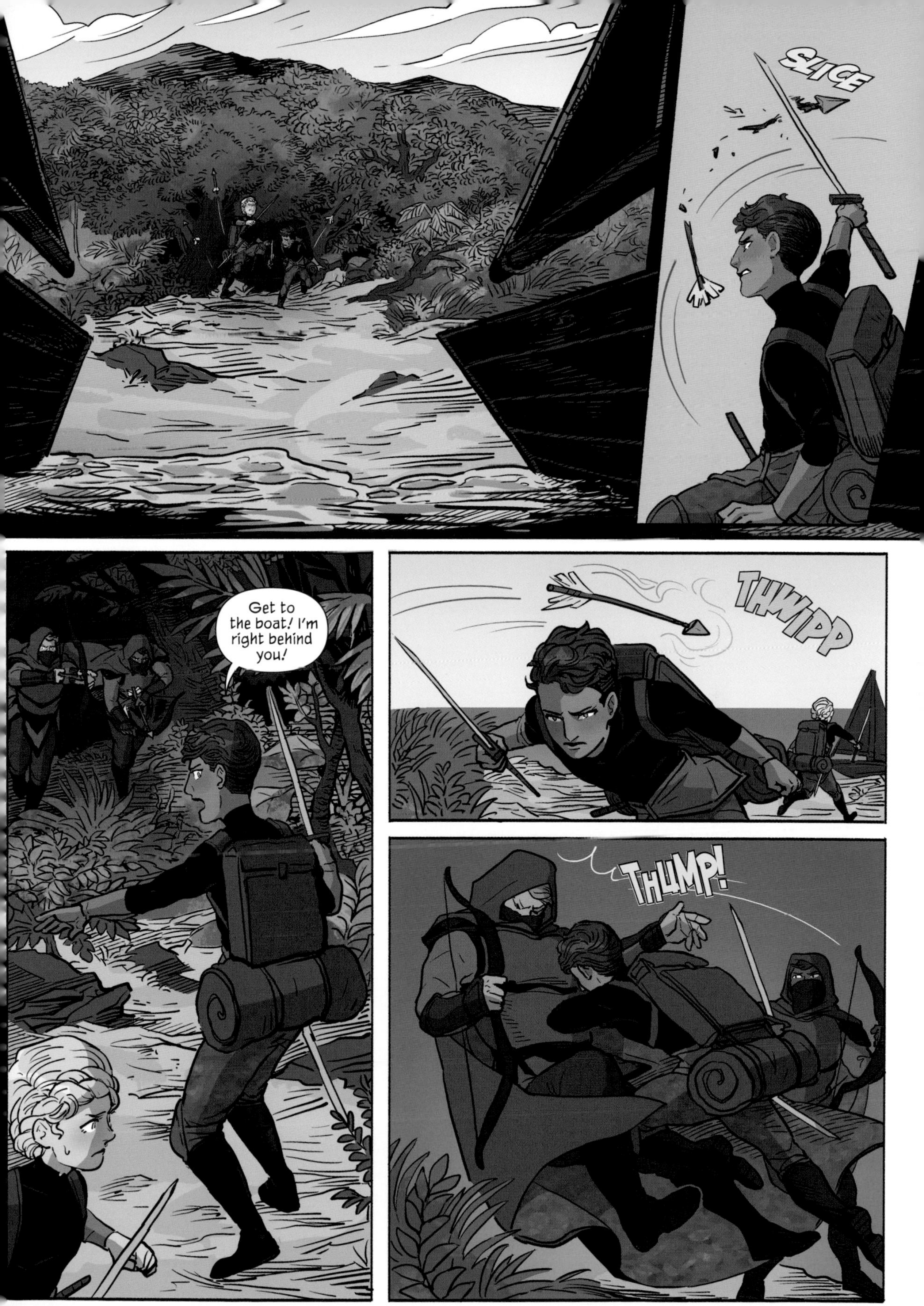
SLICE
Get to the boat! I'm right behind you!
THWIPP
THUMP!

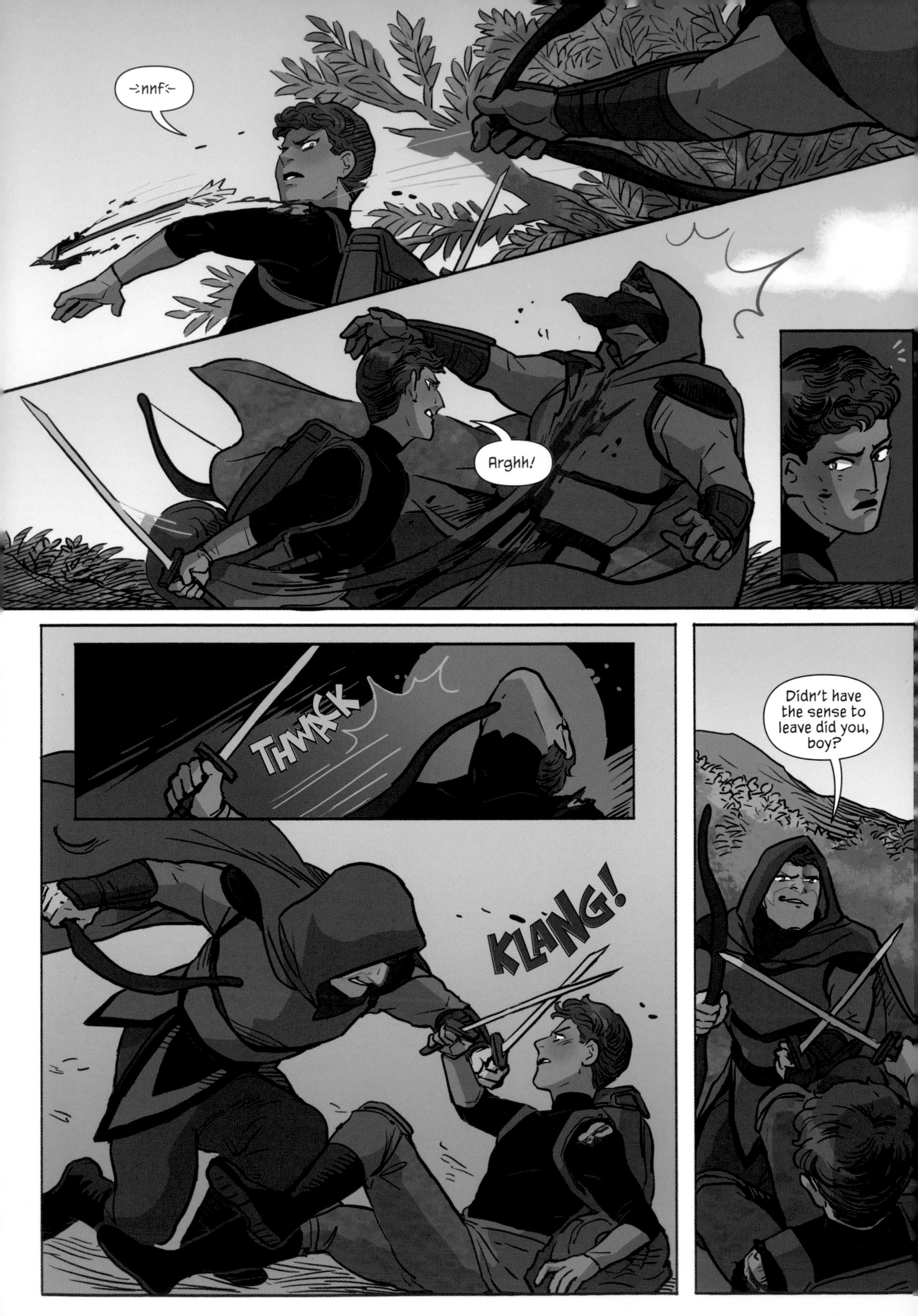
-nnf-
Arghh!
THWACK
KLANG!
Didn't have the sense to leave did you, boy?

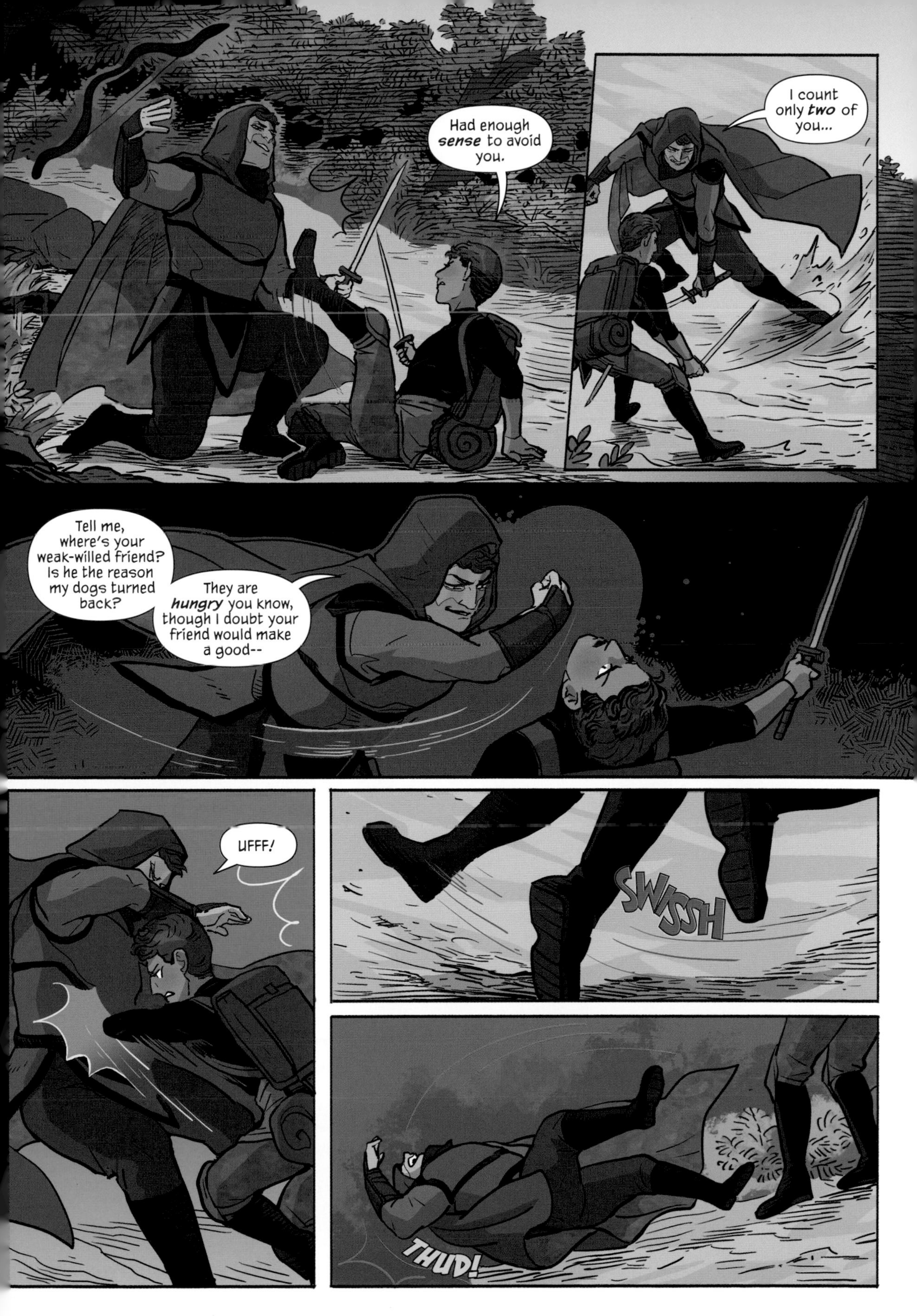
Had enough *sense* to avoid you.
I count only *two* of you...
Tell me, where's your weak-willed friend? Is he the reason my dogs turned back?
They are *hungry* you know, though I doubt your friend would make a good--
UFFF!
SWISSH
THUD!

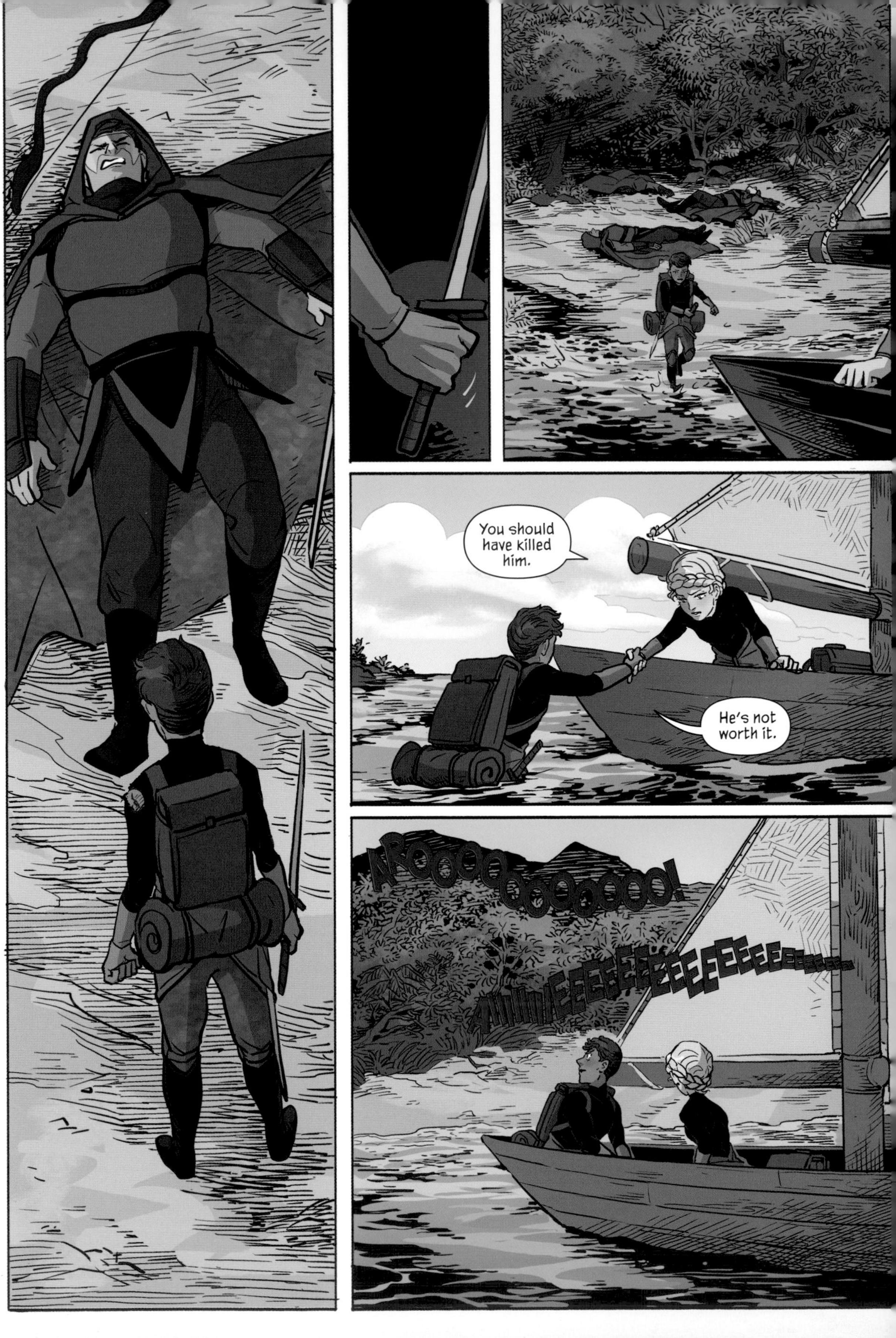
You should have killed him.
He's not worth it.
AROOOOOOOOOOOOO!
AHHHHHEEEEEEEEEEEeeeeeee...

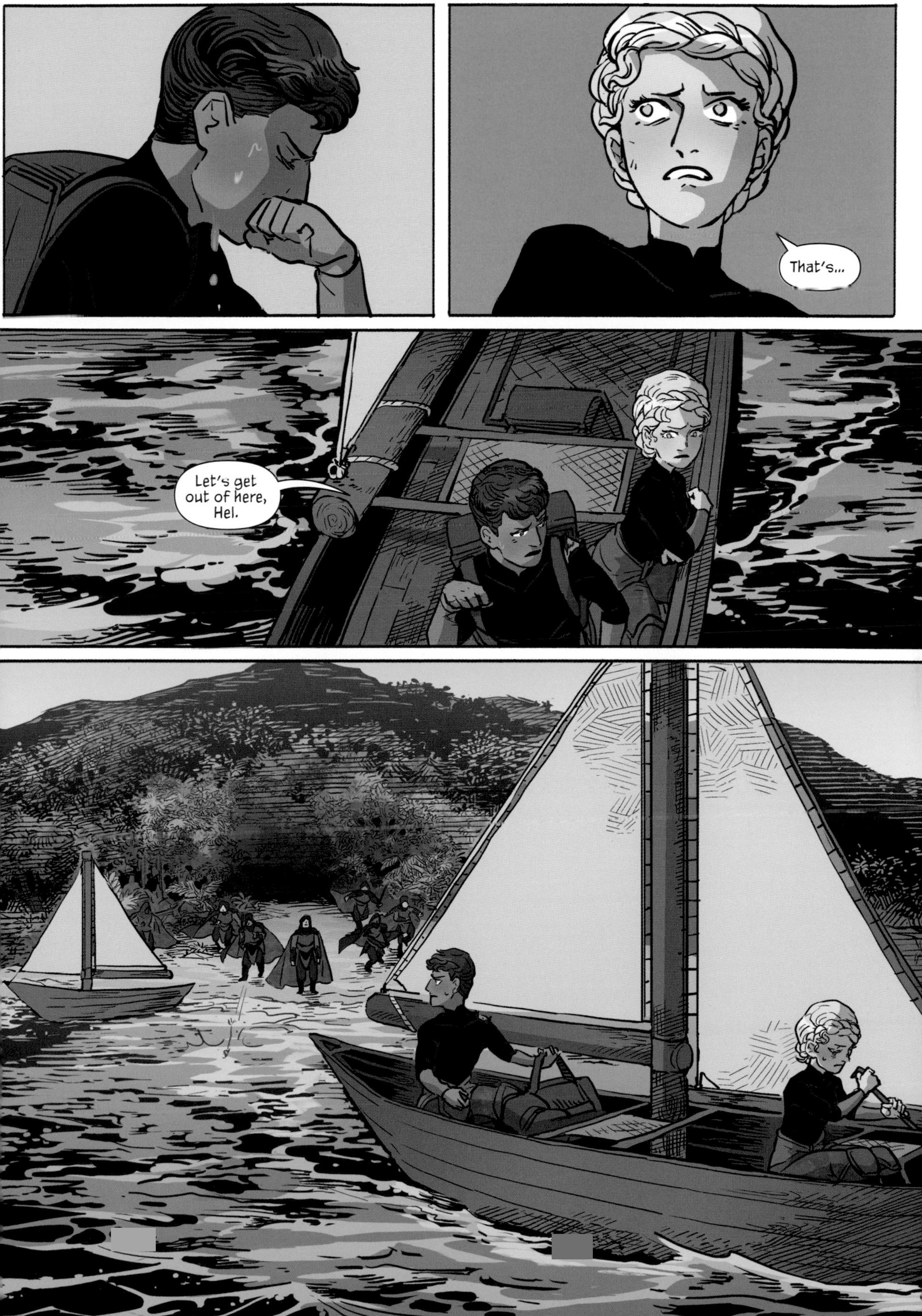
That's...
Let's get out of here, Hel.

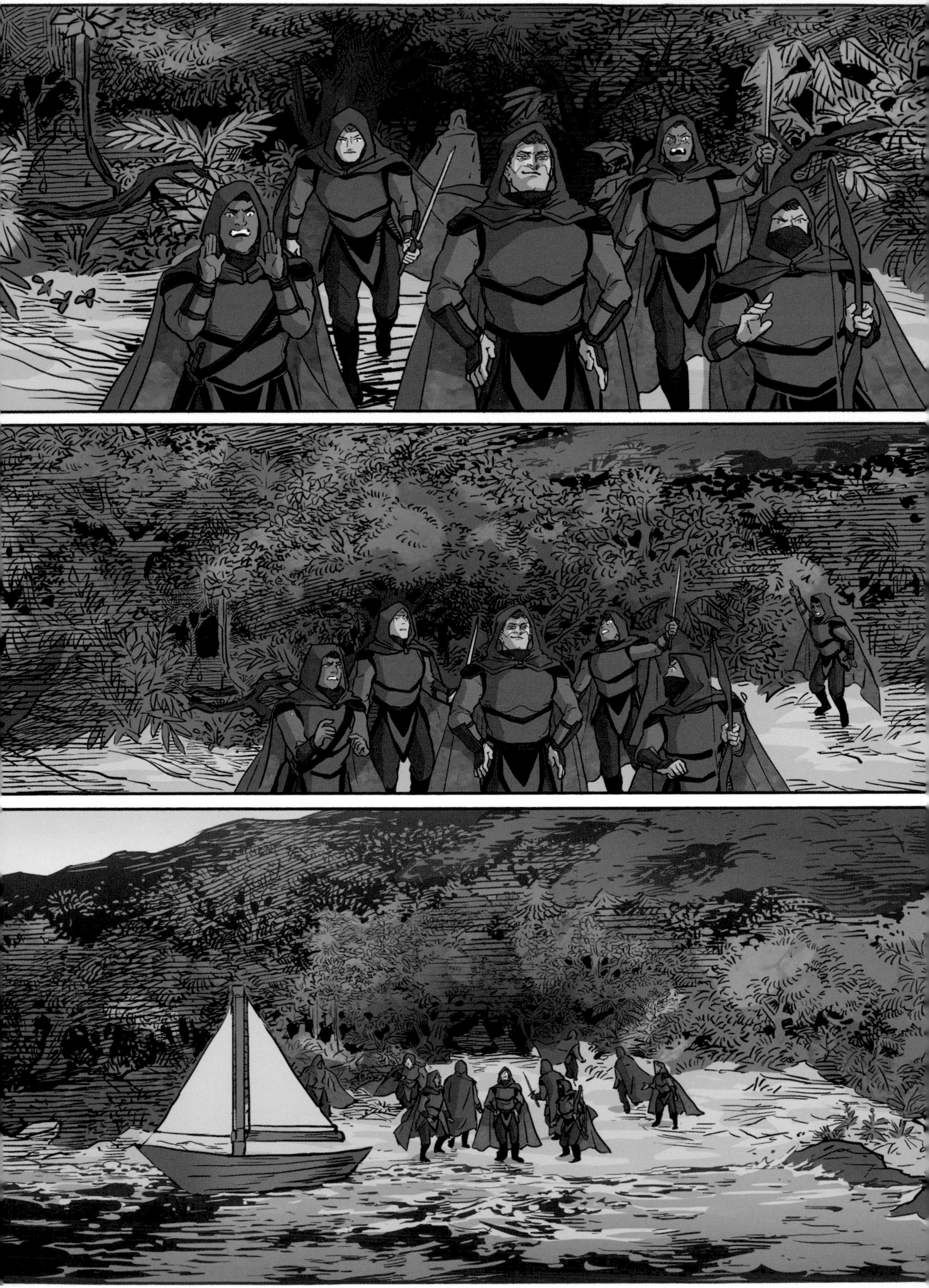

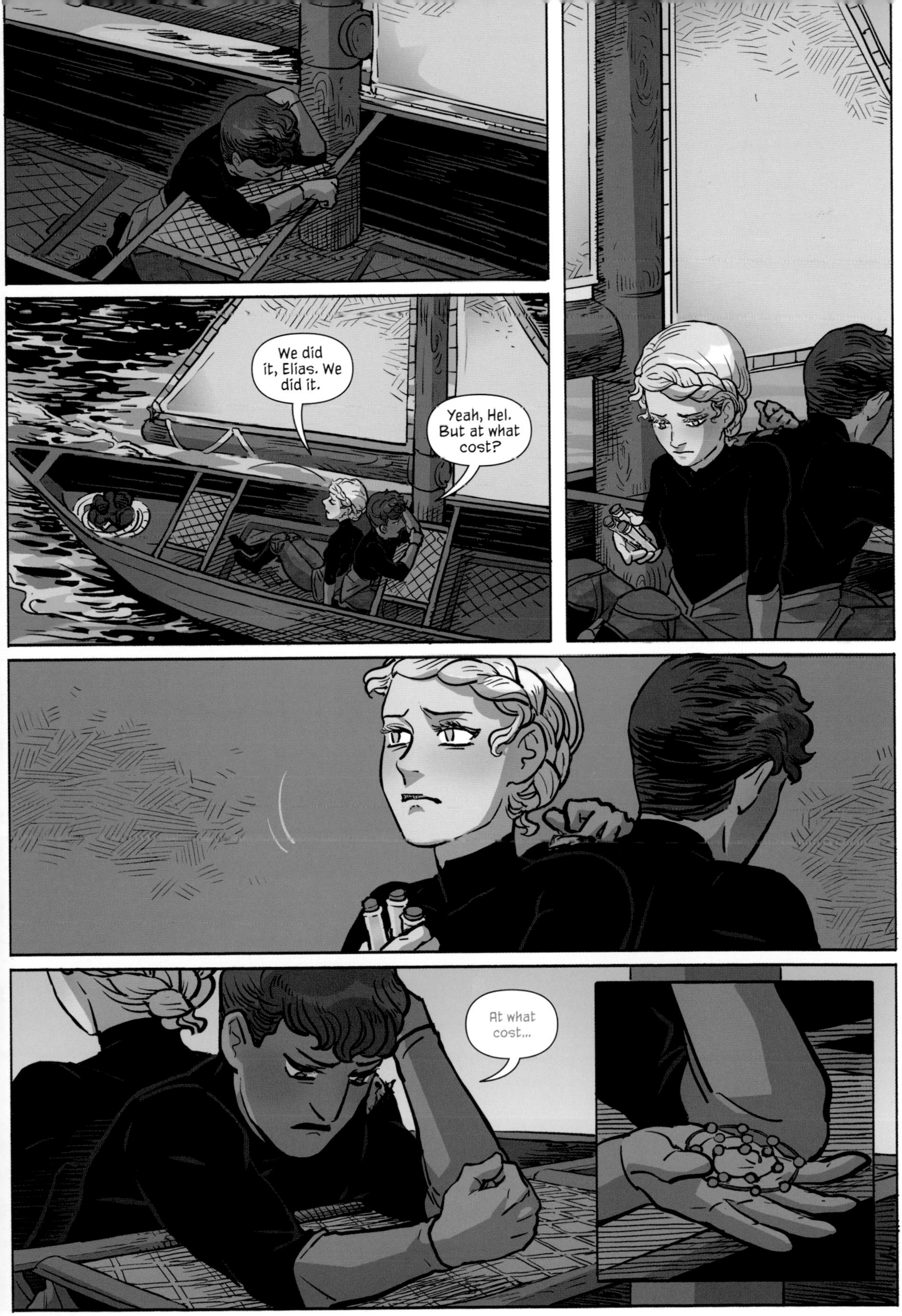

We did it, Elias. We did it.
Yeah, Hel. But at what cost?
At what cost...

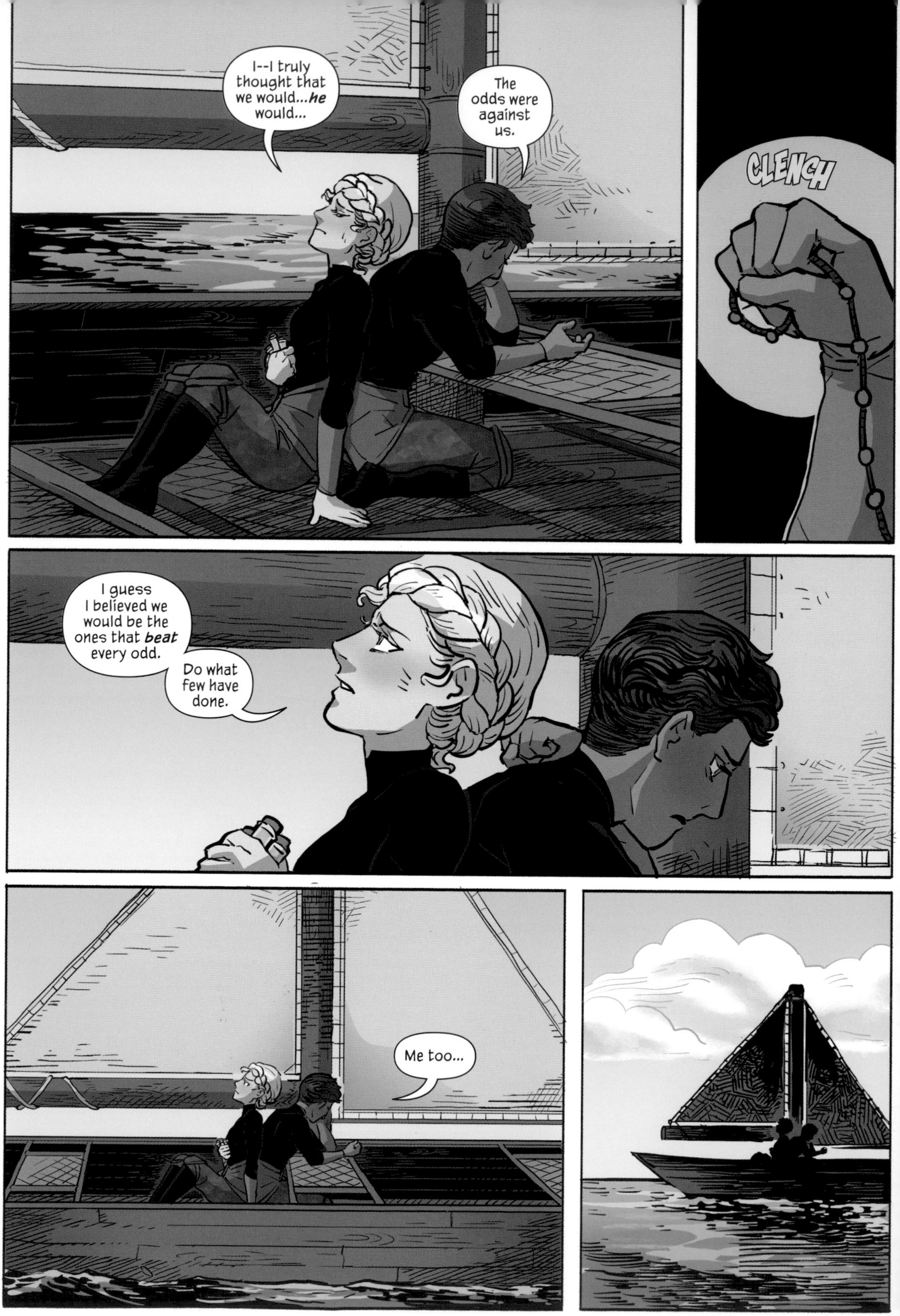
I--I truly thought that we would...*he* would...
The odds were against us.
CLENCH
I guess I believed we would be the ones that *beat* every odd.
Do what few have done.
Me too...

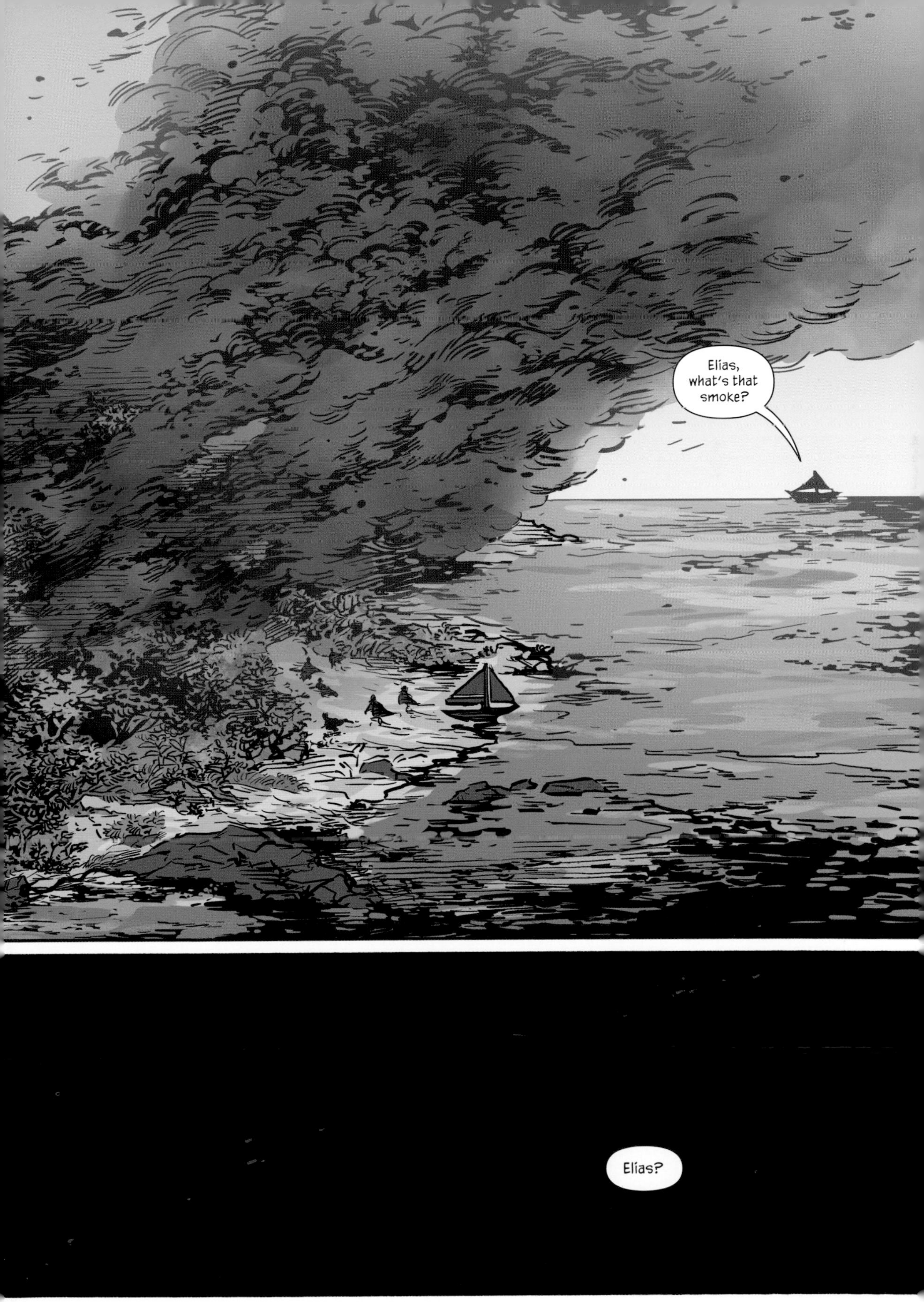
Elías, what's that smoke?
Elías?

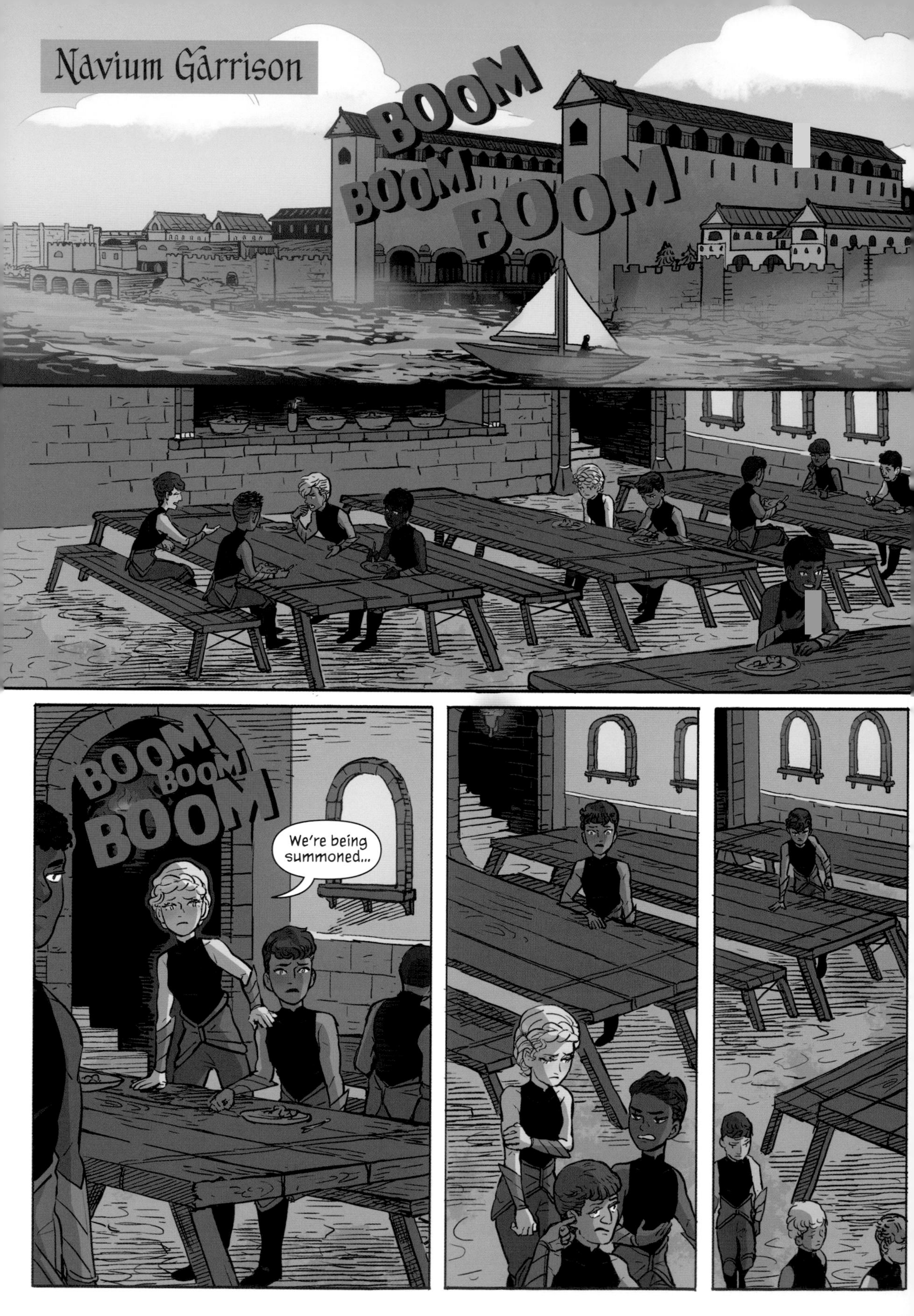
Navium Garrison
BOOM
BOOM
BOOM
BOOM
BOOM
BOOM
We're being summoned...

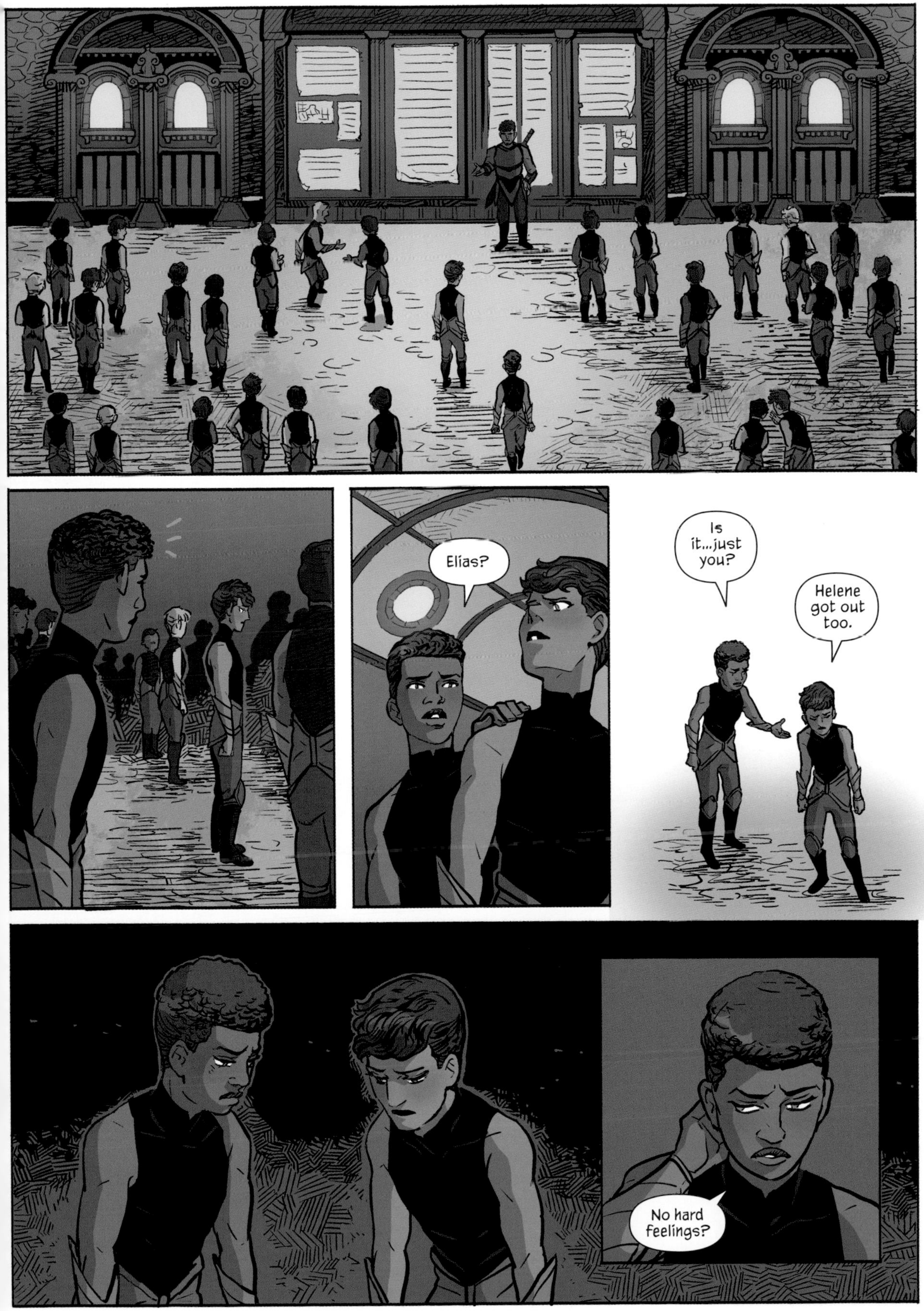
Elias?
Is it...just you?
Helene got out too.
No hard feelings?

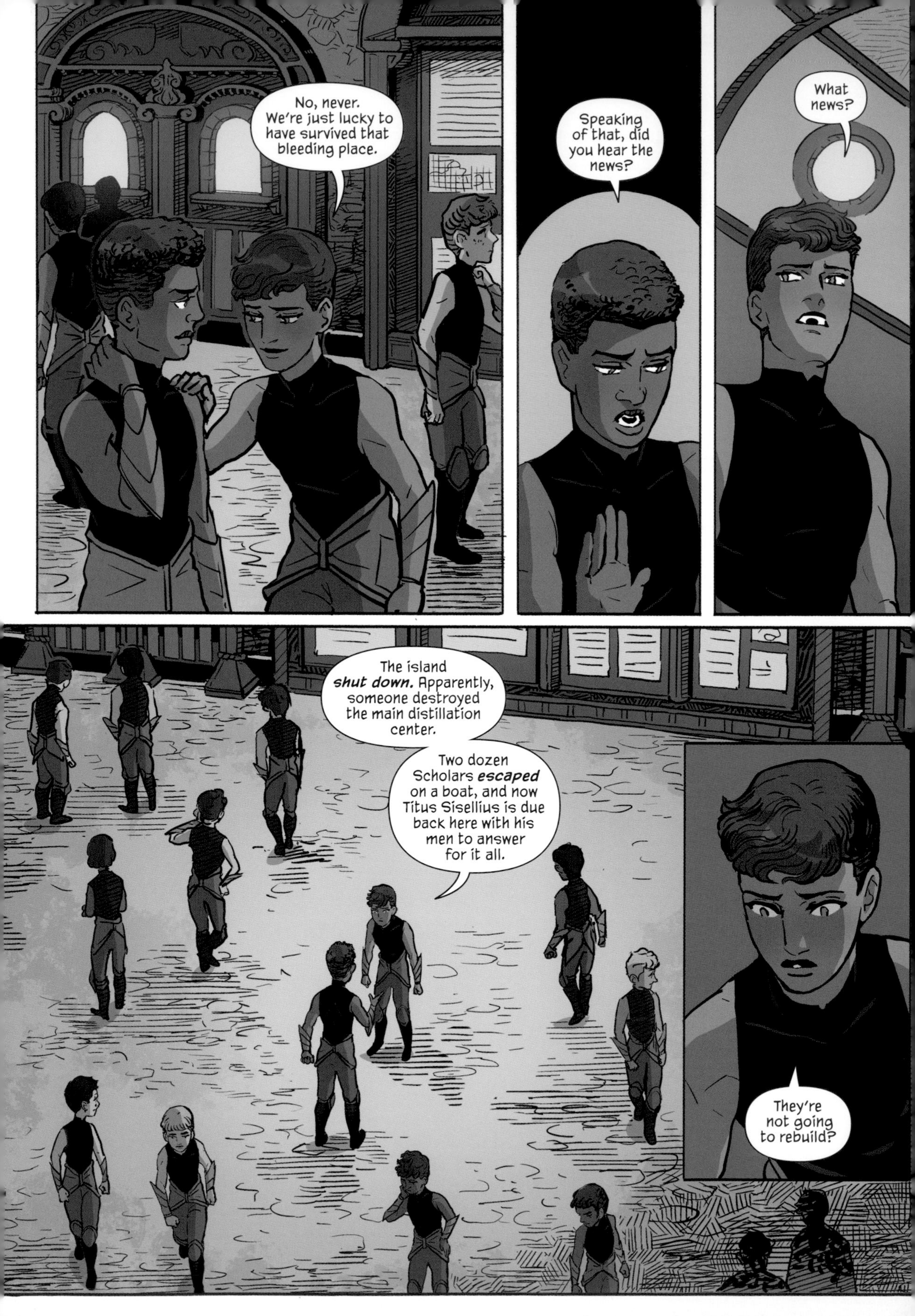
No, never. We're just lucky to have survived that bleeding place.
Speaking of that, did you hear the news?
What news?
The island *shut down.* Apparently, someone destroyed the main distillation center.
Two dozen Scholars *escaped* on a boat, and now Titus Sisellius is due back here with his men to answer for it all.
They're not going to rebuild?

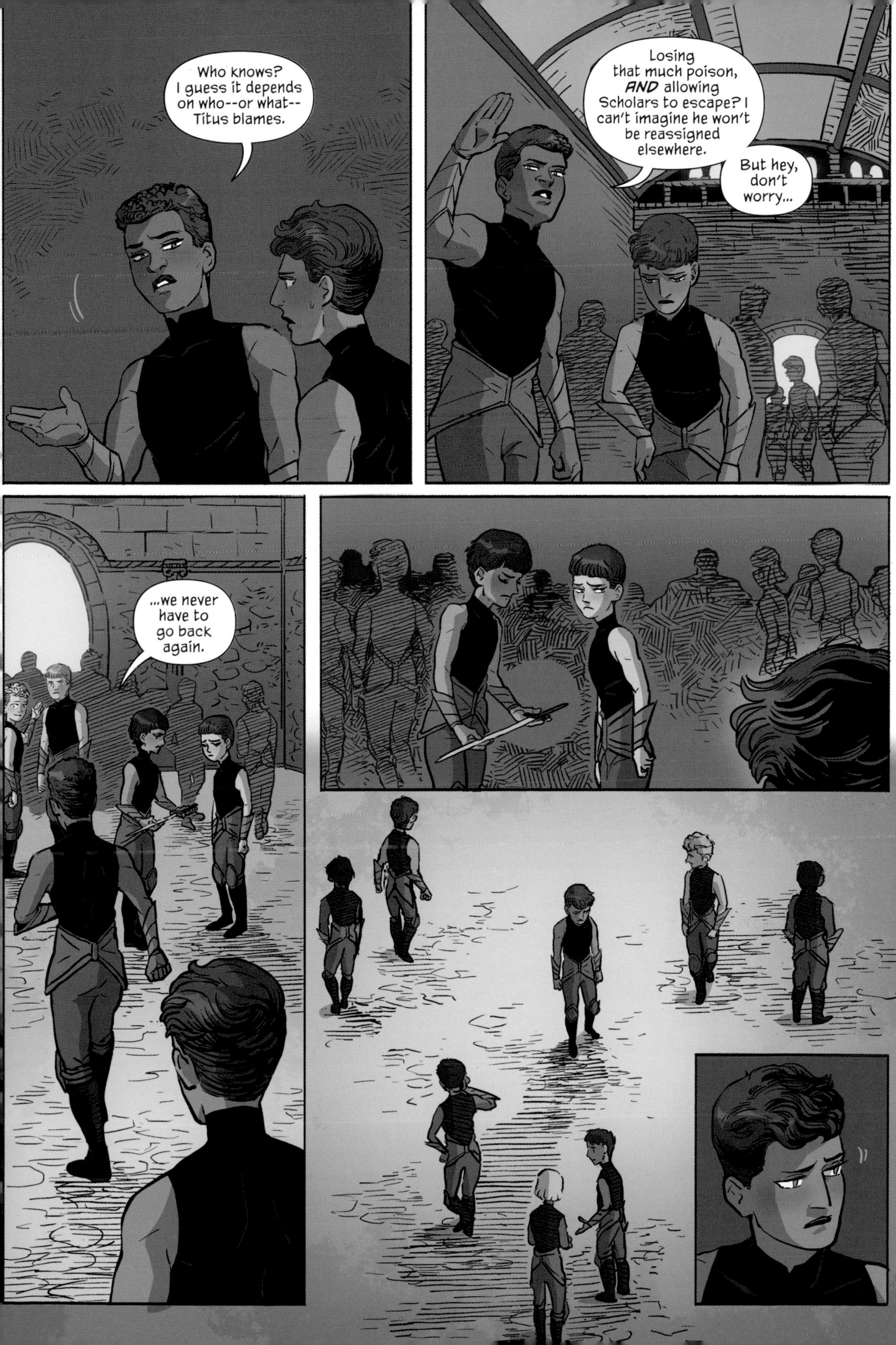
Who knows? I guess it depends on who--or what--Titus blames.
Losing that much poison, AND allowing Scholars to escape? I can't imagine he won't be reassigned elsewhere.
But hey, don't worry...
...we never have to go back again.

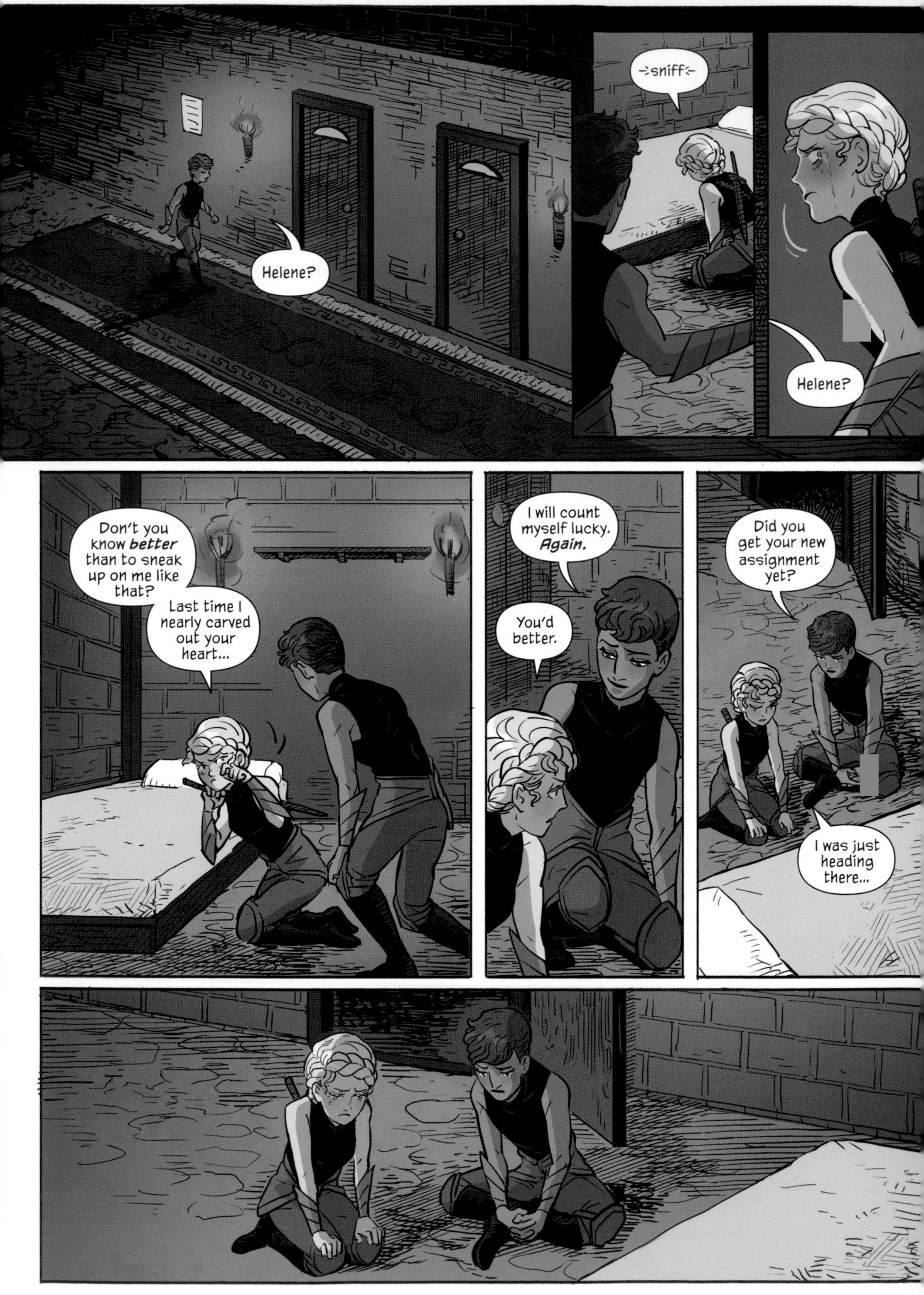
Helene?
-sniff-
Helene?
Don't you know *better* than to sneak up on me like that?
Last time I nearly carved out your heart...
I will count myself lucky. *Again.*
You'd better.
Did you get your new assignment yet?
I was just heading there...

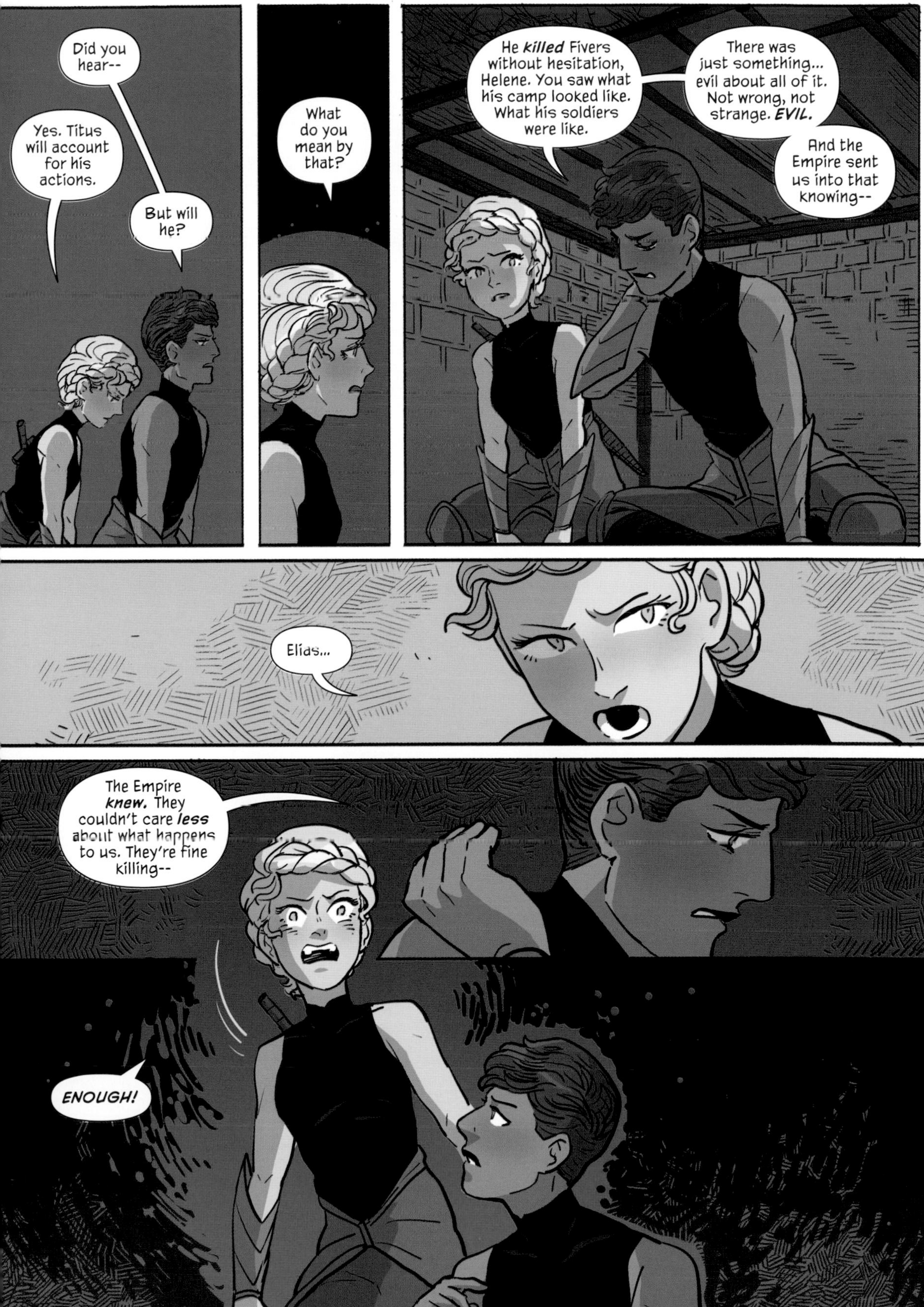
Did you hear--
Yes. Titus will account for his actions.
But will he?
What do you mean by that?
He ***killed*** Fivers without hesitation, Helene. You saw what his camp looked like. What his soldiers were like.
There was just something... evil about all of it. Not wrong, not strange. ***EVIL.***
And the Empire sent us into that knowing--
Elias...
The Empire ***knew.*** They couldn't care ***less*** about what happens to us. They're fine killing--
ENOUGH!

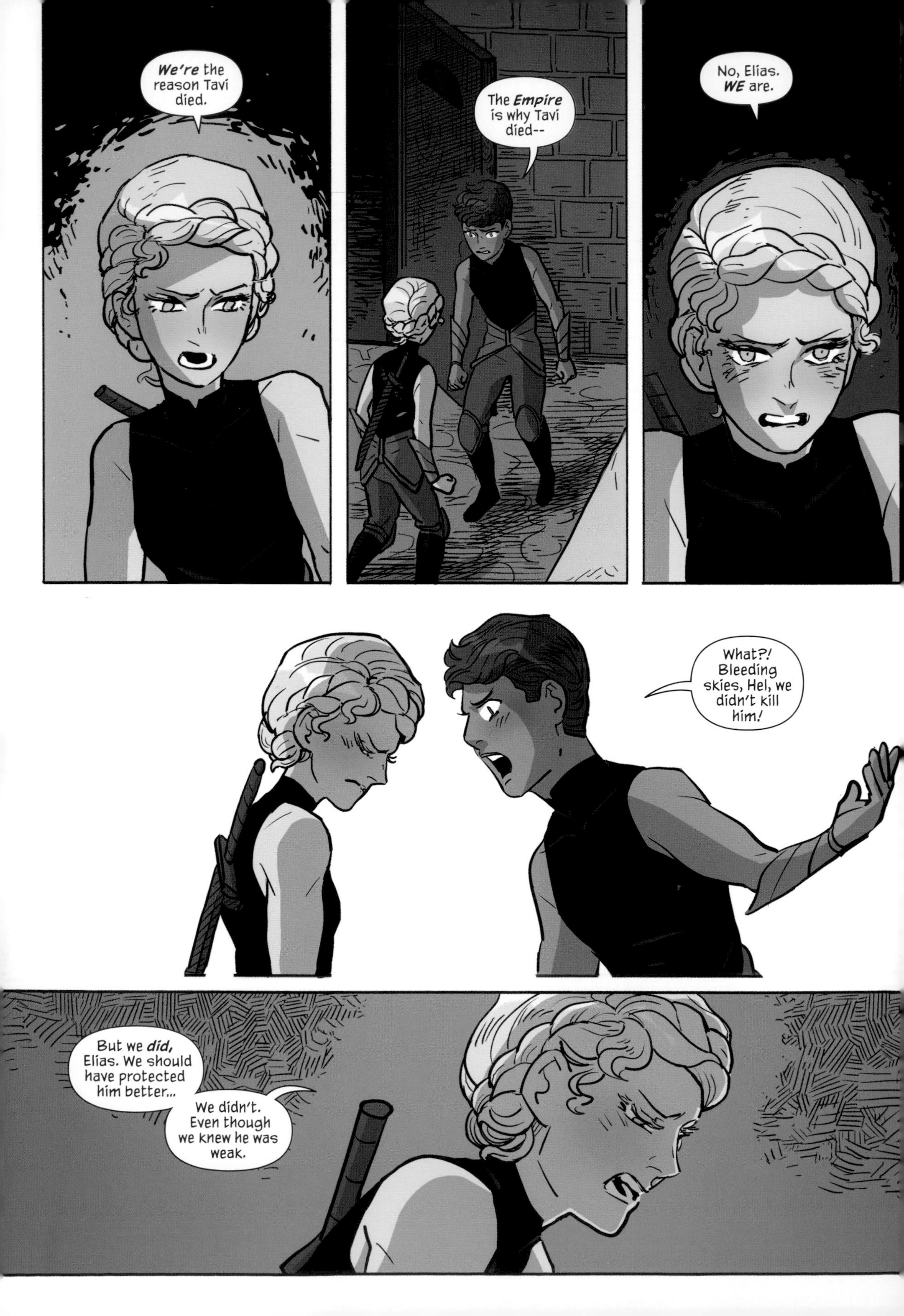
We're the reason Tavi died.
The *Empire* is why Tavi died--
No, Elias. ***WE*** are.
What?! Bleeding skies, Hel, we didn't kill him!
But we *did,* Elias. We should have protected him better...
We didn't. Even though we knew he was weak.

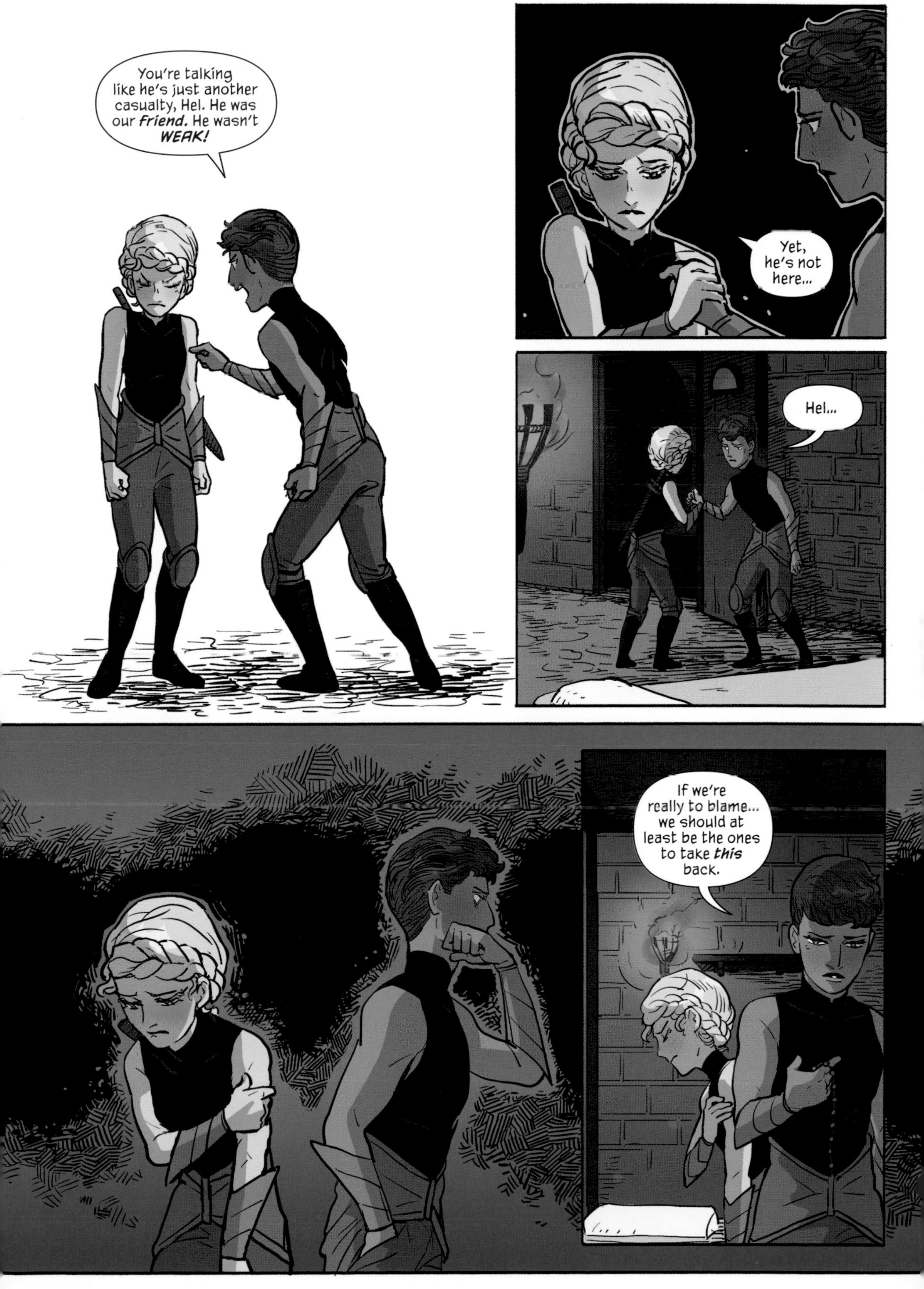
You're talking like he's just another casualty, Hel. He was our *friend.* He wasn't ***WEAK!***
Yet, he's not here...
Hel...
If we're really to blame... we should at least be the ones to take ***this*** back.

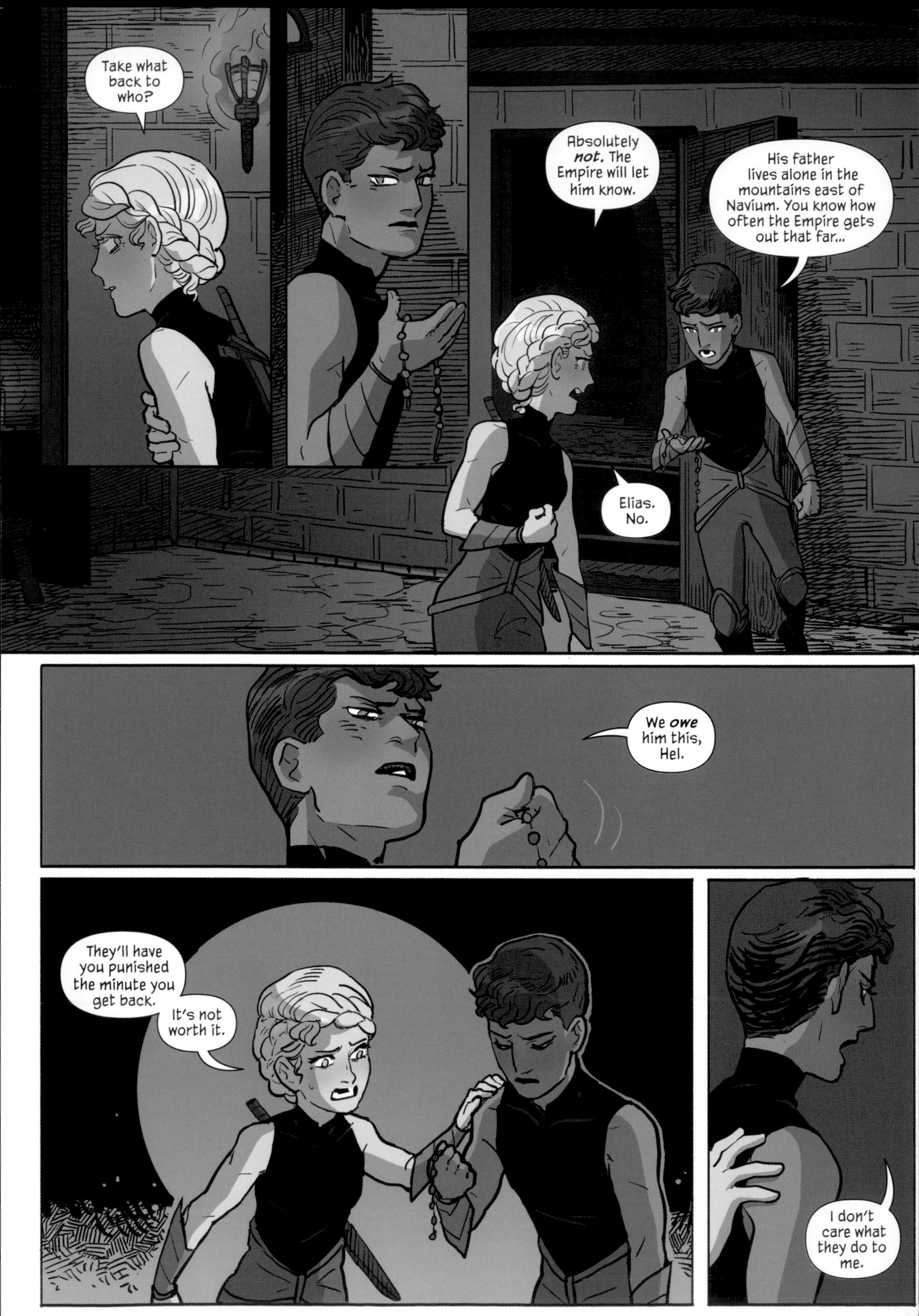
Take what back to who?
Absolutely *not.* The Empire will let him know.
His father lives alone in the mountains east of Navium. You know how often the Empire gets out that far...
Elias. No.
We *owe* him this, Hel.
They'll have you punished the minute you get back.
It's not worth it.
I don't care what they do to me.

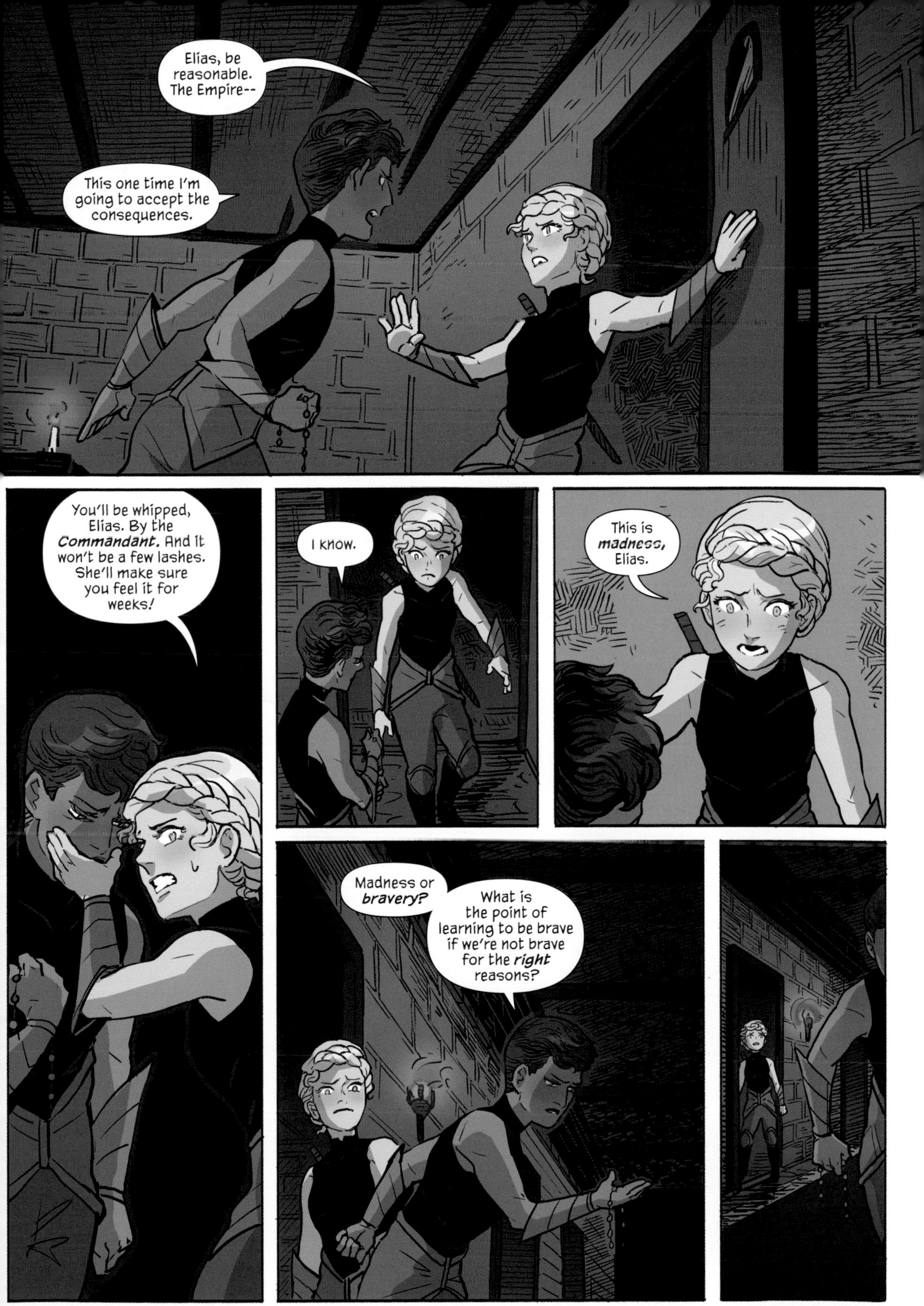
Elias, be reasonable. The Empire--
This one time I'm going to accept the consequences.
You'll be whipped, Elias. By the *Commandant.* And it won't be a few lashes. She'll make sure you feel it for weeks!
I know.
This is *madness,* Elias.
Madness or *bravery?*
What is the point of learning to be brave if we're not brave for the *right* reasons?

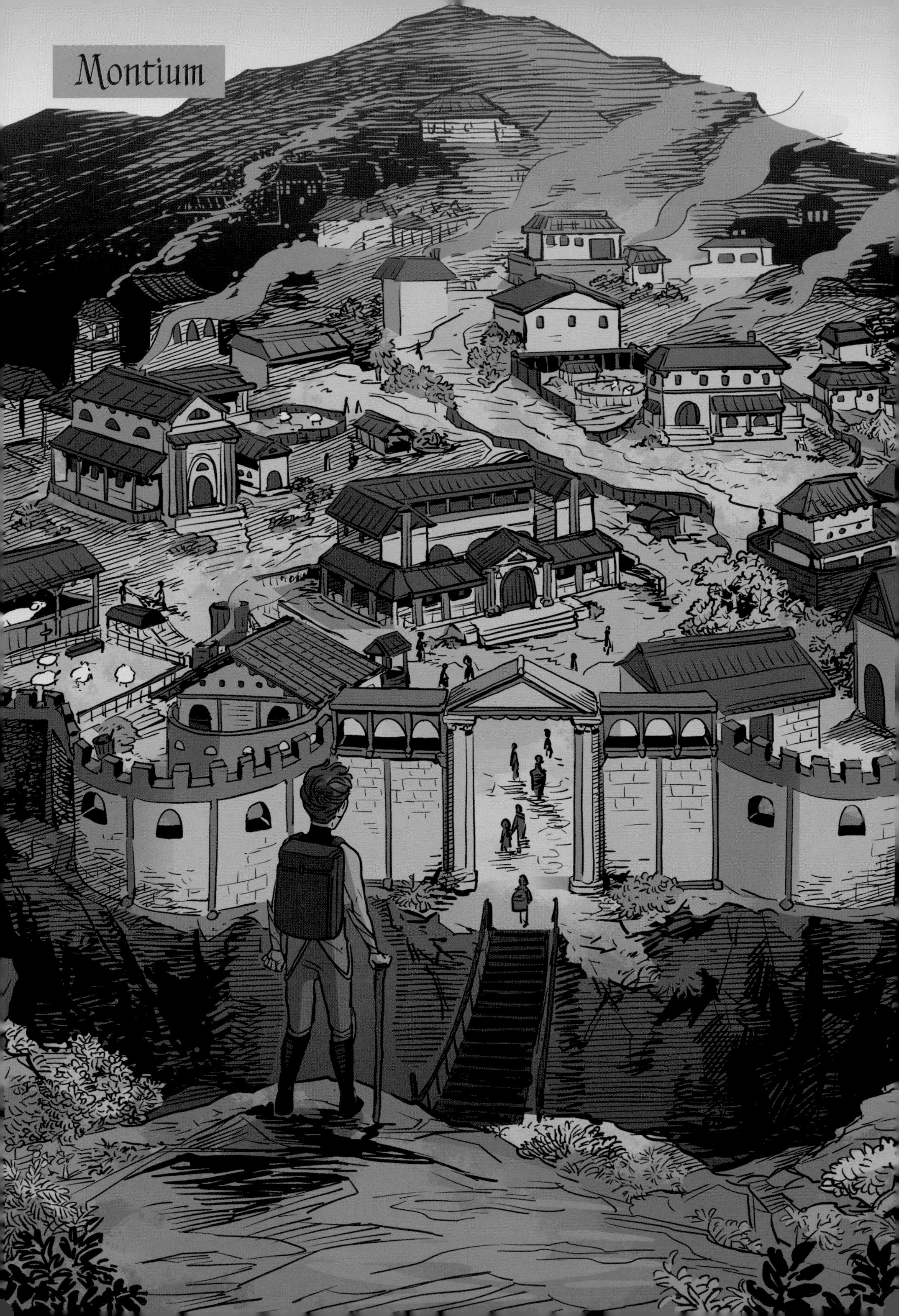
Montium

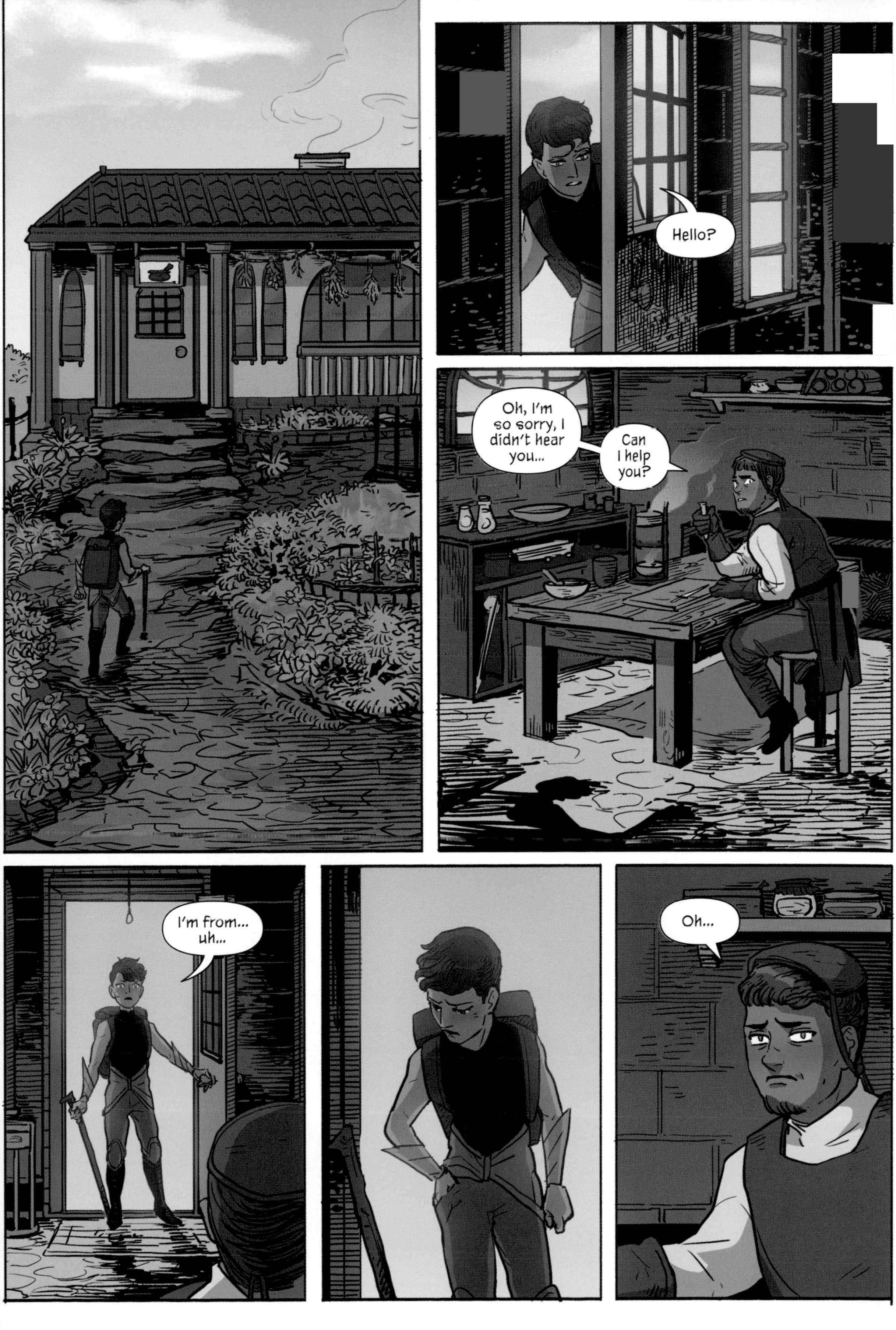
Hello?
Oh, I'm so sorry, I didn't hear you...
Can I help you?
I'm from... uh...
Oh...

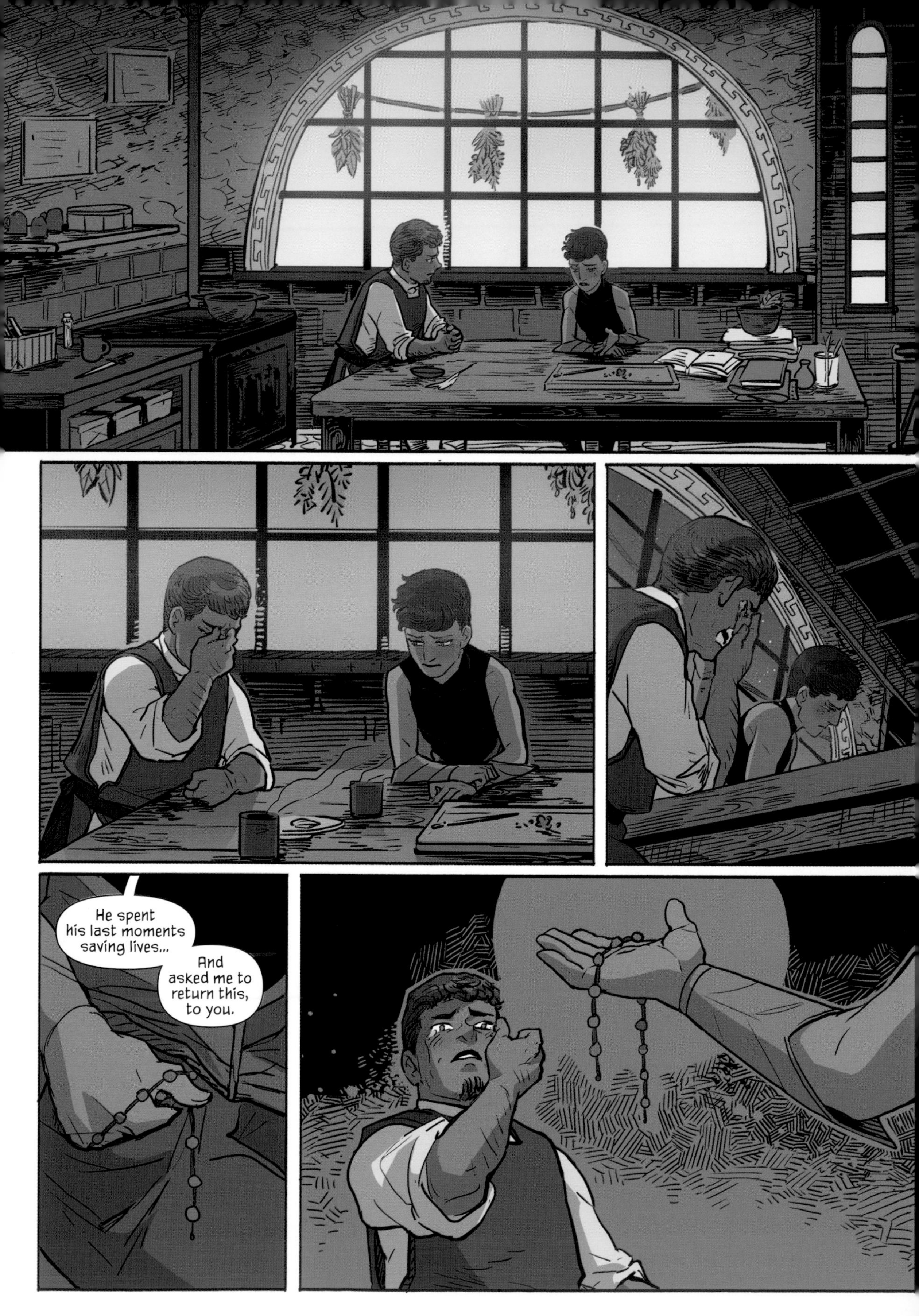
He spent his last moments saving lives...
And asked me to return this, to you.

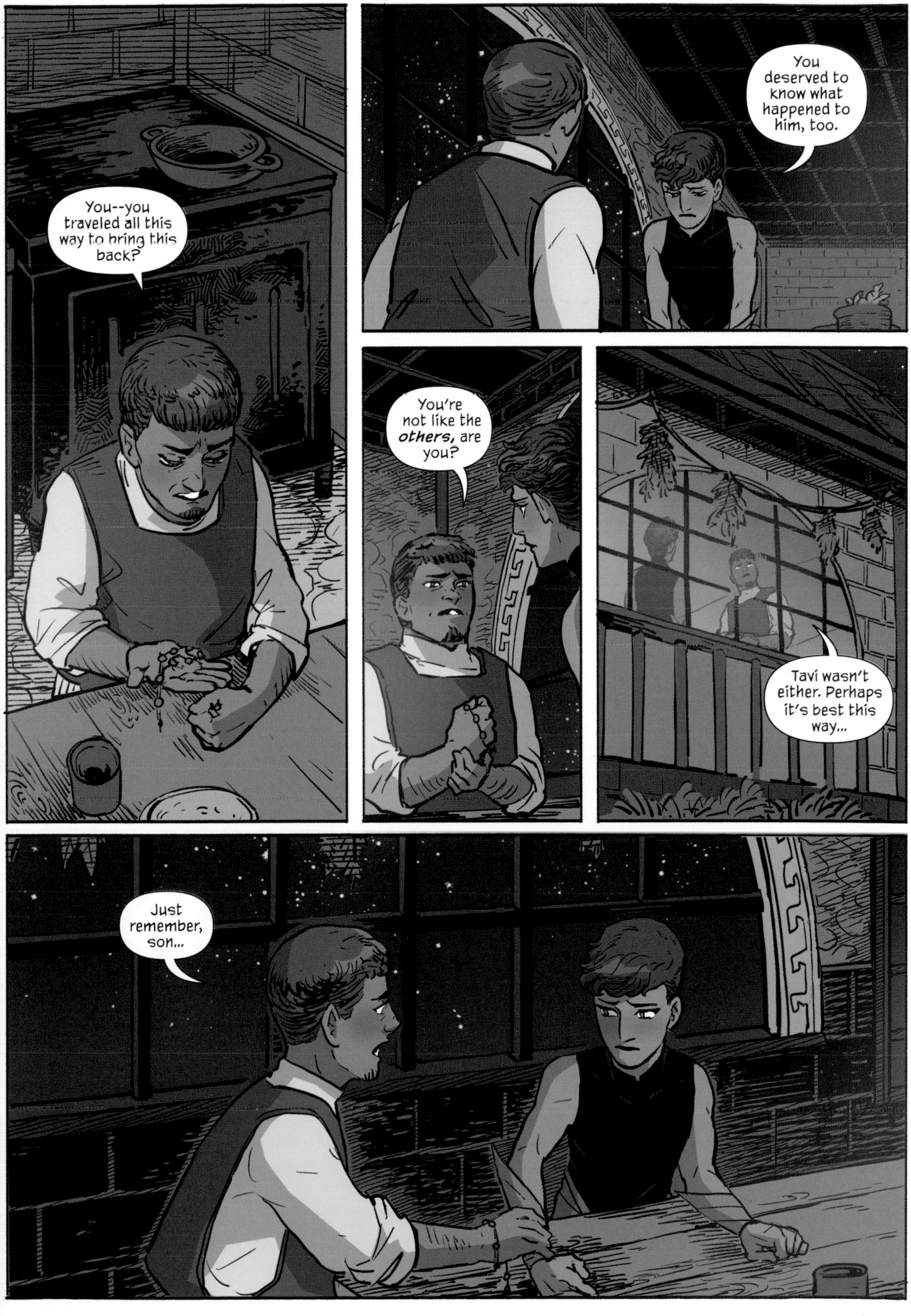
You--you traveled all this way to bring this back?
You deserved to know what happened to him, too.
You're not like the *others,* are you?
Tavi wasn't either. Perhaps it's best this way...
Just remember, son...

...don't let them destroy your spirit.

When your body is broken, and your heart is crushed. When they've honed you and molded you and beaten you into their perfect soldier...

...your *spirit* is still the one thing they cannot touch.

Remember that. For me...

...for *him.*

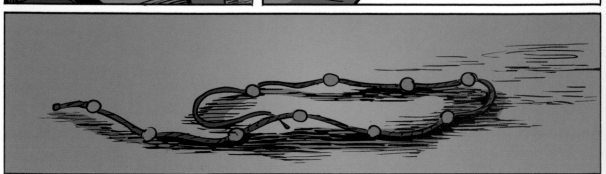

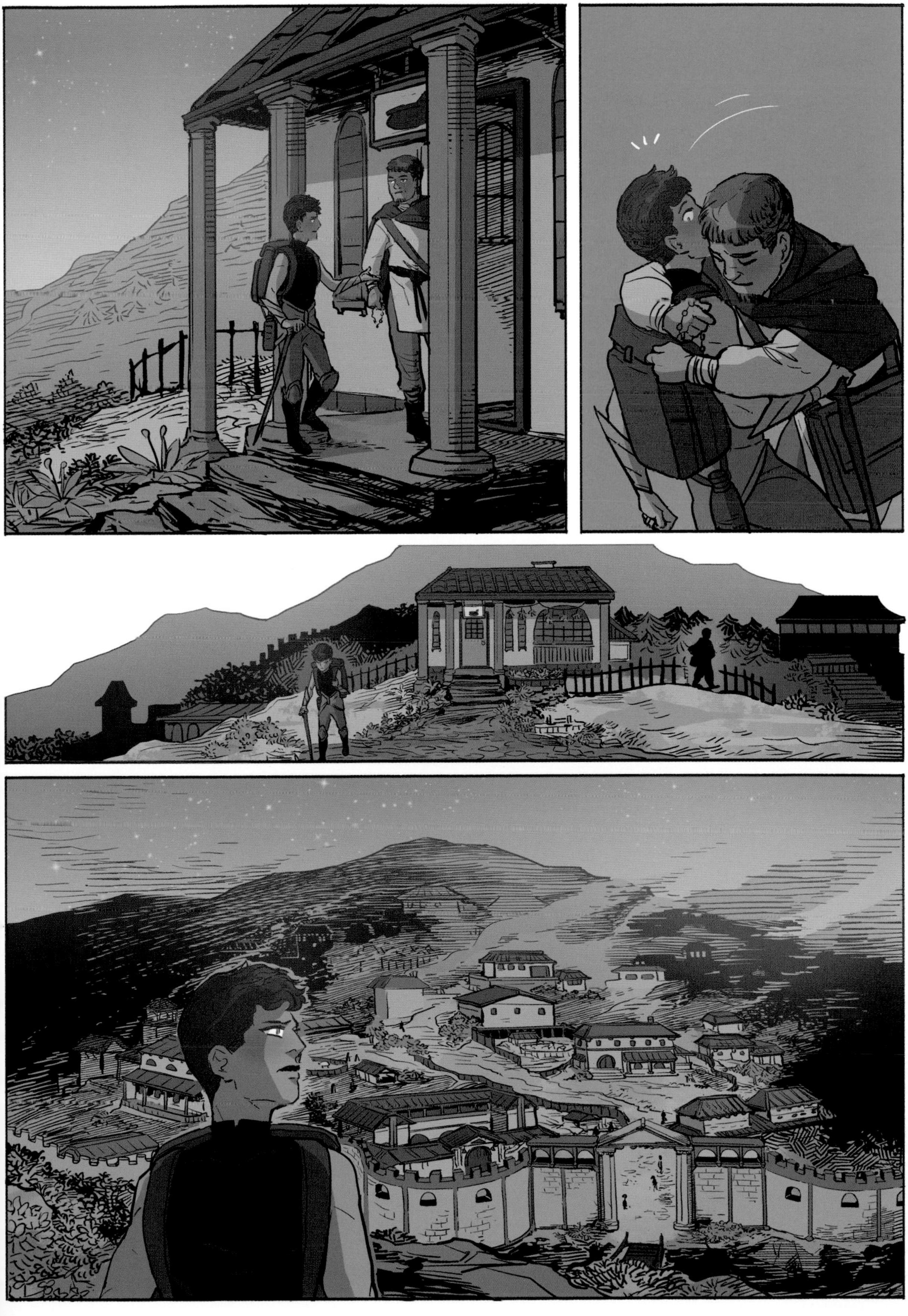

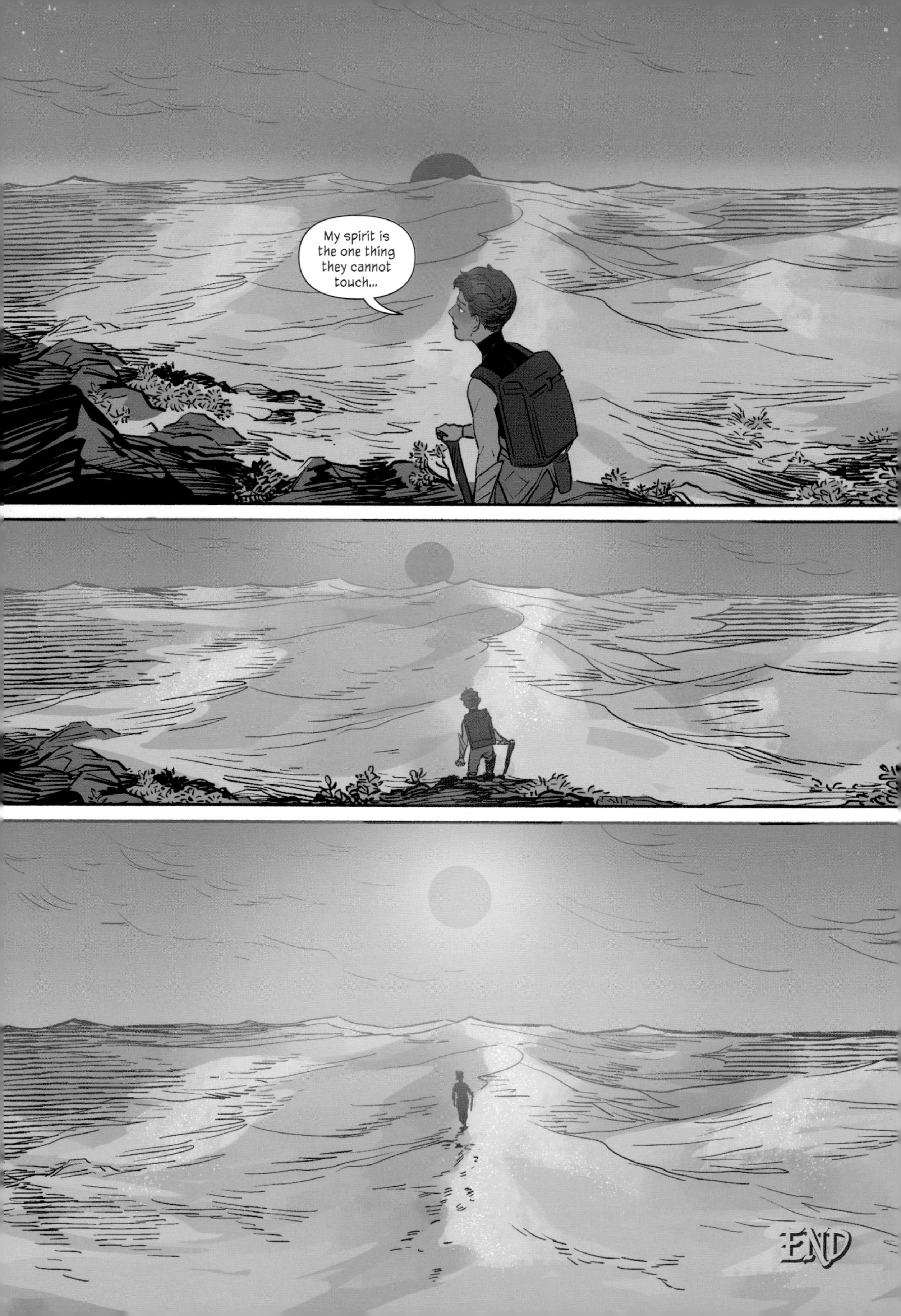
My spirit is the one thing they cannot touch...
END

ABOUT THE CREATORS

Sabaa Tahir is the author of the *New York Times* best-selling An Ember in the Ashes series. She grew up in California's Mojave Desert at her family's eighteen-room motel. There, she spent her time devouring fantasy novels, raiding her brother's comic book stash, and playing guitar badly. She began writing while working nights as a newspaper editor. She likes thunderous indie rock, garish socks and all things nerd. This is Sabaa's first graphic novel collaboration.

Nicole Andelfinger is a comic book writer who has written for series such as *Jim Henson's Dark Crystal: Age of Resistance, Adventure Time, Regular Show, Rugrats,* and *Steven Universe* from BOOM! Studios, as well as the *Munchkin* series for Simon & Schuster, based on the popular card game from Steve Jackson Games.

Sonia Liao is a comic book artist based in Westford, Massachusetts. After graduating from MICA with her BFA in Illustration, she completed an internship at Fablevision and began life as a freelance artist. She's done work for publishers such as BOOM! Studios, Sourcebook Fire, Red 5 Comics, and Global Tinker.

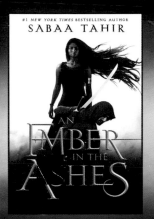

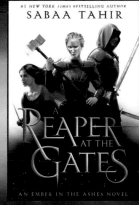
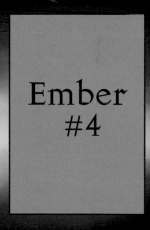

DISCOVER
GROUNDBREAKING TITLES

ASAF HANUKA
THE
REALIST

LONG WALK
TO VALHALLA
ADAM SMITH MATTHEW FOX

THE
MARCH
OF THE CRABS
THE CRABBY CONDITION
ARTHUR DE PINS

Jane
ALINE BROSH McKENNA
RAMÓN K. PÉREZ

ROYDEN LEPP
RUST
VOLUME ONE
VISITOR IN THE FIELD

MOUSE GUARD
THE BLACK AXE
DAVID PETERSEN

The Realist
Asaf Hanuka
ISBN: 978-1-60886-688-5 | $24.99 US

The Realist: Plug and Play
Asaf Hanuka
ISBN: 978-1-60886-953-4 | $24.99 US

Long Walk to Valhalla
Adam Smith, Matt Fox
ISBN: 978-1-60886-692-2 | $24.99 US

The March of The Crabs
Arthur De Pins
Volume 1: The Crabby Condition
ISBN: 978-1-60886-689-2 | $19.99 US
Volume 2: The Empire of the Crabs
ISBN: 978-1-68415-014-4 | $19.99 US

Jane
Aline Brosh McKenna, Ramón K. Pérez
ISBN: 978-1-60886-981-7 | $24.99 US

Rust
Royden Lepp
Volume 0: The Boy Soldier
ISBN: 978-1-60886-806-3 | $10.99 US
Volume 1: Visitor in the Field
ISBN: 978-1-60886-894-0 | $14.99 US
Volume 2: Secrets of the Cell
ISBN: 978-1-60886-895-7 | $14.99 US

Mouse Guard
David Petersen
Mouse Guard: Fall 1152
ISBN: 978-1-93238-657-8 | $24.95 US
Mouse Guard: Winter 1152
ISBN: 978-1-93238-674-5 | $24.95 US
Mouse Guard: The Black Axe
ISBN: 978-1-93639-306-0 | $24.95 US

The Cloud
K.I. Zachopoulos, Vincenzo Balzano
ISBN: 978-1-60886-725-7 | $24.99 US

Cursed Pirate Girl Coloring Book
Jeremy A. Bastian
ISBN: 978-1-60886-947-3 | $16.99 US

ARCHAIA™

AVAILABLE AT YOUR LOCAL COMICS SHOP AND BOOKSTORE
To find a comics shop in your area, visit www.comicshoplocator.com
WWW.**BOOM-STUDIOS**.COM

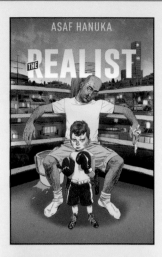

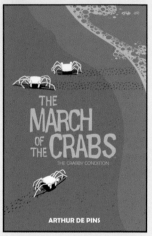

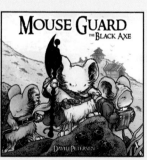

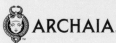